[LONDON IN A BOX]

Studies in

THEATRE HISTORY *and* CULTURE

Edited by Heather S. Nathans

[LONDON]
in a box

ENGLISHNESS *and* THEATRE
in REVOLUTIONARY AMERICA

• • •

ODAI JOHNSON

UNIVERSITY OF IOWA PRESS

Iowa City

University of Iowa Press, Iowa City 52242
Copyright © 2017 by the University of Iowa Press
www.uipress.uiowa.edu
Printed in the United States of America

Design by Richard Hendel

No part of this book may be reproduced or used in any form or by any means without permission in writing from the publisher. All reasonable steps have been taken to contact copyright holders of material used in this book. The publisher would be pleased to make suitable arrangements with any whom it has not been possible to reach.

The University of Iowa Press is a member of Green Press Initiative and is committed to preserving natural resources.

Printed on acid-free paper

Library of Congress Cataloging-in-Publication Data
Names: Johnson, Odai, 1959– author.
Title: London in a box : Englishness and theatre in revolutionary America / Odai Johnson.
Description: Iowa City : University of Iowa Press, 2017. | Series: Studies in theatre history and culture | Includes bibliographical references and index.
Identifiers: LCCN 2016040304 | ISBN 978-1-60938-494-4 (pbk) | ISBN 978-1-60938-495-1 (ebk)
Subjects: LCSH: Douglass, David, –1789. | Theatrical producers and directors—United States—Biography. | Theater—United States—History—18th century. | Theater and state—United States—History—18th century. | United States—Civilization—English influences. | BISAC: PERFORMING ARTS / Theater / History & Criticism.
Classification: LCC PN2287.D543 J64 2017 | DDC 792.02/33092 [B]—dc23
LC record available at https://lccn.loc.gov/2016040304

3 1327 00640 4313

In the memory of my father

[CONTENTS]

Acknowledgments *ix*

[PREFACE]
"The Velim Lyth Bare":
A Note on Absence and Other Sources *xi*

[PROLOGUE]
The Most Well-Connected Man in America Receives a
Letter from Congress, and Is Put Out of Business *1*

[CHAPTER 1]
A Season of Great Uncertainty: New York, October 1774 *11*

[CHAPTER 2]
A Disastrous Arrival: New York, October 1758 *18*

[CHAPTER 3]
Building a Network: 1759–1760 *25*

[CHAPTER 4]
London in a Box *40*

[CHAPTER 5]
This Wandering Theatre:
Newport, New York, Charleston, 1761–1763 *57*

[CHAPTER 6]
Heart of Oak, and Other Transatlantic Transformations:
April 1764–October 1766 *69*

[CHAPTER 7]
Murder in the Greenroom, and Other London Interludes:
1764–1765 *81*

[CHAPTER 8]
Sailing on an Unwelcomed Ship: 1765–1766 *95*

[CHAPTER 9]
The Politics of Frugality: 1767–1769 *113*

[CHAPTER 10]
Associations and Binges: 1770 *132*

[CHAPTER 11]
Lords of the Turf: Maryland, 1770–1771 *151*

[CHAPTER 12]
Great Reckonings in Small Rooms: 1773–1774 *160*

[CHAPTER 13]
Christopher Gadsden's Wharf: Charleston, Summer 1774 *193*

[CHAPTER 14]
The Second America: New York, Winter 1774 *202*

[EPILOGUE]
Final Reckonings: New York, January 1775 *216*

Notes *223*

Works Cited *253*

Index *271*

[ACKNOWLEDGMENTS]

This book has been a decade and a half in the making, and has met with many helpful allies over the years, from Spanish Town, Jamaica, and Charleston, South Carolina, to Edinburgh, Scotland. If I may single out the more persistent advocates for David Douglass and his theatres in America, it is that convivial knot of architectural historians at Colonial Williamsburg—Cary Carson, Carl Lounsbury, Willie Graham, and Ed Chapel—who gave inspiration to a biographical history when they uncovered the 1760 Douglass Theatre in Williamsburg. In the years since then, they have sponsored research and hosted symposiums in preparation for rebuilding the theatre, and it was my great good fortune to be among their guests when conversations about the 1760 Douglass Theatre in Williamsburg and the symposium hosted there first gave rise to the project. Since its discovery, that theatre has met with more misfortunes than a hero in a Henry Fielding novel, but I remain hopeful that one day the Douglass Theatre will indeed be rebuilt.

Along the way, to the many helpful staff members of Colonial Williamsburg and the Rockefeller Library and for the support of the Rockefeller Foundation, I owe a great debt of thanks. I am equally grateful to have been the recipient of a Floyd Jones Endowment, which has allowed both time and travel away from my home institution for the research, writing, and rewriting of the book. This last part of the process was facilitated by the kind editorial team at the University of Iowa Press, to the indefatigable Heather Nathan, and to the initial readers on the project for their enthusiastic responses. To all, my thanks.

Earlier versions and excerpts of some of the material (the *Heart of Oak* chapter and Jefferson's theatre-going) have appeared in the *New England Theatre Journal* and the *Virginia Magazine of History and Biography*.

[PREFACE]

"The Velim Lyth Bare"
A Note on Absence and Other Sources

• • •

In the conservatory wing of the DeWitt-Wallace museum in Colonial Williamsburg sleeps Charles Willson Peale's portrait of Nancy Hallam in the role of Imogen (disguised as Fidele) in Shakespeare's *Cymbeline*. Her portrait helped to advance Peale's career, socially and artistically. The theatre, with its brilliant assemblies, offered a perfect arena for advancement—except for the actors within it.

Nancy Hallam never owned this image, nor could she carry away the nearly life-size portrait with her on their coastal packet down to Williamsburg when the company packed up and moved south.[1] Theirs was an itinerant life, and the actors owned no more than what they could carry in trunks; the archives and portraits that documented their life and work remained behind. This goes to the heart of the historiographical problem of the book: even the evidence of performance was not owned by the actors, who never preserved it.

There are no known surviving letters from any of the twenty or more actors in the American Company: not a single note back home (where was home, for most of them?). A few public notices, a few hastily penned business notes by Douglass to a printer to settle accounts, call in debts, or announce a departure, an occasional defense of their profession survive, but no personal documents to chronicle their lives. They left homes for new places, fell in love, had children, fell out of love—traveling, always traveling—and in the thick of historic events that birthed a nation, the actors remained historically unavailable. No proper account book, no letter book, no memoir, no confessions. Instead, a few receipts for a wig or a buckle in Williamsburg, a scrap of a line about borrowing money in Jamaica, a carriage for sale, and postholes where a theatre once stood are all that remain.

We have little by way of audience accounts of what transpired inside the theatre prior to the Revolution, though everybody who would be an "actor" in the events to come attended night after night.[2] We don't even have a good riot over a controversial play (an occasional

London occurrence), despite the staging of the same contested titles. Hugh Kelly's *Word to the Wise* sparked riots where Kelly was damned as an anti-Wilkes placeman and required David Garrick himself to intervene when it opened in London, but Douglass chose the same play to open his last seasons in Philadelphia, New York, and Charleston and no one even commented on it.

At the end of twenty-five years acting and managing a company, it cannot even be claimed that Douglass enjoyed his profession. Given the chance in Jamaica, he left the theatre and returned to printing, the profession of his youth. In his fifties he settled down, married again, and raised a family. He largely reinvented himself as the king's printer and public office-holder and left little record of his prior life on the stage behind.[3] At his death, not even a play title remained in the very detailed inventory of his estate.[4] His is a story that largely resists telling, of a life lived in public yet remaining intensely private. Like his theatres, little remains of the lives within—mostly holes.

In 2001 archeologists at Colonial Williamsburg confirmed the site of the Douglass Theatre, "the theatre by the capitol," from its only tangible remains: the postholes outlining where the building once stood. Not much to go on, but the holes confirm the dimensions and suggest something of the theatre's relationship to the city's other civic spaces.

Conversely, in the National Archives of Scotland there are, for example, a modest bundle of accounts, receipts, and invoices belonging to David Ross during his construction and outfitting of the Theatre Royal in Edinburgh in 1768. Ross was part of exactly the same project of exporting London culture to the British provinces and at exactly the same time, the 1760s. Mr. Ross's building receipts reveal who his purveyors were, what his building materials were, and the cost of erecting a theatre, as well as who his subscribers were ("By Cash from A. Douglass, esq. D[itt]o from the Duke of Queensbury"). All the properties belonging to the stage are recorded there (e.g., "A Mahogany Pembroke Table; a Mahogany French elbow chair covered with leather and brass nails"; "A Sheild for the Character of Douglas of rattan Mahogany covered with Leather and brass nails"; as well as the interior fittings, e.g., "Six window sashes with pullys"). From his receipts we know the size of the crown molding (7 in.), the color of the carpet on the stairs (black and yellow carpetine), but also the size of the stairs, as it required 12¾ yards by ¾ of a yard in width. "35½ yards of white linen for lyning the slips." Even their safe: "A Mahogony strong box with 25 drawers for holding cash." We can even reconstruct the size of the scenery (8 ft × 5 ft) by the dimensions of the fir wood for the frames ("26 [×?] 7⅝ sheafts of white wood Fir for the Scenery." We have the fully documented playhouse on the same British provincial circuit in the same years, in this case 1768.[5] The list of invoices is astonishing in its detail, down to the six dozen square-headed screws, and indeed, so complete is the inventory, that the theatre could be reconstructed and David Ross would recognize it.

The theatres Douglass built in America were similar in dimensions to other British provincial theatres erected in the same decade, and like them functioned as part of the same civilizing process. But little of them is left. Hence the history of scraps: of tavern receipts and memorandum books ("Pd. at the playhouse 7s"); of shipping news, self-authored "puffs," want ads, play bills, and club notes—a reading of traces, working from corners, from edges, from memoirs that were not remembered, for a subject who frankly preferred to be left out of history, for people who walked away from their own images.

In the absence of voices from within the theatre, I have relied on an abundance of primary material about the theatre and the times: newspapers, diaries, letters and satires and pamphlets, memorandum books and playbills. The theatre in early America has been chronicled for a century now. Among the local sources I have leaned on: for Philadelphia, Thomas Pollock, *The Philadelphia Theatre in the Eighteenth Century*; for New York, George Odell, *Annals of the New York Stage*; Eola Willis for *The Charleston Stage*; and my own and the late William Burling's documentary calendar. Still the most solid summary narrative of the company-by-company culture of theatre before the war remains Hugh Rankin's *Theater in Colonial America*. Interpretive studies of the period tend to concentrate more on performance during the Revolution and the early republic but include useful opening chapters and summaries of the prior decade. Jason Shaffer's *Performing Patriotism* has provided very helpful material for the performances during the war; Heather Nathans's *Early American Theatre from the Revolution to Thomas Jefferson* offers a valuable reading of the economic hostility toward theatre in New York, Boston, and Philadelphia throughout the pre- and post-revolutionary period, while Jeffrey Richards's *Theatre Enough* explores the image of theatre on the culture at large.

Mine is a very local study, concerned with what it meant for a specific mixed audience to be in the theatre on a specific night in a specific city, and how what they saw and heard and participated in shaped their understanding of the events around them. But these local audiences were also part of a larger transatlantic citizenship of shared culture, and hence studies in transatlantic culture have also been enormously useful for seeing the colonies as part of the larger British Atlantic world before they were American, and how that Britishness was produced, reproduced, and circulated. Julie Flavell's *When London Was Capital of America*, Elizabeth Maddock Dillon's *New World Drama: The Performative Commons in the Atlantic World, 1649–1849*, Daniel O'Quinn's *Entertaining Crisis in the Atlantic Imperium, 1770–1790*, David Shields's *Civil Tongues and Polite Letters in British America* all consider performance as a space ("commons") and a nationalizing force in the transatlantic world.

Equally helpful were the studies in material culture, that brilliant turn of the field that considers the ideology of goods. I would note in particular the works of T. H. Breen, *The Marketplace of Revolution: How Consumer Politics Shaped American Independence*, "An Empire of Goods: The Anglicization of Colonial America, 1690–1776," and "Baubles of Britain"; Richard Bushman's *The Refinement of America: Persons, Houses, Cities*; and Cary Carson's *The Consumer Revolution in British America: Why Demand?* as well as his edited collection *Of Consuming Interest: The Style of Life in the Eighteenth Century*; together with the recent work of Christina Hodge, *Consumerism and the Emergence of the Middle Class in Colonial America*, and Kate Haulman, *The Politics of Fashion in Eighteenth Century America*. Though, curiously, few consider theatre in the context of what Christina Hodge has called the "Genteel Revolution,"[6] all helped to map the vast desire for gentility within a landscape of goods, manners, and acquisitions and that slippery way in which goods, manners, and acquisitions played into the making and unmaking of national identities.

For the complicated and still underexplored area of patronage in an immigrant new world ("scratching") and its relationship to the arts in British America: Nicholas Butler's *Votaries of Apollo: The St. Cecilia Society and the Patronage of Concert Music in Charleston, South Carolina, 1766–1820*, which explores the patronage network of Charleston; Bernard

Bailyn and Philip Morgan's edited collection, *Strangers within the Realm: Cultural Margins of the First British Empire*, particularly Maldwyn Jones's contribution, *The Scotch-Irish in British America*; and Alan Karras's *Sojourners in the Sun: Scottish Migrants in Jamaica and the Chesapeake* all point to a largely unexcavated new field of study of how such social networks shaped identity in the eighteenth century.

Studies on the Revolutionary War from the Stamp Act forward are a prolific industry, with new biographies (and now musicals) of founders appearing annually. Most useful in this vast field were those works which address the abiding questions of the period, namely, how in the course of a dozen years British-Americans became Americans. Short titles of my shortlist for various approaches to the question of the emerging notion of nation and the chaos that accompanied that realignment of identity: Jack P. Greene, "An Uneasy Connection"; Neil Longley York, *Turning the World Upside Down*; Edmund and Helen Morgan's *The Stamp Act Crisis*; Peter Thomas, *British Politics and the Stamp Act Crisis*; Robert Middlekauff's *The Glorious Cause*; Carl and Jessica Bridenbaugh's *Rebels and Gentlemen*; Gordon Wood's *The Radicalism of the American Revolution*; Leonard Sadosky's *Revolutionary Negotiations*; Ronald Hoffman and Peter Albert (eds.), *The Transforming Hand of Revolution*; and H. T. Dickinson (ed.), *Britain and the American Revolution*, all so helpful in situating one actor's life in the thick of such enormous political and social change.

Finally, an invitation. The medieval chronicler John Capgrave in his *Chronicle of England* undertook to write an early (very early) history of England (he commenced with the Fall of Man). Fully aware of the immensity of a field unknown to him, writing as he was ca. 1450, more than a few gaps appeared in Capgrave's historical record. His solution was to leave blank pages in his book for others to fill. The "velim lith bare," he wrote, or, translated into more contemporary English, "the vellum lies bare": "If other studious men, that have more read than I, or can find that I found not, or have old books which make more expression of those stories that fell from the creation of Adam onto the general Flood that I have, the velim lie bare, save the number, ready to receive that they will set in."[7] I too, painfully aware of the gaps in the study, would leave plenty of blank pages in each chapter for subsequent historians to amend the record and fill in the many gaps and speculations. Most poignantly absent, and hence the most pressing gap, are the actors' voices. I have done what I can to reclaim their position, but the life of their lives, the subjects themselves, remains removed, somewhat aloof, almost indifferent to the mighty spectacle of transformation in which they played such an important role.

[LONDON IN A BOX]

[PROLOGUE]

The Most Well-Connected Man in America Receives a Letter from Congress, and Is Put Out of Business

• • •

THE MISSING LETTER: NEW YORK, LATE OCTOBER 1774

If one went looking for the tipping point in the run-up to the American Revolution—that point of reckoning beyond which violent separation was inevitable—it would not be the destruction of the tea in Boston harbor, or the blockade of Boston by British warships, or even the gathering of the First Continental Congress, all of which, though monumental events in the revolution to come, held out some promise of compromise. Rather, I think (playfully perhaps, but the work is all about serious play), the moment wherein the full gravity of the separation of nations that would come was first revealed in a small congressional decision in late October of 1774 to close the theatres in British America.

Closing the theatres wasn't the first act of open defiance of the Crown—the extra-legal gathering at Philadelphia was defiance enough. But the numerous resolutions of the Congress—the declaration of their rights as English citizens to assemble, to petition, to enter into non-importation agreements to boycott British goods, to encourage economy and frugality—were all declarations of rights in the struggle with Great Britain. To close the theatres that operated by the authority of Crown-appointed colonial governors openly usurped royal authority over a pet favorite of the Crown. Theatres operated "by Permission of the Governor," as the topmost line of every playbill read; "Vivant Rex and Regina" read the bottom line. To open or close them was not in the discretion of anybody except the Crown-appointed governors, and the theatre's vexed history in British America had been a reflection of that troubled authority. To close them was a small and radical act of the Continental Congress among far weightier measures, but a hard shot across the bow of British culture. To suppress "the American Company of Actors," as the only professional troupe then performing in the colonies was known, was more than asserting Congress's authority; it amounted to refashioning the name "American" from geography to nation.

The theatre in America, after all, had been the single most concentrated school for manufacturing Britishness: British manners, British identity, British taste, British values, and British material and social culture for British-Americans a long way from London; and many congressmen, including the president, Peyton Randolph, had educated themselves in it. To retire it now, in late 1774, uncoupled the hyphenated British-American and intimated a permanent severing.

After the Congress penned its resolves, local institutions appeared to police them: citizen committees, technically vigilantes, were formed. These were the same "sign or die" committees that had terrorized merchants during the protests against the Townshend Acts in 1767 and 1768. In late October 1774, when Randolph wrote a personal letter to David Douglass, the manager of the American Company of Actors, then in New York preparing to open the John Street Theatre for a winter season, to inform him that there could be no winter season of plays, it was understood that the Crown-appointed governor no longer had any say in the matter.[1]

For twenty years Douglass, a Scottish immigrant, actor, and manager of the American Company (and modestly, the founder of the American theatre), had been in the business of making British-Americans British. Now, his patrons declared they had no further use for that service. It must have seemed a Rubicon of an ominous finality.

In the scheme of events, closing the theatres was a small moment, but deeply portentous, and riddled with irony. Amid all the overtures of peace and reconciliation, all the possibilities of compromise, repeals, alternative plans of unions, and shared governance that were floated across the pond in the summer and fall of 1774, closing the theatre was not just another belt-tightening resolution, like curtailing the expensive practice of giving out gloves at funerals (also banned). To renounce this most British of institutions was a quiet declaration of a new identity, one that no longer required the same arenas of civility, such as the side box in which Colonel Washington and General Gage had sat together just a year prior in that same John Street Theatre. More than any other goods or services in British America, the theatre had been the quintessential salon of civility, and the revolutionary generation avidly consumed the latest London plays, performed by London-trained actors, and imitated their diction, carriage, and poise. The theatre had taught provincial Americans to speak like urbane Londoners, that is, to speak correctly, and how to carry themselves within and above their station—a critical skill in a nation of self-fashioning immigrants. The men who signed the Congressional resolutions understood this fully, being themselves among the theatre's greatest patrons. They had prohibited not just theatre, but everything the theatre stood for—the aspiration of being British.

Throughout the escalating conflict leading up to the nomination of a Congress, in spite of the disorders up and down the colonies since the Stamp Act of 1765, there were still these preserves of refinement, these mannered social spheres and rituals, the governor's dinners, balls, and assemblies, the racing seasons, the social clubs, and the latest London plays in a Georgian provincial theatre. Here emerging Americans such as Peyton Randolph, Thomas Jefferson, Edward Rutledge, and George Washington watched plays with colonial governors one season and opposed them the next. Such mannered preserves as the John Street Theatre in New York, or the theatres in Charleston, Annapolis, and Williamsburg, had maintained the common (British) civility through times tepid and tempestuous, until October of 1774.

For David Douglass, business in America had never been better than in the fall of 1774. He owned outright a monopoly of seven theatres in six colonies. He had signed a fifteen-year lease on a lot in Charleston, South Carolina, and built an elegant new theatre ("the most commodious on the continent"), funded entirely by subscription, where his company had recently finished their most successful season in more than two decades. He had sent back to England to recruit more actors and to purchase new scenery, new costumes, and, of course, the latest London plays for the upcoming winter season in New York—a season that now obviously would not be.

After twenty years of soliciting and securing a dense network of patronage from Jamaica to Rhode Island, building and protecting a large, monopolistic circuit of provincial theatres, and providing a "school of refinement" to colonists a long way from the metropole, Douglass was deeply entrenched in the best society the colonies had to offer. He had acquainted himself with every significant figure, great and small, in the vast colonial network: every governor and lieutenant governor, every general and councilman, every legislator and Freemason, every tidewater planter, printer, "principal man," "club man," merchant, rector, burgesses, and that "vast cousinage" of Scotsmen abroad. This invaluable web of influence had allowed him the authority to build theatres against the vocal objections of moralists and frugal economists, and to operate them through the French-Indian War, the Stamp Act, and the various boycotts of British goods and luxury items during the Townshend years. He relied on his friendships, his exemptions, and a widespread coterie of patrons, including many who now sat in Philadelphia conceiving a course of action that would ultimately result in American independence and those Crown-appointed governors and generals who would oppose it. Now, in the fall of 1774, the most well-connected man in America had been put out of business by many of his best patrons.

"We will each in our several stations," read the eighth resolution of the Continental Congress, "encourage frugality, economy, and industry, and . . . will discountenance and discourage every species of extravagance and dissipation, especially all horse-racing, and all kinds of gaming, cock-fighting, exhibitions of shews, plays, and other expensive diversions and entertainments."[2]

There was little new in the resolution—they had been declaring the same ones since 1767, when John Dickinson, the Philadelphia delegate in 1774, had first articulated a platform of "oeconomy and frugality" as a response to British taxation. This time, however, they all finally seemed to mean it; and this time, they included the theatre. Throughout all the numerous non-importation agreements, good years and bad, Douglass had remained in business, and indeed, back in 1770, in Williamsburg, these same men—Peyton Randolph, Thomas Jefferson, George Washington, George Mason, and so many others—had signed the Virginia Association to boycott all British luxury goods and then promptly adjourned to their side boxes in Douglass's Williamsburg theatre. Indeed, the very week that the Virginia subscribers signed a public pledge to frugality (mid-June 1770), Washington and Jefferson purchased twenty box tickets between them and spent the next six nights out of seven in the theatre.[3]

The theatre had always been exempt; even during the protests against the 1765 Stamp Act, when the Sons of Liberty mobbed the streets, the port of Charleston was closed, and no money circulated,

Douglass had managed to keep a theatre open in Charleston throughout the winter. But 1774 was different. The theatre was the last preserve of the colonial elite, and that they were now relinquishing it meant they had finally joined the radicals. And worse for Douglass, his connections with royal governors would not serve him. In spite of his protestations of neutrality, he and his theatre had been marked as British goods.

Looking back, it seemed as if the rebellion had grown two fronts: a propertied, intellectual (and mannered) elite who reasoned their way to resistance while preserving the civil society, class distinctions, and luxury goods that marked them as British-Americans; and a mob who exhibited few of those qualities. On the one front, the polite discourse of pamphlets and essays defending rights and debating liberties was conducted largely by learned gentlemen—hot-headed and angry gentlemen, intent on something very radical—but nonetheless gentlemen of education and genteel manners, who signed themselves "Cassandra" and "Cato" and spoke to others in the classical know.[4] This class had always been among Douglass's patrons. These genteel radicals dined with their adversaries and shared boxes at the theatre with them; they shared a love of horse-racing and music, danced in polite assemblies, clubbed together, and were guests at the residences of those governors against whom they now stood. The gentlemen on both sides of the conflict would honor the conventions of engagement, would pride themselves on their honor. That population could have its rebellion and remain a polite society, really could parole prisoners on their own word, really could set aside hostilities for winter assemblies, balls, plays, and set aside animosity for independence. They really could.

But the resolves of these polite rebels, which carried no authority, were nevertheless enforced by vigilantes engaged in vandalism, street violence, and mob intimidation. These "Sons of Violence," as they were called in Parliament, displayed no civility; they were no respecters of place or station, of manners or property. They conducted mock trials who read no law; they sentenced and punished severely on rumor, destroyed printing shops in the interest of a free press, dismantled theatres, slashed artwork, and burned carriages, who could afford none of these. That lot had no use for actors teaching manners and refinement. While the gentlemen were debating in Congress, the vigilantes were patrolling the streets. In October of 1774, while Douglass sat on the steps of the not-to-be opened John Street Theatre, these spasms of violence may have seemed less the hard birthing of an independent America than the troubled rupture of two Americas. As much as Crown administrators were frightened by this Congress and its resolutions toward independence, what they represented was tame compared to the waterfront thuggery of the America on the streets. Mobs of "levelers" assaulting all signs of British rank and station, people who slashed paintings and burned carriages—was this to be the face of the new America? The birth of an uncivil society? Edward Gibbon's Goths and Vandals? Who would ever live there?

IN THE OCCASIONAL COMPANY OF FOUNDING FATHERS

Peyton Randolph could write to Douglass personally in October 1774 because the two knew each other from the Williamsburg theatre and the Williamsburg Freemasons (Randolph had been the Master Mason who initiated Douglass). Maryland delegates William Paca and Samuel Chase (the latter a congressman and both future signers of the Declaration of Independence) had managed the subscription to build a new theatre in Annapolis three years earlier, and when the company left Annapolis, the theatre was entrusted back into their care. South Carolina's representatives, John and Edward Rutledge, Christopher Gadsden, and Thomas Lynch, Jr., were all patrons of Douglass's new Charleston theatre, and the American Company manager had once spent ten weeks in Lynch's company, sailing to London.

William and Philip Livingston (New Jersey and New York delegates) had been patrons of Douglass's New York theatre since 1758. Douglass also knew them as fellow Freemasons, while Philip Livingston was the sitting president of the St. Andrew's Society, a convivial gathering of Scots. In both capacities Douglass knew them, and had handed over to their board £100 for a new hospital in the summer of 1773. The Livingstons were now part of the new Committee for Safety, which would discourage his business. Samuel Ward, delegate from Rhode Island, had been the figure with whose permission and support Douglass built his theatre in Newport, to which Bostonians drove for plays they could not see in their own anti-theatrical city.[5] But the most familiar face in Congress was that of Colonel Washington. Douglass's association with Washington may have dated back to 1751, when both men were in the theatre in Bridgetown, Barbados. The Virginia colonel was a subscriber to several of Douglass's theatres, and could frequently be seen in those in Williamsburg, Annapolis, Fredericksburg, and New York.[6] He was known to ride to all four theatres in a single year, and always in the best of company, with the governor, or fellow burgesses, buying four or five box tickets a night. Virginia assemblyman Thomas Jefferson could spend half his per diem (fifteen shillings) at the theatre daily; during court times he sometimes spent nine nights out of ten in the side box of the Williamsburg theatre in the company of Peyton Randolph or John Page. They understood class and its obligations, they understood civility, these mannered Southerners and middle colony men. They understood fine goods and courtesies, fine entertainment and polite society, and no place brought these rural planters closer to the urbanity of London than a well-acted play. This was Douglass's success: his theatres were "London in a Box" and at no point in his long career were they more profitable, more successful, or more promising than in 1774, when suddenly, very suddenly, being a mannered Londoner was no longer desirable and the theatres were shut down.

If Douglass ever paused to reflect on the influence of all this theatregoing on the events that came to pass, he never wrote about it. He left no letters, no personal records at all, except a will. Everyone else of this revolutionary generation did, though, albeit indirectly. The theatrical metaphors of the revolutionary period were inescapable. Everybody was throwing about stage language, writing of being an *Actor* on the *Great Stage*, of taking up his or her role in the *Theatre of Action* ("I long impatiently to have you upon the Stage of Action," wrote Abigail Adams to her husband, who himself wrote of this "grand scene open before me, a Congress"[7]), even dramatizing the events themselves into published and performed plays.[8] No generation stretched the *theatrum mundi* trope farther or used it more ubiquitously, applying it to the times far beyond the limits of metaphor, more than this revolutionary generation.

A small sample: "He is now commenced an actor on a busy theatre," wrote William Eddis of Maryland's governor, at the beginning of the engagement.[9] "The play is over," wrote Lafayette with the surrender of Cornwallis. General Washington, at the conclusion of the war, evoked what was the standard figure to describe his part in the times, an actor retiring from the stage: "Having now finished the work assigned me, I retire from the great Theatre of Action, bidding an Affectionate farewell to this August body under whose order I have so long acted." John Adams wrote of that performance without quotes: it wasn't like "acting" in the metaphorical sense but rather, to his mind, scripted like Shakespeare and performed like David Garrick.[10]

Nor was any generation more indebted to the theatre for providing a governing metaphor than were those who came of age in the Revolution. As private citizens, they stepped into the "great stage" of a "National tragedy" and commanded the attention of Europe, and then, with equal theatricality, stepped off into private citizenship. The rebellion became a stage, and this figural stage, so frequently and deeply evoked, saturated the cultural imagination. As Jeffrey Richards has argued, the trope of *theatrum mundi* owed much of its potency to the material stage—real actors, Douglass's actors, with real scenes, roles, and spectators (this same generation of genteel Revolutionaries)—and the trope held its currency because many of those "great actors on the stage of action" were the most prolific spectators in Douglass's theatres, and were thoroughly acquainted with the original from which the metaphor derived its life.

The real irony that few at the time could fully appreciate was the degree to which the Revolution was itself indebted to the staging of heroic ideas of individual liberty and resistance to tyranny in Douglass's theatre. The leaders of the American Revolution spoke, posed, and postured in rhetorical and cultural gestures that were indebted to the stage for their inherent theatricality. The rhetorical terms that propelled events to the extremity—"tyranny," "slavery," "tragedy"— were informed by a certain theatricality, and at times (one thinks of Patrick Henry's speeches, John Hancock's or Dr. Joseph Warren's Boston Massacre orations) excessively indebted to the playhouse.

Those who gathered in Philadelphia in 1774 to fashion a resistance movement and to imagine a rebellion that had no successful precedent, were the first generation of theatre-goers in America. They had learned a great deal about how to imagine resistance to tyranny from two decades of productions of popular plays such as Shakespeare's *Richard III* and *Julius Caesar*, Thomas Otway's *Venice Preserv'd*, and Joseph Addison's *Cato*. Tragedy, in particular, concerned itself with monarchical abuses and the resistance to them. Increasingly, from the Stamp Act of 1765 to the First Continental Congress of 1774, tragedy offered the clearest, most accessible image of the American struggle.

Occasionally—and in the early 1770s, quite frequently—the emplotment of tragedy eerily resembled the times themselves. When, for example, the delegates gathered in Philadelphia to debate the response to the blockade of Boston, the scene could have been cribbed directly from *Cato*, the most popular play in America, whose rebels gathered in their own self-fashioned senate to debate their response to Caesar's tyranny. Here is the exchange between the hot-headed Sempronius and the moderate martyr to republicanism, Cato:

> SEMPRONIUS: My voice is still for war.
>   Gods, can Roman senate long debate
>   Which of the two to choose, slav'ry or death!
> . . . .
> CATO: Let not a torrent of impetuous zeal
>   Transport thee thus beyond the bounds of reason:
>   True fortitude is seen in great exploits,
>   That justice warrants, and that wisdom guides:
>   All else is towering frenzy and distractions.
>   (2.1.23–25, 43–46)

If Sempronious sounds like Patrick Henry rising to declare "Give me liberty or give me death," it is because Henry was paraphrasing the same role, and his auditors, already familiar with it, from the stage, from the page, received it as such. Many others in Philadelphia frequently quoted it. *Cato*, quoted, paraphrased, parodied, inspired, and emplotted the resistance; it was the last play performed in America, by students, to raise money for the relief of Boston; it was one of the last performed during Douglass's final season as a civic benefit, and the theatre was so crowded the audience was sitting on the stage.

It had been chosen as a benefit because everybody knew it, and the man who had played the role of Cato in America professionally for the last sixteen years was David Douglass. From seven stages in six colonies, Douglass spoke on American soil the words that would become the mantra of the Revolution, the words that would prepare them to be Americans. As Abigail Adams wrote, "Many, very Many of our Heroes will spend their lives in the cause, With the Speach of

Cato in their Mouths, 'What a pitty it is, that we can dye but once to save our Country.'"[11] It was Douglass who spoke first against Caesar's tyranny, who publicly meditated on the need of virtuous resistance, and who, when that resistance failed, martyred himself nightly for the cause of liberty. Now, in October of 1774, having rehearsed the rebellion, the actors were being retired, and the real players were about to take the stage.

[CHAPTER 1]
A Season of Great Uncertainty
New York, October 1774

• • •

There never was a period in our history more critical than the present.
WILLIAM EDDIS, October 26, 1774

A small tax in a series of small taxes had been lately imposed on East India tea, and when a cargo of it sailed into Boston, a fiery group of radicals costumed as Mohawks, who styled themselves the Sons of Liberty, marched to the harbor and pitched the tea overboard. Even the subterfuge was marked with the same transatlantic hybridity that would characterize this generation: "Mohawks" in the cultural imagination were both the untamed tribe of native Americans they impersonated, and a gang of desperados who haunted Covent Garden in the early 1770s. William Hickey, who moved among this gang in 1771, offered a vivid portrait of their "outrageous conduct" in the theatres, taverns, and coffeehouses, and their escapades were much talked of in the newspapers.[1] If one considered their conduct in familiar London terms, the Boston Tea Party hooligans seemed exactly that kind of Mohawk, petty vandals and thugs. Indeed, even those on the American side of the question were alarmed at the "dominion of the mob." First it was stamps, now it was tea.

Whitehall was infuriated by the destruction of goods and the boycott of the tax, but mostly by the notion of American resistance to British policy, and it retaliated against the unruly colonists by closing the Boston harbor. The action catalyzed the colonies, and their delegates gathered in Philadelphia. What steps they would ultimately agree to take and upon what authority was still far from clear to those outside Carpenter's Hall, Philadelphia, in late October. The men who gathered there to debate, petition, resist, and organize were not yet the great men of history (Thomas Paine, author of *Common Sense*, had just stepped off the boat in Philadelphia, nearly broke and with few prospects); they were burgesses and planters, large-acre landholders, merchants and lawyers.[2] They also belonged to a dense network of educated, propertied gentlemen in the sparsely populated colonies and constituted a network of incalculable worth. The crucible to come would make them into generals, presidents, patriots, martyrs, and a few fence-sitters. At present, they were incensed British subjects becoming Americans, with only a vague sense of how to proceed with their grievances; they were possibly on the verge of something cataclysmic, something extraordinary and unprecedented, or else something utterly disastrous. They might very well be playing out the all-too-familiar narrative of rebellion, with its inevitable doomed conclusion.

At the close of October 1774, still months from the first shots exchanged between British regulars and colonial Minutemen that would irrevocably decide the fate of so many thousands of the uncertain, most colonists watched events and waited with great expectation. William Eddis of Annapolis was one; on the 26th of that month he wrote, "[A]ll descriptions of people are waiting for the result of their deliberations with the utmost impatience."[3] Nicholas Cresswell commented, "A General Congress of the different Colonies met at Philadelphia on the 5th of last month [October] are still sitting, but their business is a profound secret."[4] Like so many others, David Douglass waited, and like so many, not fully prepared to comprehend the enormity of the times around him. He was one of thousands of small and ordinary players caught in the uncertainty of the times. A month earlier, when Douglass was still fitting up the John Street Theatre in preparation of opening the winter season, John Adams had walked right past him, up Broadway, with Alexander McDougall ("the Wilkes of America"). It was McDougall who summarized for Adams the state of New York at the time:

> [T]here is a powerful party here who are intimidated by fears of a civil war. . . . [A]nother party are intimidated lest the leveling spirit of the New England colonies should propagate itself into New York. Another party are prompted by Episcopalian Prejudices against New England. Another party are Merchants largely concerned in Navigation, and therefore afraid of Non Importation, Non Consumption and Non Exportation Agreements. Another party are those who are looking up to Government for favours.[5]

Douglass knew firsthand that civil wars were bad for business. The last one in England closed the theatres for eighteen years. He would likely have agreed with another artist, the painter John Singleton Copley: "Political contests . . . [are] neither pleasing to an artist nor advantageous to art itself."[6] Douglass was a businessman, a merchant of high culture, and now the unemployed manager of nineteen unemployed actors and seven closed theatres. He had long-term leases and money invested in the years to come with his "theatrical force hitherto unknown" in America. And somewhere at the end of October 1774, he must have sat on the steps on his unopened theatre and wondered how it all came to this.

Merchants were maneuvering to supply the military in Boston; the Committee of 51 were marshaling to intimidate them; merchants demanded to know upon what authority they derived their force? And that was the heart of the issue: who had the authority in the city? The lieutenant governor reported to the Earl of Dartmouth "the most trifling unforeseen incident may produce the greatest events. I have already said, my lord, that I am well assured almost the whole inhabitants in the counties wish for moderate measures. They think the dispute with Great Britain is carried far enough and abhor the thoughts of pushing it to desperate lengths. . . . I have some hopes that our merchants will avoid a non-importation agreement even if proposed by the Congress."[7]

In hindsight one could say there were signs. Others would observe at the time how the king was openly cursed, how sympathetic the colonists were to the plight of Boston, that things were, as Nicholas Cresswell wrote, "ripe for rebellion." Cresswell had just landed in Virginia in mid-October, and among his first assessments of America: "Nothing but war is talked of."[8] Charles Carroll, Jr., writing to his father, observed: "I still think this controversy will at last be decided by arms: that is, I am apprehensive the oppressions of the Bostonians, & Gage's endeavours to enforce the new plan of govern[me]nt. will hurry that distressed & provoked People into some violence, which may end in blood: if that should be the case a civil war is inevitable."[9] Even the hard-nosed tidewater tobacco-broker, James Robinson, was fretful all through the summer of 1774 that "the worst is to be dreaded, as moderate men are not listened to in the present ferment."[10]

But there were those too who still spoke of the conflict as resolvable in any number of ways. For the merchants, to sever ties with Great Britain by force of arms was commercially untenable; moralists thought revolt unnatural; and the more politically far-sighted conceded that even if it succeeded, it would only leave America vulnerable to Spanish or French subjugation, or worse, throw the colonies into an intracolonial war. General Gage, meanwhile, was collecting troops, troops marching through New Jersey, sailing up the Hudson, en route to Boston. Equally visible were the broadsides at New York's Merchant's Coffeehouse urging merchants to refuse the use of their ships to transport soldiers, and pilots not to assist ships involved in the blockade of Boston. More committed merchants, like Walter Franklin, were openly ordering munitions. The contest over the tea was equally heated in New York as it was in Boston, exacerbated by the observation that the same captain who carried the stamps to New York back in 1765 now carried the tea. When they learned he had purchased the tea for private sale, an unadorned mob boarded the *London* and eighteen chests of tea were dumped in New York harbor. That had been in the spring, and the Sons of Liberty had organized and grown more dangerous since then. A heated press war was also underway: pamphlets were in high circulation, including John Dickinson's formidable Tory platform, *Essay on the Constitutional Power of Great Britain over the Colonies in America*, published and widely circulated in the late summer of 1774. Closer to home was Dr. Myles Cooper's *Friendly Address to All Reasonable Americans*, which articulated a policy of the natural maternity of Great Britain to her colonies, and pointedly noted its military superiority.[11] Cooper too was a great patron of the theatre, who had, the previous summer, sponsored plays in New York as a civic benefit for the hospital attached to Kings College (now Columbia University), and wrote the prologue for Douglass. John Adams, however, thought Cooper's maternal argument closer to the maternity of Lady Macbeth.[12] Looking back, there were plenty of signs of a mighty showdown in the making.

But at the time the idea of successful armed resistance to or independence from Great Britain was utterly without precedent. In the fall of 1774 most colonists knew that every attempt against the monarchy of Great Britain since the English civil war had failed. A century of Irish uprisings, most recently the Heart of Oak uprising (1762), Scottish highland revolts, the "Forty Five" (the Jacobite rebellion), had all been quashed mercilessly. On the American continent the same was true for a century of Indian uprisings, including, Pontiac's Rebellion, the Cherokee wars in South Carolina, and the French-Indian War of 1756–1763. Servant and slave revolts in the colonies and on the islands of the Anglophone West Indies had also failed. There had been many attempts to rise against Great Britain, but there was no precedent to suggest that a new armed rebellion would end differently. One hears the voice of Cato, a role Douglass himself played for fifteen years, coolly reasoning: "Let not a torrent of impetuous zeal / Transport thee thus beyond the bounds of reason."

A general boycott of all British goods seemed equally improbable, despite John Adams's injunction: "Frugality, my Dear, Frugality, parsimony must be our refuge. . . . [L]et us eat potatoes and drink water, let us wear canvas."[13] Douglass had just spent eight months in Charleston, one of the busiest trading ports on the coast. Charlestonians were certainly not wearing canvas, not the beaus onstage, where they sat because the theatre was so crowded, night after night, and the ladies there described as "dazzling" and "superfine," where one could lose a jeweled bracelet there "set with Brilliants, Rubies and twelve strings of Oriental Pearls" and advertise for its recovery.[14] At the close of that season, some of the actors in his company had sailed to Philadelphia with one of South Carolina's most radical delegates, Christopher Gadsden, who had just completed the longest wharf in America, capable of unloading any number of ships at the same time. Surely merchants (and representatives) such as Gadsden and Henry Laurens were not about to forfeit their business.

More likely, cooler heads would pull back from this brinkmanship and restore civil order, reestablish commerce, and allow level-headed men of business on both sides of the pond to return to making money. Douglass, who had kept his theatre open right through the Stamp Act crisis, had weathered these tempests before. "Bad this year, the better the next," as Douglass himself would speak from the stage; "[w]e must take things rough and smooth as they run."[15] Many merchants endured periods of suspended business. John Jay's former legal employer, the New York firm of Benjamin Kissam, had to recess during the Stamp Act crisis, and Kissam wrote to Jay on its repeal: "As upon the Repeal of the Stamp Act, we shall doubtless have a Luxuriant Harvest of Law, I would not willingly, after the long Famine we have had, miss reaping my part of the crop."[16] Even this selected boycott of goods would be a matter of negotiation (in South Carolina rice was exempted, but not wheat or hemp; in Virginia spars and saltpetre were exempted).[17] These patriots were very boisterous at the moment, but at its core, America remained a land of merchants, bound up with the merchants of England. Commerce impassioned the trans-Atlantic world, not rights, and men of sense would soon restore—if not harmony, at least the climate for trade. So reasoned many, and so may have Douglass reasoned, because he remained in New York for the next three months.

The Association of Mechanics in New York fretted out the same anxiety. In early November of 1774 they wrote to the New York Committee with "anxious solicitude for the restoration of that harmony and mutual confidence between the parent state and America."[18] The lieutenant governor, Cadwallader Colden, concurred: "I am well assured almost the whole inhabitants in the counties wish for moderate measures. They think the dispute with Great Britain is carried far enough and abhor the thoughts of pushing it to desperate lengths. In the city a large majority of the people wish that a non-importation agreement may not be proposed by the Congress."[19] William Cunninghame, a Virginia tobacco-broker, assumed the parties would compromise: "Meanwhile, our violent patriots, of which there are a number, will cool and they will consult reason and their own interests."[20]

Even this great display of arms, militiamen carrying off gunpowder, drilling on the parade, seemed all show. One Scots merchant asserted: "It was the general opinion among civil and military men that our provincials would not fire a single gun in the contest, and all their preparations were meant only to intimidate and to exhort terms." "Notwithstanding the noise of arming and mustering," wrote another, "the colonists will not attempt fighting."[21] Over and over one finds levelheaded voices convinced that armed resistance would be too devastating to be seriously entertained. So the actors did not leave New York, and New Yorkers noticed. And then more actors arrived. New recruits from London appeared, anticipating work. Peyton Randolph's letter to Douglass was followed by a visit from Philip Levingston and John Jay of the New York Committee of Safety, another by-product of the first Congress, citizens delegated to patrol the new resolutions. Levingston, whom Douglass knew from the St. Andrew's Society, reconfirmed personally the will of the Congress.[22] Cadwallader Colden would also have noticed that though Douglass did not leave, neither did he open the theatre, though he had secured the requisite permission. Colden and his family were all long-time acquaintances and patrons of Douglass. Douglass had relied on character letters and support from the lieutenant governor for years, and was familiar enough with the Colden family to carry letters for them in his own travels, such as the letter from David Colden to Alexander Garden that Douglass carried to Charleston, which spoke with great detail, great interest, and at some length about Douglass and his success in the business of theatre.[23] Suddenly, to open or not to open became a question of political identity in which neutrality was an increasingly difficult position to occupy.

The Sons of Liberty reminded Mr. Douglass that the last company that played New York in 1766 during the Stamp Act crisis had faced a mob that whipped the actors and demolished the playhouse, and "carried the pieces to the common, where they consumed them in a bonfire." One unfortunate young man had his skull fractured, "his recovery doubtful."[24]

For three months at the close of 1774 and the opening of 1775, Douglass watched and waited, while local militias formed, munitions unloaded on the wharfs, British warships arrived, and dispatches flew back and forth across the sea. He waited, like so many others, during these most critical months in American history, with nineteen unemployed actors, and watched from the wings of an empty theatre the preparations of what John Adams called "the Theatre of Action."[25]

It is difficult to look beyond the charisma of 1776 and everything that followed, but to those caught up in the confusion of the times that preceded the Declaration of Independence and the war, to those who could see beyond the rhetoric of slavery and liberty, it must have seemed incredible to think of severing ties with Great Britain, the largest power in Europe. As Douglass waited in New York for a civil outcome of the current uncertainty, the only comfort was—if there was any comfort—that he had been here before. He had been shut down before in New York, sixteen years earlier during his first assault on the city in 1758.

[CHAPTER 2]

A Disastrous Arrival

New York, October 1758

• • •

Perhaps it was a good omen that the cannons at Fort George in New York harbor sounded in welcome that morning, and the houses shone in a grand illumination the evening Douglass first sailed to New York. But the celebration was not in honor of an obscure company of strolling actors from the West Indies sailing in the thick of the hurricane season. Rather, it marked the arrival of Major General Jeffery Amherst, hero of the French-Indian War. Amherst had arrived in New York the night before; by Friday morning word had spread, and by evening "most of the houses in town were handsomely illuminated and a general joy appeared in every countenance."[1] Still, a festive town promised business.

It was Douglass's first time in America, though he and his company were a well-traveled troupe. Most of them had originated in England, Ireland, or like himself, Scotland, and had been touring the Anglophone islands of the West Indies for nearly a decade, branching out from their base in Kingston, Jamaica, for short engagements at other plantation islands of the Caribbean. They appeared in Jamaica, Barbados, Tortola, St. Croix, Antigua, and no doubt many of the other Leeward Islands, where they might cobble up a theatre and run a month's season of plays.[2] Along the way, Douglass had developed a useful social network of Caribbean patrons, lieutenant governors, planters, and merchant families connected to New York, Charleston, and Newport interests. Most recently, the company had sailed from St. Croix, where Douglass had made two influential contacts: the Danish governor of that island, Baron von Prock, whose letter of recommendation Douglass carried with him to New York, and a prominent merchant, Nicholas Cruger, from the Cruger family of traders who operated shipping houses in St. Croix and New York. His brother, John Cruger, was mayor of New York, and Douglass likely also carried a letter from Nicholas Cruger in St. Croix.

His new wife, Sarah Douglass, the former Mrs. Hallam, and her son,

Lewis Hallam, Jr., had both acted in New York six years earlier, when the Hallam Company (The Company of Comedians from London) toured the principal cities of North America. That company had arrived in Virginia in the summer of 1752, played a season in the capital, Williamsburg, and the countryside hamlets (Norfolk, Fredericksburg, Alexandria) for eleven months before alighting in New York in the summer of 1753, then moving on to Philadelphia and down to Charleston. Only fifteen during his first tour, young Lewis Hallam was now the company's lead actor. The Hallams still carried a letter of recommendation from their last tour, some five years earlier:

> On Friday last arrived here from the West Indies a Company of Comedians, who hope to obtain leave to entertain the town during the winter season: Part of it was here in the year 1753. They have an ample Certificate of their private as well as public qualifications from the Lieutenant Governor of Pennsylvania, and many of the principal Inhabitants of the city of Philadelphia. They were lately at St. Croix, and succeeded so well there as to procure Credentials from his Excellency the Baron Von Prock, Captain General and Governor in Chief of his Danish Majesty's Settlements in America. They flatter themselves they shall be able to acquire the same Reputation here.[3]

New York had grown to a town of roughly twelve thousand inhabitants, a bustling metropole compared to the company's tiny Caribbean island circuit. One of New York's earliest historians, William Smith, Jr., described the city in 1757 as "[o]ne of the most social places on the continent."[4] New York also had a sporadic tradition of supporting a playhouse that dated back to the early 1700s, an appetite whetted by the absence of a professional theatrical season since the Hallams' departure in the winter of 1753–1754. That year the pamphleteer William Livingston had complained about the enormous popularity of such "annihilating Amusements." His critique of his countrymen may sound harsh to modern readers ("too many of my Fellow Citizens of Both Sexes, among those especially call themselves the Polite and Well-bred, Hours, Days, and Months are sordidly wasted in one continual Circle of such trifling Amusements"), but extravagance was music to a theatre manager's ear.[5] New York had hosted three separate companies briefly between 1752 and 1753. And now, in the fall of

1758, armed with character letters, Douglass, his wife Sarah, her son Lewis, and thirteen other seasoned actors returned with every expectation of a lucrative season. They enjoyed the support of a least one prominent merchant family, the Crugers, who rented them a warehouse on the wharf to convert into a temporary theatre.

Douglass found a powerful patron in the Cruger family, particularly John Cruger, who was the mayor of New York (1757–1758). In the fall of 1758 Mayor Cruger was also running for the General Assembly, which had recently been dissolved by Lieutenant Governor James De Lancey, who sought more favorable assemblymen. Cruger's rivals in the contest included Oliver De Lancey, (James's son) and Philip and Robert Livingston.[6] The Livingstons, Crugers, and De Lanceys represented old merchant families with deep political bloodlines and deeper antagonisms that remained unresolved right through the Revolution. Into this deep play stepped Douglass, who began remodeling the warehouse on Cruger's wharf in the thick of Cruger's campaign against the lieutenant governor's son. "The election which ensued," wrote William Livingston, "was unfavorable to the De Lancey party."[7] And so when Douglass commenced the round of social calls necessary to promote his season of entertainments, things turned sour. Before he had even completed his remodeling, the father of the defeated candidate denied him permission to perform.

We will never know all the sordid details, but Douglass's alliance with Cruger likely undermined his project. Perhaps it was the way he began the conversion of a warehouse to a playhouse before he had secured permission to play? Perhaps the public perception was that the players were Cruger's men? Perhaps the imposing politicos of the city concurred that if they could not defeat Cruger, they could at least kick his tenant. The shocked Douglass went public:

> Mr. Douglass, who came here with a company of comedians, having apply'd to the gentlemen in power for permission to play, has (to his great mortification) met with a positive and absolute denial: He has in vain represented that such are his circumstances, and those of the other members of his company, that it is impossible for them to move to another place; and tho' in the humblest manner he begg'd the magistrates would indulge him in acting as many plays as would barely defray the expences he

and the company have been at, in coming to this city, and enable them to proceed to another; he has been unfortunate enough to be peremptorily refused it. As he has given over all thoughts of acting, he begs leave to inform the publick, that in a few days he will open an Histrionic Academy, of which proper notice will be given in this paper.[8]

Circumventing the civic injunction under the guise of a teaching academy was a device theatre managers had been using in England for twenty years, since Parliament passed the Licensing Act (1737) that limited the right of performance to two London theatres, Drury Lane and Covent Garden. Theatres, like William Hallam's at Goodman's Field, that had operated if not entirely legally at least unharassed for years, on and off, found themselves criminalized and developed strategies that capitalized on the many loopholes in the act, including the wording that no company could play for "hire, gain, or reward." Managers quickly noted that nothing technically prohibited anyone from playing for free. Hence they advertised "gratis" performances following a concert (for example), with tickets for the music that resembled the same pricing structure of the playhouse. David Garrick had made his debut in *Richard III*, gratis, after just such a concert.

The "concert format" allowed illegal theatres to continue their repertory of plays as concerts, "between the parts of which will be offered, gratis, Romeo and Juliet." Managers also devised the "moral lecture," in which various actors would display, for example, the dangers of jealousy, by offering the "parable" of Othello. They propagated the "histrionic academy," or acting school device, in which the manager (the professor) offered a free "exhibition" of his students' skills. Charles Macklin had offered an acting academy, where he displayed "rehearsals" of plays. Theophilus Cibber had used the histrionic academy device as late as summer of 1756.[9] The most famous remained Samuel Foote's picture auctions, which offered plays interspersed among the bidding. When confronted with a similar problem in New York, Douglass responded by advertising "A Histrionic Academy," and at first glance it should have worked. If his audiences were truly provincial, they would be fooled, and if truly urbane, they would understand. It should have worked. It didn't.

The subterfuge fooled no one and angered many. Douglass was informed in no uncertain terms that any attempt to circumvent the city's authority would be prosecuted. The humbled manager did the only thing he could: he went public with his apology.

> Whereas I am informed, that an advertisement of mine, which appeared some time ago in this paper, giving notice that I would open an Histrionic Academy, has been understood by many as a declaration that I proposed under that colour, to act plays, without the consent of the magistracy: This is therefore to inform the public, that such a construction was quite foreign to my intent and meaning, that so vain, so insolent a project never once entered into my head; It is an impeachment of my understanding to imagine, I would dare, in a publick manner, to aim at an affront on gentlemen, on whom I am dependent for the only means that can save us from utter ruin. All that I proposed to do was, to deliver dissertations of subject, moral, instructive and entertaining, and to endeavour to qualify such as would favour me with their attendance, to speak in public with propriety. But as such an understanding might have occasioned an inquiry into my capacity, I thought the publick would treat me with greater favour, when they we're informed that I was deprived of any other means of getting my bread; nor would that have done any more than barely supplied our present necessities. The expenses of our coming here, our living since our arrival, with the charge of building, etc. (which let me observe, we had engaged for before we had any reason to apprehend a denial) amount to a sum that would swallow up the profits of a great many nights acting, had we permission. I shall conclude with humbly hoping that those gentlemen who have entertained an ill opinion of me, from my supposed presumption, will do me the favour to believe, that I have truly explained the advertisement, and that I am, to them, and the publick, a very humble, and very devoted servant, David Douglass, Decem 8 1758.[10]

The company had been in town for nearly two months with no income. The expenses accrued by sailing from the islands, their board and lodging, converting a warehouse to a playhouse continued to mount. The remodeling remained incomplete, Douglass was running out of money, and now he had earned the wrath of the city's authorities.

In early December of 1758, for all intents and purposes, the nascent American theatre became a casualty of political naiveté.

Everything a new manager could have done wrong, Douglass did. He played merchants against magistrates and the magistrates trumped. He allied himself with one candidate and the losing candidates retaliated. He published his presence before he secured his permission. He began the expensive business of remodeling without permission to play. He undertook the cost himself and was out of pocket after the closure. Once denied permission, he sought to evade his denial, and then denied his evasion. The only thing he did right was publicly prostrating himself as the city's "very humble, and very devoted servant." That may have softened a few hearts on the council. George Odell's conclusion appears the most likely: "[D]oubtless certain people of influence desired to see plays."[11] Sufficiently chastened, Douglass received grudging permission to perform for thirteen nights—enough to see them out of town without debts.

In spite of a tempestuous introduction, the company met with terrific success in New York, opening on December 28, 1758, to an overflowing (ware)house, and playing three nights a week, "generously encouraged."[12] Among those in attendance were the generals Webb and Lounden, who "both devoted themselves to such amusements, concerts, theatrical performances, assemblies, etc. as the city afforded."[13] This brace of high brass as clientele likely trumped all local authority.

Like most companies on the provincial circuit, the repertory of plays consisted primarily of familiar playwrights such as Otway, Shakespeare, Dryden, and Farquhar, but even these dated works filled the small house, and more importantly, secured the company's credit and invitation to return. They had blundered and stumbled, but in the end they filled the house and were invited back.

When Douglass opened on December 28, 1758, with a prologue of his own composition, he spoke of this "unlucky time."[14] The war with France was playing out on British-American soil, the constant fear of the French invasion had led to press gangs from General Loundon's fleet snapping up as many as eight hundred men in one night. Though the company would have been eager to propitiate, some of their titles suggest a wry commentary on local politics in the winter of 1758–1759, particularly concerning the raising and billeting of troops. When Governor Delancey summoned the assembly to meet at the close of January 1759, the raising of troops loomed as the most pressing issue. The governor promised to recruit 2600 men by offering bounties to the recruiting officers. Douglass had recently staged Farquhar's *Recruiting Officer*, a play that parodied this very scenario.

The company closed their brief season with Shakespeare's *Richard III* on February 7, 1759, and promptly disappeared to the provinces. To his credit, the debacle of the "New York Histrionic Academy" would be Douglass's only major tactical error in his career on the continent.

New York had proved an academy after all, and Douglass learned two significant lessons. First, he had a commodity people wanted. He had London high culture, plays, music, dance; he had, in short, London in a box, and colonists had a strong desire to emulate that urbane capital. He had the best actors on the continent (the only ones), and if his first season in America had not been curtailed by a civic battle, he could have played three very profitable months in New York. He also learned the need for cultivating his relationships with men of authority and his reading of local politics, and in the third quarter of the eighteenth century this would be very complicated. It would become a lifelong social project that would ultimately promote both Douglass and theatre itself into the highest echelons of colonial American society. After the first disappointment in New York, Douglass would insinuate himself into every available social network, club, party, class, and organization in the colonies. He would never again invest his own money in building a theatre without permission. He would never rent someone else's building. And most importantly, he would make sure he knew every governor, lieutenant governor, and general, every mayor, every councilman, every principal gentleman, every Grand Master of every Freemason lodge, every printer, planter, and horse-racer, every merchant and man of property in every colony in America that he entered. He would become the most well-connected man in America.

[CHAPTER 3]
Building a Network
1759–1760

• • •

Patronage held everything together.
ALLAN KARRAS, *Sojourners in the Sun*

PHILADELPHIA

When young London rake William Hickey exhausted his father's patience and was shipped to Calcutta, Hickey carried with him nearly two dozen letters of introduction: "I believe there never was a man better recommended than myself."[1] Two dozen letters attested to his promise (composed by friends and family relieved to be rid of him); and if twenty-four letters seems excessive, it was. But any newcomer moving in the vast network of British imperial power relied on letters of character to serve as a foundation upon which to build his reputation. Introductions to the "quality" often proved the first order of business upon arriving in a new colony. Such letters constructed a social network across vast distances and served as social accelerators. The further afield one traveled, the more letters one needed. The young George Washington and his brother Lawrence presented their letters upon disembarking in Barbados and immediately received introductions to the best people of the island. The young Alexander Hamilton used a fulsome letter from Hugh Knox on St. Croix to open doors in Elizabethtown, New Jersey, that would have been closed to an unconnected young man from the West Indies. Conversely, a tepid letter could utterly damn with the faintest of praise.[2] The biggest criticism anyone offered of the social aspirant was to arrive someplace, as Thomas Paine arrived in America, "without connections."[3]

Douglass began the long and laborious process of building a network of patrons that eventually guaranteed him the long business plan of monopolizing the theatre in British America. There were, of course, other models at hand. Many traveling companies simply treated the cities of colonial America as a one-time pirate raid: enter anonymously, play illegally, take plenteously, and decamp before the debts were called in. The Hallams had toured British America exactly this way. And there were others with worse practices. The criminal tactics of William Verling's New American Company in the late 1760s left seventeen pages of pending legal suits in the Ann Arundel court registers.[4]

But rather than moving through the host cities as vagrants, playing and preying, Douglass chose to become a resident of America, and his conception of citizenship, of belonging not to a colony or a city but to a larger dominion, the social network of cultured colonial British America, reveals the obscure sea change sweeping over the land in the decades to come, fashioning Americans out of provincial British colonists. To succeed in such a landscape, Douglass would have to build an intra-colonial network from the trading class, the plantation class, the moneyed, the urbane, and above all, the ruling class. He transplanted his network from colony to colony, exploiting the intra-colonial associations and clubs, alliances and loose affiliations, taking full advantage of every contact he could: pressing letters from Virginia into service in Newport, exporting patronage from New York to Charleston. Nor, as a native Scot, could he rely solely on the densely established but overtaxed Scottish web that monopolized certain industries, such as trading houses, shipping, and sugar.[5] Luckily for him, neither Douglass nor his product had a rival in America. His vocation had the professional advantage of being socially fluid, particularly in the hands of one graceful enough to pass in polite society.

While New York had been a disaster financially and politically, it proved a social success. When Douglass left, he carried permission from Cadwallader Colden to return, and he would build a proper theatre the following year. But for now, he let the political dust settle and surfaced next in Philadelphia, in early 1759. There Douglass went straight to the power,[6] presenting himself on April 5, 1759, before William Denny, the lieutenant governor of Pennsylvania, to secure permission to erect a theatre and perform in the city. Before their encounter, he secured the recommendations of several gentlemen of that city who had patronized his playhouse in New York and encouraged him to attempt Philadelphia.

Denny proved an easy mark. In his early days in London he had circulated among literary, urbane, and ribald circles, three populations he missed in his new post in Philadelphia. He was, for example, one of the original members of the Dilettanti Society, that amiable group described by Horace Walpole in the following way: "The nominal qualification is having been in Italy, and the real one, being drunk."[7] The Dilettanti represented a curious combination of amateur antiquarians and professional hedonists, and many of their portraits display their appetite for their holy trinity: the classical, the garter, and the punch bowl. Denny's name appears among the club's first documents, and after his recall from America he returned to the group. His more diplomatic critics dismissed him as bookish ("retired to his library"), or absent ("the master of the ship is at Athens among some curious antiquities"), while the worst lambasted him as "scandalously indolent and luxurious so that he minds his own ease and belly more than concerns of the government."[8] To be fair, the governor inherited an unsolvable situation in Pennsylvania, more divisive than most colonies, but with the additional disadvantage of a Crown-chartered frontier land grant of enormous proportions whose only city was a Quaker stronghold. The governor found himself stymied by infighting, assembly against council (his own appointment derived from the Penn family, whom the assembly openly labeled as "tyrants"), and well aware that all parties resented him as a newly minted, Crown-appointed placeman. Denny had recently been promoted from captain to colonel, that he might have the appropriate rank to govern the province, but this pleasure-loving scholar was clearly in over his head. His first response was a frank assessment: "The people [of Pennsylvania] are divided into parties, violent and obstinate beyond imagination," and they remained so until his recall later in 1759.[9]

The arrival of a company of actors shone as the one bright spot in his administration, and Denny, despite his indolence, sensing the complicated political landscape, granted Douglass permission to play, with two astute conditions: Denny communicated his permission in a private letter, not a council-approved motion, and he requested that Douglass build his playhouse outside the city limits, and consequently, outside the city's jurisdiction. It was just as well, given the civic imbroglio that ensued. The Quaker-controlled assembly strenuously opposed to the players, and the city council divided on the issue. The theatre's strongest supporter, beyond the governor, was the prominent, forward-looking patron of the arts Reverend William Smith, provost of the College of Philadelphia.

William Smith possessed a forceful personality. He had come to Philadelphia in 1755 to promote a plan for higher education. On the recommendation of Benjamin Franklin, Smith was appointed provost of the College of Philadelphia, as well as the Charity School. The supervision of the city's education system did not offer sufficient scope for Smith's talent, abilities, and ambitions. Philadelphia historians Carl and Jessica Bridenbaugh describe Provost Smith as "a force second only to Franklin in many phases of its [Philadelphia's] cultural life." But the force often carried Smith far afield from academia, as pamphleteer and publisher. Franklin wrote to George Whitefield in 1756 that he wished Smith would "learn to mind Party-writing and Party-politics less and his proper Business more."[10] His political writings, published in his own periodical, the *American Magazine*, caused the assembly to jail him twice in 1757–1758. Additionally, Smith was more than a theatre supporter: he introduced academic theatre into his curriculum at the college, and he adapted *The Masque of Alfred* for student productions in 1756–1757. Smith wrote articles and editorials in favor of introducing theatre into the city. He also fervently opposed the Quakers and the Quaker-controlled assembly.

The assembly, in their turn, had no love for Smith. They resented his use of lotteries to raise money for his college. When the assembly drafted this current act for suppression of plays, they attached a rider also preventing lotteries. This bill used anti-theatrical legislation to undermine Provost Smith's position. As Bridenbaugh argues, "by prohibiting lotteries, then one of the chief sources of income for the Academy, the Quaker legislators hoped to procure his overthrow, or at least his serious embarrassment. This partisan measure they shrewdly combined with legislation for suppression of the theatre, in order to secure the backing of dissenting groups."[11]

Douglass thus found himself in the middle of another battle for local power, in which the contest over theatre had little to do with the theatre itself. To the Quaker petition were also added petitions from the Lutherans, the Baptists, and the Presbyterians. On May 22, 1759, Presbyterian Richard Treat penned an elegant appeal from the synod of New York and Philadelphia to Lieutenant Governor William Denny of Pennsylvania:

With the greatest concern for the interests of virtue and Religion, we beg leave to inform your honour that we understand there is a Proposal of erecting a house within this city or Suburbs peculiarly designed for exhibiting plays. That we cannot but believe in the common method they are conducted, they prove a most powerful engine of debauching the minds and corrupting the manners of youth, by encouraging Idleness, extravagance, and immorality, which are of most fatal consequence to the publick weal. That the present war with France and the critical conjuncture of our publick affairs, render the entertainments of the stage peculiarly improper [?] at this time. Therefore we as the ministers of Christ and the friends of mankind humbly intreat your honour to discountenance this pernicious design. We presume not by this address to dictate to your honour, but only to discharge what we judge to be a duty incumbent on us in present circumstances; and flatter ourselves we shall obtain your ready concurrence in an affair of so much importance which we doubt not will be extremely agreeable to the good people of this city and Province, and particularly oblige . . .
[Signed] Richard Treat.[12]

Denny had warned the assembly that the act was unreasonable and reminded them that Pennsylvania, as a British proprietary colony, had no authority to prohibit plays, and that all such earlier prohibitions — dating back to 1692 — had been routinely repealed in Parliament. The city council found fault with the yoking of the suppression of lotteries to the bill, as being harmful to the college, and uncoupled the measures, leaving the anti-theatrical legislation a stand-alone bill. If Douglass thought he was in dire straits again, this was nothing compared to the fears of his builder. Alexander Alexander, a "smith," on the strength of the governor's private letter to Douglass, had already begun building the playhouse, at his own expense. When he heard about the petitions in circulation among the Quakers, Lutherans, and Presbyterians, he wrote to the governor. Alexander and the painter on the project, William Williams, petitioned that if the bill passed Douglass be exempted, that they might get paid for their labor: "That your petitioners [Alexander and Williams] relying on the said permission to be genuine, and not entertaining the least doubt that anything cou'd intervene to prevent Mr. Douglass's design of acting, your Petitioner, Alexander, was prevailed on to build, at his own charge, a large building for a Play House, for the use of Mr. Douglass and his company, which when finished, will cost your Petitioner £300 and upwards."[13] That Douglass had commissioned builders in advance of his license indicates a certain confidence on the manager's part that an arrangement with the city would eventually be worked out.

Still, it must have been mortifying for Douglass to learn that eight days later, the Commonwealth of Pennsylvania, acting on the Quaker petition, passed a law forbidding plays with a £500 fine for violation.[14] The legislation suggested an implicit bid for self-governance, a defiance of parliamentary law, and a severing from the codes of greater British culture. Four times in the past Pennsylvanian anti-theatrical legislation had been repealed in London and missives sent reminding the colony that it lived under parliamentary law, including the right to operate theatres, and four times Pennsylvania had responded by rescinding that permission.[15]

Eventually, some deft behind-the-scenes politicking by Denny temporarily thwarted the theatre's opponents by deferring the new law's commencement until January 1, 1760, thus effectively allowing Douglass to play until the end of the year, by which time the law would have been repealed at the King's Council in England. It was an astute move, but Douglass knew that license to play from the governor was no guarantee of popular support. Still, it was point and match for Douglass in Philadelphia: he had the governor's support, and in America in 1759 that was largely what counted. The Quakers gnashed their teeth and penned diatribes against the vices of play-going, but Douglass (and incidentally Alexander and Williams) gave a great sigh of relief, and the theatre opened beyond the reach of its firmest opponents.

Douglass built his theatre on Society Hill (the corner of Vernon and South Streets), just two blocks beyond the town's jurisdiction, which had been a pleasure district of illicit entertainment since the 1720s, when William Moraley arrived there and "spent many a pound."[16] Here, beyond the prying eyes of zealots and the light of street lamps, Alexander built a rough barn of a building and called it a theatre. To the company that had been without income for two months, it must have seemed like flush times. Once opened, in June of 1759, Douglass and company played three nights a week for the rest of the year. And as a thanks to Provost Smith, Douglass donated benefit proceeds from the *London Merchant* "towards the raising of a Fund for purchasing an Organ to the College Hall in this City, and instructing the Charity Children in Psalmody." These gestures secured him not only the credit to return, but enormous currency of character.

MARYLAND

At the start of 1760 Douglass and company traveled the coach road south into Maryland, where he had plans to construct a theatre in the tidewater capital. To this end he introduced himself to Governor Horatio Sharpe, who granted him permission to build a playhouse in Annapolis and perform there and elsewhere in the colony. The first public notice of the project appears in the *Maryland Gazette* of February 7, 1760: "By permission of his Excellence the Governor, a Theatre is erecting in this city, which will be opened soon by a Company of Comedians, who are now at Chester-Town."

How he was able to arrive in a new colony, introduce himself to the governor, secure permission to play, select a site, lease or purchase a lot, hire a local contractor, and erect a playhouse in less than eight weeks is a wonder that Douglass would repeat many times. Douglass made two key refinements in his business plan. First, before establishing themselves in Annapolis, the company stopped in Chester, where they could play in the market house with only the mayor's permission while the larger project of entering the capital, securing permission, and building a theatre could be undertaken without the expense of idle actors the company had experienced in New York and Philadelphia. Second, to secure permission in Maryland, Douglass carried letters of introduction from Philadelphia. He gathered up governors because they spoke most directly to each other. A letter from Governor Denny or the "principal gentlemen" addressed directly to Governor Horatio Sharpe would go a long way toward establishing his credentials.

His entry into the first of many social clubs, the Honorable Society of Freemasons, also stood him in good stead. In many colonial towns, the Freemasons offered the easiest access to important social networks. If, for example, Douglass made the first week of February meeting of the Masons in Annapolis, he would have found Governor Sharpe in attendance, and he would have met the secretary of the Masonic lodge, Jonas Green. Green was an alderman in Annapolis, as well as a printer who published the only newspaper in the colony. He later supplied the playbills and play tickets for Douglass, and sold theatre tickets as well. That connection delivered auxiliary connections: Green was also the secretary for another wealthy, influential club, the Annapolis Racing Association—that horsey crowd of plantation aristocrats—with whom Douglass would ingratiate himself by offering "the theatric purse" of £50. Green was also the master of ceremonies for the Tuesday Club, the talented gentlemen who later penned prologues for the playhouse and provided the chamber orchestra. And the lots next to where Douglass built his playhouse belonged to Green. As Lawrence Wroth summarized, "[T]here seems to have been no local activity of any importance in which the 'printer to the Province' was not concerned."[17] And every colonial city seemed to have a Green or two, someone whose hands were in a great deal of the city's business, usually a printer, like Green, or Robert Wells in Charleston, William Bradford in Philadelphia, and they became enormously useful connections for Douglass.

Douglass purchased two lots near Acton's Cove, at the lower end of town—as William Eddis would describe it later, "inconveniently situated"—but the inconvenience notwithstanding, he attracted the best of Annapolis society to the waterfront. When the theatre opened on March 3, 1760, the house was full, and Governor Sharpe joined the audience. As a signal of support, such a presence was invaluable. The company played regularly (advertising play titles for Mondays, Thursdays, and Saturdays) until an Easter recess, after which the court season opened in Annapolis, the town filled with tidewater litigants, and the actors worked every night except Sunday. All told, they played for two and half months, and won numerous supporters. But perhaps the company's most enthusiastic patron was a clergyman, the rector of St. Paul's, for whom the arrival of the players recalled for him his youth in London, as a playwright.

As a young man at Trinity College, Dublin, James Sterling (1701– 1763) became infatuated with the playhouse. His *The Rival Generals* was performed at the Smock Alley Theatre, Dublin (1720), and printed in Dublin and London. Flush with success, Sterling married Nancy Lyddel, an actress from Smock Alley, and in 1722 they traveled to London for Mrs. Sterling's engagement with John Rich's company at Lincoln's

Inn Fields. Sterling's second play, *Parricide* (1726), followed, as well as poetic translations and various prologues and epilogues for the playhouse. Mrs. Sterling became a well-known actress during the 1720s, both in London and Dublin. The Sterlings further cemented their attachment to the profession when Henry Giffard, manager of Goodman's Inn Fields, married Mrs. Sterling's sister.

But after his wife's death in 1732, Sterling put his theatre career behind him. He became a minister and immigrated to America in 1736. He applied first at Boston, but his checkered past preceded him, and the town would have little to do with a playhouse parson. When an opening arose in Maryland, Sterling traveled south and secured his first post in All Hallows Parish in 1737. Eighteen months later he was appointed by Governor Samuel Ogle as rector of Saint Anne's in Annapolis. Soon afterwards, he resigned that post and moved to the more lucrative parish of St. Paul's, in Chestertown, Kent County, where he remained for the next twenty years.[18] He remarried, twice, accumulated a fine estate, and though he published occasional poems in William Smith's *American Magazine* (1757–1758) to maintain his reputation as a gentleman poet, to all appearances his theatrical career seemed the folly of a London youth.

That is, until one day in February of 1760, when David Douglass and his company of players arrived in Chestertown while Douglass was building a new theatre in Annapolis. During their brief stay the parson's passion for the boards re-ignited. The American Company played Chestertown briefly (perhaps a month, no more than six weeks), and when the company departed for the capital, Sterling traveled with them. Douglass opened the new playhouse on March 3, 1760, and Sterling wrote a special prologue for the new season, as well as the epilogue. The prologue was published in the *Maryland Gazette*, and by desire, spoken again on March 13.[19] Jonas Green wrote a fine review of the opening:

> Monday last the theatre in this city was open'd, when the tragedy of the Orphan, and Lethe (a dramatic satire) were perform'd, in the presence of his Excellency the Governor, to a polite and numerous audience, who all express'd a general satisfaction. The principal characters, both in the play and entertainment, were perform'd with great justice, and the applause which attended

> the whole representation, did less honour to the abilities of the actors than to the taste of their auditors. For the amusement and emolument of such of our readers as were not present, we here insert the Prologue and epilogue, both written by a Gentleman in this Province, whose poetical Works have render'd him justly Admir'd by all Encouragers of the Liberal Arts.

The presence of men like Sterling underscores that the liberal arts in America emerged due to the talents of a few zealous individuals who, assembled in clubs (like Dr. Hamilton's Tuesday Club, or in the next decade, the Hominy Club, both in Annapolis). And they arrived against the objections of more pragmatic intellectual leaders, such as Benjamin Franklin, who considered the mid-century introduction of the arts into America as premature.

> Thus poetry, painting, and music, (and the stage as their embodiment) are all the necessary and proper gratifications of a refined state of society, but objectionable at an earlier period, since their cultivation would make a taste for enjoyment precede its means. All things have their season, he would say, and with young countries, as with young men, you must curb their fancy to strengthen their judgement. . . . To America, one schoolmaster is worth a dozen poets.[20]

This opinion suggests why some of America's fiercest anti-theatricalists could enjoy it elsewhere. Men such as Henry Laurens, merchant of Charleston and later president of the Congress, knew Douglass personally, but thought the company "a set of strollers fleecing the city." Yet Laurens insisted on carrying his son to see plays while in London. Or Josiah Quincy, Jr., who resisted introducing theatrical entertainments in Boston, but enjoyed them enormously whenever he traveled, including to Douglass's theatre in New York (of which he wrote, "I believe if I had staid in town a month, I should go to the theatre every acting night"[21]).

To others, such as Sterling, the arrival of the arts ushered in a golden future for America, yet an America that was both the proper extension of Great Britain and at the same time a contestant for supremacy, an America in which the arts would be a hallmark of the refinement of character. Sterling put it thus, onstage and page:

Lo! to new Worlds th' advent'rous Muse conveys
The moral Wisdom of dramatic lays!
She bears thro' Ocean Phoebus' high Command,
And tunes his Lyre in fair Maria's Land;
And rising Bards in Western Climes inspires!
See! Genius wakes, dispels the former Gloom,
And shed Light's Blaze, deriv'd from Greece and Rome!
With polish'd Arts wild Passions to control;
To warm the Breast, and humanize the Soul!
By magic Sounds to vary Hopes and Fears;
Or make each Eye dissolve in virtuous tears!
Til sympathizing Youths in Anguish melt,
And Virgins sigh for Woes, before unfelt!
Here, as we speak, each heart-struck Patriot glows
With real Rage to crush Britannia's Foes!
To quell bold Tyrants, and support the Laws,
Or, like brave WOLFE, bleed in his Country's Cause!

Europe no more, sole Arbitress, shall sit,
Or boast the proud Monopoly of Wit;
Her youngest Daughter here with filial Claim,
Asserts her Portion of Maternal Fame!
Let no nice Sparks despise our humble Scenes,
Half-Buskin'd Monarchs, and iten'rant Queens!
Triflers! who boast, they once in Tragic Fury
Heard Garrick thund'ring on the Stage of Drury!
Or view'd, exulting, o'er each gay Machine,
The Feats of Covent-Garden's Harlequin!
Athens from such beginnings, mean and low!
Saw Thespis' Cart a wond'rous Structure grow;
Saw Theatres aspire, and with surprize
Ghosts, Gods, and Daemons, or descend or rise!
To Taste, from Censure, draw no rash Pretence;
But think Good-Nature the sure Test of Sense!
As England's Sons, attend to Reason's strains;
And prove her Blood flows richly in your Veins;
Be what we Act, the Heroes of our Parts;
And feel, that Britons here have Roman hearts!

The values encoded in the prologue represent a wealth of American aspirations, to both join and outdo their European ancestry. Sterling voices the desire for inclusion in the long genealogy of empire—Greek, Roman, and British. Such sentiments trade on the theatre's role in nation-building, in manufacturing Britons whose own mythic identity was half Roman. The prologue also speaks with urgency about its own belatedness. It positions Douglass's venture as the microcosm of the civilizing force of the arts, the whole of Athenian performance tradition collapsed into a single generation.

Moving on from Annapolis, Douglass secured his character letters and met the horse and jockey crowd from northern Virginia, who encouraged his company to seek permission in Williamsburg, the capital city. During the wait for permission, the company enjoyed a brief layover in Upper Marlborough. There Douglass promised to accommodate "such ladies and gentlemen who choose to go home after the play" by beginning the performance at 4:00 instead of their customary 6:00. Douglass had missed the semi-annual assembly that convened in Marlborough in late April, but one English traveler, Andrew Barnaby, visited Marlborough and encountered Douglass during his stay there. Barnaby had left George Washington's plantation with the colonel's borrowed coach and traveled up to Marlborough. "I here met with a strolling company of players, under the direction of one Douglass. I went to see their theatre, which was a neat convenient tobacco-house, well fitted up for the purpose."[22] Barnaby did not stay for the production, but his account demonstrates that Douglass frequently introduced himself to travelers of distinction. The company played in Upper Marlborough through June of 1760, within an easy ride of Mount Vernon, though it is unknown if Washington attended, as his diaries from May 1760 to May 1761 are missing.

WILLIAMSBURG

During the fall of 1760, while Douglass made his way to the capital, the company played tidewater towns including Alexandria and Fredericksburg. He carried his letters of introduction from Horatio Sharpe to Virginia's lieutenant governor, Francis Fauquier, who had his hands full with a major Indian uprising. Among the issues discussed at September's council meeting was an attack on the regiment from Fort

Loudoun. Fort Loudoun had been under siege, its inhabitants in distress, reduced to four ounces of horseflesh per day. A large band of Cherokee and Creek Indians fired on the garrison sent to relieve them, killing all the officers and imprisoning all the enlisted men. What recruits could be raised were hastily drafted. William Byrd III described his troops as two-thirds mob, "new-raised men, who at this moment are neither clothed or armed."[23] Under such circumstances, granting permission to a troupe of players may have been the last thing on the council's mind.

Or not. What might theatre offer to a community carving out its niche in civilized society? While men on the frontiers consumed rationed horseflesh, pinned down in by Indians, the very notion of importing European culture as a buffer against the wilderness had distinct appeal. Fauquier could recognize the irony of Douglass's civilizing project at such a moment. He was, as Jefferson described him, the most refined man in the colony. The young Jefferson, along with his mentor from the College of William and Mary, William Small, and George Wythe, with whom Jefferson studied law, constituted a convivial quartet at the governor's table, of which gatherings Jefferson later wrote: "At these dinners I have heard more good sense, more rational and philosophical conversations, than in all my life besides. They were truly Attic societies. The governor was musical also, and a good performer, and associated me with two or three other amateurs in his weekly concerts."[24]

Into such refinement Douglass would be welcomed in Williamsburg. He needed now to buy or lease land and raise a subscription to build a theatre. The quickest way to meet such patrons would be the quarterly assembly of the Freemasons. Peyton Randolph, the Master Mason, was also among the governor's gatherings, "always good humored," as Jefferson described him in his autobiography. Douglass's name appears on the earliest preserved list of the Virginia Masons.[25] There Douglass met the social elite of the colony and was granted permission to play, secured the land, hired a contractor, and delivered a template plan for a theatre. Douglass arrived sometime in August and had opened the new theatre by October 2, 1760. It was fast work, but among his subscribers who helped forward the project was a familiar face, Colonel Washington, who recorded a payment of £7. 10. 3 "for the playhouse."[26]

The Fall Court season in Williamsburg provided an essential semi-annual market for the players. Each year in the spring and fall the town would swell with incoming planters, traders, representatives, and litigants. A French traveler visiting Williamsburg in 1765 recorded: "I suppose there might be 5 or 6000 people here during the Courts."[27] The Fall Court season began sometime around the 10th of October and could last for twenty-four days or more. The House of Burgesses also met fall and spring. The visitors also availed themselves of the heavy social calendar: court seasons (chronicled in calendar records for 1752, 1768, 1770, 1771, 1772) also became popular times for balls, horse races, and theatre.

Court in Williamsburg also proved a dense site of intersecting spheres of influence—economic, juridical, and social. Unlike Charleston, Boston, or New York, Virginia had no single urban center, no natural entrepôt. Rather, it had a network of navigable rivers and small trading hubs from Norfolk on the coast to Petersburg, Fredericksburg, and Alexandria inland. Towns remained relatively modest in size, with vast populations spread among a wide geography. This population of planters, merchants, and traders gathered during the Public Times in Williamsburg for the General Court (in April and October) and the lesser court of the Oyer and Terminer, in June and December, when, as Governor Fauquier wrote to the Board of Trade, "persons engaged in business of any kind" converged on the capital.[28] Claimants came to court to settle disputes and debts. James Robinson, an overseer of a chain of tobacco stores, gathered his clerks at court session to pay salaries, while the cartel of tobacco dealers met to set their prices. Bankers set interest rates. Speculators and place seekers found employment. A kind of grain exchange informally transpired in the coffeehouses of Williamsburg at court times.[29]

To finance the construction of the new playhouse, Douglass offered a subscription scheme. Subscribers like Washington would advance money, and Douglass would advance tickets. Washington purchased the equivalent of twenty box tickets, providing Douglass the up-front money to underwrite the construction of the new theatre, a scheme he would use in Annapolis, New York, and Charleston.[30] The theatre opened sometime in October; Washington would leave the capital on November 6, giving him a solid month in town, during which time he purchased an additional twenty-four tickets.

At the close of 1760 Douglass had on his list of elite the governors of New York, Pennsylvania, Maryland, and Virginia and the principal men of three middle colonies with good markets, two of which held semiannual courts, and a fine racing season. He now owned three theatres and an American monopoly on his goods. He would return to New York next, build another theatre there, and then reconnoiter Newport, Rhode Island. What became very clear very early was that he was selling something highly desirable: he was selling London, and he carried it in a box.

[CHAPTER 4]
London in a Box
• • •

'Tis a devilish thing to live in a village a hundred miles from the capital, with a preposterous gouty father, and a super-annuated maiden aunt. — I am heartily sick of my situation.
ISAAC BICKERSTAFF, *Love in a Village*

Looking over the wealth of images of provincial English theatres, such as those in James Winston's *The Theatric Tourist,* the eighteenth-century provincial theatre does not always look like a particularly attractive place. Many appear little better than frumpy barns on the outskirts of town, tarted up with a portico. But in spite of the raw appearance of colonial theatres on the provincial circuits, the theatre was, in its day, the richest place in town; and in the same breath it should be noted that neither the town that hosted the theatre nor the theatregoers who frequented it could really afford such a luxury. That they demanded it nonetheless speaks to the genteel desires of the period that theatre represented in its most extravagant form. If the urbane society of London proved out of reach for backcountry planters, villagers, and country squires in the colonies, the desire for it was not. The inside of a well-lit theatre was as close to London as many provincials ever got, and in this regard the theatre in colonial America was "London in a Box," and Douglass a purveyor of European taste, fashionable manners, and gentility. Among the second sons and social aspirants of early America, he found a ready market. Playwright Oliver Goldsmith noted the acute desire for London fashion in that wry way of all London transplants:

> MRS. HARDCASTLE: I vow, Mr. Hardcastle, you're very particular. Is there a creature in the whole country, but ourselves, that does not take a trip to town now and then, to rub off the rust a little? . . .
>
> MR. HARDCASTLE: Aye, and bring back vanity and affectation to last them the whole year. I wonder why London cannot keep its own fools at home. *She Stoops to Conquer* (1.1.1–10)

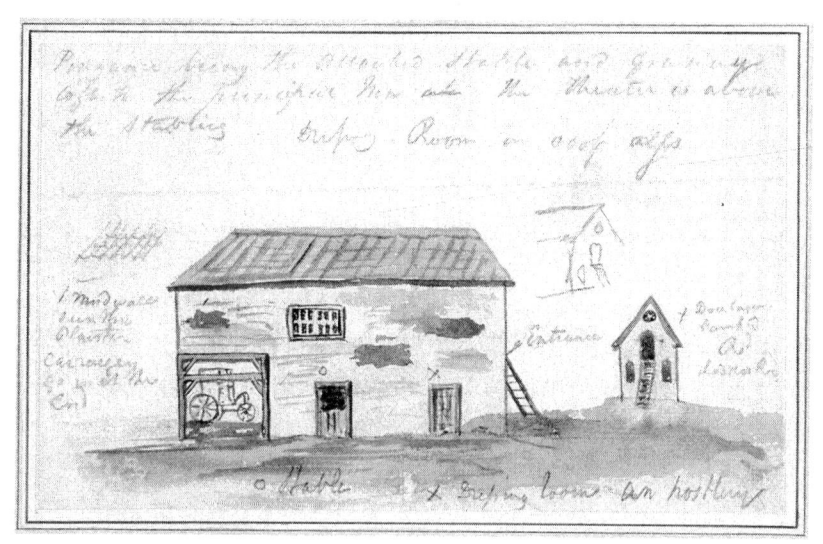

Figure 1. Penzance Theatre, Penzance, Cornwall, England, watercolor by Daniel Havell. Reproduced in James Winston, "Notes for 'The Theatric Tourist,'" HEW 13.4.2, 2:10, Harry Elkins Widener Collection, Houghton Library, Harvard University, Cambridge, MA.

Figure 2. Stroud Theatre, Gloucestershire, England, watercolor by Daniel Havell. Reproduced in James Winston, "Notes for 'The Theatric Tourist,'" HEW 13.4.2, 2:52, Harry Elkins Widener Collection, Houghton Library, Harvard University, Cambridge, MA.

The best London plays all ridiculed those who lacked London manners, or worse, were too ignorant to aspire to them. To be stuck in the country with nothing but a dull curate, awkward servants, and a Saturday game of whist with the maiden aunt was the most despised fate on the London stage from the Restoration to the end of the eighteenth century. Sir George Etherege's *Man of Mode* (1676) closes with a forlorn evocation of life outside of London:

> HARRIET: Emilia, pity me, who am going to that sad place. Methinks I hear the hateful noise of the rooks already, kaw, kaw, kaw!—There's music in the worst cry in London, "My dill and cucumbers to pickle." (5.2.449–453)

And it remained so a century later for Goldsmith's audiences who came to town to rub the rust off and to the theatre to acquire their affectation.[1] The deplorable figure was the country squire who aspired to manners he could not emulate, or the poor country girl who "can do nothing but dangle her arms, look gawky, turn her toes in, and talk broad Hampshire," as the naive Peggy is described in Garrick's *The Country Girl*.

The highest echelon of colonial society, who could afford to travel abroad and acquire taste directly, were few but enormously influential: the sons of Charleston's elite—Peter Manigault, John Rutledge, Ralph Izard, Thomas Lynch, Jr., Arthur Middleton, Charles Coteworth Pinckney, and John Laurens, for example—indoctrinated themselves in European taste and manners during their London sojourns, returning to the colonies as models of refinement and setting the standard of taste for the colony. Young Peter Manigault, son of South Carolina's attorney general, developed a "great taste" in London first and later transported it across the Atlantic. "The plays are now come in," he wrote home to his mother outside Charleston, "which makes London the pleasantest place in the World, and the Resort of all People of Fashion."[2] But for the bulk of residents who could not travel abroad, such as the young William Patterson, who dreamed of visiting London with his friend John MacPherson, "frequenting playhouses, operas and balls, a professed admirer of every fashionable amusement," Douglass strategically positioned his theatres as finishing schools for acquiring gentility. They formed part of that genteel revolution that Richard

Bushman has called "the refinement of America."[3] The theatres in America first established in that extraordinary generation, the third quarter of the eighteenth century, were part of what scholars have labeled "the consumer revolution" that reshaped the social landscape of colonial America. Like developing trade in tea equipage, porcelain, pewter ware, carriages, silk, or Turkish carpets, the theatre became an acquired, expensive, but necessary habit of the new Georgian taste that redefined "gentility" into material terms of consumption and display. As Bushman, writing of Wedgwood vases, remarks, "[g]enteel culture was not an inheritance; it could be acquired by purchases."[4]

The process was not only about acquiring imported material goods, but about acquiring the manners to use them—if not the "bona fide metropolitan manners, and what they could get you," as Julie Flavell writes of London, as close as a provincial dweller could get.[5] When John Adams visited New York en route to the first Congress in Philadelphia in 1774, he lamented the great want of good manners: "With all the Opulence and Splendor of this City, there is very little good Breeding to be found. . . . I have not seen one real Gentleman, one well bred Man since I came to Town. At the Entertainments there is no Conversation that is agreeable. There is no Modesty, no attention to one another. They talk very loud, very fast, and altogether."[6] If Adams found refinement lacking, others in that congressional company knew how to acquire it: "I know of nothing more entertaining and more likely to give you a graceful manner of speaking than seeing a good play well acted," wrote John Rutledge to his brother Edward.[7] The implication was, as Flavell writes, that "[g]enteel manners were a cheap accessory for those who had the knack of imitation."[8]

Theatre managers such as Thomas Sheridan in Dublin and Douglass in America sold the culture of gentility to provincial gentry uneasy about their social positions. Mid-century America boasted a core of social elite, but they were, with few exceptions, an aristocracy founded on merchant money, often hastily acquired, and some of dubious foundation; their claims were not based in bloodlines, titles, or generational privilege, and they were aware of the shortcomings.[9] Through energy, public spirit, and genteel manners, many families quickly rose from obscure origins to positions of prominence, and suffered the ridicule of those who knew them as immigrants: "Every Tradesman is

[now] a Merchant, every Merchant is a Gentleman, and every Gentleman one of the Noblesse," began an anonymous satirist of the Charleston aspirants:

> "The Sons of our lowest Mechanics are sent to the Colleges of Philadelphia, England, or Scotland, and there acquire, with their learning, laudable ambition of becoming Gentlefolks. . . . Persons of small fortune, Clerks and Apprentices, dress in every Respect equal to those of the first Rank and Eminence. . . . The Merchant leaves his Counting house for the Ball-room, and the country Gentleman his Affairs for the Amusements of the Turf."[10]

Though these colonists inhabited the backwoods and provinces, to go to the theatre was to be a little closer to London, and this desire largely explains why theatres dotted the colonial American landscape, from Halifax, North Carolina, to Halifax, Nova Scotia, even in towns that could not afford the luxury.[11] The theatre in America became a poor man's finishing school for the socially mobile. New Bern, North Carolina, for example, a town of fewer than a thousand citizens, in 1769 boasted five notable buildings: a courthouse, a jail, a tobacco warehouse, a hemp warehouse, and a theatre. And as one plantation owner wrote from the isolated Leeward island of Antigua: "We begin to feel somewhat alive here, the theatre is established."[12] The most articulate expression of this civilizing force was a Philadelphia editorial describing Douglass's new Southwark Theatre as an affordable, in-city substitute for the Grand Tour:

> The Americans are become now so refined, that an intimate knowledge of the customs, sports, and fashions of Europe, is become absolutely essential to a genteel and liberal education, and is found to be no other way attained, than by a tour to Italy, France, and England. The moment our young gentleman is released from the schools, he pants for his departure, and the fond indulgent parent, hoping thereby to see his darling boy shine in future, foremost in the ranks of his country's honors, scrapes together his hard got gold, and consigns it with his blessing, to the advent'rous youth; tis true he returns with every notion of taste and politeness that can render him the envy of his fellows

at home. But alas, these are all the visible returns of his adventure—he brings back new desires, instead of the wherewithal to gratify them, and again fleeces the old gentleman, to support those passions, himself consented to the acquirement of. Thus the country is annually robbed of a considerable sum, to the great grief of all true American spirits; to remedy this growing evil, sure, nothing could more fortunately have happened than the present establishment of the Theatre; where our youth may hear and view, at a trifling expence, every refinement of politeness, every sentiment of honour, and every scene of debauchery and villainy represented in the most striking colours."[13]

In a world of second sons and London-hungry aspirants, to be seen in the theatre was also to be "refined," and theatrical reviews of the period praise the audience's refinement as much as the actors' execution, describing the theatre as a "School of Politeness."[14]

The theatre in colonial America existed in towns too small to sustain a permanent playhouse. In 1760 the largest cities in America, such as New York and Philadelphia, sheltered fewer than fifteen thousand residents, and a southern capital such as Williamsburg, Virginia, could only exceed a thousand during court season. Yet between 1758 and 1775 Douglass built nineteen theatres in the towns of colonial America and the Anglophone Caribbean. They were not imposed on the landscape by traveling managers, but rather allowed by permission of governors, mayors, and city boards. Subscribers such as George Washington, who fronted £8 on the 1760 Williamsburg theatre; Maryland governor Robert Eden, who headed the list of subscribers who raised £600 for the new theatre in Annapolis in 1771; and those ladies and gentlemen of Charleston who encouraged David Douglass in the thick of the Stamp Act crisis, when there was no money in circulation—all conceived of such spaces as desirable for a cultured way of life. Most colonial cities, for example, had theatres long before they had hospitals. "Many people who, at this time, would not give one penny towards paving the streets, &c, would give ninety times that sum to see Cato well acted," wrote one editorial in Baltimore. Another in New York observed, "[T]he money thrown away in one night at a play would purchase wood, provisions and other necessaries, sufficient for a number of poor, to make them pass thro' the winter with tolerable comfort."[15] But the tolerable comfort of the poor was not part of what I have termed elsewhere "the anatomy of desire."[16]

Advancement, or survival, within the fragile and occasionally fraudulent stage of self-fashioning required the stability of certain signs—manners, dress, speech—through which one's station could be recognized, and these were all public acts. As critics of the young Benedict Arnold made clear, "[h]is manner was that of a gentleman's while he was silent; but his conversation betrayed a vulgar education."[17] Private markers—letter writing, penmanship, Latin quotations—could all be fabricated, but speech, as well as carriage, education, and manners, could not. Washington utterly redesigned his carriage, his writing style, even his penmanship when he began to cultivate a prominent persona, giving over his florid expressions and hand in favor of a more standard gentlemanly script.[18] To those still waiting in the anteroom of polite society for the finishing, there was the stage. In short, the well-bred body looked like an actor's.

THE BARBADOS JOURNAL

To get some sense of the theatre's role in the fashioning of young men into young gentlemen, consider the first experience of the theatre for the young George Washington. He first saw David Douglass onstage in Barbados in 1751, the only time Washington ever traveled off the continent.[19] He was nineteen at the time, and had sailed with his ailing brother Lawrence in the hopes of improving his health. The young men arrived in Bridgetown in November of 1751, and introduced themselves to Mr. Carter, councilman and chief justice of the island, who in turn introduced them to the theatre in Bridgetown, where Washington and his brother saw a production of George Lillo's *The Tragedy of George Barnwell, or The London Merchant.*

Washington's Barbados journal reveals the self-fashioning project upon which the young man had already embarked. From the wilds of Virginia, he was learning how to seem to be urbane without the advantages of London society. The young Washington, with next to little experience of such things, wrote briefly of his first theatre-going that night; but how he wrote of it—haltingly, constantly correcting himself—reveals a great deal about the refining process of such a space. He begins, "Was treated with a play ticket," but adds a little editorial carrot in the text, perhaps remembering his courtesy, and superscribes the addition "by Mr. Carter," before continuing, "to see the Tragedy of George Barnwell acted. The character of Barnwell and several others was said to be well performed."[20] "Said to be well performed": not having the experience himself, he acknowledges that the quality of the performance was best left to the judgment of others, presumably the more experienced Mr. Carter. He defers his own judgment, and in deferring learns the standards of performance. He was, in essence, being taught what constituted a good performance. He further notes, "There was a band of Musick ["a band of" was crossed out] adapted and regularly conducted by Mr.   " When Washington, like others of the rough, saw musicians gathered, he termed them according to military associations with music: regimental assemblies were called "bands," the term being used in the same way as in the account books of the Royal Theatre New York during its military season: "its Band of Music."[21] But theatres, as every experienced eighteenth-century theatre-goer knew, employed "orchestras," not "bands." It was a new, urbane model of concert music, so he crossed out "band." Further, to note that the music was "adapted" required somebody else's experience—perhaps again Mr. Carter's? Adapted from what? Abbreviated from the original, perhaps, but did he know the original? Somebody in the party did. And "regularly conducted" begs the question of how much chamber music young George was familiar with. Most revealing is the name of the conductor himself: not a satirist's dash that conspires with the reader, but rather it was not completed: he knew enough to acknowledge the conductor but was not familiar enough to use his name. He nods an acknowledgment without introductions; in short, he is recognizing both what is polite behavior and his own social shortcomings as a novice to the circle. As he wrote of his social experience on the island: "Hospitality and a genteel behavior is shewn to every gentleman stranger by the Gentlemen inhabitants."[22] The redundancy of "gentleman" is telling in this context.

Gordon Wood has written of Washington's compulsion to seem genteel: "He wanted desperately to know the proper rules of behavior for a liberal gentleman, and when he discovered these rules he stuck by them with an earnestness that awed his contemporaries."[23] In the theatre in Barbados, Washington is learning real behavior in a real space, not the proscriptions of his youthful "Rules of Civility" copied

London in a Box

[47

out and so earnestly adhered to ("8th rule: At play and at fire, its good manners to give place to the last comer").

The new map of British provincialism favored the assimilated, and no other public space offered the standard of genteel behavior quite like the stage. On the frontiers of the British Atlantic world, second sons, Irish immigrants, lowland Scots already absorbed by the union of 1707, all had a higher desire for Anglicization and advancement. As Eric Richards has noted, "The American colonies (and indeed England) constituted not so much an escape as an opportunity, less a refuge than an avenue of advancement. . . . Having failed to carve an independent Scottish empire, they elbowed their way into England's."[24] Others in pursuit of advancement were not content to observe the manners of actors. More than one biography of John Paul Jones attributes much of his character to his training on the stage. The young naval officer not only attended but in a time of want took to the stage in Jamaica, as an actor in the same company David Douglass trained in—and Phillips Russel thought it was Jones's training onstage that allowed "this gardener's son . . . his distinct speech and easy self-possession."[25]

The charismatic preacher George Whitefield, drawing crowds in Charleston and Philadelphia, learned his elocution from David Garrick, the best actor in London. When Mrs. Douglass spoke her epilogue on her husband's benefit night before the Masonic brotherhood, she knew it had been praised before for "all the Graces of gesture, and Propriety of Elocution, and met with universal and loud Applause."[26]

In the provinces of British culture, from Edinburgh to Annapolis, actors taught the elocution and deportment of gentlemen. The Irish actor-manager Thomas Sheridan was making a fortune at training lowland Scotsmen to sound like high-born Englishmen, or at least to speak broad Augustan English. In the summer of 1761 Sheridan (father of Richard Sheridan) left his management of the Smock Alley playhouse in Dublin to undertake a lecture tour teaching elocution to those lowland Scots anxious to assimilate, at a solid guinea per lecture.[27] Sheridan's elocution lectures, which were subsequently published and widely read (including in the bookstores and colleges of America), position the provincials as unfortunate, primitive, pre-British bodies, culturally damaged, like the misshapen feet of Chinese women or the flattened skulls of "barbarians" in "some savage countries," both examples quoted by Sheridan in his text.[28] Linguistic correction, to Sheridan, equaled cultural promotion. Sheridan's lectures on elocution stressed the study and rehearsal of proper (British) speech, complemented by the most eloquent modes of delivery, and the best examples, he advocated, were actors. His model: "Comedians [actors], whose profession it is, to speak from memory, the sentiments of others, and yet to deliver them, as if they were the result of their own immediate feeling."[29] London-trained actors on the provincial stage, suggested Sheridan, provided the nearest road to the urbanity of London. As Dr. Johnson quipped, the Scotchman's best prospect was the high road to London, and his biographer, the young Scotsman James Boswell, was the quintessential case study in assimilation. Boswell was one of those who attended Sheridan's (pricey) lectures, then studied privately with Sheridan to rid himself of his Scottish tongue and loose carriage.[30] Boswell certainly learned a great deal about manners, poise, and diction from his close association with actors, including Sheridan, and wrote frankly about his own make-over: "Since I came up, I have begun to acquire a composed genteel character very different from a rattling uncultivated one which for some time past I have been fond of. I have discovered that we may be in some degree whatever character we choose."[31]

High-culture assimilation was good business in America as well. Sheridan's lectures on elocution were sold in bookstores from Boston to Georgia; they were available at the Philadelphia Library, advertised in newspapers, included in the very first order of books for the new library at the College of Providence (Brown University), and a required part of the instruction of grammar schools and colleges alike.[32] For those a long way from the lecture hall, Douglass and his company were offering the same product of genteel manners, elocution, and deportment to colonists of "vulgar education," "poor extraction," and a long way from the capital, at five shillings for the pit. Here in the playhouse, complained one tradesman in New York, his daughter picked up manners above station and compounded the money spent with valuable working hours in front of a mirror mimicking the speech and manners of the actors.[33] Rising gentry, such as tradesmen on their way to becoming merchants, always stood in danger of falling, and seeming to be was essential to maintaining position. Seen in this light, the "Histrionic Academy" that Douglass offered in New York as a ruse to evade the authorities was not altogether a subterfuge. He was teaching gentility, fashioning Britishness: in Paul Goring's phrase, "forging British bodies" (91).

"THE GREAT FONDNESS"

The great desire for London goods met its availability in the 1760s, and British urbanity was more accessible than ever in the colonies. Benjamin Franklin spoke to this before the House of Commons during the Stamp Act debates of 1766. Describing the relationship of the colonies to the Crown Franklin openly concedes: "They had not only a respect, but an affection for Great Britain, for its laws, its customs and manners, and even a fondness for its fashions, that greatly increased its commerce. Natives of Britain were always treated with particular regard; to be an Old England man was, of itself, a character of some respect, and gave a kind of rank among us."[34]

By the 1760s, "the great fondness" had translated into a great market. However, unlike common products such as wooden tableware or high-end products like portraiture, a night at the theatre left one no better off materially, that is, one didn't come away with anything that could be inventoried in probate after death. John Galt, the biographer of Benjamin West, also in New York in 1759, wrote of a city "wholly devoted to mercantile pursuits. A disposition to estimate things, not by their . . . beauty, but by the price which they would bring in the market."[35] Hence the objections to money lavished away at the playhouse carried a certain truth about them.

The actor John Bernard relates an amusing anecdote of an itinerant trader whose goods were so ordinary he had to manufacture his own market. A "hickory dealer," or seller of common wooden tableware, traveled to Virginia with a well-laden wagon. He was already at a market disadvantage in a culture that desired ceramic ware, over the more primitive stock of their pioneering forefathers. But unfortunately the hickory-seller also arrived during an outbreak of yellow fever. "The ravages of the plague were at this time so dreadful that it will be supposed there was a general tendency to try the most desperate and absurd expedients to avert it." The peddler, capitalizing on the distress of the populace, dressed himself as respectably as possible and rode to a printing office in Williamsburg, where "under an assumed name, he had a hundred bills struck off to this effect: WANTED IMMEDIATELY, Wooden Ware in any quantity for the fever hospital at Philadelphia, such being found not to convey the infection." He then sent a boy to paper the town, creating a panic that fed on both an immediate desire for woodenware and a suspicion of all other utensils. "The doom of crockery was pronounced"; piles of old earthenware were pitched to the street ("which looked a pottery after an earthquake"), and then, "about noon, when the work of destruction was at its height, a wagon made its way into the village, with a man vociferating with all the powers of his lungs, 'Wooden Ware!' His arrival was hailed as a God-send, a crowd collected round him as to a magician who brought talismans, and in less than two hours his plague-averting platters were all disposed of at exorbitant prices."[36] The hickory-seller sold what nobody really needed and thus had to create a need for his wares, and there were those who thought the theatre was not that dissimilar: it too fabricated its own market.

Even those who did not attend the professional theatre (most Bostonians, for example) could be *au fait* with the latest London plays. Though Douglass boasted the first American production of Cumberland's *The West Indian* in October of 1771, in Williamsburg, Virginia, Abigail Adams had already read the play and discussed it six months earlier.[37] She had it from her cousin, Isaac Smith, who sent back plays and reports of the theatre from London. She and Mercy Otis Warren conducted a grand correspondence over the latest London plays that neither had seen. Both recognized that knowing the latest London plays was an essential part of any educated English person's conversation.

The colonies in the third quarter of the eighteenth century were attracting specialty craftsmen of all kinds. The first waves of immigrants and backwoods settlers had given way in mid-century to a generation of consumers who were the market for London goods. Specialty craftsmen such as jewelers, carriage makers, wood-carvers, bookbinders, peruke makers, dancing masters, and portrait painters found themselves in demand in the capitals of America. Charles Carroll of Carrollton and ten other contributors raised money for the young Charles Willson Peale to travel to London to learn painting and return to Maryland to practice the art. In the following decade, the fine arts would follow: portrait and landscape painters, historical painters like Benjamin West, poets and composers. The gentrification was driven by a desire for goods, crafts, and talent hitherto unavailable in America.

The theatre's attraction to a generation who drank coffee, read the latest newspapers, and purchased the latest books at the famous Old London Coffee House in Philadelphia or the London Coffeehouse in Boston or the English Coffee House in Williamsburg was its Londonness; they drank porter imported from London, though brewers in America could brew their own, and read newspapers with the latest London news set with type imported from London. Plantation estates, like Washington's Mount Vernon, emulated English country seats and were fashionably painted on the inside with colors derived from imported pigments (Prussian blue, verdigris green); Washington also ordered his civilian clothing from London. Wigs were sent out of London, though they chanced a poor fit, and the aspirant paid dearly for them and their upkeep. New York had its own Vauxhall Gardens and Raneleagh, both modeled on London's resorts of the same name, and over its theatre was the familiar motto of Drury Lane; both music and musicians were imported from London connections, like Peter Valton and his harpsichord, whose immigration to America was sponsored by the Charleston St. Cecilia's Society. Polite society gathered at concerts, theatre, balls, and entertainments, where one was expected to dance, and the acquisition of this fundamental social skill was also a theatrical by-product. The young Alexander Graydon, in Philadelphia, related his forced tutorial in the gentle art that was, nonetheless, an essential part of any gentleman's or gentlewoman's social tool kit, and a sine qua non for advancement:

> [H]e [Major George Etherington] gave me a pretty sharp lecture upon a resolution I had absurdly taken up, not to learn dancing, from an idea of its being an effeminate and unmanly recreation. He combated my folly with argument, of which I have since felt the full force; but which, as they turned upon interests, I was then too young to form conceptions of, they produced neither conviction nor effect. Fortunately for me, I had to deal with a man who was not thus to be baffled. He very properly assumed the rights of mature age and experience, and accordingly, one day, on my return from school, he accosted me with "Come here

young man, I have something to say to you" and with a mysterious air conducted me to his chamber. Here I found myself entrapped. Godwin, the assistance of Tioli, the dancing master, was prepared to give me a lesson. Etherington introduced me to him as the pupil he had been speaking of, and saying he would leave us to ourselves, he politely retired. The arrangement with Tioli was, that I should be attended in the major's room until I was sufficiently drilled for the public school; and the ice thus broken, I went on, and instead of standing in the corner, like a goose on one leg (the major's comparison) "while music softens and while dancing fires" I became qualified for the enjoyment of female society, in one of its most captivating forms.[38]

James Godwin, an actor and dancer with Douglass's American Company, taught Graydon to dance. Godwin, a former student of the Italian dancing master Mr. Tioli, joined Douglass in 1765 and worked with the company until after the Revolution. Any theatrical production included dancing—playbills advertised dances, and Douglass paid well for a good dancer (Godwin earned £4 per week).

After his dancing lessons, the theatre, wrote Alexander Graydon, "was yet useful to me in one respect. It induced me to open books which had hitherto lain neglected on the shelf. . . . Now I became a reader of plays, and particularly those of Shakespeare, of which I was an ardent and unaffected admirer. From these I passed to those of Otway and Rowe, and the other writers of tragedy, and thence to the English poets of every description." And from the study of poetry, he learned a genteel hand at writing, both in style and penmanship, and corrected his disadvantage (by his own admission) of "being wholly unapprised of the structure of the sentences." Theatre taught Graydon the appreciation and later imitation of the graceful body, the literary hand and comprehending mind.[39]

The rector Jonathan Boucher, a country parson with literary ambitions, betrayed the same anxiety of class and manners that his Potomac neighbor Washington had. Boucher's own wife described him as "often awkward, yet always interesting, perfectly untaught and unformed . . . incapable of making a bow like a gentleman, yet far more incapable of thinking, speaking, or acting in a manner unbecoming a gentleman."[40] When Boucher was offered the pulpit at St. Anne's

Annapolis, he found a genteel society to improve his social deficits and a theatre to advance his literary talents. "A very handsome theatre was built while I stayed there by subscription, and as the church was old and ordinary, and this theatre was built on land belonging to the church, I drew up a petition in verse in behalf of the old Church, which was inserted in the Gazette, and did me credit. And this, I think, was one of the first things that made me to be taken notice of. I also wrote some verses on one of the actresses, and a prologue or two. And thus, as I was now once more among literary men."[41] Boucher went on to found the Homony Club of Annapolis, a select society of literary men.

Colonial theatre offered a transatlantic memory of a memory of a genteel, aristocratic world, a simulacrum of urbane refinement for those who could not participate in the original. Provincial newspapers carried the gossip of the stage luminaries of London—of Garrick and Cibber and Samuel Foote.[42] A rising tidewater cordwainer by profession, Allen Quynn, who would become a trustee of the Annapolis theatre, had, at the time of his death, portraits of David Garrick and Sarah Siddons in his house in Annapolis.[43] Letters from London frequently mention the theatrical doings with familiar detail, even to residents in rural backwaters like the young James Iredell ("Now for news in the ladies way: the theatre has sustained a great loss in Mr. Powell, who is now allowed to be one of the greatest actors this age has produced. Curiosity led me, when in town to see Mr. Sheridan in the character of Hamlet").[44] Colonists read of Garrick's roles, the witty exchanges in the boxes, of Mr. Foote's misfortune and his return to the stage, deaths and elopements, and one can clearly hear the snobbery in the voices of those who actually made it to the London theatres. John MacPherson gloated in his letters to his friend William Patterson: "I was several times there [the Haymarket]. . . . Foote you know is only a mimic, and it is therefore impossible to make any remarks upon him intelligible to one who never saw him."[45]

When colonists could not travel to see plays, they read them. John Mein sold, described, and recommended the best plays at his London Book Store, as did William Bradford at his London Coffeehouse in Philadelphia.[46] They also learned to be critics: "As the practice prevails in our mother country," began one op-ed, "I hope you will have no objections against inserting in your paper the observations that any gentleman may decently make concerning the actors on our little theatre here."[47] Touring actors would be compared to London standards of acting, as editorials went on to do: "I'm sorry Mr. Hallam . . . does not take copy from the inimitable Garrick. . . . Miss Wainwright is a very good singer, and her action exceeds the famous Miss Brent."[48] More frequently, reviewers advertised their own London experiences, like the anonymous "YZ" (William Eddis?) who rhapsodized of Miss Hallam's performance in Cymbeline: "[M]ethought I heard once more the warbling of Cibber in my ear!" YZ was reminding his readers of the lovely voice of Susannah Cibber and his own time spent in a box at Drury Lane.[49] Or the poor farmer in the wilds of Windsor, Nova Scotia, who missed the visit of a small company in Halifax: "I am very sorry I cannot go down immediately, as our Hay-making is not quite over. Please to let us know what stay the Players are like to make and what pieces they propose to Act. I hope the Provok'd Wife is among the Number: Sir John Brute is an amiable Character."[50]

The reshaping of the social landscape that played out in the third quarter of the eighteenth century in many colonial American cities was little different from the same gentrification that occurred in the provincial cities of Great Britain. Writing to James Iredell in Edenton, North Carolina, Margaret Macartney described Bristol in 1773 with a fondness for its progress: "[I]ts so alter'd you would Scarce know it again. They have thrown down Narrow lanes and are building fine Streets. It is this Winter I hear the Gayest Place in the world, Concerts twice a Week, the Balls as usual, and Plays three times."[51]

Writing just before the Revolution, the actor John Bernard was astonished to find so many colonists with such developed European tastes, and was particularly surprised to find them so acquainted with theatre culture:

> Their furniture, pictures, and musical instruments were all imported from Europe. But this did not surprise me as much as the tone of their conversation. Their favorite topics were European, and I found men leading secluded lives in the woods of Virginia perfectly *au fait* as to the literary, dramatic, and personal gossip of London and Paris. . . . At one house I met with a gentleman who had participated in my revels at the London clubs. His memory was a storehouse of anecdote which he flavoured by a

peculiarly happy faculty of imitation, the rapturous manner in which the company recognized the originals often making me look round to see if I was not once more snugly ensconced over the piazza at Covent Garden."[52]

This was the legacy of David Douglass and his theatres: a generation of theatre-going would make Americans Londoners abroad, just in time for a most unmannerly rebellion that would utterly unmake their Britishness.

[CHAPTER 5]
"This Wandering Theatre"
Newport, New York, Charleston, 1761–1763
• • •

And business was good. Douglass's first tour of America—New York, Philadelphia, Newport, Williamsburg, Annapolis, Charleston—assured him that he had a product that the colonists wanted. He built theatres—and a rolodex of influential clientele—but at a cost.

"THIS MOTLEY LIFE . . ."

Among the many pleasures denied the itinerant actor: a permanent home and address for receiving mail and visitors (Douglass had dead letters waiting in Newport and Philadelphia for months), year-round acquaintances, a church pew of one's own, a garden.[1] Richard Ketchum notes that in New York in 1760 "nearly every house lot of any size had a garden";[2] the same was true in Williamsburg. But itinerant players had neither house nor land. Douglass and his wife Sarah rented their lodgings on short leases; their actors boarded at ordinaries. They ate tavern food, sat as guests in the back of the parish church, and owned no more than they could carry in trunks, much of which comprised professional tools such as scripts and costumes. Thomas Wall carried his plays and playbills, his mandolin and sheet music; the trunk was stolen and he advertised the contents. They were true strollers struggling against their centuries-old reputation as rogues and vagabonds, and the small markets of colonial America guaranteed it would be the lot of their vocation.

Consider the life of Mrs. Douglass, née Sarah Smythe and widow of Lewis Hallam, Sr. Sarah Smythe Hallam Douglass had married into the profession with her first husband, Lewis Hallam, Sr. Driven out of London by the Licensing Act, she bid farewell to her two youngest children and traveled to America in 1752, then to the islands of the Caribbean, then back to America in 1758. She did not see her two children or her London family for thirteen years. But that was only a visit; she returned to the traveling life, strolling with Douglass and the American Company until her death in 1777.³ She spent twenty-five years constantly on the road; her longest engagement lasted five months.

This life of travel wearied many, like the young Henry Gifford, son of a London theatre manager, who played in North Carolina in the 1760s. Gifford applied to Governor William Tryon for a letter of introduction to the bishop of London that might take orders and assume a clerical position somewhere. He was, he wrote to Tryon, "wearied of the vague life" of playing. Tryon recommended Gifford, but the bishop would not have actors in the pulpit. Gifford was still a strolling actor on the provincial circuit a decade later, but working even smaller markets than Douglass and his company, playing in Halifax, Nova Scotia, and the Leeward Islands.⁴ Henrietta Osbourn, whom Douglass recruited in London and brought to America, wrote and delivered a prologue on her benefit night, January 19, 1768, in Norfolk, Virginia, that spoke to the same travel-weariness:

> For 10 long years this motley life I've led;
> And felt (as rapidly throu life I've whirl'd)
> All changes of this April-weathered world!
> One day, have gaily bask'd in sunshine warm,
> The next, have shivered underneath a storm;
> Yet tho' thus doom'd perpetually to roam,
> Still, when at Norfolk, thought myself home;
> And wish'd, yes often wish'd, but oh! In vain,
> With such dear friends, I ever might remain.
> But fate decrees, I no such bliss shall know,
> Still bids me wander, and resigned I go.⁵

Henrietta finally left the profession to open an import mercantile in Annapolis, in time for the Revolution that would boycott such imports. Strolling was a hard life, and it was a rare actor in the company who would remain a "lifer." Most of the company, a dozen or more, who came and went, would all at some point weary of the strolling life and settle into other careers, as printers, merchants, auctioneers, and so on.

Even a stable career actor like Stephen Woolls, whom Douglass recruited in London in 1765, would long for permanence. Sometime after his summer singing engagement at the Vauxhall in New

York (1767), he left the company, took up the profession of land surveyor, traveled to western Pennsylvania, and there met and married an Indian woman, receiving a tract of land as dowry, which, as John Bernard relates, "he soon contrived to convert into a handsome independence."[6] But for unknown reasons he returned to the company the following summer in Williamsburg and remained an actor until his death in 1799, more than three decades after his American debut.

Apart from the actor's salary, each season (and there could be several seasons a year) every actor received a benefit, the proceeds of the night. The proceeds of a good benefit could net an actor £60 or more (minus the "charges," or expenses of the house), and in a good year that could be the case for each town they played.[7] A small collection of playbills preserved from 1781 documents that Thomas Wall cleared £60 an evening in the smallish burg of Baltimore, during the war. A few pages from a very slim account book of William Wignell, from Jamaica, testify to the financial troughs and crests of the strolling life. Wignell stepped off the boat from London the same winter that Congress shut down the theatre. The first records in his account book begin with his borrowing money from Hallam and Douglass when the company opened in Spanish Town, Jamaica—until he enjoyed his first benefit night, and then he was flush again.[8] Most theatre managers did a little better, operating on a sharing system, with a split of the profits, and reserving extra shares (called "dead shares") for their trouble. Compared to other trades, actors did well enough, but they also experienced extended periods of travel, down time, delays in construction or denied permission, and revolutions, all of which put a strain on the purses and pocketbooks of idle actors.

OPPOSITION IN THE NORTH

After a socially and financially successful run in Virginia in 1760–1761, playing the capital and the James River towns, Douglass sailed with his company to Newport, Rhode Island. Newport was a popular summer resort, with social and commercial ties to Virginia and South Carolina. Many southern elite escaped the heat with a summer home in Rhode Island.[9] Encouraged by this familiar migration, Douglass proposed to erect a theatre and entertain the town for a short time, but local opposition refused his application. Willard reports that on the first day of

August "a special town meeting was called at the request of a number of freemen, by warrant of the town council, and it being put to vote whether the freemen 'were for allowing plays to be acted in town or not,' it was voted, not."[10]

But that same day, August 1, the Boston diarist Nathaniel Ames (and Harvard classmate of Joseph Warren) recorded that he was in Providence to watch plays. He saw *Douglas* on August 1, "with Harlequine," and the following day saw *The Distress'd Mother*. This suggests that in spite of Newport's opposition, Douglass was already in business in Providence, likely operating under some kind of subterfuge, like the "histrionic academy" he had attempted in New York.

When Douglass heard of the vote, he countered by publishing his character letter from Virginia in the *Newport Mercury* of August 11. When Douglass left Williamsburg, in June of 1761, he carried with him a character letter attesting to his company's merits and signed "by near one hundred of the principal men of the colony." A few of the names were sure to be familiar among his Newport audience. It was recent enough (dated from Williamsburg, June 11, 1761) to carry currency:

> The Company of comedians under the direction of David Douglass has performed in this colony for near a twelvemonth; during which time they have made it their constant practice to behave with prudence and discretion in their private character, and to use their utmost endeavours to give general satisfaction in their publick capacity. We have therefore thought proper to recommend them as a company whose behavior merits the favour of the public and who are capable of entertaining a sensible and polite audience.

Douglass also purchased support among the legislators—or so one writer claims—when he "complimented the House with tickets" (i.e., the House of Representatives). The same writer also claims Douglass employed many "indefatigable measures . . . to draw persons of every rank into the game."[11] The tactics worked. Willard astutely reasons that the "enemies of the theatre were more numerous than powerful, and were ignorant how to proceed under the circumstances."[12] So the governing classes prevailed; Douglass received his license, a temporary playhouse was built, and they prepared to receive the opening night audience on September 2, 1761. Willard claims the initial performance was September 7,[13] but a fine review of their opening—extracted from a letter from Newport dated September 10, sent to Boston, and printed in the *Boston Gazette* of September 21, 1761—places the initial performances on September 2:

> As to the opposition and clamour against the Play-House erected here, it was much too vehement to continue, and, like the snow or hail of midsummer, melted gradually away. The house was open'd on the second of the month with the Fair Penitent, and Aesop in the Shades: and I cannot think you ever saw the Royal houses of Drury and Covent Garden fuller (without being crowded) or any audience there more deeply attentive or better pleased. On the evening of the fourth Jane Shore with the Toy-Shop were perform'd to the highest satisfaction of a very full house. On Monday and Tuesday last the Provok'd Husband with the Miller of Mansfield were perform'd with the greatest applause. Last evening George Barnwell with the Mock Doctor were exhibited before a great many of our General Assembly, and as many others as then could be admitted, and I can assure you that the audience were greatly mov'd and affected with the distress and fate of the unhappy hero of that very moral and virtuous entertainment. Upon the whole I not only invite you here on this occasion, but encourage you to give all your friends ample assurances that the Company of Comedians here, more than verify their just letters of credence from Virginia, and are indeed capable of entertaining a very polite and sensible audience.

With that business settled, Douglass returned to New York to secure permission there for his next stop. It must have given him great pleasure to read: "Last week his honour the Lieutenant Governor was pleased to give Mr. Douglass permission to build a theatre, to perform in this city the ensuing winter. That settled, he returned to Newport for a civic benefit.[14]

Douglass certainly knew that civic charities were part of his rent. He also certainly exploited the publicity of an early charity benefit. Their third performance in Newport (September 7) raised £50 for the benefit of the poor. The gesture drew praise from the press, but an astute

Bostonian op-ed observed that "the motives are so obvious. . . . [The benefit] artfully contrived to accomplish the design [i.e., establishing the theatre], in opposition to the avow'd sentiments of the town." The author concludes:

> However well the pretended charity has been adapted, a theatre is in no respect adapted to the state and circumstances of this poor, small town.—Can any man in his senses, not abandon'd to pleasure, think a place so young can throw away three or four thousand pounds a week at a play-house, or can he probably imagine, that a thousand pounds given to the poor to still, what is term'd a popular clamour, can be an equivalent for the loss of £30,000 consum'd in the short space of eight or ten weeks, besides a great loss of time.—To all such charities, may not the following maxim be justly applied, he steals the goose and gives the giblets in alms.[15]

The money was delivered to George Gibbs, who, Willard tells us, "expended it in the purchase of corn, which was stored until the succeeding winter, and then distributed among the deserving poor."[16] The claims of the critics (albeit financially exaggerated) were in part just and uniform throughout colonial America. For all the scholarship lavished on the moral opposition to theatre in colonial America, more often than not the objections were based on frugality and concerns about players carrying money out of the colony, leaving the town culturally richer but economically the poorer for it.

These objections resurface from Charleston to Halifax. From Philadelphia in 1766: "At a time when most Masters of Families are complaining of the great Scarcity of Money, and of the Stagnation of Trade, and are retrenching their Expenses, very great must their Infatuation be, who thus circumstanced, give Encouragement to a Sett of strolling Comedians."[17] In New York, Douglass went so far as to publish his expenses, every ticket receipt in and every bill sticker he paid out, to document the meagerness of his profit.

Towns were small and seasons were short in colonial American cities, usually lasting a few months at most. Even a capital like New York could see only five months at a stretch before the season of plays exhausted audiences' desires and disposable revenue. So Douglass kept on the move, traveling from New York back to Rhode Island, then to Williamsburg in the fall of 1762, before moving on to Norfolk and Petersburg.

By spring 1763 they were back in Williamsburg, and George Washington was back in attendance. On at least five occasions between April 26 and May 5, 1763, Colonel Washington took a box. Indeed, minus gazettes for the period, Washington's box receipts and the council's character letter remain the primary evidence of the company's residency in Williamsburg.

The year 1763 saw the close of the Seven Years' War and the signing of a treaty that put an end to hostilities on the continent. Pro-British feelings ran high among the colonists, and anti-French sentiment created a common antagonist. America was remapped: the French lost their holdings; the British gained sole dominion of the eastern seaboard and seemed the manifest proprietor of the western promise ("a New World, to George's Empire won," as James Sterling put it[18]); and the native peoples were pushed further to the west. At no point was British America more British than at the close of the Seven Years' War. A map commissioned for the occasion featured a crest of the Appalachian Mountains that marked the extent of the Anglo holdings: "This land reserved for the Indians." The ink was no sooner dried before the Cumberland Gap was opened and those fertile Ohio River valleys "reserved for the Indians" were poached by second sons. Threatened by the incursions, a loose confederation of tribes under the Ottawa leader Pontiac waged a last stand of resistance, attacking the forts of the Ohio country. The frontier would remain uneasy, but with the treaty Great Britain had emerged as the dominant military power in Europe and America. In a flurry of celebration, authors composed and circulated anthems on both sides of the Atlantic. They sang "Rule Britannia, Britannia rule the waves" and "Hearts of Oak are our ships, Hearts of Oak are our men; / We always are ready, steady, boys, steady, / We'll fight and we'll conquer again."

Douglass and his wandering theatre now moved down to Charleston, South Carolina. A theatre had been in and out of operation on Queen Street, Charleston, since the 1730s. The first, short-lived venture had been initiated by Henry Holt and Charles Shepherd in 1736 and dissolved by 1738. The building was advertised for sale in 1741, hosting balls the following year, and Hugh Rankin suggests it was destroyed in the 1752 hurricane.[19] When the Hallam Company arrived two years later, they built a new theatre, and to distinguish it from the former one they styled it "The New Theatre." When Douglass arrived in Charleston, he found Hallam's New Theatre vandalized: "[s]everal malicious and evil-disposed persons [having] cut and destroyed the scenes and furniture of the [play]house."[20] Another new theatre would have to be built, his fifth in three years.

PLAYERS, SMALL POX, AND OTHER PLAGUES

"It is now upwards of a month since any person has been seized with the small pox in Charleston, which may therefore now be reckoned entirely over," announced the *South Carolina Gazette*, September 10–17, 1763. All that summer small pox had raged in Charleston. Those who enjoyed the privilege of country estates left the city. Fear of inoculation led to quarantines, and travel was discouraged. Apothecaries advertised every kind of medicine. A Small Pox Hospital opened expressly for the treatment of slaves, costing their owners a hefty £15 per head. Inoculation was initially practiced widely, until it became suspect and physicians ceased the practice.[21] By mid-October one finds advertisements that offered lodging with no risk of small pox. The dreadful summer had passed when the actors arrived.

The colonial governor of South Carolina, William Henry Lyttelton, granted his consent; Douglass secured a lease and contracted with a builder to raze the old playhouse entirely. The appearance of the company was noted in the *South Carolina Gazette*:

> A Company of Comedians arrived here last Monday from Virginia who are called the American Company and were formerly under the direction of Mr. Lewis Hallam, till his death. Amongst the principal performers we hear are Mr. David Douglass (the present Manager, married to Mrs. Hallam), Mr. Lewis Hallam Jr., Mr. Quelst [Quelch], Mrs. Douglass, Mrs. Harman, etc. They come warmly recommended from the Northern colonies where they have performed several years with great applause, and in their private capacities acquired the best of characters. A theatre is already contracted for 75 feet by 35 feet, to be erected near where that of Mssrs. Holiday and Comp. formerly stood and intended to be opened the 5th of December next.[22]

Before the new theatre opened, someone thought fit to reprint an extract from Dr. Watts's "On the Education of Children and Youth." "Dr. Watts' Remarks on Playhouses" reminded the readership of the *Gazette* of the hazards of such "midnight assemblies." With the danger of plague still in the air, it evoked the threat of contamination that the playhouse would present to the innocent: "The youth of serious religion that ventures sometimes into this infected air, finds his antidotes too weak to resist the contagion."[23] The paper reprinted the essay the following week, admonishing the town for supporting so frivolous a pastime.

Theatre enthusiasts remained determined and the theatre-building proceeded. The *Gazette* notes that the company played Monday-Wednesday-Friday, and the theatre was described as "elegantly finished."[24] Mrs. Anne Manigault, wife of the colony's treasurer, Gabriel Manigault, was an occasional visitor, traveling to town from their country seat to watch plays, and briefly recorded her visits.[25] After the opening, the first grand night would have been St. John's night, December 27, which the Masons celebrated by attending Farquhar's *The Beaux' Stratagem*. Several members of the company, including Douglass, Hallam, and Quelch, were Freemasons, and this special evening was tantamount to a bespoke for this influential and charitable social club.

By the first of year (January 4) the General Assembly convened; Douglass was playing to sold-out houses and making "all imaginable success," so noted Alexander Garden, who attended frequently. A letter of February 1, 1764, from Dr. Garden to David Colden, son of Cadwallader Colden, offers a firsthand account of the general reception of Douglass's company in Charleston that winter:

> Sir: Your favour of Jan 26th 1763 was sent to me some time in November by Mr. Douglass. I was then confined in my room & had been for many weeks, as soon as I was able to see Company I begged Mr. Douglass to favour me with his & I found him perfectly answer the Character which you drew of him. You may depend on this that I will not omit any opportunity to shew Every service in my power to him or any person whose acquaintance you are so obliging as to offer me.
>
> He has met with all imagined Success in this place since their theatre was opened, which I think was the first Wednesday of

December, since which time they have performed thrice a week and Every night to a full nay a Crowded house. Hitherto they can't possibly have made less than £110 sterling [each] night at a medium for some nights they have made between 130 and 140 sterling in one night & I do believe never under £90 sterling & that only for one or two rainy Evenings. This will shew you how much the people here are given to gaiety, when you compare this place in numbers of Inhabitants to York which is at Least double if not Treble in number to us. Mr. Douglass has made a valuable acquisition in Miss Cheer who arrived here from London much about the time that Mr. Douglass arrived with his company. Soon after that, she agreed to go on the stage where she has since appeared in some Chief Characters with great applause particularly Monimia in the Orphan and Juliet of Shakespeare and Hermione of the Distrest Mother. Her fine person, her youth, her Voice, & Appearance &c conspire to make her appear with propriety—Such a one they much wanted as Mrs. Douglass was their Chief actress before & who on that account had always too many Characters to appear in."[26]

Douglass had visited Garden shortly after his arrival in Charleston and carried a letter to Garden from David Colden in New York. The letter assisted Douglass in securing support among polite society, including that of the lieutenant governor, William Bull, a fellow amateur botanist. And all, not incidentally, were Scotsmen.

Dr. Alexander Garden was a physician and natural historian in Charleston, educated at Aberdeen. He was also the first American member of the Royal Society of Arts. But Garden's spirit of inquiry extended beyond the natural history of America. He wrote on all manner of colonial life, scientific and ethical: how to improve the economy of rice production, the treatment of slaves, silkworm culture. He presided over the St. Cecilia's Society, Charleston's famous music club. He was a familiar of the Colden family, acquainted with the governor's library, went on botanical expeditions in the Catskills with Jane Colden, and corresponded with the governor's son, David.[27] He was also an intimate of the lieutenant governor, William Bull, who had trained as a doctor before abandoning that practice for politics. Bull had presented Garden with his own copy of Linnaeus's *Fundamenta*

Botanica.[28] When tensions developed between the colonists and the Crown, Garden tried to remain neutral, but after the siege of Yorktown, his country estate was confiscated and he returned to London. Douglass's connections to Garden as a patron who could introduce him directly to the lieutenant governor of the colony illuminates the circles in which the manager now moved.

Another person in the house attended as frequently as she could: Mrs. Ann Manigault, the speaker's wife. Her abstracted diary (the original has been lost) records the activities of a house that was, as the biographer aptly writes, "an open house during the period of his active business life, having guests almost every day at one or more of the four meals."[29] Her diary records the dense social network of the most influential members of Charleston society: the Pinckneys, the Rutledges, the Deas, the Gardens, the Gadsdens, the Izards, and the Lynches, and her weekly trips to the theatre interspersed with laconic entries of the social news—"To the play, the Conscious Lovers"; "Lady Anne married"; "to the play—Jane Shore"; "To the play Love for love"—throughout February, March, April, and May of 1763 confirm the attraction of the theatre for her and her class.

As Garden noted, business was good. The first five years on the continent had afforded Douglass a sound reconnaissance of the provincial British market in America from Newport to Charleston and had enlisted strong supporters among the governing class to establish his company in enough of a circuit to sustain themselves. He had established a monopoly on the continent and moved readily between New York, Philadelphia, Annapolis, Williamsburg, Newport, and then back to New York, back to Williamsburg, down to Charleston. He had built seven theatres, secured the patronage of six governors, and bought or leased land in five colonies, as well as the innumerable converted market houses like those in Chestertown, Maryland, and Petersburg, Virginia, where the young Jefferson rode from Shadwell to watch the plays. To ensure continued success, he prepared to embark on a recruitment trip to restock his acting company. He had been playing the same repertory for five years, trafficking in the memory of London. Business would not continue to be brisk without the "latest goods from London."

Though the company played Charleston until mid-May (at least), Douglass and his wife pulled out of the season early to travel to London to recruit new actors, musicians, and singers; to purchase new scenes; and to visit family.[30] Mrs. Douglass had a daughter she had not seen since 1752. The company were to return to the island circuit they had left in 1758 and would reconvene with Douglass in Charleston in the fall.

A month earlier, the Rhode Island–based Jewish merchant Moses Lopez sailed into Charleston harbor with the intent of unloading both his cargo and the ship that brought it. His sojourn in Charleston offers a merchant's view of the economic landscape at the time. On May 3, 1764, he wrote to his brother, remarking how considerably the city had grown since his last visit: "It has increased with sumptuous brick houses in very great number. One cannot go anywhere where one does not see new buildings and large and small houses started, half finished, and almost finished."[31]

It was all so promising, and so deceptive. Douglass's first five years on the continent showed him there was money to be made in America. But when he returned in the fall, he would find a very different America, one beginning its inexorable march toward uncoupling its British-American identity, and Douglass and his theatres would be left on the British side of the hyphen.

[CHAPTER 6]

Heart of Oak, and Other Transatlantic Transformations

April 1764–October 1766

• • •

Mr. De Speculo: How much must a man be worth per annum to be entitled to the appellation of "Esquire"? Yours, J. T.
Unanswered letter to "The Mirrour," *New York Gazette*, January 4, 1768

CARPENTER MARKS

That J. T.'s query went unanswered is some indication of the confusion over the use of titles in British America, but it is also some indication of the extraordinary possibilities of the long eighteenth century that even actors could acquire titles. Somewhere in the mid-1760s David Douglass began to style himself "gentleman," and by the close of the decade "Esquire," a rank below a knight, above a gentleman, and the distinction between upper and lower gentry. The title was technically not dependent on salary but was assumed by virtue of holding a public office, such as mayor, justice of the peace, a military rank above captain, or a degree from Oxford or Cambridge—none of which Douglass technically enjoyed. When and how exactly his social promotion occurred is not clear, but in less than half a decade Douglass moved from strolling actor to upper gentry.[1] It was a small claim in a nation of self-fashioning strangers, but how it came about is central to understanding the possibility of reinvention in America, individually for immigrants and then collectively as a nation consciously fashioning a new identity. Making Americans out of British colonists followed the same trajectory that so many immigrants traced. A consideration of how self-fashioning played out for the individual illuminates something about how the nation modulated its identity.

Jonathan Swift satirically traced this genealogy of social advancement:

> A Beggar had a Beadle,
>   A Beadle had a Yeoman;
> A Yeoman had a prentice,
>   A prentice had a Freeman:
> The Freeman had a Master,
>   The Master had a lease;
> The Lease made him a Gentleman,
>   And Justice of the Peace.[2]

So Swift tracks the social mobility upwards through knights, lords, dukes, kings, emperors, and a pope—peaking, of course, with the lawyer. But this trajectory was multigenerational, each installment begetting minor, accumulative social advances. In America, the ascension of so many second sons accelerated, compressing the promotion into a single meteoric burst: transported felons became schoolmasters, rectors, traders, and landholders; indentured servants became freemen, bought land, slaves, or other indentured servants, and retired, thirty years later, landed gentry and esquired gentlemen.[3]

No place offered a more fertile ground for rapid social elevation than America, and David Douglass, Esq., was one of a legion of self-fashioned gentlemen. Charles Woodmason—no friend of titles—disparaged the rise of Rowland Lowndes, speaker of the house of South Carolina, this way: "[H]e was a parish orphan boy, nor knows his own origin, taken from the dunghill by our late Provost marshal, made his valet, then learn'd to read and write, then became Gaoler, then Provost Marshal, got money, married well, settled plantations, became a planter, a magistrate, a senator, speaker of the House and now Chief judge."[4] Woodmason's vitriol reminds us that all these risings were shadowed by erasures that seemed never complete and certainly never outpaced memory. Secret histories and buried pasts abounded in America, some utterly hidden, others more carelessly left lying about.

It was common family history but never shared abroad that the Scotsman William MacGregor had come to America to escape execution. He had fought at the battle of Sherrifmuir during the first Jacobite uprising. But when the cause collapsed and rebels were hunted down, MacGregor took refuge in the house of one Mr. Skinner, adopted the name, and fled Scotland. He settled in Philadelphia as William Skinner and became a schoolteacher. Under his new identity he secured the sponsorship of the bishop of London, took orders, and was appointed Rector of St. Peter's Episcopal Church in Perth Amboy, New Jersey. He married well; their son became the attorney general for the colony, and their daughter—the rebel's granddaughter—married an Irish peer.[5] The fugitive past was never circulated outside the family. But another rector, James Sterling, immigrated to begin again in the same generation and was far less careful of his history. His first congregation would have nothing to do with a former playwright who had married an actress, of all things. It was inevitable that all those erasures of renegade pasts would leave the odd trace: scars of rash enlistments, criminal reputations lingering in the memories of old associates, old-country accents, awkward bows, open vowels that betrayed highland origins, like dirty fingernails on the hands of the gentry who rose too quickly to mind all the details, like carpenter marks left on the woodwork of so many esquired immigrants.

Cadwallader Colden, in spite of his age and title, still carried the stigma of being a drummer boy in the first Jacobite rising in 1715, a memory the Sons of Liberty resuscitated with his effigy fifty years later, during the Stamp Act riots. Lord Ogleby, in Coleman's *The Clandestine Marriage*, as he marries into the Sterlings, a rising merchant family, bartering his bankrupt title for their new money, puts it this way: "Mr. Sterling will never get rid of Blackfriars, always taste of the Borachio" (i.e., betray his low origins; 2.1). Jonathan Boucher, the Annapolis rector, likewise not to the manor born, all his life remained incapable of making a proper bow, but he nevertheless rose in that self-fashioning and clumsy way that America allowed.

If we are considering this art of stowing away the past and assuming the promise of a new continent of self, no place made it easier than shipboard on a transatlantic crossing. Passengers left their homeland (their old names, identities) and in the open expanse of opportunity became anew in America. One passage of one voyage in particular left a few legible traces of this sea change on each of its passengers, including David Douglass, Esq., making visible the process of transformation, arresting the ghosts before they were utterly stowed.[6]

THE *HEART OF OAK*

Prior to the close of the Charleston season in April 1764, Douglass and his wife returned to London. Their venture in America had been a successful though trying five years, profitable enough to take a half year off, sail back to England, and restock their trunks with the latest London goods.

David and Sarah shipped on the *Heart of Oak*, Capt. Henry Gunn, a ship that advertised "extraordinary accommodations."[7] Like other passengers on board, they had prior ties with the ship's owner, Charleston merchant and future president of the Congress, Henry Laurens.[8] Laurens was one of the wealthiest men in the colony, and the ship was both a crucial image and vehicle of that success. It was a new ship, a large ship (two hundred tons), and a tight ship (as it carried rice and indigo, it needed to be very dry), built in Charleston in 1763 and christened with a muscular and familiar name from a popular song originally written by another actor-manager, David Garrick, the most famous actor of his century, with music by William Boyce, organist, King's Chapel, Westminster. The piece was currently performed in the London theatres, both as orchestra music and as a new dance routine with a rousing chorus that celebrated the British naval victories of the recently concluded French-Indian War:

> Hearts of Oak are our ships, Hearts of Oak are our men;
> We always are ready, steady, boys, steady,
> We'll fight and we'll conquer again.

The piece quickly became one of those stock patriotic songs played as curtain raisers and occasionally used to defuse tensions when audiences threatened disturbances, like the one James Beard, manager of Covent Garden, experienced on May 16, 1763, over a pricing dispute. The orchestra was called on to play "Hearts of Oak," "Britons Strike Home," and "Rule Britannia." The idea was that by chorusing these anthems the management could reassert the common British community of auditors and actors. "Hearts of Oak" had only recently made it over the water and was, we would say, still on the charts when Henry Laurens christened his new ship. The use of a military name for a commercial ship was part of a subtle reclamation of power underway between the transatlantic partners: the chiasmus of American commerce intersecting with British imperial might.

Laurens's investment in the *Heart of Oak* was a major installment in his own self-fashioning project.[9] He had built a substantial fortune on transatlantic trade, exporting the raw goods of America, and importing the fine goods of England and offering them for sale. With his new ship Laurens became a freighter and was now formally out of the shop; he had recently purchased sizeable acreage and had begun to build a country seat, the aspiration of a "gentleman." But like many other southern merchants with substantial fortunes, his earlier career rested heavily on the sale of slaves. Lots of them. In seven years alone (1751–1758) Laurens imported or brokered forty-five slave cargos.[10] Having built his fortune on "the African foundation," by the early 1760s he had diversified into freight, shop-keeping, and shipping. By 1763, when Laurens christened his new ship, he had disengaged himself from any active trading in slaves, excepting the odd domestic transaction.[11] His money (and reputation) would now be laundered in indigo, rice, and green tar, two hundred tons at a time, and these raw American goods would be translated into fine European imports, like the "neat Windsor riding chairs, imported in the ship *Heart of Oak*, from London . . . with a fine light coloured cloth, painted a strong chocolate colour . . . likewise a very elegant Chimney glass" it carried on its return in September 1764.[12] It also brought Peter Valton and his harpsichord to Charleston, sponsored by the St. Cecilia Society, of which Laurens was an active officer. Valton had been recommended by William Boyce, who trained him, and Boyce wrote the music for the song after which the ship was named.[13]

American raw goods went out, British luxury goods came back, and raw Americans like the ship owner and his sons whom he would send to London for refining all floated upwards. Both trading partners required each other, and both profited from the partnership: crucial points to recall when Bostonians and Virginians began clamoring for trade boycotts. Laurens would also sell cargo room to other traders, for a percentage in freightage, and other retailers would purchase goods directly off his craft, or import for another percentage in freightage, and they too would float upwards. Laurens became very wealthy and assumed his place among the oligarchs of Charleston, with civic posts and colonial appointments that would culminate in four terms in Congress. His trade brought wealth, his wealth brought office, and his office brought respectability. Whatever else it transported, the *Heart of Oak* carried Laurens from slaver to one of the principal men of the colony of South Carolina. He was in no way unique in this rise.

When the *Heart of Oak* departed from Charleston, it carried several passengers involved in the same transatlantic transformation: a few discerning travelers, all acquaintances of Henry Laurens, all part of the same dense intra-colonial network were all refashioning themselves as he had done. They would all leave Carolina from one position and return somewhat elevated, as if the crossing itself were a rite of social promotion. The young men who went to England for finishing school hardly needed to claim the title of gentleman on their return; the journey itself was diploma enough.[14]

Joining the Douglasses on board was Sir Egerton Leigh, another of the wealthiest men in the province and in station second only to the lieutenant governor of South Carolina. He held many positions in Charleston: he was one of the city's few genuine knights, later a baron, a substantial landholder, a practicing lawyer, a member of the Governor's Council, surveyor general, and judge of the Vice Admiralty court. Married to Laurens's niece, he was a prominent member of many social clubs, including the St. Andrew's Society, and he served as Grand Master of the Freemasons. His rise in Charleston society had been meteoric, and now, at the age of thirty-two, he occupied the highest stratum. Laurens sent him to England with a very generous note of credit on his own account, a courtesy hardly needed.[15]

Sir Egerton was sailing to London to secure his newest appointment as attorney general for the colony, and as such, his inaugural piece of business was the first official transmission of the Stamp Act on his return in the summer of 1765.[16] His appointment as enforcer of British colonial policy would mark the beginning of his equally meteoric descent in Charleston society. He would be seen and despised as a "royal placeman" now obligated by his new post to enforce the Stamp Act, setting himself apart from the populist spirit of the colonies.[17] He would never recover his reputation. Even as his appointments rose, his income declined from £1,200 when he sailed to London to less than £100 in 1774. "He was probably correct in believing," concludes Robert Calhoon, "that an unofficial boycott existed of all

Crown services which involved paying him a fee."[18] The overlapping appointments also embroiled him in a conflict of interest, prosecuting shipping cases for the Admiralty Court and deciding on them as attorney general. One litigant: the shipowner, Henry Laurens, his brother-in-law.

Their dispute would go public, with a flurry of printed pamphlets on both sides, and would reveal, among other pieces of dirty laundry, Sir Egerton's affair with his wife's younger sister, who was also his ward. It was a scandal of trans-Atlantic proportions, damaging his reputation in Charleston and London, and the whole nasty business would culminate in an unwanted pregnancy, an indelicate shipping off to England of mother and child, the death of the child at sea, a duel between the two men (proposed but never executed), a pamphlet war, and Leigh's complete disgrace.[19] His final efforts to recoup his standing led him to compose a dramatic parody on his dispute with Henry Laurens, one of the first efforts at dramatic composition by a Charlestonian.[20] He would offer it to the man who now sailed with him, David Douglass, who, wisely, declined to produce it.

That Leigh would turn to playwriting as the last weapon in his arsenal of public dispute reveals the public potential of the theatre. By then, 1769, Sir Egerton was on very good terms with Douglass, a popular patron of the actors, and when his sharp decline began, people remembered his association with actors, not his new baronage. One hears the sneer in the voice of James Laurens when he wrote to his brother Henry: "[But] His Spirits have been lately Supported by a Company of Players who have been fleecing the town since November last, who when they do not entertain him at the Theatre (where by the by he has met with much disrespect), get drunk with him at his own house."[21] Getting drunk with common players reminded both parties of the dubious pasts of both baron and esquire.

But for now, in 1764, Leigh was sailing on Laurens's ship, and he and Douglass would have time enough during the crossing to explore their dramatic interests, over a quarter cask of madeira, courtesy of fellow passenger David Deas, soon to be Esquire. Deas was another Charleston merchant; he had arrived in the colony in 1738 from Leith, Scotland, joined by his brother John. Together they ran a retail shop, imported and brokered the sale of goods and slaves, and by the close of the 1750s had outgrown the shop. Deas followed Laurens out of the slave business, becoming a trader of high-end London goods, a property broker, and just recently a planter.[22] In 1764, when he sailed to London, Lieutenant Governor William Bull had just nominated him and Henry Laurens to serve on perhaps the most important body the colony could offer: the Board of Trade. It negotiated the exchange of duties on goods, and with the appointment came the new title: Esquire. Deas would return to Charleston "Esq.," run for the assembly, win, and secure his place in the enormously influential Carolina oligarchy.

Another Scotsman, Dr. Samuel Carne, also shipped on the *Heart of Oak* for a formative crossing. He had arrived in Charleston as an apothecary—one step up the medical ladder from barber-surgeon—but he too had branched out into the more profitable business of trading. The ship carried some 4,445 pounds of his indigo in the hold, his first major venture, and he was traveling to London with his goods to secure a British trading partner. Having secured one, he would leave off his practice as druggist to become an esquired merchant, amass a fine library, and float upwards. To present himself in his new role, he was traveling flush, having just pocketed £579 from the sale of his domestic slaves, sold to, yes, Henry Laurens.[23]

The youngest passenger, Thomas Lynch, Jr., was also engaged in the London transformation. The young man was going to study law at Middle Temple, and would return to Charleston a finished lawyer in 1772, run for office, and lose his first election to the House of Assembly to his shipmate, David Deas, in a contest for the seat vacated by Henry Laurens.[24] Lynch would later be elected to the Provincial Congress, then the Continental Congress under Laurens, and would be among those who signed the Declaration of Independence.

In such company traveled David Douglass, whose refashioning project was perhaps the most pronounced of any of the men on board. He left America in the spring of 1764 as the strolling manager of a company of players, and when he returned in the fall of 1765, he began to style himself a gentleman. He announced himself as such in London: "A Gentleman has arrived in town [London] from Carolina, in order to engage a select company of players"; and when he returned to America he began to sign his name David Douglass, Esq., a designation he would use until his death in 1789.[25] He would wear a wig (offstage), when wigs were the badge of gentry, and purchase a four horse phaeton, "genteely ornamented," for sporting around a tidewater town less than half a mile long.[26] Exactly where and when this social promotion occurred is not recorded, nor is it clear exactly how the claim was earned or substantiated. He did not use the title prior to his departure and he did on his return, as if the passage itself had somehow promoted him.

Perhaps by associating himself with gentry, Douglass had become gentry. He sidled up to their circles, joined their societies, their clubs. David Deas, John Deas, Sir Egerton Leigh, and the ship captain, Henry Gunn, were all members of the St. Andrew's Society, a benevolent organization of Scots that boasted the wealthiest men of the colony in its membership. Naturally Douglass joined.[27] Leigh was also Grand Master of the Charleston Freemasons, and naturally Douglass joined and sponsored benefits for the local lodge at the theatre.

He also refashioned his "Company of Comedians from London." His first five-year tour exploited the cachet of "London" in the provinces, but when he returned, the company would now be called "The American Company" exclusively, and the tide of cachet would reverse. For Douglass, defending a monopoly, the new name—more geographic than political at this point—referred to his circuit, but the shift from the mid-1760s onward inexorably carried an increasingly pronounced ideology of nation and identity.

One finds these kinds of dense associations all over the social network of colonial America, for example, the Jockey Club in Annapolis that could host three governors and four signers at a single race; the same was true of the monthly Freemasons meetings, or a concert at the St. Cecilia's Society, or a side box at the playhouse. But few occasions were quite so concentrated as a captain's mess on a seven-week voyage. There, playhouse and politics—the two great theatres—would make and unmake many relationships, throwing together some and severing others by nation, by family, by calling, by cause. Sir Egerton would return to England, incensed at America; Deas would become a Royalist; Lynch would rise to sign the Declaration of Independence; and Douglass too would have to choose a side.

But in the late spring of 1764, before the storm, Sir Egerton, the attorney general who wrote dramatic dialogues and drank with the actors; a young man going off to study law; rising Scottish immigrants turned gentlemen; apothecaries and actors-all were going to London to parlay their careers and characters into gentility, or their gentility into nobility, slavers becoming traders, strollers becoming gentlemen, Scotsmen becoming Englishmen. They sailed on a ship whose name Charlestonians knew as an exporter of raw goods and an importer of the best of London goods. A year later its reputation would undergo a radical change: the *Heart of Oak* would be the ship that brought the Stamp agent, George Saxby, to South Carolina. The city would riot on its arrival.

The Stamp Act crisis would itself transform many British colonists, such as Henry Laurens, radicalized into something new and brave and utterly unknown, but certainly no longer British. Others would be loyalized, such as Leigh and Dr. Carne, who found themselves so divided from their constituents and clients that they departed the colonies at the outbreak of hostilities.[28] And the crisis would take that popular English song from the theatre, "Hearts of Oak," and remake it into an American anthem of resistance. John Dickinson (delegate to the Continental Congress and the author of *Letters from a Pennsylvania Farmer*) rewrote the lyrics and sent them to James Otis in Boston. Otis took the liberty of publishing them, and the new words would appear in newspapers from New York to Charleston: "A New Song, to the tune of Hearts of Oak." The tune would now be known as "The American Song of Liberty" and would remain in the hymnal of the Sons of Liberty right through the Revolution.[29] When the original boasted:

> America's islands our thunder alarms
> and all its vast continent bows to our arms—

under Dickinson's pen it now became:

> No tyrannous acts shall suppress your just claim
> or stain with dishonour America's name

In the original, the third stanza began with the declarative statement:

> To King George, as true subjects we loyal bow down.

In Dickinson's rendering:

> Come join hand in hand, brave Americans all,
> And rouse your bold hearts at fair Liberty's call.

And the chorus transmogrified into an anthem of commercial resistance:

> In Freedom we're born, and in freedom we'll live
> our purses are ready
> > Steady, friends, steady,
> > Not as slaves, but as freemen our money we'll give![30]

The refashioned lyrics spoke to the merchant class, this powerful, newly risen class and the new weaponization of commerce. This was a power lodged not in the British naval fleet or in Whitehall's centralized authority, but in the commercial power of American merchants. The potency of this new force lay precisely in the individual consumer, whose purses were ready, "steady, friends, steady," to spend or to boycott. For the next decade, the appeal to non-consumption, boycotts and embargos—commercial warfare—transformed British colonists into Americans.

When, a few years later, in 1770, the loyalist Alexander Mackrabie tried to celebrate St. George's Day in Philadelphia and end his disappointing evening in the theatre, he endeavored to coerce a community of good British loyalists into chorusing national anthems, but the bonhomie of the years after the French-Indian War seemed a long time distant. Mackrabie found little support when he tried to make "the people all chorus 'God Save the King' and 'Rule Britannia' and 'Britons Strike Home' and such like nonsense."[31] Notably, the popular "Hearts of Oak" had dropped out of the British patriotic repertory entirely, so thoroughly had the Stamp Act reclaimed the piece.

Rewriting texts—histories, origins, station, self—was what America excelled at. And so a Scots refugee from the '45 Jacobite uprising, printer's apprentice, and strolling actor on the Caribbean circuit, now the manager of an itinerant company of actors and the owner of a chain of theatres, stepped off the boat in London with money in his pockets and announced himself a Gentleman from Carolina. Adding "nation" to the sea change (promoting British America to America) was only the extension of a process well under way and commonly deployed in the decades prior to the Declaration of Independence. That moment was a kind of carpenter's mark left on the unfinished project of nation-building. A paralegal body of representatives forging a new—in this case national—identity had been the personal genealogy of colonial America. Speaking of the British Americas before Parliament, Edmund Burke might argue against those intractable spirits who would make the colonists barbarians, "We cannot, I fear, falsify the pedigree of this fierce people," implying they were, like his auditors, British by disposition. But falsifying their pedigree is exactly what Americans themselves had been doing for decades, and that slippage of identity, that unmooring and refashioning, would allow the emergence of a new national self in the 1770s.[32] Self-fashioning a nation was the product of the imagination of self-fashioning citizens. America's accelerated emergence from dependent state to independent nation only reproduced the promotion of so many of its restless residents. America's passage, was, in this regard, just another *Heart of Oak* sea crossing.

[CHAPTER 7]

Murder in the Greenroom, and Other London Interludes
1764–1765

• • •

*A gentleman is just arrived in town [i.e., London]
from Carolina, in order to engage a select company of players of
both sexes, for the new theatre open'd last winter in Charles-Town, with
great applause. —New scenes, machinery, and abundance of other
playhouse decorations, are now shipping for the same place.*
New York Post-Boy, July 5, 1764, reprinted as London news

The urgency of the shipping news was a bit of a stretch: Douglass had only just arrived in London and would dawdle in town for well over a year, before he and his new recruits, scenes, and machines would return to America.[1] Moreover, the news of his arrival likely could not have reached New York by July 5, as he had disembarked in mid-June.[2] The news likely wasn't from London at all, but rather, I suspect, had been penned by Douglass himself in Charleston and forwarded on to New York. It is not likely that the great metropole of London took the slightest notice of an actor-manager from America, but if other members of his small profession noticed him and his wife, their presence would have caused more than a few raised eyebrows. This venture in America had been, after all, the joke of the theatre world back in 1751—the "greenroom jest" that actors were sailing to the back of beyond to do theatre for the savages, for Irish felons transported to the Carolinas, and here they were again, flush with a profitable circuit of new theatres, rumors of a royal patent, loading up actors and scenery and going back for more.[3]

For Douglass, London was more than the capital of the Anglophone world; it was the epicenter of culture, the very heart of the theatre profession, where the very best actors could be found. For Mrs. Douglass, London was home. Sarah Hallam Douglass had, after all, married into the largest dynasty of actors of the eighteenth century, the Hallam clan, three generations of extended family, and all actors, and much of their history had ended disastrously, some of it tragically-like the greenroom murder that brought them all to America in the first place.[4]

MURDER IN THE GREENROOM: LONDON, 10 MAY 1735

Douglass knew about it, of course, the murder. All the actors knew. It had been the talk of the trade years ago. Poor Hallam, murdered for a wig. Mrs. Douglass knew as much about it as anyone. It was her father-in-law who died so grotesquely, killed by another actor with the thrust of a walking cane through his eye socket and into his brain. His death ultimately forced the Hallams to leave London and seek out markets in America. Though it might seem to be a fine venture in the 1760s, they came home to the dirty secret: the American theatre was built on a greenroom murder.

In 1735, Thomas Hallam was one of few in his clan legitimately employed in a patent—or officially sanctioned—theatre. The sons Adam, George, William, Lewis, and daughter Ann Hallam were struggling in what would shortly be termed "unlicensed theatres" at the Haymarket, New Wells, and Lincoln's Inn Fields, or employed in provincial companies. After the Licensing Act of 1737, these fringe venues played a cat-and-mouse game with the Lord Chamberlain's office, and increasingly were squeezed out of business. Thomas had the legitimate gig, until one night a simmering quarrel broke out in the greenroom.

For a man who had performed so many tragic deaths onstage, his own death was utterly graceless: a walking cane through the eye while sitting backstage in the greenroom, still in costume, engaged in a sputtering quarrel over a wig for the afterpiece. What's more, the play was still going on, and the man who so violently wielded the cane, Charles Macklin, was obliged to finish the play. Claiming the privilege of first line actor in the company, he desired a particular wig held (tightly) by Thomas Hallam, who insisted he was every bit as much a gentleman as Macklin and equally entitled to wear the wig. It belonged to neither of them, being a company wig. But hard words followed, besmirching the parentage of both contestants, interrupted by the scenes that required one or both of the actors to appear onstage, then resumed again in the greenroom. Macklin's temper finally got the better of him, rash words gave way to rash actions, and he struck Hallam with a cane. He intended, so the deposition ran, to crack his head, but the tip thrust through poor Hallam's eye and into his cortex. Macklin immediately realized the severity of the blow and in revulsion threw the cane in the fire. Hallam collapsed into a chair, his eyeball crushed and oozing down his cheek. A young boy entered from the stage, dressed as a young girl—young Master Arne, the son of the composer Thomas Arne, who was present backstage and later, when the murder came to court, offered his deposition. It was to the shocked young Arne that Hallam muttered his last words: "Whip up your skirt, you bitch, and urine in my eye."

Young Arne was so horrified by the sight of the wounded man that he could not perform the requisite act (urine was thought to be a poor-man's disinfectant). Macklin himself obliged the dying Hallam, and then returned to the stage to act the remainder of the afterpiece. A surgeon was called for and trepanned the skull to release the pressure caused by the blow. Needless to say, between the injury and the treatment, Thomas Hallam never recovered: he died the following morning. Macklin fled, returned, and was arrested and tried for the murder. But with the intercession of Charles Fleetwood (the manager of the theatre) and a host of character witnesses, Macklin pleaded the ancient ruse "benefit of clergy" (he could recite the Lord's Prayer in Latin), and the sentence was commuted to a branding on the thumb (later further commuted and performed with a cold iron). It was, after all, just a dispute between actors—hardly something to bother the courts about. Macklin went on to have a substantial career on the stage.[5]

With Thomas Hallam dead, so too died the Hallams' hope for legitimacy. The sons had a few good years, but after the Licensing Act of 1737 Parliament closed all the theatres except Westminster and the two patent-holding houses, Covent Garden and Drury Lane. The theatres at Lincoln's Field, New Wells, and Goodman's Field were now technically illegal, and though they dodged the authorities with "concert formats" throughout the 1740s, in the end, harassed by the court and creditors, the Hallams hawked all but the costumes and commissioned an agent, Robert Upton, to explore markets in the New World. He sailed for New York with the family's last reserves of capital and then absconded; they never heard back from him. Threatened with foreclosure, the Hallams outfitted a small company and sailed to Virginia in the summer of 1752. The actors in London called it the "green-room jest"—and never expected to hear from them again.

The Hallams' "Company of Comedians from London" toured the British colonies for four years—the first London-trained company to do so. They played each of the principal cities exactly once, then left the continent—debts and all—for the Anglophone islands of the Caribbean, where most were heard from no more. Sarah Hallam survived, as did her son, Lewis Jr., but Lewis Sr. and his brother William died and the remainder of the company (twelve in number) left little trace of their disappearance. That was the mid-1750s, and now here was Mrs. Hallam (alive and remarried), back from the islands from which no one returned, and moreover, successful.

When Sarah Hallam first left London in the summer of 1752, her sons Lewis Jr. and Adam traveled with the company, but she had left behind a young daughter, Isabella. Now, twelve years later, Isabella had not only taken to the stage but was a rising star, with a high-profile engagement at Covent Garden. And little Isabella was not so little anymore; in fact, she was about to elope.

DECLARING INDEPENDENCE (A DOMESTIC FARCE)

Mrs. Douglass also still had a gaggle of former in-laws in town, as well as their actor spouses, together with the seventeen-year-old Isabella, who had been left with her aunt when she was only four. Answering an inquiry late in her life, Isabella described that time: "When I was only four years old . . . my Aunt with true sisterly affection, prevail'd on my mother to leave me under her protection."[6] The date is a little troublesome, as her preserved christening records (St. Mary Whitechapel) for May 25, 1746, would make her nearly six when her mother left. That point aside, the young Hallam daughter grew up in the household of John and Ann Barrington.

Mrs. Barrington was herself a very capable actress, with a long career on the boards, and had a daughter from her first marriage, Mary-Ann, about Isabella's age. In 1752 Ann had appealed to her sister-in-law to leave the young Isabella behind, and so Isabella grew up with her cousin in her aunt and uncle's household. She and the Barringtons all had seasonal and summer engagements, tall cotton as far as the acting profession allowed: the winter season was spent at Covent Garden, while the summer had lately been spent with the company at Bristol, where there was talk of a patent and a subscription scheme was under way to erect a new playhouse. They were doing well, for actors, and had raised their ward well, giving her a general education, acting experience, and musical training.[7]

In the summer of 1764, when mother and daughter met, again there was news to share. America proved prosperous, with Isabella's brother Lewis thriving as the lead.[8] That Douglass was the sole manager of a small touring circuit of theatres without competition must have been table talk for more than the Hallam family. News of his success gave rise to the public (and published) rumor that a royal patent would be issued for a theatre in New York.[9] It proved only rumor. But the theatrical community must have known Douglass was doing well enough to go back with new scenes and fresh recruits.

Young Isabella's news was bigger still. She had debuted at Covent Garden as Juliet, and on the strength of her debut had secured a contract for the upcoming season. She looked like the rising fortune of the family. Of greater importance, to a seventeen-year-old, she had a beau. He was George Mattocks, a twenty-seven-year-old dandy, and he too was an actor and singer in the Covent Garden company. He sang the leads in the ballad operas (Macheath in *The Beggar's Opera*, Tom in *Tom Jones*) and had small comic roles in the straight plays. More promising, he had assumed the management of Plymouth's summer company as a lieutenant to Madame Capte Deville, a dancer, who had appointed him to oversee the company back in 1760. The following year Mattocks bought half the property of the Frankford Gate Theatre at Plymouth and managed it from 1761 to 1763. For the summer company he hired the Barringtons and the young Miss Hallam. In the end, it did not prove to be a lucrative arrangement for owner, lieutenant, or company, but they were all working actors, winter and summer, town and country. In the summer of 1764, when Isabella's mother returned to London, Mr. Mattocks was "paying his addresses" to Isabella, and she, in turn, was pleading the merits of the match to a family who clearly thought otherwise.

And with good reason. George Mattocks had maintained an open affair with Harriot Pitt, another actress in the Plymouth company, with whom he had coauthored two illegitimate children and then abandoned them. When he proposed to Isabella Hallam, the Barringtons were deeply opposed. Enter mother from America, after twelve years' absence. Whatever conversations followed, they were not meant for the public ear; but it must have been a rocky summer. George Mattocks was disentangling himself from a messy liaison with one actress while courting another in the same company, ten years his junior, who was in love against the wishes of her guardians. And as if it wasn't bad enough that she couldn't get the support of one family, a second one popped up from the back of beyond and was also set against her.

The whole scene played out like an afterpiece written by George Coleman. For a large theatrical family whose members had been playing such farces for three generations, it should have come as no surprise that a pair of determined young lovers—including one who debuted as Juliet—would find a way to thwart the parents' desires. Isabella Hallam and George Mattocks eloped to France and were married.[10]

It must have been a difficult spot for Douglass, who could see the advantages to having George Mattocks and Isabella Hallam join him and her mother on the American circuit. They were exactly what he came for, promising young actors in a singing way, experienced in playing the big houses as well as the provinces, desired and talked about in the capital, attractive, talented, the latest goods from London—and even better, they were family, so they couldn't quit. Isabella in particular showed promise (she would, over her career, far outearn her husband). But Douglass could not make such an offer against the will of his own wife and the Hallam family, who saw that Isabella's prospects were far better in London. Nor could he likely offer a contract to the one and not the other, or persuade the pair to abandon London for Williamsburg, Virginia. So here were his best two recruits, in his own family, and Douglass couldn't have them.

He did, however, find plenty of other good talent. When the Covent Garden season opened in the fall, joining Isabella and Mr. Mattocks was one Miss Sarah Wainwright, who debuted November 12 in *The Guardian Outwitted*, a ballad opera by Thomas Arne (father of the young Arne who couldn't . . .). She was a pupil of Arne's, and this production was listed as "her first appearance on any stage." Douglass approached her with the offer to come to America, an offer that seemed more attractive because her roles had been diminished in favor of Isabella Hallam-Maddocks. Douglass also picked up another of Arne's pupils, Stephen Woolls. Though he had little stage experience at the time, he was a melodious singer and would remain with the American Company for the next thirty years. Since both Wainwright and Woolls were "actors in a singing way," Douglass purchased the latest musicals, such as Bickerstaff's *Maid of the Mill, Love in a Village,* and *School for Fathers,* in which he saw Mattocks, his niece, and Miss Wainwright all perform. Then there was the scenery to contract, costumes to order, new plays to pick up, and, one hopes, leisure enough to enjoy the capital and its entertainments, including the seven-year-old Mozart in town that summer. But the real story that summer and fall was John Wilkes, and all the inexorable events that moved toward the crisis to come in ways that eerily foreshadow the issues a decade later.

WILKES AND LIBERTY

The fate of Wilkes and America must stand or fall together.
WILLIAM PALFREY to Wilkes, February 21, 1769

Anybody in any London coffeehouse would have read the story, including those Charlestonians who gathered at the Carolina Coffeehouse to exchange news of America and London and reconnect with acquaintances across the water. And at the heart of coffeehouses was politics. Any stranger in London after late May of 1764 would have heard much criticism of John Stuart, Earl of Bute, Scotsman and Tory, who was consolidating power and roping in satirists of all walks to sponsor journals and rout the Whig opposition. For its part, the Whig opposition found a spokesman in John Wilkes, whose disturbances of the last year still left the ringing echo of "Wilkes and Liberty" in the streets. Wilkes, MP for Aylesbury, had led public opposition to the policies of Lord Bute, culminating with the publication of the infamous #45 issue of Wilkes's journal, the *North Briton,* in April 1763. Wilkes's attack on the despotism of Bute's ministry found willing readers—willing, that is, to burn boots as effigies amid cries of liberty.

This was London, not Boston. Wilkes's populism was mixed with a heavy dollop of anti-Scottish sentiment directed against Lord Bute (whom Wilkes refers to as "The Scot").[11] He wrote, "I cannot sufficiently admire the prudence they have discovered in sending a Scotch regiment to quell the riots about the king's bench prison. Was it in order to allay the animosities, which unhappily run already but too high between the two kingdoms? . . . In plain language, if the ministry act from ignorance, they are the most blundering; if from design, they are the most treacherous set of ministers, with which this kingdom has been cursed for this century past and upwards. Some indeed alledge [sic] another reason and say, that the ministry sent a Scotch regiment, because no English regiment would fire upon the people" (*North Briton*, #48). When Douglass arrived, Wilkes had just been arrested, tried for libel, exonerated, and carried home in triumph by a large crowd, amidst bonfires and shouts of liberty. He would be threatened with a second trial for libel and would flee to France, but the call of "Wilkes and Liberty" and the rights of men were in the very streets of London.[12]

The Wilkes affair provided a grammar of dissent, and Americans followed his campaign studiously. The manner in which his objections to the court party's policies had been vilified, he himself had been exiled, and he had been denied the seat in Parliament to which he had been elected after his return animated readers in the colonies. In Boston Alden Bradford acknowledged, "The case of Wilkes occupied much of the public attention. And the contest was so warmly maintained, as to the legality of his election, and his retaining a seat in Parliament, after being chosen, that it excited an uncommon interest through the greater part of the kingdom, and arrayed almost the whole population either for or against the political principles he professed."[13] Nor was the polarizing effect of the Wilkes affair the topic of one summer. Again and again elections were called and again and again Wilkes won and again and again he was denied his seat. It became clear to any coffeehouse patron that government was no longer in the hands of its representatives, and this sense of disenfranchisement was another London product that traveled across the pond.

Even the language of dissent found a first expression in the Wilkes affair. "[I]t is now become the fashionable style," wrote Wilkes in *North Briton* #49 (May 21, 1768), "at the court end of the town, to treat all those as mob, who presume to find fault with the conduct of the ministry." This tone would underlie the basic assumption of the opposition in America as well. Opposition was a mob, a word that came readily to the tongues of British ministers abroad and hard-nosed governors at home like Cadwallader Colden. "Mobs," continues Wilkes, "are always dangerous; but I know that they are dangerous only in proportion to the despotism of the government. No mobs are to be seen in Turkey; because there, almost always, mobs are attended with a revolution in the state."

The *North Briton* was recalled from the printer and publicly burned; consequently, it was widely read. Rewards were offered for intact copies. Charles Burney, the famous doctor of music, prized his copy. Hugh Gaine, a New York printer, somehow secured a copy, reprinted it, and advertised it openly, along with the description of Wilkes's arrest and trial.[14] Other papers printed excerpts. William Carmichael, a Scottish planter in Chestertown, Maryland, loaned his folio of the *North Briton* to Henry Callister, a tidewater tobacco-broker, who wrote back with this prescient assessment: "[I]f the present ministry [of Lord Bute] do not give way with a good grace, I apprehend there will be bad doings indeed, where England, Scotland, Ireland and America will probably be entangled—If a civil war should break out, France will have a hand in it, and it may produce another revolution which God avert we cannot expect a better than the last."[15] The Wilkes affair gathered up much of the simmering opposition to British policies in America and would remain an icon of resistance right up until the outbreak of open hostilities.

And then there was theatricalizing of the affair, an eighteenth-century proclivity. After Wilkes's indictment, the *North Briton* carried an allegory titled *The Fall of Solomon: A Tragedy*. The reimagining of events as theatrical representations that would characterize the American Revolution (as one "Cassandra" wrote, "the Acts of our National Tragedy has begun"[16]) had its precedent here in just such theatre-thinking. Both Wilkes and the reimagining of Wilkes in theatrical terms reveal how potently the theatre informed the cultural imagination. The *Mousetrap* of Hamlet offered a moral parable for royal guilt; the set speech of Hotspur (*Henry IV, Part I*) did the same for the excised word "Massacre" at the trial of Donald Maclane, the Scottish soldier who had fired and killed one of the rioters at St. George's Field. After the judge admonished Maclean for using the word to describe British soldiers firing on the mob outside the prison where Wilkes was held, the *North Briton* published this verse:

> They would not have me mention MASSACRE
> Forbid my tongue to speak of MASSACRE
> Yet, I will find them when they lie asleep
> And in their ears I'll holla, MASSACRE!
> Nay, I will have a starling taught to speak
> Nothing but MASSACRE, and give it them,
> To keep their Guilt still before them."
> (North Briton, #63, 378)

The Wilkes affair provided a model and language of dissent that could be exported. The Boston massacre became a "massacre" because it reproduced this earlier "massacre." In New York, during the Stamp Act riots, the fiery pamphlet author Alexander McDougall was imprisoned for libel "only to be hailed as the Wilkes of America."[17] The radical leader Christopher Gadsden in Charleston sponsored the founding of the John Wilkes Club, or "Club Forty-Five" as it was known, and hosted an election barbecue in October 1768 (where he secured the votes of the Charleston mechanics against Henry Laurens), after which they decorated a Liberty Tree in honor of Wilkes with forty-five lights and forty-five rockets. Later that evening the same company assembled in Dillon's tavern, "where the 45 lights [were] placed upon the table, with 45 bowls of punch, 45 bottles of wine."[18] Henry Laurens complained, "I have always disliked those stupid Garnishings of No. 45, Wilkes and Liberty, and drinking 45 toasts to the Cause of true Liberty 450 times."[19]

The Club Forty-Five was a force in South Carolina politics right up to the election of delegates to the First Continental Congress. They had, for example, pledged a sizeable contribution to the Wilkes fund, a debt on the books still in 1774. Wilkes was a potent transatlantic model of popular dissent that endured past his initial popularity, partly because of his association with an equally potent theatrical tradition: Addison's *Cato*. One encomium to Wilkes:

> Great is the man, and great is his reward,
> Who pays despotic rulers no regard;
> But wide expands the spirit to be free,
> And perseveres in glorious Liberty:
> On him at once both heaven and earth shall smile
> All hail to Wilkes! the Cato of our isle.[20]

When Wilkes was released from prison in March 1770, supporters carried him to the theatre for a sponsored production of *Cato*. This gesture offers a telling metaphor for how the resistance movement was marketed around Wilkes and also beautifully embodies the transatlantic transformation of the Wilkes affair. What was in England a symbol of ruffianism became an elevated model of American dissent. When the notion of Wilkes crossed the sea, it was classicized, washed of indecencies and petty scandals, and came out of the pond more like Cato of old.

But one didn't need to read of "the late disturbances" of the Wilkes campaign in the papers: class unrest was happening all across London. Many of these seemingly unrelated incidents were driven by the same class anxiety Douglass had encountered in New York. In London servants rioted at Ranelagh Gardens, a fashionable pleasure resort, because coachmen and footmen were not allowed in. Swords were drawn and two men run through before the brutal business ended in court.[21] When the Vauxhall, another pleasure garden, installed a railing to separate the coaches from the gentlefolk, the servants broke down the rails and knocked out the lamps.[22]

And the uproar over Wilkes didn't go away. In June the fourteen journeymen printers who had been jailed for their part in publishing *North Briton* #45 had their day in court and received their settlements for false imprisonment. In July, Wilkes himself was tried for publishing the piece and fled to France.[23] Though he was absent, his cause remained and would inspire America throughout the 1760s.

THEATRE NEWS

When Douglass visited London that decisive year, there were two very large headlines in the theatre's long story—that is, beyond the petty gossip, greenroom chatter, and elopements. The first was the huge influence that David Garrick exerted over the field, even in his absence. Douglass would have read of Garrick's tour of Italy in the summer of 1764. He was writing open letters (a sort of eighteenth-century blog), building his own personal fame, but the collateral benefit spread to the whole profession. It was not just that he was a national celebrity becoming an international celebrity, but that, like any truly great figure, he was elevating his profession. Acting was becoming more respectable because of David Garrick. His unblemished personal life and network of influential patrons, his enormous talent and meteoric career, had accomplished astonishing promotions in the social status of acting. At his death, Edmund Burke eulogized him for raising "the character of his profession to the rank of a liberal art, not only by his talents, but by the regularity and probity of his life and the elegance of his manners."[24] That was Garrick's revolution.

But in the 1760s many of the old and less respectable associations remained. The most concentrated brothel district in London was still just off Covent Garden, where actors like Ned Shuter debauched himself nightly until he passed out. Young rakes like James Boswell or William Hickey could sport in the theatre for the express purpose of finding a wench. When Hickey, on his last night in London, "went the rounds of Covent Garden and Drury Lane," he wasn't seeking the pleasure of the plays. The two most notorious houses Hickey visited (Weatherby's and Murphy's, establishments that shocked even the seasoned profligate) were a quick wink from the theatre, while his usual haunts stood on Bow Street, Covent Garden.[25] These houses were Douglass's immediate neighbors while he visited London. His wife's family, the Barringtons and her daughter, lived on Bow Street, Covent Garden, on the corner of Broad Street, and her brother, Adam Hallam, was also a Bow Street resident.[26] That part of the profession's reputation traveled, and Douglass strained against it in America.

The other inescapable item had a more direct bearing on Douglass. Theatre was no longer just a London phenomenon. One of the by-products of the Licensing Act was the proliferation of playhouses in the provinces, and by the mid-1760s, theatre was everywhere. With the capital closed to all but two companies, actors and managers sought their business in circuits in and around provincial towns, and quickly stitched these circuits into seasons. Covent Garden's John Arthur assembled a summer company and ventured into the southern circuit at Bath, Portsmouth, and Plymouth from 1758 to 1763. A competent architect, he designed and remodeled Bath's Orchid Street theatre and built Plymouth's playhouse out of three unfinished buildings.[27] Tate Wilkinson operated the northern Yorkshire circuit.

Mr. Ivory, the proprietor of the theatre in Norwich, built a new playhouse in Colchester, which had just opened in the summer of 1764. The season also saw the establishment of the new company in Bristol, whose building was remodeled, according to the designs of John Arthur, in 1765. Another theatre had opened in Sheffield in 1762, and two years later Samuel Johnson opened a new playhouse in Chichester.[28] The new theatre at Richmond also opened that summer. Douglass's circuit in the colonies was part of this provincial playhouse building spree, as the rumor that a royal patent would be issued for a theatre in New York revealed. Theatre as a nationalizing, civilizing force was spreading across the English countryside.

Such a proliferation meant that acting opportunities were expanding enormously. Douglass found a tough market recruiting. He shopped performers at various theatres in London during the 1764–1765 season. At the Haymarket he met Thomas Llewellyn Lechemere Wall, who advertised himself as "from the Theatre Royal Drury Lane and the Haymarket," though his name is curiously not found on the preserved cast lists of either. He had trained in Sheridan's company at Smock Alley, Dublin, in 1757–1758. When he came to London is unclear, and if he ever played Drury Lane he did not meet with great success there. His association with Foote's company may have been equally brief, and the prospect of a world elsewhere tempted him to leave the metropolis. Once in America, Wall would be a long-standing figure on the colonial stage, remaining well into the 1780s—indeed, staying through the Revolutionary War, when the rest of the American Company departed. He was captured, set up a theatre in a prison camp, and once paroled seeded the first company of the new America, even before the war was over.[29]

Douglass also signed Henrietta Osborne, according to what few records remain of her a temperamental itinerant who played with nearly every company on the American circuit. She was a member of the original Murray-Kean Company that had played briefly in Philadelphia and New York in 1749–1751, then joined Robert Upton's assembly in the winter of 1751–1752 before returning to the Murray-Kean in 1752. Both of these were scratch companies strolling America before the Hallams arrived. Osborne drifted to Jamaica in the mid-1750s, where she likely met Douglass, who was playing with John Moody's company. She returned to London in 1758. Tate Wilkinson claims she returned pregnant, with Moody the godfather "or some kind of father," and delivered her baby in the fifth act of *The Mourning Bride*.[30] She strolled with Kennedy's "Brandy Company" in 1760–1761, before she was hired at Covent Garden for the 1762–1763 season, and in the summer of 1763 she was also acting with Foote's company at the Haymarket. When she was "between engagements"—as the courteous phrase goes—in the summer of 1764, she was recruited by Douglass, and both knew what they were getting into. She was a seasoned provincial player and knew firsthand the pitfalls of the strolling life. Douglass, for his part, must have known something of her temperamental disposition.

Despite the competition, he signed five seasoned actors, most in a "singing way," and acquired the latest musical comedies. After Garrick had returned many of Shakespeare's plays to the repertory, we see American debuts of *Coriolanus*, *King John*, *King Lear*, and *Cymbeline*. Douglass also purchased anthologized musical scores, such as *The Musical Companion: Being a Collection of all the New Songs sung at the Playhouses and all the Public Gardens*.[31] The latest music was every bit as important to the colonists as the latest fashions. Many of these numbers were on the lips of Londoners through the singing of his own daughter-in-law, Mrs. Mattocks. Douglass also called upon the services of Nicholas Dahl, scene painter to Covent Garden, and the manager would advertise his new brushwork among the latest goods of London.

With new actors, new songs, new plays, new scenes—no patent, but all in all, a successful trip—Douglass, his wife, and recruits boarded a Carolina ship for Charleston late that summer. The plan had been to rendezvous in October with Lewis Hallam and the remainder of the corps who had been playing in Barbados for the past winter season. The wayward islanders, however, found the Bridgetown market rather comfortable and chose not to leave the island—another revolt in the making. Instead of his company, Douglass found only a letter waiting for him in Charleston. The mutiny of actors was, however, the least of his worries. It is not likely to have been common knowledge among the high-spirited passengers, so Douglass and his recruits may have been well at sea before they discovered they were all sailing back to America with a cargo of stamped paper and a British stamp agent determined to enforce the Stamp Act.

[CHAPTER 8]
Sailing on an Unwelcomed Ship
1765–1766

• • •

TAXING PLAYHOUSES

It is an odd thought, but quite thinkable in 1765: a tax on the London theatres might have prevented the Revolution and loss of the British colonies in America. It was actually proposed but dismissed in favor of the stamp tax. More the pity, as it would certainly have mollified the dissent that followed the enactment of the Stamp Act. Odder still, but to suggest a tax on the London theatres was a potentially dangerous notion. Parliament first debated imposing a tax on the playhouses during the Restoration, but the bill was quashed when Charles II reminded Parliament that the actors played at the king's pleasure. When Sir John Coventry asked, not sotto voce enough, if His Majesty's pleasure lay with actors or actresses, he was ambushed that night and two assailants slit his nose to the bone. The disfigurement made for delicate conversation on the subject for decades afterwards. Even during the parliamentary debates about the Licensing Act in 1737, there was little serious talk of a tax.

But in 1765 the debate was renewed: "Talk of laying a stamp duty on all playhouse tickets is again renewed," reported the *Gazetteer, or Daily Advertiser* as early as April 6, 1765. In the end, Parliament exempted the theatre and looked elsewhere for revenue. At some level Parliament still perceived the theatres to play at the king's pleasure. Though the discussion was to be resumed "with the next session"—that is, in the fall—in the end the conversation turned to a tax of a broader nature: a stamp tax on all paper goods.

The Stamp Act had its origins at the close of the French-Indian war, in 1763, when George Grenville, Bute's successor, argued that the colonies themselves must bear part of the enormous expense of defending them. This was no small charge. The annual expense of maintaining ten thousand troops was estimated at more than £220,000. As chancellor of the exchequer it was Grenville's responsibility to balance the war budget, and given the backlash against Bute's taxes, he need an external source. A tax of some nature was the obvious solution, but the specifics were in need of research. No one in Whitehall knew enough about how the shipping, receiving, sales, and distribution of American goods and services functioned to prepare a suitable measure to take to Parliament. For example, were land grants (being royal gifts) taxable? How would the additional taxation of American manufactured goods affect the transatlantic market? Would a direct tariff on the colonies essentially transfer manufacturing to the British West Indies? Would a stiff tariff expand black-market trade? What goods could be taxable? It was a problem that occupied Grenville for eighteen months.

It was not until early 1765 that a draft resolution was circulated, including to the colonists in the hope of inspiring self-imposed levies that would make legislation unnecessary. The colonists, however, were not inspired. Grenville's bill was introduced in Parliament in February 1765, rushed to passage by the close of March, and slated to become effective November 1, 1765.[1]

By late summer of 1765 it would have been apparent to any reading person that stamps were going to America and would directly impact many businesses that involved paper, including theatres. How this new legislation would be received was not just anybody's guess. Whitehall had a strong inkling of the hostility that awaited and deliberately chose several American representatives as stamp agents, among them George Saxby for South Carolina.

For a merchant like Douglass, who throughout the escalating rift between the colonies and Great Britain endeavored to remain politically neutral, it is ironic that he most likely sailed back from England on the same ship that carried the spark of the Revolution. Kenneth Silverman writes that "[q]uite certainly" the same *Carolina Packet* that carried the stamped paper "brought to Charleston from London David Douglass and several members of his American Company."[2] Silverman may be mistaken, as the identity of the stamp ship was not public knowledge. In the small flotilla that gathered at Deal to wait on a favorable wind in the second week of September 1765 were three vessels bound for Charleston: *Planter's Adventure*, *Carolina Packet*, and *Heart of Oak*; one had the stamps, one had the stamp agent—George Saxby—and one carried the actors.[3]

The first to arrive was *Planter's Adventure*, anchoring with its stamps off Fort Johnson on October 18. It had sailed faster than expected, arrived early, and off-loaded its volatile cargo unbeknownst to the crowds of Sons of Liberty who had prepared a forceful resistance. The trouble began the next day. The 19th saw a gallows erected (20 inches high at the prominent intersection of Church and Broad Streets), with an effigy of George Saxby hanging from one side and a boot (the icon for Lord Bute) on the other. The effigy remained on display throughout the day, with a dire warning against anyone who should attempt to dismantle it. It was later paraded and publicly burned.

Troops were dispatched to the fort, and the town simmered throughout the week, uncertain about the location of the stamps. On the night of October 23, rumors that the stamps had been lodged at Henry Laurens's house prompted a mob to gather there and demand a search. Peter Timothy of the *South Carolina Gazette*, the most liberal of the Charleston papers, softly described the events of that Wednesday night: "[I]t was reported, that the stampt papers had been brought up to town, unobserved, and lodged in the house of a gentleman at Ansonborough, upon which a number of people went thither to be satisfied of the truth of the report; but finding none, they returned quietly, without offering the least insult to any person whatever."[4] Laurens (the "gentleman at Ansonborough"), the victim of the raid, took a less generous view:

> At midnight of the said Wednesday I heard a most violent thumping & confused noise at my Western door & chamber Window, & soon distinguish'd the sounds of *Liberty, Liberty & Stamp'd Paper, Open your doors & let us Search your House & Cellers*. I open'd the Window, saw a croud of Men chiefly in disguise & heard the Voices & thumpings of many more on the side, assured them that I had no Stamp'd Paper nor any connexion with stamps. When I found that no fair words would pacify them I accused them with cruelty to a poor Sick Woman far gone with Child & produced Mrs. Laurens shrieking and wringing her hands adding that if there was any one Man amongst them who owed me a spite & would turn out I had a brace of Pistols at his service & would settle the dispute immediately but that it was base in such a multitude to attack a single Man.

Sailing on an Unwelcomed Ship [97

Laurens went on at great length about the assault, which lasted for an hour and a quarter, complete with cutlasses at his throat, but the search produced no stamps, and so the marauders departed—peaceably, he adds—leaving his garden untrampled.[5]

To prevent further assaults, on Thursday morning Lieutenant Governor Bull had the clerk of the council print the news that the stamps were lodged in Fort Johnson on James Island. When the *Carolina Packet* sailed into Charleston on Friday, there was "some little appearance of tumult, but it subsided as soon as it was known no stamp officer was on board. Mr. Saxby had taken his passage and was on board the *Heart of Oak*, Capt. Gunn." An angry crowd had gathered at the dockside, but no agents, only actors. Welcome to America.[6]

Saxby and *Heart of Oak* arrived the next morning, on October 26. The violence that met him at dockside must have alarmed the new actors. Mobs had gathered (the *Gazette* estimated two thousand on Saturday) and had been agitating all week. Saxby no sooner disembarked than he was forced to flee to Fort Johnson, where the Charleston stamp distributor, Caleb Lloyd, was already holed up. After two days' imprisonment in the fort, during which their houses were rifled, their tenants robbed, and their effigies burned on the streets, both agents agreed to resign their posts. By the time Saxby and Lloyd rowed back from the fort to surrender their office, an enormous crowd had gathered. "Upon their landing, a lane was instantly formed, amidst the greatest concourse of people that ever were assembled here on any occasion (being supposed upwards of seven thousand souls) and a new declaration was publickly read."[7] Their renunciations were publicly read, printed, and accompanied by the tolling of bells.

The conclusion of the affair was reported in the last issue of the *South Carolina Gazette* before the Stamp Act went into effect: "[T]he air rang with the musick of bells, drums, hautboys, violins, huzza's, firing of cannon, &c. &c. and the flag before mentioned being carried before them the music continuing, they were conducted to Mr. Dillon's tavern, and, after taking some refreshment there, to their own houses."[8] By Black Friday, the day the act was to take effect, the mob's numbers "[became] more formidable & Riot [was] in Fashion."[9]

All across America and the Anglophone Caribbean, street violence erupted at the landing of the stamps and their agents. The people of Boston set the first bonfires, and their actions quickly became legendary, but New Yorkers mobbed with equal violence and results. They burned effigies of the stamp men, ransacked the house of Major Thomas James, and made a bonfire of the lieutenant governor's carriage.

How incongruous it must have been to read of the arrival of an acting company with the latest London operas in a town experiencing the worst citywide violence in its colonial career. Douglass announced his arrival in the last paper before the act was to commence:

> On Friday last, Mr. Douglass, director of the Theatre in this town, arriv'd from London with a reinforcement of his company. We hear he has engaged some very capital singers from the theatres in London, with a view of entertaining the town this winter with English operas. It is imagined, when he is joined by the company from Barbados, that our theatrical performance will be executed in a manner not inferior to the most applauded in England. The scenes and decorations, we are informed, are of a superiour kind to any that have been seen in America, being designed by the most eminent maker in London."[10]

But Douglass was clearly in a very different America than the one he left. If he had any notion of opening his theatre soon, the unrest of the town would soon have disabused him. On Black Friday the town was effectively shut down. "Tomorrow, most of the business in publick offices will cease," wrote Robert Wells in his paper, "and from this day the publication of the *South Carolina Gazette* will also be suspended, it being impossible to continue it without great loss to the printer, when the numerous subscribers thereto have signified, almost to a man, that they will not take in One stampt newspaper, if stamps could be obtained." The account book of James Poyas, a dry-goods merchant, which normally filled two pages a day of receipts, recorded not a single transaction for that entire first weekend of the act.[11]

The courts also closed. They too ran on paper, and as no stamped paper was to be had, no writs, no deeds, no bills, no contracts, no foreclosures, no leases, and no court dockets would be issued. No paper also meant no trade: no ready money in circulation; no newspapers, hence, no advertisements. For the indebted, there were no writs of prosecution, no collecting on outstanding debts, and no courts in which to press the claims; it was a debtor's holiday. Certificates of debt were issued as an emergency measure to satisfy creditors. No stamps would apply to the ports as well, which required clearance slips to land cargo, load more cargo, and depart. Ships could enter, but they could not unload their cargo, nor sell their goods, nor depart to sell them elsewhere. In a city of transatlantic merchants, a port bottled up with slack-water ships meant a complete commercial standstill.

And here was a theatre manager trying to restart a luxury business in a simmering town with no money, offering the latest London operas when London meant Lord Bute, placemen like Saxby, and British tyranny, who had secured permission from a man (Lieutenant Governor Bull) who would insist he use stamps for his playbills; and a mob who could be guaranteed to pull down the theatre if they saw so much as a single stamped playbill. The fears were quite real: later that same season in New York, the Sons of Liberty completely destroyed his Chapel Street theatre.

THE WRECK ON CHAPEL STREET, AND OTHER EXPRESSIONS OF AMERICAN LIBERTY: NEW YORK

Opposition to the Stamp Act in the colonies was swift and surprisingly well organized, and it unified the colonies as no previous issue had. But it also created two discrete bodies of power: an intellectual agency that authored "circular letters" and appeals to action, enjoining delegates to meet in the Stamp Act Congress in New York; and a second, mobile body on the street that enforced such appeals. This second America was the triumph of the first body (the Sam Adamses, the John Hancocks, the Christopher Gadsdens), but once animated, the Sons of Liberty would take on a political role of their own whose agenda was, in critical ways, altogether different from that of the men who first activated them.

Unlike earlier revenue-generating acts (like the Sugar Act of 1764), the Stamp Act affected everyone, and this ability to unify the disparate colonies, if only temporarily, has led many to invoke the first of the theatrical metaphors of the period: it was the prologue of the drama to come. Delegates from nine colonies gathered in New York in October 1765 to sound out consensus among such disparate markets as Boston and Charleston, share strategies, and carry back what today we would call "action plans." The delegates drafted written protests and the individual colonies hired agents to represent their objections in Whitehall. Some colonies passed resolutions not to support the act. A general boycott of British goods was also proposed. But by far the most successful component of this new congress was the creation of the Sons of Liberty.

Centered in Connecticut, this organization of radical tradesmen rapidly spread to Boston, Philadelphia, New York, and Charleston. The articulate, reasoned opposition of the delegates in assembly encouraged mob actions by the Sons of Liberty, who burned effigies, erected gallows, threatened merchants, staged mock funerals, put up Liberty Trees, and generally showed little or no respect for property. If the unfortunate stamp distributor was known, the Sons were becoming a second America, and they would force him to resign his office or threaten to pull his house down. Or both. This second America was a new and powerful weapon, but it was a sword without a sheath, and once drawn it remained out, jabbing its rude way through polite society. It was unschooled power, raw, dockside thuggery, but very useful against willful bad policy.

The ministry was willful enough to resolve to apply the Stamp Act by force if necessary. The colonists, for their part, had already expressed their abhorrence of the act in petitions to Parliament. By early November 1765 news had reached London of the resignation of the stamp distributors for Maryland, New Jersey, and New Hampshire, and similar reports from other colonies followed. General Gage in New York summarized the opposition to the act with uncharacteristic cogency: "The question is not of the inexpediency of the Stamp Act, or of the inability of the colonies to pay the tax, but that it is unconstitutional, and contrary to their rights."[12]

Suspicions also fell on the growing division between the classes. It was popularly believed, as General Conway wrote to the colonial governors, that the resistance "can only have found Place among the lower and more ignorant of the People; the better and wiser Part of the Colonies well know that Decency and Submission may prevail."[13] This certainly played out in New York. But in many colonies, the disturbances of "lower sorts" were demonstratively an extension of the "wiser Part." In Charleston, the Sons of Liberty had the backing of prominent merchants, assemblymen, and lawyers. And that alliance was not lost on anyone. When the "mob" assaulted Henry Laurens's house, he recognized many of the men on the shadowy edges of the torchlight. The lieutenant governor of South Carolina, William Bull, wrote: "Although these numerous Assemblies of the People bore the appearance of common populace; Yet there is great reason to apprehend they were animated and encouraged by some considerable Men, who stood behind the Curtain"[14]—another theatrical metaphor.

The very real fear was that if the "lower sorts" began to view the playhouse as a preserve of the wealthy, the theatre would become collateral damage. As it did. Douglass had rented his theatre in New York, the Chapel Street Theatre, that winter to two actors formerly of the American Company, John Tomlinson and his wife Ann, who assembled "a company of young gentlemen," secured permission from Lieutenant Governor Colden, and performed a few plays in the spring of 1765. Tomlinson had planned a small winter season, but then came the stamps and the turmoil that followed. He carried his small company out of the city—where, we do not know—but his return in the spring of 1766 was noted by the same Sons of Liberty who had been audacious enough to make a public bonfire of the lieutenant governor's carriage.[15]

Captain Montresor, a military engineer stationed in New York, recorded the arrival of the actors and the city's response: "A Grand meeting of the Sons of Liberty to settle matters of moment, amongst the many whether they shall admit the strollers, arrived here to act, tho the General [Gage] has given them permission. . . . Some stamps as tis said found in the streets were publickly burned at the Coffeehouse together with some playbills, all to prevent their spirits to flag."[16] The playhouse was one issue of many, but Montresor singles it out for satire. However, the mob's primary business was not the players, but rather a large cache of stamped paper recently found. It had been part of a cargo bound to Philadelphia on the ship *Ellis* that wrecked. The paper was retrieved, bundled off to New York, and when discovered, "seized by the Sons of Liberty, and purified [burned] at the Coffee house last Friday, before a Thousand Spectators."[17]

To which blaze they added playbills, expressing their hostility to the theatre as something licensed by the British general. Tomlinson countered that he had secured permission, that the repeal of the Stamp Act was imminent, but to no avail. When he opened the theatre anyway, midway through the second act a signal was given and the destruction began. A Maryland newspaper later reported,

> A rumor was spread about town, on Monday, that if the play went on, the audience would meet with some disturbance from the multitude. This prevented the greatest part of those who intended to have been there from going: however many people came, and the play began; but soon interrupted by the multitude who burst open the doors, and entered with noise and tumult. The audience escaped in the best manner they could, many lost their hats and other parts of dress. A boy had his skull fractured, and was yesterday trepanned, his recovery is doubtful; several others were dangerously hurt; but we have heard of no lives lost. The multitude immediately demolished the house, and carried the pieces to the common, where they consumed them in a bonfire.[18]

For the first time in the growing conflict, the theatre found itself on the un-American side of the question. The salon of the mannerly had just been demolished by a mob.

If Douglass was in the business of making Americans Londoners, that is, fashioning urbanity and civility, the Sons of Liberty were in the business of making unmannered Americans violent levelers, hostile to class distinctions. Where the theatre taught class, rank, and distinction, the Sons of Liberty were demolishing distinctions, targeting "rank" and all its signs, including books, carriages, artwork, and now the theatre. They were, in this spirit, Douglass's fiercest antagonists. They were building a different kind of America, one with no use for the theatre and its elite clientele. John Adams might take pride in "the people, even to the lowest Ranks" becoming "more attentive to their Liberties, more inquisitive about them, and more determined to defend them," but they had also become more violent, more anarchistic, more divided, and easily mobilized.[19]

In the midst of the Chapel Street fray, enter Hallam. Not Lewis Hallam the actor, not Sarah Hallam or Nancy Hallam, actresses, but Lieutenant Thomas Hallam, the actors' uncle, Sarah's former brother-in-law, the white sheep of the clan, the only one who did not take to the stage, the odd Hallam who entered service in His Majesty's navy.

Sailing on an Unwelcomed Ship [103

Thomas Hallam was stationed in New York during the winter of 1765–1766, on board the man-of-war *Garland*. He earned the particular hatred of the Sons of Liberty when he intimated that "their proceedings were equal to the Proceedings in Scotland in 1745," and then invited them to "be damn'd and kiss his arse." They in return demanded that he be handed over with a halter around his neck. Hallam remained on board except when he honored their paralegal committee by appearing "to give satisfaction" for his comments. He denied their allegations, they produced affidavits to the contrary, and Hallam refused to recognize any authority of the populist court of self-empowered waterfront thugs. The business would have gotten downright nasty if General Gage had not intervened. Hallam returned to his ship with a threat hanging over his head. Next to Cadwallader Colden, for many weeks that spring Lieutenant Hallam was the most hated man in New York.[20] It is just as well for both parties that the rest of his family didn't show up to entertain the opulent.

A BROKEN SEASON: CHARLESTON

Douglass and half his company remained in Charleston, with a huge problem on their hands. Theatres ran on paper. Douglass relied heavily on printers to advertise the play in newspapers and in playbills, hundreds of them for each playing night. From the account books of Philadelphia printers Franklin and Hall we know the printers struck off between four hundred and six hundred handbills for each performance. The British military, when they performed in Philadelphia during the war, would run off one thousand bills for each performance.[21] Douglass hired bill-stickers to paper the town with playbills. That was where he met the public, through the posted bills. And then there were the tickets, also printed. In Charleston Douglass relied on Robert Wells, who had already announced a suspension of his press. Even if Douglass could solve the advertising problem, how does one run a theatre without tickets? And with business shut down, who would come?

These were the material problems. The larger issue was one of alliances. The company played by permission of the royally appointed governors or their lieutenants, yet it played for an audience that was increasingly and sometimes violently opposed to Great Britain's American policies. Like the newspapers that attempted to be "open to all parties," the playhouse might not announce a position, but Douglass needed to be allied with those in power. His position would need to be known, one way or another.

It was all uncharted territory, and unlike other businesses—printing, for example—Douglass had no commercial counterparts elsewhere from which to take his cue. He owned all the theatres in America. Newspapers modeled their responses on each other. Many, like Timothy's *South Carolina Gazette*, strategically decided to suspend publication during the heat of the crisis, while others side-stepped the act by claiming, as Hugh Gaine did in New York, that "no stamped paper was to be had." Printers William Bradford, Philadelphia, and William Goddard, Providence, both belonged to the Sons of Liberty[22] and openly defied the Stamp Act.

Printers were at particular risk, relying as they did on both public support and government contracts; like the players they were licensed, and that license could be suspended at the governor's discretion. Mechanically, their business relied on the fragile imported typesets, easily scattered or destroyed; Andrew Steuart, for example, risked publishing the *North Carolina Gazette* and witnessed the destruction of his shop. Conversely, some printers were threatened by the Sons of Liberty to remain open, defying the act. John Holt, printer of the *New York Gazette*, received the following warning on the day before the act took effect: "[S]hould you at this critical time shut up the press, and basely desert us, depend upon it, your house, person, and effects, will be in imminent danger. We shall therefore expect your paper on Thursday as usual."[23]

Colonial resistance to the Stamp Act also meant that the wayward American Company, which had remained in Barbados instead of meeting Douglass in Charleston that October as planned, now could not come to the mainland at all. After the first of November, ships could not be cleared to sail or land without stamped paper, with the net result that nobody was sailing anywhere. Six weeks later, Charles Crouch published a list of over eighty ships waiting to clear at the Custom-House.[24] And that was only mid-December. Their crews were stranded, bored, unpaid, and prowling Charleston.

The return to Carolina that had begun with such promise had soured utterly. Douglass did the only thing he could: he went public with his dilemma.

To the Public:

A sense of past favours, and an ambition of convincing my friends that they were not thrown away, but conferred upon a heart truly grateful that pants for an opportunity of acknowledging them, were my motives for planning an Entertainment this winter, which, I flattered myself, would not have been altogether unworthy the attention of so respectable and judicious an audience as the ladies and gentlemen of Carolina compose: To that end, I collected in London, some Performers, who, when joined to the company now at Barbados, would have enabled me to execute my Entertainments with a superior degree of excellence to any that have hitherto appeared in America; and it was my pride to produce them first in this town, where my former labours had met with such distinguished, such uncommon marks of approbation.

I had also employed the proper artificers to refit the Theatre, and make such commodious and elegant alterations, the construction of it would admit. The new scenes I have brought over with me, with those in the possession of the company at Barbados, as they would have given a diversity, so they would have been a considerable improvement to our representations.

But these flattering hopes, in which I fondly indulged myself, are now at an end: — I received, on Friday, letters from Barbados, which to my utter astonishment, inform me, that the company cannot possibly leave that island before the end of March! Notwithstanding I had taken every previous measure necessary as I thought, to effect a junction here by [in?] October.

Great as this disappointment must be to a person in my situation, in regard to the expences I have been at, I feel more concern to find myself obliged to baulk the expectations [the town?] had conceived, from my declarations, of an Entertainment. Than [torn] . . . my own particular interest may sustain.

Under these circumstances I would have embarked immediately for Barbados, had there been an opportunity; but none offering at this time, I must have contented myself with waiting until I could have procured a vessel, and consequently given over all thoughts of performing here this winter, had not some ladies and gentlemen insisted upon my opening the Theatre with the little strength I have brought from London with me, and presenting such pieces as the thinness of my company will permit me to exhibit [torn]; in order, as they very politely observed, to enable me to defray some part of the expence I have incurred: It was to no purpose that I urged, the [contemptible?] light I might stand in with many, for presuming to treat the publick with plain dishes after having giving them so sumptuous a bill of fare—I was obliged to submit, as there is nothing a Carolina audience can ask, that I dare refuse.

Therefore, considering myself once more listed under the banners of the publick, I shall proceed with the utmost dispatch to refit the Theatre, which I hope will be in proper order to receive an audience on Monday the 11th instant; when, by permission of his Honour the Lieutenant-Governor, I propose to open it, with a Play and Farce, which will be expressed in the bills for the day.

And, that I may demonstrate my inclinations to remove every cause of complaint, I shall voluntarily reduce the prices of the tickets from the accustomed rated of forty, thirty and twenty shillings (which I find there are some objections to) to thirty-five, twenty-five, and fifteen; which, I am confident, if properly considered, will be acknowledged to be as low as we can possibly perform for.

                I have the honour to be the Publick's
                      Most obedient,
                            Most devoted, and
                                    Most humble servant
                                        D. Douglass

Charleston
November 4, 1765[25]

It is a curious feature of the document (a handbill housed in the South Carolina Historical Society) that the top right-hand corner (perhaps where the stamp would be affixed) is missing. The mere existence of the document begs the question of how Douglass printed and circulated it while still remaining in good standing with the government. He also noted that he would be employing playbills to advertise his productions—"as expressed in the bills of the day." How was he ex-

Sailing on an Unwelcomed Ship

pecting to circulate playbills without stamps? Private encouragement from the highest levels may have circumvented the need for Douglass to wholly honor the act. Somebody was supporting the idea of a winter season of plays, and that support allowed Douglass to open his theatre, advertise his plays, and remain open through the winter.

Remarkably, the theatre in Charleston was exempted from the intra-national contest between Great Britain and the colonies that season. Even many of the most vocal opponents of the Stamp Act were in the side boxes during the thick of the crisis. The populist spokesman Charles Woodmason accused the "Liberty Boys" and their leader, Christopher Gadsden, of being great hypocrites, encouraging a general boycott on British goods on the one hand and "rioting in Luxury and Extravagance" on the other. Among the extravagances singled out by Woodmason: "Private Dances, cards, dice, turtle feasts, above all, A Playhouse was supported and carried on."[26]

In spite of the dire effects on business that the Stamp Act produced, the business of pleasure was well supported. Musician Peter Valton had arrived on the same *Heart of Oak* that brought the stamp agent, (and maybe the actors) and was organizing a benefit concert for November 13 to introduce himself to Charleston. Douglass used the same occasion to introduce Miss Nancy Hallam (Mrs. Douglass's niece) and Miss Sarah Wainwright, fresh from Covent Garden with the latest London songs. Douglass was reestablishing himself with the St. Cecilia Society, the amateur musical group that sponsored the concert and was well stocked with Charleston's elite. This and the subsequent concerts sponsored by the Society maintained a preserve of gentility in spite of the times. Such too would be the theatre, a quiet, genteel salon in the midst of the unrest.

On the streets of Charleston, it remained a winter of discontent: port closed, courts closed, ships and crews stranded, and a lot of merchant money sitting idle in the harbor. The operating metaphors of the Stamp Act crisis, liberty and slavery, inspired the real slaves in Carolina's midst to consider their own freedom. Fears of an uprising were real enough that the governor dispatched militias on the streets, and in the backcountry he hired Catawba Indians. Mrs. Manigault registered it: "[I]t was feared there would be some trouble with the negroes."[27]

Scanty records remain of the season, as Douglass wisely did not advertise much. The media silence was only broken late in February 1766, when the caution of his actors gave way to self-interest and they began to publicize their own benefits in the only newspaper that defied the act. Henrietta Osborne initially broke the press silence for her evening on February 27, 1766. Mrs. Douglass risked visibility for her benefit a week later. Other actors followed, presumably without repercussions. Douglass's choice of plays for the civic benefit on April 16, 1766—Addison's *Cato*—was not a thoughtless one. He needed the support of the entire city, both Lieutenant Governor William Bull and the Sons of Liberty. Both parties could feast on the patriotism the play offered.[28]

It must have been a disappointing time for a manager with new talent and new scenes and such plans. He rounded out his half company with some local talent, but all told it was a slight company of singers and utility actors: himself and Mrs. Douglass, William Verling (local), Henrietta Osborne, Stephen Woolls, Thomas Wall, Miss Wainwright, Mr. Emmet (local), and Nancy Hallam. The remainder of his old company likely were sorely missed during that Charleston winter season, most notably his leads, Lewis Hallam and Margaret Cheer, but also Owen and Mary Morris, Mr. and Mrs. Allyn, and John and Catherine Harman, as well as the minor actors, Mr. Quelch, Adam Hallam, Miss Crane, and Mr. Barry. This corps remained in Barbados well into the next spring. The company Douglass pieced together played the winter and into the spring of 1766, but one senses that the season did not live up to even its apologetic promise. Occasionally a notice appears (e.g., March 4, 1766) praising the performances, but there's a strong scent of puffery as the company geared up for the benefit season.

Then an unusual cold snap in January brought snow and ice to this southern seaport and destroyed the citrus orchards. Meanwhile, the port remained closed to outgoing vessels, and the owners and merchants clamored for a resolution of the standoff. Charleston resident and botanist Dr. Alexander Garden wrote of the city's plight in late December 1765: "The courts of justice are shut up, navigation and commerce stopt, the produce unvendable, and credit going to decay, and all correspondence with Britain at an end!"[29] At its peak, upwards of fourteen hundred stranded vessels stopped up the harbor, all with idle crews unwelcomed and unpaid until their cargos could be unloaded and reloaded; and this population presented a greater threat

Sailing on an Unwelcomed Ship

than the Sons of Liberty.[30] Robert Weir writes of this problem: "By January widespread violence seemed inevitable unless the impatient sailors left town. Bull and the Sons of Liberty appear to have thereupon reached a tacit compromise, for a number of the largest vessels in the harbor from British home ports quietly cleared and sailed, in all probability using stamped paper acquired in Georgia (where it was available)."[31] Pressure mounted from merchants and lawyers to resume business, and recognizing that any vigorous attempt to enforce the act would only result in great violence, in February Governor Bull began issuing special certificates, stating that no stamped paper was available. By March the port, if not normalized, at least was able to clear the backlog of vessels, as customs officials began to regularly issue clearances on unstamped paper.

In such bleak and troubled times, the theatre—howsoever poor—may have been the one bright spot. To break the monotony of the unseasonable cold weather, closed ports, and no goods, Mrs. Ann Manigault traveled frequently to Charleston to buy what she could: a seat at the playhouse. Here are her entries for the month of January 1766: "Jan. 4. Cloudy cold day. Snowed very hard at night. 5. Exceedingly cold. Sometimes snow, wind, and drizzly. 6 Very cold and clear. 12 Mr. Milligan's son died of a sore throat. 17 Went to the play—the Distressed Mother. 30. My daughter brought to bed of a son at 3/4 past 11 at night. He was called Peter. 31. I went to the play—Douglass."[32] A trip to the playhouse was an island of pleasure in a cold life where a child could die of a sore throat.

The Stamp Act and the agitation that surrounded it has frequently been referred to as the "prologue to the Revolution." This is not so much an after-the-fact construction by historians as a recognition by the astute at the time.[33] Garden broke off communication with his British collectors, writing to one: "This fatal Stamp Act is likely to put an end to our intercourse. You have imposed a taxation in America, which the Americans say they will not receive. Every colony upon the continent has risen in opposition to King, Lords, and Commons on this occasion. . . . The die is thrown for the sovereignty of America!"[34]

The hated Stamp Act was rescinded in March of 1766, but the news did not reach the colonies until mid-April. When the repeal was formally announced, it was popularly celebrated in Charleston—with Governor Bull hosting an elegant entertainment at Dillon's Tavern.

Douglass's contribution was the last advertised play of that season, *Cato*, offered as a benefit for the poor on April 16. One wonders how Cato's indictment of tyrants went over after this winter of discontent.

Financially the season had been a bust. Still, Douglass had escaped a dangerous time without damages (except for the theatre in New York), and he could not have chosen a better city in which to weather the storm than Charleston. Though opposition was vocal and sometimes violent, Charleston was not the tinderbox to spark the revolution that New York might have been or Boston was to be. Some thanks were in order. On the day before the civic benefit, April 15, 1766, Douglass published a note of thanks to Charleston's audiences: "Mr. Douglass returns the public his most sincere thanks for the many favours he received this winter as an actor; he assures them, he will ever retain a most grateful sense of the obligations he has to this province, which have so amply rewarded his imperfect, though well-meant, attempts to contribute to their entertainment."[35]

The Stamp Act crisis had produced some very valuable lessons. These disparate colonies could be united forcefully in a single cause. Many counted the reconciliation proposed by its retraction a firm victory. Nevertheless, independence (what Dr. Garden called "American Sovereignty") had been made thinkable, and once imagined it could not be unimagined. That tool of popular dissent was hanging in the shed—not in hand, but the shed was not far away, and the idea could and would be pulled out again.

Germane to Douglass's business, from here on whatever he played onstage, whatever history, whatever myth of monarch and subject—Roman, Shakespearean, tragic, or comic—would be read with American sovereignty in mind. Innocent texts would become politicized, comedies of manners would lose their manners, historical texts would lose their history, everything would be available to a new and topical application. The possibility of independence turned theatre into a weapon.

CODA: HARD WORDS AT DOCKSIDE

By May 6 Douglass had posted his departure notice in the *South Carolina Gazette*, soliciting those with outstanding debts to discharge their accounts, as he was "intending to depart this province very soon."

"Very soon" dragged on as he waited for his Barbados corps, and we find him still in the city at the end of the month, when on May 30 he advertised for a "man's blue cloak . . . found some time ago at the Theatre."

The wayward island company, meanwhile, had their season concluded for them when, on the night of May 13, 1766, the theatre in Barbados, along with hundreds of other buildings, burned down. The fire started somewhere on High Street, Bridgetown, at 11:00 at night. Pushed by strong winds and unhindered by the fire brigade's inadequate water supply, by 9 o'clock the next morning most of the city had been consumed.[36] What the fire spared the fire brigade destroyed, blowing up buildings in an attempt to contain the damage. Twenty-six acres at the center of the town were destroyed, from High Street to the waterfront, including 1,140 buildings, all of the public offices, and 400 private houses.[37] For the actors, it must have been an anxious night, with all hands on deck rolling scenery and packing costumes ahead of the fire and the house leveling. Six months later Thomas Underwood, a lieutenant with the marines stationed there, wrote: "I never saw so ruinous a place as Bridgetown."[38] Nicholas Cresswell, who traveled to Barbados in 1774, noted that most of the city had yet to be rebuilt.[39]

Lewis Hallam and the actors sailed back to Charleston—a sympathetic city that had donated £785 to the survivors of the Barbados fire.[40] Douglass may have contributed to the fund—it would have been expected—but he, perhaps, was less charitable to his son-in-law. In the body politic of the American Company, the "colonies" tottered on the verge of open revolt. In Lewis Hallam's defense, one might kindly ascribe the long delay in rejoining Douglass to the effective closure of the port of Charleston to transport. Still, with Hallam eight months late to their rendezvous, one readily imagines that Douglass and the young man exchanged more than a few words at dockside.

[CHAPTER 9]
The Politics of Frugality
1767–1769
• • •

Our purses are ready, steady, friends, steady
Not as slaves, but as freemen our money we'll give.
JOHN DICKINSON

Q: What used to be the pride of the Americans?
A: To indulge in the fashions and manufactures of Great Britain.
Q: What is now their pride?
A: To wear old clothes over again, till they can make new ones.
The Examination of Doctor Benjamin Franklin
before an August Assembly, Relating to the Repeal
of the Stamp Act, 1766

THE RIOTER'S CREDO: NEW YORK, MAY 1766

The targets of the destruction in New York and Boston during the Stamp Act—the houses of the placemen, the carriage of the lieutenant governor who enforced the policies—were understandable targets in the assault on unpopular British policy. These men were charged with overseeing the act. But the destruction of New York's Chapel Street Theatre a full month after the repeal? The residual rage vented on the building was perhaps less the last spasm of anger toward a bad policy than the first eruption of a deeper distrust, class antagonism unloosed by the Stamp Act that marked the playhouse as luxury British goods during a campaign favoring homespun frugality. Why the theatre was singled out for the last aftershock of mob violence alerts us to the changing attitudes toward the theatre and their role in transforming British subjects into American citizens in the Revolution.

Somehow, even in the first euphoria of the repeal, the Sons of Liberty and the population they represented continued to see the theatre as a preserve of the wealthy. It is worth exploring how the theatre came to earn its association with luxury that was now targeted by populist antagonism. Douglass spent 1766–1768 in Philadelphia and New York, and both cities during this relatively peaceable time were the sites of fierce hostility to the theatre—more so than any other time in his long tenure in British America. In the same years, Douglass also attempted to secure permission to play in Boston, only to be met with the passage of new anti-theatrical legislation spearheaded by no less a figure than John Hancock. Why this violent response at this otherwise rather euphoric time?

Traditionally, historians have attributed this anti-theatrical campaign to an ongoing moral backlash against the largely Restoration reputation of the stage. This argument dates back to the first plays performed in North America. But it's curious that the moment of loudest objection erupted not upon the introduction of professional theatre in the 1750s, or even during the months of the Stamp Act when Douglass played in Charleston, but rather during the years of the Townshend Acts (1767–1770), and the objections against the theatre were one part morality to three parts economy. Under this outbreak of populist hostility may have resided a deeper distrust, not of the innocent diversions of those who could afford them, but rather the surrogation of a leveling spirit. The new theatre offered the most visible target in a campaign to promote the critique of genteel consumption from a social indulgence to a political position, until the very Londonness that the theatre offered was branded as another Crown institution that imposed British goods upon American colonists. To a certain population, the theatre may have come to stand for something that was the very antithesis of the living lean they called "oeconomy" at a time when frugality was the platform of resistance to British policy.

The repeal of the Stamp Act was followed by a series of smaller duties (collectively known as the Townshend Acts) imposed on the colonies. At their core the new acts asserted the right of Parliament to tax the colonies. The new acts also replaced the antagonism against a single revenue target—stamps—with a more general boycott against British goods that took the form of non-importation agreements. When men like John Dickinson in Philadelphia, Sam Adams and his Caucus Club in Boston, Charles Woodmason in Charleston, and the Sons of Liberty everywhere began denouncing the taxes by pledging a platform of economy as protest, an evening of rational entertainment in the side boxes of a new theatre suddenly represented a gross rejection of that campaign, perhaps even tacit support for British policies in America.

One of the ways to hear the reverberation of quiet unrest that runs through the non-importation years is to attend to the campaign against the theatre. This campaign had the effect of congealing "American" identity around a leveling spirit that would prove invaluable in the years ahead. What began as moral campaign against a new theatre in Philadelphia (the Southwark Theatre, 1766) modulated into a grumble of working-class dissent, until, to a large part of the new political force (mechanics, tradesmen, the Sons of Liberty, and the readership of Dickinson's *Letters from a Farmer*, about which I will have more to say), the theatre had become another British "duty"— another subterfuge, like the duty on paper and glass—to be resisted. Douglass's performance of genteel London culture had somehow become London policy.

In the story of the American Revolution, the intermission between the repeal of the Stamp Act (March 18, 1766) and the flare-ups associated with the non-importation agreements that culminated in a contest over the tax on tea in 1773 has been characterized as a wound more skinned over than healed. The euphoria of repeal gave way to a "trough of exhaustion," as Middlekauff put it, "a detente of sorts," some mending of administrative bridges, a cooling off of open hostility, and a return to commerce, but the dissent never wholly disappeared.[1] Statues of former prime minister William Pitt and King George III were erected in New York and Charleston, but troops were also quartered. Behind the immediate "rush of good feelings" was also a permanent dislocation of identity. A new and antagonistic subject had been conceived and validated by the repeal and would never wholly be unconceived. This new "American" identity might recede in peaceful times, might return to its toasts and loyalties, but the fundamental subject status had been redesigned. The difficulty that always surprises the historian (and drives so much recent good scholarship) is how quickly Americans became American (what Gordon Wood has called the change "from subject to citizen"[2]), and as the roots of the political citizen can be traced back to the organized revolts of the Stamp Act, so too can one find traces of a simmering unrest present even in those relatively hale times after repeal.

Apart from the familiar flashpoint events that threatened to deprive British Americans of their liberties (stamps, tea, soldiers), another sort of enduring discontent simmered in colonial America, waiting for larger events to endow it with a sudden focal gravity. What was called with some chagrin a "leveling spirit" that would flatten the hierarchies from the monarchy on down and without which no democracy could be adequately conceived had been very present in America since Bacon's Rebellion in the 1670s, though it seldom erupted as an independent issue. The fundamental notion of the rebellion—the full extent of a liberty available to every (white, male, property-owning) citizen—was itself a critique of privilege. James Iredell, a North Carolina planter steeped in the genteel culture of London, satirized this leveling spirit viciously, and in doing so explained a great deal of its force. In his *Creed of a Rioter* he imagines the credo of the mob to be simply "I am a sworn enemy to all gentlemen. I believe none in that station of life can possibly possess either honor or virtue."[3]

This distrust of privilege and its trappings was available to more people than the backcountry settlers, mechanics, and small tradesmen. "At all times," wrote Alexander Graydon in Philadelphia of his revolutionary generation, "leveling principles are much to the general taste, and were of course popular with us," a notion with which observers on both sides of the contest concurred.[4] When Ambrose Serle, secretary to the British general Lord Howe, arrived in America in 1774, he was mildly shocked to discover that "Subordination and Distinction of Ranks in Society" is "much wanted [i.e., lacking] here."[5] If the leveling principle could not stand alone as a solitary platform of open class war, it was certainly an essential part of the grammar of resistance, and when the right issues appeared, this simmering body of dissent quickly folded into the larger disorders and ferociously deployed against targets of wealth and privilege. It was anger held in reserve, banked up against the next violation and then spent with drunken abandon. Tracing this enduring, subterranean stratum one hears not a loud or a focused signal, but something like the reverberations of a low, irritating hum.

For example, the extraordinary reception enjoyed by John Dickinson's *Letters from a Farmer in Pennsylvania* (1767), published in a Philadelphia newspaper, reprinted across the colonies, then republished as a pamphlet, exposes a hungry market for this unadorned distrust of class privilege.[6] Dickinson's posture as a farmer (albeit an educated gentleman farmer) appealed to the humble of station, while his submissive tones belied his radical intentions: though Parliament had the right to regulate trade in British America, he argued, it had no right to raise revenue with new taxes on American commerce while denying the colonies the right to their own manufacturing. The Townshend Acts did just this, and Dickinson proposed that the peaceable weapons of frugality, economy, and home manufacturing—all available to the most common of readers—were not only the quickest remedy but themselves politically potent. "Let us take another step," he wrote, assuming petitioned redress would fail. "Let us invent, let us work, let us save." "Her [Great Britain's] unkindness will instruct us and compel us, after some time, to discover in our industry and frugality surprising remedies."[7]

Under this claim, working and saving, industry and frugality, became political positions, "American" positions, available to a large intra-colonial constituency of working, saving, industrious folk. Their opposite—leisure, luxury, genteel consumption, and frivolous spending—available to the privileged (idle) few—sustained British injustice. Dickinson, who had rewritten the "Hearts of Oak" lyrics to weaponize commerce ("Our purses are ready, steady, friends, steady"), voiced this new critique of genteel consumption, and it found a large pool of dissenters already present, people to whom this new ideology of "oeconomy" spoke with the greatest urgency. William Franklin wrote to his father that Dickinson's ideas sat "very well with great numbers of the common people."[8]

What broadened the appeal of Dickinson's (Quaker) reasoning was that it did not demand unlawful assembly or violent, extra-legal action that had been the signature of the Sons of Liberty during the Stamp Act protests; it required only frugality. Nothing more was needed but to gird one's purse against the unnecessary British goods one couldn't afford anyway. Almost twenty years earlier Josiah Tucker had astutely predicted that the colonies would revolt as soon as they were self-sufficient.[9] "Save your money and you will save your country," was the motto deployed up and down the colonies.[10] Almost immediately one begins to see the language of frugality translated into acts of economic defiance against all manner of spending, eschewing all manner of pleasures. And what target could be more visible than itinerant London-trained actors and new theatres?

Enter David Douglass, like the hickory-seller with a cartload of unnecessary wares, eighteen idle actors, and a plan to build new theatres in Philadelphia and New York. And if that took, Boston would be next. For three years, 1766–1769, the company moved between Philadelphia and New York, finding market enough for their wares, but finding also a persistent platform of dissent.

DOUGLASS'S REBUTTAL

It may have started with morality, but it was never about morality. Before Douglass had even opened his new theatre in Philadelphia, a synod of Quakers penned a petition to Governor John Penn expressing their trepidation. Their "Remonstrations against Erecting a Theatre" expressed the danger of plays "to subvert the Good order, morals, & Prosperity" of the community. To be fair, the Quaker campaign against the theatre had been going on long before the first actor arrived in Philadelphia. When Douglass experienced the pattern in 1759, the governor would allow it, the Assembly of Pennsylvania would prohibit it, and Parliament would repeal the assembly's prohibition.[11] In spite of the Quaker legislature, acting companies had nonetheless found a market in Philadelphia.

In this latest installment in 1766, the petition was only the beginning. The assault against the new Southwark Theatre widened once the theatre opened in the fall with a flurry of anti-theatrical editorials peppering the papers. One "Censor," praising God for dispelling the last troubles (over the Stamp Act), pointedly asks his readership: "Would you have supported these people [the actors] had the detested Stamp Act been unrepealed?"[12] That association would be difficult to unstick. "The Absolute Unlawfulness of Stage Entertainments, fully demonstrated" was fully demonstrated in successive issues of both the *Pennsylvania Chronicle* and the *Gazette*.[13]

Opponents of the theatre vigorously carried on their campaign throughout the winter, and it was vexing enough to prompt an exasperated manager's public rebuttal. In March of 1767, Douglass wrote:

> To the Printers of the *Pennsylvania Gazette*:
> I have with all the composure imaginable, overlooked the torrent of incomprehensible abuse which has been, of late, so plen-

tifully bestowed on the Theatre, those who countenance it, and the performers; nor do I now intend to enter into a controversy with the gentlemen who have attacked me in so indecent, so illiberal a manner: People of understanding, who are unprejudiced, will judge for themselves; nor will it be in my power, or that of my doughty adversaries, to bias them: But as I have reason to think that the greater number, by far, of those who are enemies to the Theatre, are unacquainted with the nature and tendency of Dramatic Entertainments, I am of the opinion that the following essay, written at New York about five years ago, but not published, as the opposition to which it refers subsided, will not, at this time, be an improper address to them, as it presents an impartial view of the good effects a well regulated Theatre must undoubtedly have on the manners of a people.[14]

There followed Douglass's essay on the utility of theatre, composed for the edification of his detractors. Its 244 lines in 10 paragraphs dominated the pages of the *Pennsylvania Gazette* and the *Pennsylvania Chronicle* from February 23 to March 2, 1767, and the *Pennsylvania Journal* on February 19, 1767. The work displayed a certain erudition—from the Horatian head quote to the verses from Addison and Pope, and it summarized a century's arguments: theatre, if well regulated, was a moral and rational institution that improved citizens and polished character. The most respected writers recognized its merits, and those who did not like it should stay away without preventing others from enjoying it. The trouble was, Douglass was fighting the wrong fight: he was defending the morality of theatre, and his detractors were stalking a far bigger beast.

Douglass responded as his counterparts in Bath, Bristol, Dublin, or Edinburgh might have.[15] Tate Wilkinson on the York circuit complained of exactly the same opposition from the Methodists; David Ross in Scotland battled the Presbyterians. "The Playhouse in Glasgow," reported the *Gentleman's Magazine*, "has been disapproved of by the Presbytery there, and the ministers in general have been instructed to dissuade their hearers from frequenting it."[16] The preachers, the ministers, and the rectors were always railing against the theatre—George Percy did so in Charleston, and the charismatic George Whitefield preached against the players in Philadelphia.[17] Though zealous and unpleasant, these moralists were not a force sufficient to damage Douglass's business. But this new approach of conflating the theatre with luxury and luxury with British policy—this was a new and dangerous platform, one Douglass was neither prepared nor equipped to combat.

The manager's alliance with the Crown-appointed governors didn't help. Douglass was required to secure permission from the governors to open, but to the Philadelphia objectors he had become altogether too cozy with his latest patron, the new governor of Pennsylvania, John Penn. The grandson of William Penn, John Penn had lived in Philadelphia as a young man returning from a Grand Tour. His first stay, from 1752 to 1755, thoroughly depressed him; after Italy, Philadelphia was sadly provincial and morally rigid. He took up the acquaintance of an Italian musician and scandalized Philadelphia with his prodigality. He was recalled to England in 1755. Perhaps the intervening eight years matured the young spendthrift. When James Hamilton, exhausted by the Indian wars, was replaced in 1763, John Penn came back to Philadelphia, now as the colony's governor.

Artistic, born of privilege, John Penn seemed decadent to the Quakers, who called him "effeminate." Worse still, he freely associated with the actors. Thomas Wharton complained to Benjamin Franklin:

> The inhabitants of this City (I mean the Sober and Religious Part of them) have met and prepared a Memorial to the House, requesting them to offer to the Governor, A Bill for the putting a stop to the exhibition of Plays in this Province. I cannot doubt of their cheerful Concurrence; and I think it will much puzzle the G—r to know, how to conduct himself therein. Tis said that, he constantly attends them, and that, he has had the Players to dine, or sup with him. To such a State is Pennsylvania reduced, that when N. York, and the other Colonies had refused those wretches an Asylum; they found this their only Sanctuary![18]

Wharton's comment points up the dilemma Douglass faced: courting the ruling class often put him at odds with the populace. In February the governor did indeed entertain the promised remonstrance to expel the actors, and as Wharton suspected, Penn did nothing whatsoever. The press debate, however, continued. "Theatricus" and "Anti-thespis," "Censor," "Democritus," "Philolethes," and the rest of the tribe poured on the invective. Some of the arguments were as old as Tertullian: bad models corrupt absolutely. Others, more nuanced, recognized the potency of portraying doomed heroes, but found its potency far too seductive.

One solution was a series of benefits for the town. It was first suggested by the anonymous "Philoanthropos" on March 30, who wrote to William Goddard, publisher of the *Pennsylvania Chronicle*:

> Mr. Goddard. I could not help observing an odd contrast in the Postscript to your paper of February 23—On the one side, we were pathetically recommended to a view of misery in the inhabitants of the jail, and on the other, had a tempting invitation to the Play-house. It immediately occur'd to me that a visit to the latter might be of admirable advantage to the former, if only one performance were exhibited expressly for the benefit of the prisoners.[19]

The same issue recounted a morality tale about a prodigal stroller from a London newspaper. This Barnwellesque figure offers his miserable experience as a warning to "prevent the destruction of any other young fellow, and serve to remove that unhappy propensity to a theatrical life." Another parable featured the memoirs of an octogenarian who, as a youth, fell victim to the enticements of the stage but was soon convinced of their dangers, and described the utter financial and moral poverty of the strolling life.[20] *The Absolute Unlawfullness of the Stage* continued in weekly installments like a bad Dickensian serial through the spring and summer of 1767.

Still, there was support enough for the American Company to play into July and reprise a season in Philadelphia for two months of the fall. When it finally sputtered to a close in November 1767, Margaret Shippen (a Philadelphia resident who would later marry Benedict Arnold) wished a hearty good riddance to the company: "The players must soon leave off here and will not be again permitted to act these two years. They are going to New York but it is believed that the Opposition will be strong enough to prevent their acting there."[21] Indeed, New Yorkers talked of such a bill, but as "Dramaticus" noted in the *Gazette* "some of the first rank and figure among us refused to countenance a measure, which two or three busy people had concerted to discourage it. Their example, I think, should silence popular clamour."[22] But the "clamour" would not go away; it proved instead to be the low hum of a class antagonism that would set the populace against the "first rank" and use the theatre against the elite.

THE TRADESMAN'S STRUGGLES

The season of 1767–1768 was another year of battles for Douglass, this time in New York. But without the Quaker opposition, there was no moral stratum to the argument; it focused solely on extravagance at a time of economy. Asked one "Tradesman": "Are our circumstances altered? Is money grown more plenty? Have our tradesmen full employment? Are we more frugal? Is grain cheaper? Are our importations less? Not to mention the play-house and equipages, which it is hoped none but people of fortune frequent or use. . . . Surely it is high time for the middling people to abstain from every superfluity in dress, furniture, and living."[23] In the new spirit of industry and frugality, sewing parties became fashionable and women stitched up homespun in public displays of political anti-fashion.

Douglass had arrived in the summer with a one-man show, Stevens's *Lecture on Heads*, but his real intention was to raise a subscription and build a new theatre, the John Street Theatre, and that project met with success. It opened on December 7 of 1767, and by coincidence, the newspapers that printed the first notice of opening night also carried the first installment of Dickinson's *Letters from a Farmer*. On one page the argument to spend, on the other to be American and economize. Throughout December *Letters from a Farmer* occupied half of the news, rounded out by editorials of "A Tradesman" and "Philander," who argued insistently, "Save your money, and you will save your Country!" "Our enemies know that . . . to impoverish us is the surest way to enslave us. Therefore if you mean still to be free, let us unanimously lay aside foreign superfluities."[24] Next page, playbills offering the latest London plays, at seven shillings sixpence a box seat.

Even the grievances of the new theatre seemed luxurious—the great congestion of carriages ("to prevent Accidents by Carriages meeting, it is requested that those coming to the House may enter John Street from the Broadway")—must have seemed perfectly frivolous.[25] The desire Douglass sold—to be seen, to acquire—was pricey, and objecting to those who paid that price was pointedly partisan during a campaign of economy. Douglass might answer, "[I]f you can't afford it, don't go," but many who could not afford it went anyway and blamed the shopkeeper for dangling the wares. One anonymous editorial in the *New York Mirror* complained of the demands on his humble household this infatuation with the theatre had caused. "A Tradesman" regretted that his wife and daughter had caught the theatre affliction:

> One of my neighbors, you must know, has a daughter of about the age of mine, who has been gallanted several times to the play; there being some intimacy between them; my daughter had often heard miss talk in raptures of the play, so that she could [not] conceal her own inclination to go. I told her that I could not afford it, and endeavoured to reason with her about the matter, but all would not satisfy her. I kept her off however sometime as well as I could, till, unhappily, her mother had got into her head as strong a notion to go to the play, as the daughter had; and thus being doubly attacked, I was obliged to give up. When the girl had gained this conquest over me, you can't imagine how overjoyed she was, and till play night came, her head was full of nothing else.
>
> It is natural to suppose, that I would not let my wife and daughter go alone to the play, and therefore I was obliged to accompany them. I proposed to go into the gallery, where I thought we might see enough of the play, and save a good deal of our money. But believe me, my wife and daughter both turned up their noses at it, and said, no, not they; they would not go among a set of ragamuffins, and if I could not afford to accommodate them with a better place, they rather chose not to go at all. . . . I next proposed that we should sit in the pitt [*sic*] but here pride raised another objection: They told me that no reputable woman, or of any kind of fashion sat in the pitt, and that surely I could not desire them to go among such cattle as were generally to be found there. The result of all was, that they must go into the boxes; and in short they prevailed on me to go with them; and you may judge too, that we were obliged to spruce up a little extraordinary to mix with such genteel company. I wish I had time

to tell you what pains were taken for this purpose. This night, by the bye, was a loss to me of 24s dead, besides about two shillings expended in oranges and sugar plums.

The "24s dead" was pure loss—the trader acquired nothing for the experience but lost revenue. Furthermore, the daughter returned from the playhouse with such a passion for plays that she gave over all her work time to idle reading, then assumed the parts of characters, practicing before the mirror and badgering her poor father to return to the theatre. He concluded: "I really think in my conscience, that the rich people who encourage and support the Play House will have much to answer for: Nor do I think that industry and oeconomy will ever thrive among us, as long as this cursed engine of pleasure, idleness, and extravagance remains."[26]

This populist narrative played out repeatedly in the winter of 1767–1768. The *New York Post Boy* termed the new theatre a "tax" on the people; the *New York Journal* concurred, asking, "What an enormous tax do we burthen ourselves with? It is computed at least £300 a week," and lamented the money that went toward "foreign finery."[27] The conclusion, like that of the "Tradesman," was concise: "Luxury and extravagance is the bane of the age."[28]

As if to compound the problems, the theatre was wrapped in the Crown's authority. "Vivat Rex and Regina," began the playbills; the play existed "by permission of his excellency the Governor," or "by command of Lady Moore"—the governor's wife. Competing command performances by Governor Moore and General Gage during their squabbles over precedence (not between themselves but "with respect to their Ladies who cannot agree which shall stand first couple in a country Dance"—a dispute so serious that the husband threatened a duel) only added to the public's sense that this "rational entertainment" was becoming a frivolous sport of "foreign finery."

The invocation of the tainted labels "tax," "duty," and "foreign" was forcibly shifting the theatre's reputation upwards and eastward (i.e., aristocratic and English). The unspoken argument was that theatre was not a populist institution in British America; and as the hyphen in that "British-American" identity was strained and eventually broken, theatre and its culture of refinement remained firmly on the British side. Populist voices, such as those of the New York tradesman, Dickinson, and Woodmason, might denounce the hypocrisy of the radical elite, enjoying their plays when frugality was a political platform, but theatres, in spite of their gallery seating, were never designed for the hoi polloi. "Democritus" might weigh in on the matter, but he, like the "Tradesman," was thoroughly priced out of the theatre.

Consider it economically: Colonel Washington paid his white laborer, Jonathan Palmer, five shillings a day to harvest the wheat— ten hours or more outside in the sun. That entire day's wage was the price of the cheapest seat in the nearest theatre: a gallery bench in Annapolis.[29] Douglass might claim that plays like *The London Merchant* would improve the apprentice's morals, but not if apprentices had to steal something to attend. The expense alone prompted one editorial to conclude: "I do not know any commodity that can be better spared in these his Majesty's colonies [than actors]."[30] In the follow-up issue to the same conversation, players were damned in harsher, medieval terms: "Vagrants and Vagabonds should be set to hard labour, and proper punishments devised for those, who harbour and encourage these pests to society." The proper place for the player was "picking oakum in the workhouse."[31]

It is not incidental that this editorial was published alongside Dickinson's *Letters from a Farmer in Pennsylvania*. The criticism of actors even shared a few phrases with Dickinson's criticism of British officials: actors, said the editorial, were "idle drones," the same phrase being currently applied to placemen, as in James Wilson's denunciation of them as "a set of idle drones" and "lazy, proud, worthless pensioners."[32] When the "Tradesman" concluded that "a society in which there is little money, must supply their wants by industry and oeconomy," he had articulated Dickinson's appeal exactly: hard work and economy were the colonist's best response to London. Dickinson's line of reasoning, that opposition to small taxes was required to forestall setting a precedent, equally applied to the playhouse: "In abstaining from them [plays], you will serve your country while you are saving yourself. Remember, that unless an effectual discouragement be given to the Play-house now, it is likely to be intailed upon us."[33] "What an enormous tax we burthen ourselves with? . . . You who love your country, think what ruin this brings on us!"[34]

Nor, honestly, was the theatre in the service of "Democritus." It courted the elite. Whenever possible, theater managers converted gallery and pit seating to the more expensive boxes, or shut the cheaper seats entirely. Fine folk at high prices watching London manners and comedies of manners: that was the theatre's truck in trade. But in New York after the Stamp Act, "Democritus" was legion in New York, and he named the theatre as elitist and foreign. "As to playhouses," wrote another, "cock-fighting, fox-hunting, horse-racing . . . they are all of British extract, and brought in practice by British gentlemen, and others, especially theatrical performances, of which there have been none in this city these two or three years, and when attempted about a year and a half ago, the house was pulled down."[35] Keeping theatres upright in such leveling times required the full apparatus of colonial authority against a growing insurgent America with little use for British luxury goods.

And that was the easy part. The theatre acquired two further associations in the Townshend years that further troubled its status in America: with the military and with Parliament, the two most hated institutions in British America.

MAJOR MONCREIF'S *OTHELLO*

The campaign against the extravagance of theatre was taking its toll. With few new markets Douglass overstayed his welcome in both New York and Philadelphia. In New York Douglass reduced performances from three per week to two and reduced his advertisements to a lean play title. His actors were suffering "embarrassments"—couldn't pay their landlords is usually what the phrase meant. Douglass leaned on his prominent patrons—the Freemasons (March 27), the "Grand Knot of the Friendly Brothers of St. Patrick" (March 17, April 3)—for bespoke performances, before doing something he had not before, that is, accept the assistance of amateurs: gentlemen from His Majesty's Sixteenth Regiment, currently quartered in New York. The American Company shared the stage with the soldiers for a production of *Othello*: "The part of Othello to be attempted by a Gentleman, assisted by other Gentlemen, in the characters of the Duke and Senate of Venice. From a benevolent and generous design of encouraging the theatre and relieving the performers from some embarrassments in which they are involved."[36]

For the occasion, Douglass charged box prices for the benches in the pit and was obliged to justify himself: "[T]he reasons why the pit is made box price this evening are first, in compliment to the gentlemen who are to perform; next, on account of a new set of scenes, which were painted at great expense for the occasion; and because the demand for boxes has been so great that the director of the theatre could not otherwise accommodate one half of the ladies and gentlemen who have applied for places."[37] Joseph Ireland deduced that the gentleman in the lead role was Major James Moncrief. Some years later, when the British occupied New York and the officers opened the same John Street Theatre, Major Moncrief reprised the role.[38] The other gentlemen were likely other members of the same regiment, and the crowded audience that night comprised none other than the military.

Moncrief carried no ordinary reputation. He was a Scotsman by birth, which made have eased his acquaintance with Douglass. His father had fought in the '45, but he himself had been schooled in London and joined the British military, serving in America for nearly two decades. During the Revolution, General Clinton singled him out for praise for his work in the siege of Charleston, but by then his loathing for Americans was fabled. "Pre-eminent in malignity stood the engineer Moncrieff," wrote Dr. Alexander Garden.[39] The persistence and violence with which he pursued the British cause during the war would lead Major Moncrief to assemble a company of slaves in Carolina to fight against the rebels in exchange for their manumission. Even after the surrender of Cornwallis, the major volunteered to continue the war with his black company. And lest we assume any kindly attitude toward African Americans because of his playing a blackface role and his raising the black regiment, Moncrief was also a major slaveholder in Florida and the West Indies, and he reneged on his promise to his regiment, selling as many as eight hundred of these men back into slavery on Spanish plantations in the Caribbean or holding them in service on his own estate.[40] Such he would be in the war. For now, for one night in April 1769, officers joined the American Company, Major Moncrief blacked up and played Othello for a crowd of soldiers paying full price, Douglass filled his coffers, and the actors discharged their "embarrassments." That the military bailed out the theatre might have been weighed in the balance sheets of many "tradesmen."

JOHN HANCOCK'S SIGNATURE

If New York was hostile, Boston with its religious roots was downright impenetrable. Douglass never did build a theatre in Boston, the only principal colonial city that did not have a professional theatre, and why he couldn't is the story. There was certainly market enough: Bostonians were riding by stage as far away as Providence, Rhode Island, and Portsmouth, New Hampshire, to see plays. Certainly there were elites who desired their London culture. And the troops who had arrived in late 1768 at the request of Governor Francis Bernard would make a good market.

Even in Boston itself, where a harsh 1750 prohibition was in effect, there were amateur companies playing. In spite of a harsh 1750 prohibition, complaints of amateurs gathering for theatricals persisted, most recently in the spring of 1767.[41] An editorial of March 30 reveals a substantial practice and suggests "had the present actors an opportunity seeing a play well exhibited, I am confident some of them might make as considerable a figure as any of those credible gentlemen." The next issue extended an overt invitation to Douglass: "The acting of plays and tragedies in this town is now practiced with impunity.... PS. It is apprehended that when the American Company of Comedians, who are now at New York or Philadelphia, hear there is so great an inclination for such entertainments in this place, they will endeavor to introduce themselves."[42] Alden Bradford relates that there were "repeated attempts" made throughout the spring to revoke the colony's anti-theatrical legislation, but they were quiet—we read nothing of them in the newspapers. To counter them, a bill was introduced into the assembly, on June 6, 1767, and a committee of five legislators, including John Hancock, pushed through a bill restating the colony's prohibition of stage plays.[43]

Hancock was not only one of the wealthiest men in New England, but also the most connected. John Adams had claimed that "not less than a thousand families were, every day of the year, dependent on Mr. Hancock for their daily bread."[44] He was the city's largest shipowner, its wealthiest working merchant. He had gathered the city's merchant association when news first arrived of the Townshend Acts, and he urged a partial boycott of English imports—particularly luxury goods.

Hancock's "Hancock" was enough to keep Douglass out of Boston in

1767 and 1768—until, that is, the act was tested under circumstances bound up with everything of consequence that happened afterwards to Boston and the nation-to-be. In October 1768, in response to Governor Bernard's request, two regiments of British military and their artillery entered Boston to stay. Twelve hundred soldiers disembarked and marched into a town of fifteen thousand, "with drums beating, fifes playing and colours flying," up King Street onto Boston Common "as if taking possession of a conquered town," wrote the governor.[45] Troops camping and drilling on the Common, ships anchored with their cannon facing the city, General Gage securing peace on the streets: it must have looked like an occupation. And so in the late winter of 1769 when the soldiers began to stage plays for their own amusement, the contest between colonial law and parliamentary law was a further expression of English provocation.

It began when an objector queried, in print, why the military were staging plays "in open violation of an act of this province." In the following issue the objector was reminded: "That there is an Act of Parliament licensing theatrical performances throughout the King's dominions, which I take upon me to say (and no one can contradict) intirely supercedes [sic] the Act of this province, the assembly are restricted to making laws not contrary to the laws of England."[46] The contest was never about theatre, but rather about whether parliamentary or colonial law held primacy. Lost to many in the euphoria of the repeal was a reassertion of "the absolute, unlimited supremacy of Parliament": the Declaratory Act, bundled into the repeal as a face-saving measure. This act was, as David Ramsay related, "more hostile to American rights than the Stamp Act; for it annulled those resolutions and acts of the provincial assemblies."[47] The performance of plays was the test case in Boston. As in Philadelphia, parliamentary law trumped, and these military performances declared the authority of the local assembly null and void. The soldiers continued to stage their plays, and the theatre became the playground of the military in defiance of colonial law.

When two more regiments arrived, Bostonians considered their presence tantamount to a permanent standing army. But word of the military theatricals reached Douglass, and scenting a market, he traveled up to Boston in the summer of 1769, rented a long room in the Bunch of Grapes tavern, and began to exhibit the same one-person show he had performed in New York—George Alexander Stevens's *Lecture on Heads*—to feel out the town's inclination. The Freemasons met at the Bunch of Grapes on June 24 (forty-one of them, including Joseph Warren, John Rowe, Paul Revere, and John Hancock), and no doubt Douglass, a mason, introduced himself to that network, as he did in other cities. He certainly met John Rowe, the Grand Master of the lodge, who attended one of Douglass's performances and wrote about it.[48] Rowe was dining twice a week with John Hancock and somewhere a conversation occurred: a few discouraging words from the well-connected would nip the project in the bud. It might not have been the Masons; the Bunch of Grapes was also the meeting place of the Committee of Merchants, whose chair was also currently occupied by John Hancock. Their objections were the loss of ready money. The same tavern also hosted the Independent Corps of Cadets, a ceremonial Boston militia that was becoming far less ceremonial and far more militant; these proto-minutemen were commanded by Colonel John Hancock. In short, in would have been difficult for Douglass to avoid meeting Hancock, and it was Hancock who had initiated the legislation against the theatre in Boston.[49]

If Douglass persisted, he would have had to visit Governor Bernard (who was departing that very week for England and had appointed Thomas Hutchinson lieutenant governor). Perhaps it was privately intimated that any proposal that either Bernard or Hutchinson endorsed and the military supported was not likely to make Douglass or his actors popular in Boston in the winter of 1769–1770. If that conversation occurred, it was not recorded. So Douglass performed a few solo shows (Rowe recorded laconically "went to hear Mr. Douglass Lecture on Heads. He performed well"), but the town was tetchy. On the departure of Bernard it celebrated, but trade, goods, and spending were all watched carefully. On August 4, Rowe himself recorded that he received a very sharp lecture from the merchants "about the importation of some Porter on board Jarvis."[50]

The resistance to Great Britain in Boston was deep, from the streets and from the pulpit. What Peter Oliver called "Mr. Otis' Black Regiment"—the dissenting clergy encouraged by James Otis who preached against importation, luxury, and extravagance of any kind—squarely positioned the theatre as a British institution.[51] If an established Boston man like John Rowe suffered hard words for importing English beer, what would the town's residents make of visiting actors? Douglass thought better of the venture and bid farewell to Boston.

Shut out in Boston, where to play next was a serious problem. New York and Philadelphia were exhausted markets. Douglass had sent an actor, John Henry, back to Charleston to seek permission to play, but he was denied in that friendliest of markets. The company reassembled in Philadelphia at the close of September, and Douglass penned a desperate letter to John Penn pleading that "nothing but an Exertion of that Humanity, which you possess in so eminent a Degree, can save us from Destruction."[52] The plea resulted in a final fling in Philadelphia. It was no better than a roof in a rainstorm, and at the close of a dire season, Douglass wrote to his printer, William Bradford, begging off his debts: "You are no stranger to our very bad success this season. . . . I am oblig'd to carry the Company away directly to Williamsburg that I may not lose the June court, and am much [stretched] for money."[53] Bradford had withheld the money from the ticket sales for the last night's performance against an outstanding printing bill. Douglass promised to settle his debts and retreated to the one reliable market left: Virginia and Maryland. On June 5, a general meeting of Philadelphia's tradesmen, small merchants, and mechanics was called to continue their support of non-importation and non-consumption. Wrote Henry Drinker: "[I]t will be carried without much difficulty to continue the present plan."[54]

The company sailed down to Williamsburg in time for the June court.

[CHAPTER 10]

Associations and Binges

1770

• • •

PLAYING FOR THE HOUSE OF RADICALS:
WILLIAMSBURG, VIRGINIA, 1770

The Townshend years were difficult. They were times of great solidarity against taxation and luxury, but they were also times of great inequity, when the price of patriotism was administered on a sliding scale that favored the elite and punished the small merchant. Markets for London manners were in short supply in British America, and Douglass remained in his retreat in Virginia. Virginians had been supporting a rival company in Douglass's absence, the short-lived New American Company, and Douglass's return to the South may have been, in part, an attempt to reclaim his market share.[1]

It was already court season in Williamsburg when the actors disembarked at Capital Landing in June of 1770. "Public times" in the capital meant that the small tidewater town was crowded with backcountry planters, claimants, merchants, burgesses, and pleasure-seekers, who converged for its brief semiannual flurry of business, litigation, and nightly convivial gatherings. The spring court was particularly litigious this year. Apart from the usual stack of suits for debt recovery and tenant and title disputes that were contested in the taverns, argued in the courts, and settled in the coffeehouse, there was the additional pressure of small merchants suffering from the first year of the non-importation agreement that Virginia and other colonies had subscribed to. As in the North, the more vocal patriots had formed a Virginia Association agreeing to boycott the trade in many staple and luxury goods to protest British policy. George Washington and his Fairfax County neighbor George Mason drafted Virginia's first agreement, which the burgesses (colonial legislators) and merchants had endorsed at last year's spring court.

Now, twelve months later, its effects were being felt at home as well as abroad. Wrote one merchant, "The shopkeeper or dry goods merchant must suffer greatly, especially if their stock in trade is small and they follow that business for a mere support. If their conduct is the result of choice it is patriotism indeed, but I apprehend it is otherwise: that they are obliged to comply with the popular clamour through the influences of some considerable men who are chiefly concerned in other branches of trade, which the Association does not hurt."[2] The boycott deferred much business and that meant debt and debt recovery; for lawyers business was brisk. One of them, Thomas Mason, advertised that he would accept no new cases "unless my fee is first paid down, or a bond given for it" and then threatened to sue all his clients in arrears.[3]

The court season coincided with the meeting of the Virginia Assembly, which brought to town the burgesses, including Colonel Washington, Robert Fairfax, Patrick Henry, Robert Munford, and a freshman burgess, Thomas Jefferson. Tobacco-broker James Robinson, like other merchants, came to the Williamsburg court to fix tobacco prices for the year and settle up business with his tidewater managers.[4] Colonel Washington advertised a meeting with former colonial military officers to settle old disputes about promised land grants.[5] Virginians could also socialize, woo, and marry at a June court.[6]

And then there was the theatre. The actors aired the playhouse in Williamsburg and were open for business on Saturday night, June 16, with John Gay's *The Beggar's Opera*, a delightfully scathing satire of former Prime Minister Walpole's administration.[7] Douglass and his company played six nights a week while court was in session, sometimes afternoons as well, and counted among their clientele some of the most influential figures in Virginia. Jefferson made a point to attend on opening night and every other night that week except one. Washington's diary entry for that day: "Dined at the Club and went to the Play, after meeting the Associates at the Capitol."[8] He too would be in the playhouse most nights that opening week, in the company of Peyton Randolph, the speaker of the house, or William Nelson, the acting governor; indeed, he and Jefferson between them purchased some twenty box tickets.

That represented an ordinary theatre bender for Jefferson and Washington. Jefferson routinely spent five nights out of six in the theatre while court was in session. Washington followed the same company of actors to four different cities that year alone, attending the theatres of Williamsburg, Fredericksburg, Annapolis, and Alexandria. But this court session was extraordinary because of the urgency of the business that brought the burgesses and merchants to town.

On the 5th of March 1770, provoked British troops had fired on a mob in Boston. It was the first exchange of open hostilities, but skirmishes had occurred all spring. Fistfights between Bostonians and British soldiers erupted into larger brawls. Soldiers fired on and killed a boy in late February; then in March a terrible melee erupted on the streets, with eleven men shot, five of them dead. The mob swelled and Governor Hutchinson, to appease them, jailed the soldiers who had fired on the crowd. John Adams and Josiah Quincy, Jr., undertook the unenviable task of their defense and subsequently won. But something irrevocable had happened; for many who stared across the bloody snow, the British regulars seemed an occupying army.

Nor were hostilities confined to Boston. Six weeks earlier, in mid-January of 1770, a street battle broke out between the Sons of Liberty in New York and the off-duty British soldiers who had chopped up their "liberty pole" for firewood. A sizeable body (perhaps three thousand) erected a new pole, and when the troops intervened, the skirmish left many wounded and one dead.[9]

News of the March "tragedy" in Boston traveled quickly; by April ad hoc committees were in heated conversation about their response to this latest expression of tyranny, and the once-imagined notion of a sovereign America emerged again. Many colonies adopted the most prudent course, a complete boycott of British goods. This non-importation agreement, originally broadly endorsed in 1769, flushed with new support, and by midsummer most of the colonies had some version of it in place, agreeing to boycott British manufactured goods until the repeal of the Townshend Acts.[10]

An advertisement appeared the *Virginia Gazette* for May 31, 1770, inviting "all Gentlemen Merchants, Traders, and others to meet the associators in Williamsburg on Friday the 15th instant in order to consult and advise, touching an Association." For a week the committee hammered out which goods were to be boycotted and which were exempted. Burgess, planter, and merchant all had their say, but at the core was the second article, which supported the principle of American industry and frugality and discouraged all manner of luxury and extravagance. The document was to advance to the House of Burgesses for approval, but the idea itself was radical enough for the new governor, Baron de Botetourt, to angrily dissolve the House before they could complete the contract. They reconvened privately and bound themselves to an association document signed by 164 of the most prominent men of the colony, many of whom then adjourned to the theatre to watch a week of British plays, written by London playwrights, in a British provincial playhouse, and performed by a company of actors London-trained to a person. Somehow the theatre, at what Washington himself wrote was "this alarming and critical juncture," was exempt from being either an extravagant luxury or "British goods."[11]

A night in a side box was certainly not taxable British goods, like tea, but it is still difficult to argue against its being a luxury good. In all the many preambles to all the many non-importation agreements, non-consumption and frugality were central to resisting British policy across the colonies. Nowhere in the many agreements were clauses of exemption for balls, theatre, or the racing season, yet they all thrived in Virginia and Maryland, and the theatre in particular found its greatest support among the very architects of pledges to "discourage all manner of luxury and extravagance." It might merely be hypocrisy, but it does reveal an elite bias. Merchants such as Henry Drinker in Philadelphia could note of the boycott: "Romans we are not as they were formerly, when they despised riches and grandeur, abode in extreme poverty and sacrificed every pleasant enjoyment for the love and service of their country."[12]

No one could question the patriotism of these Virginians. Their theatre-going was not giving over policy to pursue self-interest. Something different was at work in the South. Unlike New York, the members of this dense social Virginia arena, like their Maryland counterparts, were adept at parsing out luxury from bad policy, eliding the refined and the radical in ways the sharper divisions of class in the North did not permit. Consequently, it is worth considering what exactly was happening inside the Williamsburg theatre and how this experience was shaping those in the pit and boxes in inexorable ways. The explanation is not as facile as planter class hypocrisy—though there may have been a good bit of that—nor so pat as the manufacturing of Americans. Some deeper unsettling and refashioning was under way, in which the theatre operated as a conceptual space of a shared British culture in which the protocols of polite society shaped

Associations and Binges [135

the political conversation.¹³ What allowed these Virginia patriots to enjoy their theatre as excessively as they did was exactly their conception that such genteel settings would be essential to settling differences, even differences of enormous magnitude. The clubs, the races, and the theatre constituted the most visible zone of British culture and the last to be severed, and while it survived, so survived the possibility of a British America.

BINGEING

Some years later, after the bloody business of the Revolution had been settled, when the actor John Bernard, quite by accident, met the now-retired General Washington on the coach road a mile or so from Mount Vernon to assist in righting an overturned carriage, the two strangers recognized each other immediately: Washington from Bernard's performances at the Philadelphia theatre the previous winter, and Bernard from, well, everywhere. The conversation that followed inevitably turned to their shared tidewater acquaintances — theatre patrons like Charles Carroll and Mr. Jefferson. "There's my friend, Mr. Jefferson, has time and taste; he goes always to the play."¹⁴

And indeed Jefferson always did. Ever since his student days in Williamsburg, the prodigiously curious man followed the actors whenever he could. At nineteen, at home from his studies at William and Mary, lovesick and with an eye infection that kept him from reading law, Jefferson dreamed about a European tour he would take with his friend John Page. But this was provincial Virginia and a trip to the theatre would be as close to the Grand Tour as he would get for many years. He wrote Page on January 20, 1763, of his travel dreams, but contented himself with the local substitute: "I have some thoughts of going to Petersburg if the actors go there in May."¹⁵ He and Page knew of "the actors" from Williamsburg during previous winters, and the young Jefferson saw them there frequently over the years. Here is a page from his daily account book for his trip to the capital in June 1770:

16 June 1770   pd. for play ticket 5/
18 June 1770   pd. for d[itt]o 22/6
18 June 1770   pd. for play ticket 5/
19 June 1770   pd. for play ticket 5/

20 June 1770   pd. for play d[itt]o 5/
21 June 1770   pd. for d[itt]o 27/6
22 June 1770   pd. on signing asso[ciation] 10/
23 June 1770   pd for play tickets 20/
25 June 1770   pd for play tickets 20/
27 June 1770   pd for play tickets 22/6
28 June 1770   pd for play tickets 5/1½[16]

Jefferson, a practicing lawyer and a newly elected burgess, arrived in Williamsburg for the meeting of the General Assembly and the court session in mid-June. After attending the theatre's opening night, Jefferson hardly left it thereafter, attending eleven nights out of thirteen (setting aside Sundays, when the theatre was closed). On one occasion (June 18) he went to both afternoon and evening performances. In two weeks at the theatre Jefferson spent nearly £8. He also, notably, frequently purchased the tickets for his companions, three or four at a time (20 shillings = four seats in the pit; 22/6 = three in the boxes), twenty-four tickets in thirteen days. This is a lot of time in the theatre for a man who had just signed a pledge to curtail extravagance.

Nor were Jefferson's evenings at the theatre restricted to one rich season in June 1770. In the fall of the year, when court opened again, the actors were back in town and Jefferson was back in the playhouse, again nightly:

23 October 1770:   Pd. for play tickets 10/.
26 October 1770:   Pd. at playhouse 5/.
27 October 1770:   Pd. for play ticket 7/6.
29 October 1770:   Pd. for play ticket 7/6.
30 October 1770:   Pd. for play ticket 5/.
31 October 1770:   Pd. for d[itt]o 7/6.
                    Pd. for punch at Playhouse /7½
1 November 1770:   Pd. for play ticket 7/6.
2 November 1770:   Pd. for d[itt]o 7/6.
3 November 1770:   Pd. for play ticket 7/6.
5 November 1770;   Pd. at playhouse 2/6.
6 November 1770:   Pd. for play ticket 7/6.
                    Pd. at playhouse 1/3.
7 November 1770:   Pd. for play ticket 7/6.
8 November 1770:   Pd. for play ticket 7/6.[17]

Associations and Binges

We have a word for this kind of behavior: bingeing. This from a young man who "determined never to be idle."[18] So what commanded his interest night after night in the theatre? Clearly something was at work here beyond the attractions of *The Clandestine Marriage* and *Jane Shore*: socializing, of course; being seen in the best company, certainly; inserting himself into the colonial elite. But every night? Colonel Washington had also arrived in Williamsburg earlier in the month for the same June assembly and found the town unanimated without the theatre. His diary entries are a litany of dull nights, each recording the same line: "Dined at the Club and spent the Evening in my own room."[19] After the actors arrived, he emended the line for five nights out of six: "Dined at the club and went to the Play."[20] Washington dropped nearly £5 for the week at the theatre, treating himself and guests, including the lieutenant governor, William Nelson.

Washington's passion for the theatre has been noted before. Paul Leicester Ford, his early biographer, frequently quotes his cash ledgers, for example: "By [sic] play tickets at Sundry times [£]7. 10. 3," recorded for the fall court visit to Williamsburg in 1760. But Ford never asked what an investment the outlay represented. Seven pounds, ten shillings, and threepence would purchase twenty box-seat tickets for a month.

Theatre-going was part of a pattern of intense socializing that court time offered, highly concentrated doses of urbanity and breaks from the bucolic rhythms of rural living, even monied-estate living. Consider the rhythm of Washington's life as recorded in his laconic diary in late summer of 1773: "Sep 23: at home all day. Sep 24. Ditto. Ditto. Sep 25. Still at home all day writing. Sep 26: I set out for Annapolis Races. Dined at Rollin's and got into Annapolis between five and six o'clock. Spent the Evening and lodged at the Governor's. Sep 27: Dined at the Govr's and went to the Play in the evening."[21] A trip to town was an explosion of balls, dinners, friends, races, clubs, and evenings—nearly every evening—in the side boxes of a Douglass theatre. When Washington recorded in his personal cash book in October of 1772 "By Douglass's Company £1/19," he had placed that sum into a familiar palm, indeed, that of a man whom Washington had known for over twenty years.

Washington first saw Douglass onstage in Barbados in 1751 and regularly supported his theatres for the next two decades, in Williamsburg, Fredericksburg, Dumfries, Alexandria, Annapolis, and New York, sometimes in the same year. In 1771, for example, Washington attended performances in Dumfries in January, in Williamsburg for the spring assembly, in Alexandria in July, in Annapolis in August, and back down to Williamsburg in October and early November. In a small and well-lit house, Washington's was a very familiar face in any crowd of six cities. Moreover, he was usually in good company: in Williamsburg he attended with Peyton Randolph, the Speaker of the House, Robert Fairfax and Burrell Bassett, both burgesses, or William Nelson, the lieutenant governor; in Annapolis he shared a box with the Maryland governor, Sir Robert Eden, or Pennsylvania's governor, John Penn, down for the races; and in New York with Gouverneur Morris, James Delancey, or General Gage. Many of the most important people of several colonies eventually sat next to Colonel Washington, in the best seats in the house. This was the real commodity of the playhouse: promising men bought social visibility in the best company.

All these nights in the playhouse would mean nothing more than that Virginians loved their theatre, or that men like Washington and Jefferson were allying themselves socially to advance themselves politically—quite likely a little of both. But as the 1770s opened, the business that brought the burgesses and merchants to town became increasingly contrary to such polite, luxurious evenings with the Crown-appointed governors or their lieutenants. That business became more and more about aggressive, united responses to Great Britain's policies in America. By far the most uniformly adopted response was the non-importation agreement that sought to damage trade with an appeal to home manufacturing and a deep commitment to economy and frugality.

ASSOCIATIONS

Have you repealed our Acts yet? I wish you had,
for we want Goods most confoundedly.
ALEXANDER MACKRABIE to Philip Francis, March 10, 1770

By spring of 1770 most of the Townshend Acts had been repealed, but the damage had been done. The colonies had a weapon in their arsenal that could cripple the transatlantic economy. Proof that the trade embargos were working appeared in the newspapers and from the American merchants' own trading partners in London. "By the last advices from London," began the *Virginia Gazette*, "we learn that the non-importation of the merchants in America begins to be so severely felt by the manufactures as to render it very necessary for Parliament to do something for their relief, and that if we continue to be united, and firmly to adhere in that salutary measure, we may be sure of success."[22] Lest their readers backslide into self-interest, the story appeared alongside a reprinted account of the Boston Massacre. Washington invited Virginia merchants to the capital to renew their pledge. By contrast, in many of the northern colonies, the Sons of Liberty assumed an aggressive role in guaranteeing compliance with the associations. In Connecticut, the boycott extended even to those merchants who chose not to participate in non-importation.[23] That same spring in New York, advertisements were taken out in the newspapers identifying individuals suspected of not honoring the agreement: "[The Sons] take this opportunity to inform you that it is their pleasure you depart this city within 24 hours from this time or you may depend upon being visited in a more disagreeable manner by The Sons of Liberty."[24]

But the long-term boycott took a high toll on the merchants and traders whose livelihood lay in importing fine goods, and compliance waned.[25] A house-by-house poll in New York, a shrewd move on the part of merchants there, convinced the Sons of Liberty that their campaign for a total boycott had become impractical by the summer of 1770.[26] As James Drinker, the Philadelphia merchant, noted wryly of his neighbors: "Interest, all powerful interest will bear down on Patriotism."[27] Non-importation also required solidarity across the colonies, and even Boston reneged on its commitment to certain commodities, like tea.[28] In Philadelphia, Jacob Hiltzheimer attended a meeting at the State House "called to consult about a further non-importation of Goods from Great Britain, although the [New] Yorkers have broke their agreement."[29] Advocates needed a new and public document, and that was the order of business in Virginia for the third week of June, to renew their commitment "to avoid purchasing any commodity or article of goods whatsoever from any importer or seller of British merchandise or European goods." Hammering out which goods were included and which exempted took up most of the meeting. Medicine was always excluded from the list, as were firearms. The Charleston merchants insisted that paper be exempted, as well as broadcloth for clothing slaves. When the debates concluded, a new non-importation agreement emerged on the 22nd of June, and 164 merchants and burgesses publicly signed it, including the second article pledging that "we subscribers, as well by our own example as all other legal ways and means in our power, will promote and encourage industry and frugality, and discourage all manner of luxury and extravagance."[30] And then the authors adjourned to the theatre for a luxurious week of the latest British plays.

Peter Oliver, the Massachusetts judge, could scoff at these associations relinquishing goods the signatories could never afford ("highly diverting to see the names and marks . . . of porters and washerwomen" agreeing to boycott silks and coaches), but the Virginia associators were not porters and washerwomen.[31] They included wealthy planters and influential burgesses, many with radical inclinations, who could parse out the trade boycott and resolves against luxury from their own luxury. Somehow in the new mandate of economy and frugality, the southern theatre remained a space apart, a salon for the cultured. This exemption positioned the theatre as a venue of dubious nationality in an increasingly nationalizing debate.

Ironically, many of the goods on that newly signed boycott list appeared prominently on display in the playhouse. It modeled fashion as part of its attraction, and displayed extravagance on both sides of the footlights. The playhouse presented an odd spectacle: a house full of burgesses, planters, and merchants, fresh from the debates over which goods were to be boycotted, all signatories to a public pledge to a leaner life, gathered night after night in a theatre that unabashedly displayed the very superfine goods and fashions from London these signatories had just pledged off. Popular songs may have embraced non-importation and advocated for the homespun American to:

> Throw aside your topknots of pride
> Wear none but your own country linen
> Of economy boast, let your pride be the most
> To show clothes of your own make and spinning.[32]

If in homespun, as Rhys Isaac concluded, "lay an epitome of the Whig-republican ideal," in the playhouse in June of 1770 when the associators met, homespun proved conspicuously absent.[33] We have one fine description of the fashionable audiences who converged on the capital at court time. Hudson Muse (later delegate to the Virginia Assembly) observed to his brother:

> In a few days after I got to Virginia, I set out to Wmburg, where I was detained for 11 days, tho' I spent the time very agreeably, at the plays every night, and really must join Mr. Ennalls and Mr. Basset [Colonel Henry Basset, another signatory to the association] in thinking Miss Hallam super fine. But must confess her luster was much sullied by the number of Beauties that appeared at that court. The house was crowded every night, and the gentlemen who have generally attended that place agree there was treble the number of fine Ladies that was ever seen in town before—for my part I think it would be impossible for a man to have fixed upon a partner for life, the choice was too general to have fixed on one. About the latter end of this month I intend down again, and perhaps shall make out such another trip, as the players are to be there again, and its an amusement I am so very fond of.[34]

The "super fine" Miss Hallam (as in "superfine flour" or "superfine linen") was Douglass's niece and leading actress, Nancy Hallam, and there was nothing homespun about her. Several reviews singled her out as a figure of some fashion ("Miss Hallam, in the sprightly Miss Montagu, was as much a woman of fashion as we have seen on the stage"[35]). Muse recorded her in many roles during his eleven-night theatre binge, including the precious role of Miss Sterling in Garrick and Coleman's staple *The Clandestine Marriage*, a play that displayed London extravagance and the appetite for material luxury. It had played just two days before the associators signed (June 20, 1770), with both Washington and Jefferson in the house, and the "super fine" Miss Hallam flaunted her fashionable jewelry before the house:

> MISS STERLING: What do you think of these bracelets? I shall have a miniature of my father, set round with diamonds, to one, and Sir John's to the other. And this pair of ear-rings! Set transparent! Here, the tops, you see, will take off to wear in a morning, or in an undress. How d'ye like them?

Jewelry, snuffboxes, fashionable dress, equipage, scented paper, "remarkably elegant" costumes, and the desire for these goods partly drives the play, and that desire seems difficult to reconcile with non-importation pledges to swear off such items, encourage frugality, and wear homespun.

One of the associators, George Mason, who had coauthored a 1769 agreement with Washington, demonstrated the planter class's hypocrisy in a letter reviewing the terms of the boycott: "I have made some few alterations in it, as per memorandum on the other side," to which he added a personal postscript: "P.S. I shall take it as a particular favor if you'll be kind enough to get me two pairs of gold snaps made at Williamsburg, for my little girls. They are small rings with a joint in them, to wear in the ears instead of ear-rings; also a pair of toupee-tongs." Even as the two were working out which luxuries to forgo, "the fashions," wrote his biographer, "were not to be neglected."[36]

We are fortunate to be able to document some of the richness of the playhouse, as Hudson Muse saw it. Through the brushwork of Charles Willson Peale, Nancy Hallam's costume has been preserved, painted in September 1771 in the popular role of Fidele in Shakespeare's *Cymbeline* (performed during the 1770 Williamsburg season as well), and her costume looks rich indeed.

When "YZ" saw her in the same season in Annapolis and gushed with praise for her in that very role, he noted, in particular, that her dress seemed "remarkably elegant."[37] The brocaded silk Turkish pantaloons, printed linen jacket, jeweled dagger hilt, and spangled slippers had all been imported from London, and both her costume and her performance inspired raptures in the *Maryland Gazette*. However, no infatuated reviewer noted that much of her rich costume could also be found among the contraband items listed in the non-importation agreement. Like their Virginian counterparts, the associators of Maryland (where she was painted) had agreed to forgo "ribbons, and Millinery of all kinds, silks of all kinds, Velvets, Chintzes, and Calicoes of all sorts, printed Linens, and printed cottons, Handkerchiefs of all kinds, . . . Wigs, gloves, Hair trunks, Paintings, snuff boxes, playing cards.[38] As of 1770, the bows and buckles on Miss Hallam's superfine shoes were contraband items, as were the silk brocade on her belt, her silk patterned Turkish pants, her elaborate silk and feathered headpiece. Even the wig on the head of the manager who purchased the

Figure 3. Nancy Hallam as Imogen from Shakespeare's Cymbeline, *painted by Charles Willson Peale, Annapolis, 1771. Courtesy of the John D. Rockefeller, Jr. Library, Williamsburg, VA.*

costumes in London, the hair trunks that carried them, and the very pigments on Peale's painting that captured all this excess comprised contraband goods.[39] Yet in Hudson Muse's estimation, the elegantly costumed Miss Hallam was dull next to the scores of Virginia belles who outdressed her nightly in the theatre.

If some colonists demonstrated, as Gordon Wood has suggested, "a genteel bias" to non-importation, they shared an equally biased attitude toward "oeconomy," the partner in that dyad, and both appeared visibly on display in the theatre.[40] Economy seemed to be for those unable to afford the theatre. Not only did the theatre enjoy exemption from non-importation (certainly in the tidewater colonies), it seemed to be the one forum designed to display extravagance, to promote luxury and fashion (and hence Britishness) despite the boycott, and in this regard the theatre proved utterly contrary to the spirit of economy and frugality encouraged by the radical advocates of the American cause, even among the radical advocates in the box seats. The burgesses and planters left their boycotts at the door, and aspired to enter the playhouse as genteel and fashionable a society as London itself could offer.

American homespun—that is, autonomous manufacturing and mercantile independence—was never the stock and trade of the American Company, nor would it be a characteristic of the American theatre until the 1790s. During the Revolution, amateur American playwright Robert Munford incorporated timely political debate into his comedy *The Patriots* (1776). He included a "plain and simple" citizen, known as "Neighbor Homespun," who tolerates no finery (5.2). However, due to the wartime ban, the play never received a production. For Douglass, this kind of caricature savored too much of politics outside the theatre and hypocrisy inside. No "Neighbor Homespun" appeared on the British-American stage; rather, the fashionable auditors saw a parade of the fashionable London styles. "The costumes were remarkably elegant" appeared in numerous reviews. Certainly to the readers of the *Lady's Magazine*, in London and America, "the theatre was an acceptable setter of trends."[41] Even after the American Company left the continent during the war and British military officers deployed two of Douglass's theatres (in New York and Philadelphia) and fitted out a third in Boston to mount seven winter seasons of theatricals "for charity," surviving financial records reveal the same luxurious application of theatre culture as a refined and genteel salon, and the same extraordinary investment in fashionable costuming—to the utter ruin of the charitable aim of the project. From New York, the fifth season the British officers played, 1781–1782, they took in a remarkable £5,300; but of that vast sum, less than £300 was actually dispensed to the widows and orphans whose need prompted the season. Instead, nearly £1,100 went directly into costumes for officers and actresses. Another £1,000 went to redecorating the John Street Playhouse (and this was not startup capital, but rather their third season in an already-functioning theatre). Then came the accessories. Many of the individual receipts describe the silk and jewelry that they thought essential to their productions ("silk for Mrs. Williams—£25, 17s, 10½d"), and so £5,000 went to ensuring a fashionable resort for fashionable officers, while the pocket change went to the orphans.[42]

THE LUXURY OF ENCOURAGING FRUGALITY

Boycotting silks and snuffboxes may not seem like a substantial sacrifice, or one destined to cause financial hardship. However, to that vast assemblage of small and middling merchants and traders a far-reaching non-importation boycott punished all the wrong parties. James Robinson, a tidewater tobacco-broker, was one such. He wrote of the concern of the Virginia deliberations a fortnight after the June 22, 1770, meeting in Williamsburg:

> After some warm debates our original Associators gave the merchants an invitation to join them. Accordingly when we met at the Oyer Court, James Balfour desired that the merchants would assemble and consider the invitation. Then a rough draught of the Association was read. It underwent some considerable amendments until the one of which Mr. Payne tells me he sent you a copy was agreed to. As it stands at present it will not be of great prejudice to the trading part of the colony and you will observe an evident partiality in favour of Glasgow manufactures. . . . I hope in imitation of Virginia you will relax something in the terms of your non-importation agreement [referring to Maryland's Association]. I am indeed surprised that Philadelphia, New York, and Boston adhere to theirs so long. The shopkeeper or dry goods

merchant must suffer greatly, especially if their stock in trade is small and they follow that business for a mere support. If their conduct is the result of choice it is patriotism indeed, but I apprehend it is otherwise: that they are obliged to comply with the popular clamour through the influences of some considerable men who are chiefly concerned in other branches of trade, which the Association does not hurt."[43]

Robinson scents the hypocrisy: the first tier of associators, the plantation crowd, proposed to give up what they did not profit by, while the large traders drafted a document that supported non-importation in principle but was lenient enough not to damage their own business too dearly, a sentiment confirmed by Philadelphia merchant Henry Drinker: "[T]he burthen was unequally borne."[44]

Colony by colony, committees carved out exemptions to gain the backing of the large trading class, and applied pressure below to ensure support. An enormous amount of money was at stake. Planters built fortunes on single-crop economies (e.g., tobacco, white pine for ship masts, rice, indigo), and including these items would raise strong resistance.

Roger Atkinson, a tobacco merchant on the James River, also kept his eye on the deliberations in Williamsburg. He did not belong to the radical class; he ran a plantation and depended on an open Atlantic and a free exchange of goods between the colonies and England. He had no love for the Virginia Assembly and their talk of trade boycotts in response to British acts, and wrote to his London broker assuring him that: "The Americans are your natural Friends. They are more, they are your dependents, part of yourselves, and they are not degenerated—with the aid of America, and if you are true to yourselves, you may defy the rest of the World."[45] Atkinson writes mostly of money matters, the price of tobacco, how many hogshead he hopes to raise, weather conditions, who owes what, and how to get his leaf to market in spite of the associators. His letterbook makes little mention of the rights of colonists or the acts and abuses of Great Britain, though he too was in Williamsburg for the same assemblies that Jefferson, Washington, and Patrick Henry attended; he was there to set prices for the year. His was a merchant world, for whom this talk of arms only upset the market and created shortages and runs. Even in the extremity of a radical imagination, Atkinson's concerns remained financial. He wrote to Samuel Gisty (?) January 10, 1771, of—what else?—"The price of Tob[acco] will be at [£]20 unless a War, if there indeed be a War, may make some Alteration."

The theatre was simply another import commodity that the associators who drafted the boycotts could easily exempt. But the business of buying and selling goods was soon to be eclipsed by the recognition that commerce itself would be the first portal of protest. And Atkinson, Robinson, and so many other merchants would be gathered into the mandates, with or against their better sense. Robert Weir, surveying the association in South Carolina, described it this way: "The initial wave of enthusiasm, augmented by some coercion, was sufficient to induce most persons to co-operate."[46]

While the associators in Williamsburg were working out the exceptions—dry goods may be out, molasses, madeira, and rum from the West Indies flowed into American ports—debates and delays only made good business for Douglass. Douglass and company remained in Williamsburg in weather too hot for preachers, the only time they played the capital through the heat of summer.[47]

IN THE OCCASIONAL COMPANY OF FOUNDING FATHERS

Tempting as it is to make radical Americans of British citizens in 1770, the notion of nation is nonetheless afoot. When tidewater tobaccomen can worry about raising prices in the event of war, the perception of a deep rift, possibly a civil war, is broadcast wider than Boston coffeehouse radicals. Cadwallader Colden was quick to note that "the Virginia delegates were the most violent."[48] And these same Virginia delegates—Thomas Jefferson, George Washington, George Mason, Peyton Randolph, the Speaker of the House, associators, burgesses, councilmen, future congressmen, signers—are clearly taking a very liberal view toward the frugality and economy that the non-importation was predicated upon. Of the non-importation scheme Washington had written at its conception: "The more I consider a Scheme of this sort, the more ardently I wish success to it."[49] At the beginning of the movement, Washington wrote to Mason of his determination "[t]hat no man should scruple, or hesitate a moment to use a[r]ms in defense of so valuable a blessing, on which all the good and evil of life depends; is clearly my opinion; yet A[r]ms I would beg leave to add, should be the last resource; the *denier* [sic] resort."[50] Obviously, Colonel Washington's subsequent career would document his dedication to that last resort. But the agreement for a leaner life of homespun and frugality was not on display in one building where they all gathered. For several weeks a year, in most of the middle and southern colonies at least, everyone of station in the genteel tier could be found inside the theatre in the thick of the Townshend years. A very dense concentration of political power luxuriated in one building.

In considering the relationship between theatre and the American Revolution, Ann Fairfax Withington has wondered, "[A]mong these delegates there must surely have been men who had of an evening attended the theatre."[51] Certainly those from the middle and southern colonies were avid play-goers. Consider just the Virginians who were in the theatre during the spring court in Williamsburg (1771): Washington attended the first night in town with Colonel Burwell Basset (burgess of New Kent County from 1762 to 1775, member of four revolutionary conventions, and later senator from Virginia), as did Robert Fairfax ("and some other Gentlemen"—three others whom Washington treated to box seats), and the Speaker of the House, Peyton Randolph.[52] Thomas Jefferson was there (April 26, May 2, May 3, May 6), and so was the acting governor, Sir William Nelson (he sponsored a "Command Performance" on May 2, 1771, a night both Washington and Jefferson were also in attendance). He too identified himself, as he wrote, "an associate in principle."[53] This Virginia elite were into their second generation of supporting theatre, and many of these same names (and their fathers' before them) can be found on a list of shareholders in the first theatre in Williamsburg, going back to 1745 when they bequeathed it to the city for a new courthouse: Lewis Burwell, Sr., Lewis Burwell, Jr., William Nelson, Jn., Benjamin Harrison, Benjamin Harrison, Jr., Peter Randolph, and Beverley Randolph (Peyton Randolph's mother).[54]

None of this would mean a thing except that the pleasure-loving Virginians indulged in their theatre, but recall the tradesman in New York: "I really think in my conscience, that the rich people who encourage and support the Play House will have much to answer for."[55] These are not just the moral voices of the needy; the language is built into the very associations right up through the eighth resolution of the Congress. These are troubling attitudes to reconcile, but more so as they were shared by the very men who would give over their careers in the cause of American independence. But their America could still be a mannered sphere of class distinction, of gentility and cultivation, aristocrats, and landholding gentry, of box seats, pit seats, and a gallery. Somewhere in the years to come, this concept of America would be lost, and even that final sphere of pleasure would, finally, be given over.

One perfect image of the struggle: when excavations were originally conducted on Richard Henry Lee's house, which stood directly across the street from Douglass's theatre, several pieces of paper were found still stuck in the plaster on the outer wall. Only two sheets were legible enough to be identified: one was the Virginia non-importation agreement; the other, next to it, was a playbill.[56]

[CHAPTER 11]
Lords of the Turf
Maryland, 1770–1771

• • •

John Gordon, president of the Maryland Committee of Inspection, that self-appointed body which oversaw compliance to the non-importation agreements, summed up the movement: "Resolved: that the Non-Importation Agreement is a measure well calculated to prevent Luxury, to promote Industry, and procure a redress of American Grievances." A hundred items of boycotted goods were listed among Maryland's resolutions.[1] Colonists were weaponizing commerce "to redress American grievances." When Douglass arrived in Annapolis, he initiated a subscription scheme to build an elegant theatre. The scheme, which would have met with violence in New York or Philadelphia and been utterly impossible in Boston, was a brilliant success in Annapolis. £600 was raised.

The new theatre ("as commodious and elegant as any theatre in America") is a troubled document that reveals much of the uncertainty of the non-importation movement.[2] Annapolis already had a theatre, but it was an inelegant structure ("awkward" is how Douglass described it), and the manager at least calculated there was money and appetite enough in this tidewater capital to justify an upgrade. In the fall of 1770 Douglass floated a subscription scheme:

> [T]o the ladies and gentlemen whose publick spirit and taste for the rational entertainments of the stage, may lead them to patronise the undertaking. It is proposed then, to deliver to any lady or gentleman, subscribing five pounds or upwards, the value of their respective sums in tickets, one half of which will be admitted the first season, and the remainder the season following. The money to be deposited with William Paca and Samuel Chase, Esqrs, of the city of Annapolis.[3]

It was built in the summer of 1771 and opened September 9, 1771, "to a numerous and brilliant audience, who expressed the greatest satisfaction not only at the performance, but with the House, which is thought to be as elegant and commodious, for its size, as any theatre in America." Again, hear nothing of frugality.[4] The costumes were imported ("the dresses are remarkably elegant," wrote an observer).[5] This had been noticed with some objection in New York even before the trade boycotts had begun in earnest: "Is not foreign finery their chief expense, and their dresses imitated by our young folks?"[6] John Henry had been dispatched to London to recruit new actors. The sets were new, contracted with Covent Garden Theatre scene-painter Nicholas Dahl in the spring. The backdrop for Peale's portrait of Nancy Hallam was among those recently imported from London ("the sums lavished on the late set"), and fresher sets were to follow. That Douglass didn't hire Peale, the homespun painter, whose able brushwork elegantly captured the existing sets, reveals the cachet that London goods retained, even in the thick of the non-importation years.

To compound pleasure with pleasure, the opening of the new theatre coincided with the start of the annual racing season: two scenes of pleasure later singled out by Congress. If one were looking for the densest ambiguity in these years of frugality and economy, one might focus on the Annapolis racing season, when the beau monde of the middle colonies converged for the ponies, the balls, the dinners: where the wealthy could and did spend £1,000 on a good race horse; when rooms in town could not be found; and founders, signers, and governors crowded the turf by day and the theatre every night.

THE PROBLEM WITH JACKY CUSTIS

Jonathan Boucher, rector of St. Anne's Parish, had a problem, and it was, in miniature, the same problem the associators had. In 1770, while the planters were trying to curb their appetite for pleasure goods, Boucher was laboring to curb those of his young charge, master Jacky Custis, Washington's stepson. But the desire for "scenes of pleasure" and goods by which to satisfy that desire were so appealing, so accessible, that it was a vain battle. Washington, Boucher's neighbor, had placed the young man under the rector's care, but even under his watchful eye, Jacky neglected his studies in favor of the attractions of Annapolis. The problem was not so much that he had fallen into rich company, with the son and daughter of Samuel Galloway (the turf devotee who spent £1,000 on the racehorse Selim); their appetite for entertainment was too rich for young Jacky's blood. Or even that Jacky had developed a fond attraction for Galloway's daughter. Boucher wrote to Washington: "[I]t was about the time of the players being here [October 1770], Miss Galloway came to town. Jack has a propensity to the sex, which I am at a loss how to judge of, much more how to describe." Jacky was spending all his pocket money at the playhouse in the company of young master Galloway and his fetching sister. Young lust was challenging enough, but the real problem was one of discipline: neither Boucher nor Washington could reasonably deny the young man these "scenes of pleasures," because the two grown-ups were just as guilty of enjoying the town's entertainments. As Boucher frankly acknowledged to Washington: "[N]either you nor I can refuse his going, more especially, if we go ourselves."[7]

That was precisely the problem it took an act of Congress to settle. Both men, and many others in their social sphere, spent an inordinate amount of time and money on extravagances—the turf, the theatre—in exactly the same company as young Jacky. Washington's diary tells the story:

Oct 4   Set off for the Annapolis Races. Dined and lodged at Mr. Boucher's.
Oct 5   Reached Annapolis. Dined at the Coffee House with the Jocky Club and lodgd at the Govers, after going to the Play
Oct 6   Dined at Majr. Jenifer's. Went to the Ball, and Suppd at the Govrs.
Oct 7   Dined at the Govrs, and went to the Play afterwards.
Oct 8   Dined at Colo. Loyd's and went to the Play; from then to my lodgings.
Oct 9   Dined at Mr. Ridout's. Went to the Play and to the Govrs to Supper.

On the 10th, Washington left Annapolis after a whirlwind week of dinners, balls, racing, and nights in the theatre, but Boucher and young Jacky stayed on, spending much of the fall at the races and in the theatre (the American Company had been in residence since late August) in fine company, habituating young Custis to the "scenes of pleasure."[8] In his memoirs, Boucher, always was fond of genteel company,

Lords of the Turf   [153

described Annapolis as "the genteelest town in North America, and many of its inhabitants were highly respectable, as to station, fortune, and education. I hardly know a town in England so desirable to live in as Annapolis then was. It was the seat of Government, and the residence of the Governor, and all the great officers of state, as well as of the most eminent lawyers, physicians, and families of opulence and note."[9] Beyond the opulent residents, he further noted, "[i]t was customary for people of any fashion in the country to come and see the plays."[10] Indeed, he met his own wife in the theatre, another one of those fashionable daughters from the country.

That same fall of 1770, Douglass eyed some property next to Boucher's church and was encouraged by his success to undertake a subscription scheme to build the new theatre, of which the rector wrote with a tinge of jealousy:

> A very handsome theatre was built while I stayed there by subscription; and as the church was old and ordinary, and this theatre was built on land belonging to the church, I drew up a petition in verse in behalf of the old church, which was inserted in the gazette, and did me credit. And this, I think, was one of the first things that made me to be taken notice of. I also wrote some verses on one of the actresses; and a prologue or two.[11]

It's odd for the preacher of the largest church in the capital city to confess that he was noticed only when he wrote prologues for the theatre and verses on actresses, but it speaks to where the real action was. His verses were likely those published in the *Maryland Gazette* by "XY," one clearly enamored with Nancy Hallam's performance in *Cymbeline*:

> On finding that the part of Imogen was to be played by Miss Hallam I instantly formed to myself from my predilection for her the most sanguine hope of entertainment. But how was I ravished on experiment! She exceeded my utmost idea! Such delicacy of manner! Such classical strictness of expression! The music of her tongue—the vox liquida, how melting! Notwithstanding the horrid ruggedness of the roof and the untoward construction of the whole house methought I heard once more the warbling of Cibber in my ear. How true and thorough her knowledge of the part she personated! Her whole form and di-

mensions how happily convertible and universally adapted to the variety of her part.

When prose languished, "XY" erupted into verse:

> Hail, wond'rous maid! I grateful, hail
> Thy strange dramatic pow'r:
> To thee I owe, that Shakespeare's tale
> Has charm'd my ears once more.[12]

Such enchantment was hardly the voice of moral gravity to admonish young Jacky for his infatuations with theatre and young women, nor the voice of one encouraging frugality. While in Annapolis, Boucher and his ward lodged with Joshua Frazer, whose receipts place them in his house until the middle of December, and Frazer as well apparently spent his share of time in the theatre, because he lost his coat there and posted a note in the *Gazette*: "Left at the Play-house last week or taken from Mr. Joshua Frazer's by mistake, a new frize drab great coat. . . . Whoever has got the same, is requested to return it to Mr. Frazer."[13]

Everybody (and their landlord) it seemed was in the theatre. Washington sat with Governor Robert Eden in a side box with Reverend Boucher and young Jacky, the Galloways in another, the landlord in his new coat in the pit, the painter Charles Willson Peale, the Homony Club, the printer, "XY" and "YZ" (likely the king's surveyor, William Eddis, who also wrote about his infatuation with the Annapolis theatre): all agog over Nancy Hallam ("how was I ravished. . ."). Eddis also testified to the fine assemblage of "fashionable and handsome women" and left a good description of both theatre and assembly.[14] No homespun to be found here. The beau monde of the middle colonies, frugality notwithstanding, built themselves a new theatre for David Douglass and packed it six nights a week.

RAPTURES OVER NANCY HALLAM

Jonathan Boucher, Charles Willson Peale, William Eddis, Governor Robert Eden, former governor Horatio Sharpe, legislators William Paca, John Hall, Thomas Johnson, Dennis Dulaney, and Charles Carroll, the attorney general of the colony, Thomas Jennings, were all also members of the Homony Club, and that famous association was also in the theatre. The club was one of those elite social organizations scattered across the colonial landscape, deceptively powerful for a club who kept a poet laureate and insisted on toasting in rhymes; with a fixed number of members, it was also, frankly, as difficult to enter as the General Assembly.[15] The minutes of the club from 1770 to 1773 have survived, including a rousing sketch of their ceremonial entrance into the theatre in September 1771, to celebrate the installation of the club's new president:

> John Lookup, with a number of the Members, supported by the Master of Ceremonies, attended the theatre to witness the opera Love in a Village. It was remarkable, says the Record, that our President was, on his entrance into the Theatre, received by the whole audience with great Satisfaction & even Repeated bursts of Applause. He was pleased to express great pleasure at the Representation of this excellent composition. As the particular good spirits that appeared in all the performers upon this Occasion was manifest to the whole Audience, it may not be improper to remark that it was the opinion of several persons present (if not all) that they were much enlivened by the appearance of our President & this Respectable Society.
> n.b. It was no less remarkable than grievous to observe that our worthy member Mr. John Hall did not attend our President, on this important occasion.[16]

If one wanted to be noticed (like Boucher) or missed (like Hall), the theatre was the place to be, and a young self-taught portrait painter was among those who wanted to be noticed. When "XY" first versified his infatuation with Miss Hallam's performance in the fall of 1770, the poet concluded his encomium with a very particular wish—that her image should be captured by a very able brush:

> What Pencil, say, can paint
> Th' unlust'rous, but expressive Gloom
> Of Thee, fair, sleeping Saint!
> Or thine, or none, self-tutor'd PEALE![17]

The public plea to Charles Willson Peale was soon fulfilled. When the company returned in the fall of 1771, Peale accepted the invitation (of the rector's infatuation) and painted Nancy Hallam in the costume of Imogen, cross-dressed as Fidele. The completed portrait was hung in the (new) theatre for all to compare the brushwork and stage work, and the poet again praised his own idea:

> In thee, oh Peale, both excellencies join;
> Venetian colors and the Greek design.
> . . . .
> Shakespeare's immortal scenes our wonder raise,
> And next to him thou claim'st our highest praise.
> When Hallam as Fedele [*recte* Fidele] comes distressed,
> Tears fill each eye and passion heaves each breast.[18]

Peale, delighted with the attention, copied the lines in his own letter book. And when the Homony clubsters saw the portrait at the theatre, the club applied to Peale to paint their group portrait.[19] Peale complied, and was subsequently admitted into that elite society in January of 1772. By then, he too had used the theatre to develop more than a passing acquaintance with many of the gentlemen who would become his patrons.

And then there was the turf. The Annapolis theatre season did not coincide by chance with the racing season, already a twenty-five-year tradition in 1770, and that lavish fortnight of ponies and parties represented a singularly concentrated display of leisure, excess, and recreational consumption. The Jockey Club boasted the wealthiest tidewater and middle colony fortunes, and during the fall racing season one could find the most influential men in the mid-Atlantic at the track in the morning, the Governor's Palace for dinner, and the side boxes of the theatre at night. George Washington was a member, as were Robert Eden, John Penn, governor of Pennsylvania, and his brother, Richard Penn, quondam governor, old aristocracy like the Allen family of Philadelphia, one of the wealthiest in the province, and other deep-pocket merchants like Samuel Galloway, James Delancey of New York, Gouverneur Morris, Lord Stirling, William Paca (steward of the club), and Charles Carroll. Carroll thought some of the members, particularly the governor, "shamefully too dissipated" by the turf, attending the Annapolis races, the Marlborough, the Oxford, and leaving him little time to consider the business of the colony.[20] "The club," as Washington called it, also boasted men of more modest means (but affluent appetites) such as William Eddis, the colony's surveyor, the rector Jonathan Boucher, and the horse breeders and trainers, all converging for an intense week of dining, balls, assemblies, turf by day and theatre by night. Indeed, these convivial salons so overlapped that men like Washington attended multiple events in a day: dining with the Jockey Club, attending the races, evening in the theatre, and supper at the governor's. Douglass, for his part, would return some revenue as a race sponsor: "The American Theatrical Company's Purse of Fifty Pounds, free for any horse, Mare, or Gelding to carry nine Stone. Heat 4 miles."[21]

All these "scenes of pleasure" could be read as an intensely social urban holiday for backcountry planters, except that the colonies were waging a boycott against British goods and luxurious spending, giving their public pledges to eschew luxury, promote industry, give over frippery, and live lean. Jockey clubsters were at the races by day and theatre by night when the Earl of Hillsborough wrote from Whitehall on October 3, 1770, to Governor Eden, hoping to receive the news that the non-importation agreement was breaking down in Maryland.[22] It was but two days earlier that Douglass had initiated his subscription to build the new theatre in Annapolis.

It was noticed at the time that merchants in New York and Boston had slackened their resolve, the strain having penalized small traders and shop owners. Large merchants thrived in the exemptions, and the Earl of Hillsborough was desirous to know how Maryland was holding up in its resolve. Whole colonies had given over the struggle, to their shame; Henry Drinker sneered at Rhode Island: "[T]he little dirty colony of Rhode Island has shamefully broken faith." And though Marylanders recommitted to "Oeconomy and Frugality" as late as August 10, 1770, had Whitehall seen the September racing and theatre season in Annapolis, they would have given little credence to the American effort at non-importation and trade boycotts.[23]

In the end, the Homony Club wasn't eating hominy, though their poet laureate might promise as much. Rather, they squabbled over fresh mutton or "an excellent haunch of venison." They went to the races to watch £1,000 horses, and adjourned to their elegant new theatre. In the end, Reverend Boucher's problem with young Jackie was a fitting metaphor for the times. The "scenes of pleasure" were just too rich to avoid, and that problem would not be resolved until the Congress acted in October of 1774.

When the Maryland Association planned for their October 25, 1770, meeting, it was with little faith and a great deal of reservation. They were called "to judge the expediency of continuing the association under the particular circumstance of Philadelphia merchants breaking theirs, and that if such a meeting cannot be brought about that on that case the merchants of this town will look upon the association as dissolved and go into general importation."[24] By the close of 1770, non-importation associations cooled across the colonies, and by the following summer, talk of frugality had all but ceased. Charles Carroll of Carrollton wrote in August 1771, "[T]his is a dead time with us. . . . Politics are scarce talked of."[25] Meanwhile the theatre, so William Eddis concluded, would be "reaping a plenteous harvest."[26]

Washington's concerns about young Jacky's love of leisure were never resolved. When the young man was ready for college in 1773, his stepfather traveled to New York to place him in the care of Myles Cooper at King's College. There Washington dined with General Gage (twice) and James Delancey, and their evenings ended at the John Street Theatre, where they were treated to a new prologue written by Cooper, Jacky's new tutor.[27]

The politics of austerity as a unifying colonial position would never work where theatre thrived; frugality was at odds with the culture of the playhouse, the dense social scene of pleasure, civility, and advancement. In the southern and middle colonies, the playhouse was too tempting to give over.

There would soon come a time of reckoning, when men like Washington and his neighbor Boucher, and Myles Cooper, General Gage, and Washington's great friend Sir Robert Eden would find themselves on opposite sides of a great contest. Very soon. But in 1773, they could still share a side box in the theatre; when they could not, all civility would be over.

[CHAPTER 12]

Great Reckonings in Small Rooms
1773–1774

• • •

Madeira	£36
Madeira Com	£15
Punch Grog	£24 15s
Port	£1 15s
Clarett	£30
Beer	£7
Porter	£13 10s
Breakage	15s

Receipt of a tavern bill,
St. Andrew's Society, November 30, 1773[1]

Scratch me, countryman! And I'll scratch thee.
DAVID DOUGLASS, *South Carolina Gazette,* May 30, 1774

"PAST TIME WITH GOOD COMPANY"

Tavern bills don't tell the whole story, just the entertaining part: "the past time with good company," as Henry VIII sang it. The volumes of claret, madeira, and port lubricated a great deal of social advancement along many intersecting lines of allegiances: familiar, mercantile, and national. Clubs such as Charleston's St. Andrew's Society provided a complete rolodex of vital contacts culled from all the important strata of colonial American society: governors, planters, oligarchs and office-holders, assemblymen, large traders, small merchants, and ship captains; in peaceable times they all meant patronage. Peale found it essential in Annapolis, and David Douglass found it as vital when he was introduced to the Charleston St. Andrew's Society in August of 1773. He was formally admitted into this elite association at their next meeting on November 30 of that same year.[2]

But this amiable night of Scotsmen drinking and networking preceded the arrival of tea in Charleston's harbor (and all the violent hereafter that arrived with it). Those two forces—the convivial attraction of dense networks that constituted the necessary fabric of social and civic advancement and the undertow of a divisive nationalism that cut across that network and was precipitated ultimately by the arrival of the tea—were pulling on all parties. Societies like St. Andrew's brought together disparate interests, classes, and stations into a large and potent constellation of support, to the advantage of all parties, while the political division, exemplified best by tea, split these same populations into two irreconcilable and bitter factions. The turbulence of these two forces—the pulling together and the pulling apart—is the story of this chapter. It is about reckonings, both material and metaphoric: of intensely social gatherings (e.g., the Jockey Club, the Homony Club, the St. Andrew's Society) all celebrating a certain convivial commonality that was so essential in maintaining identity and community, before the crisis ultimately demanded a second kind of reckoning, a settling up of self, often at the expense of rupturing those very communities and reshaping those identities. These reckonings (of which Jonathan Boucher wrote to Washington: "[W]e have now each of us taken and avowed our sides") would be the dividing identity that would irrevocably rupture colonial society.[3] What was years in the pulling together was torn asunder in months, and a few evenings in the winter of 1773–1774 might very well have determined the reckoning. Many eyewitnesses wrote about this deep division, but the moment of decision is poignant. "Brothers against brothers," they wrote, in the abstract; but that moment of declaration, of recognizing the final irreparable separation within families, within clubs, was deeply, quietly dramatic.[4] Even more, it was public.

This first evening in question, November 30, 1773, began the great winter of discontent, between the arrival of the tea, the boycott, the British response culminating with the blockade of Boston, and the election of the first Congress. It was the last season of plays before the Revolution, in another new theatre, in Charleston, and it was a winter during which a certain population of colonists of all rank and station underwent a great reckoning. In the case of the St. Andrew's men, they were countrymen whose notion of country was utterly revised: some went in Scottish and came out British, some went in British and came out American; but few remained unchanged, and none untouched. Families would be torn apart, friendships dissolved, clubs disbanded. It was that kind of winter.

To get a sense of the magnitude of this rupture, we need first to consider the density and cohesion of one social network, in this case Scottish-Americans. The night before the tea arrived, they were all under one roof, at Mrs. Swallow's Tavern, where they spent £60 on their dinner (fifty-six diners) and £128 on drink (down from their 1770 bender, when they spent over £200 on bumpers). The receipts of the evening tell us who was present, and who was present was a veritable who's who of Charleston's social and political Scottish elite. These countrymen were fabled for their "scratching"—granting the favors that kept the clan so clannish.

SCOTSMEN ABROAD: "THE VAST COUSINAGE"

The account of this soggy evening comes from an extraordinary and unordered collection of the records of Charleston's St. Andrew's Society: boxes of unpublished petitions, minutes, tavern bills, membership lists, and rules that taken together offer rare insight into the social life through which politics (and particularly southern politics) have always been accomplished.[5] Founded in 1739 as an association of transplanted Scotsmen—in a colony that remained one-third Scottish until the revolution—the Society was founded "for the purpose of cultivating a good understanding and acquaintance with one another." But the colonial club was also a place where "Scotchmen abroad exercised a great though almost insensible control over each other. They became thoroughly acquainted with each other's habits, capacity and character, and they who have it in their power seldom fail to patronize and assist their deserving countrymen."[6]

And indeed, this "insensible control" is visible in the preserved minutes that record the jocular fining of members—one for remaining single, another for producing children or for not producing children, still another for marrying too young or too old—indicating that the private lives of these clubmen were public knowledge. The records detail a dense web of affluent immigrants related by business and trading interests, by marriage, by patronage, by a common Scottish descent, who clubbed exclusively, collectively dominating the colony and advancing themselves by advancing each other. As Douglass wrote, "Scratch me, countryman, and I'll scratch thee!"[7] This "scratching" was a Scottish phrase, as in "His friends to the North of the Tweed have an itch for scratching."[8] It meant to throw one's support to, as in "When Mr. Harley was going to scratch for Lord Mayor yesterday, he called upon Mr. Wilkes, and informed him that it had been declared that he promised to scratch for him on the present election; he begged him therefore to say, if he had ever given him such a promise. Mr. Wilkes declared he never did. When Mr. Harley told him he was then going to scratch against him, and that he never would give him a vote on any occasion."[9]

Throughout his public life Douglass did his best business scratching fellow Scotsmen, and his admission into the club was a scratching back of sorts. Douglass often rented from Scottish landlords (Robert Wells, Alexander Michie, John Deas). He used Scottish printers (Robert Wells, William Aikman, David Hall), he employed Scottish ticket-sellers (Robert Wells in Charleston, Alexander Hays in New York, Colin Campbell in Annapolis), and he sailed with Scottish captains (Henry Gunn, John Ogilvie, and Captain Blewer) who docked at Scottish wharfs (Robert Rowand). His civic charities were Scottish (Union Kilwinning Lodge, Charleston), or suggested by Scotsmen (Dr. Peter Middleton, president of the New York chapter of St. Andrew's between 1767 and 1770, was in charge of the New York Hospital to which the company donated benefits). Even the Scottish in the military, like Moncrief, assisted the theatre in New York. All were St. Andrew's men.

Four nights a year, at Dillon's or Mrs. Swallow's Tavern, a clubful of influential Charleston Scots all gathered. Douglass, like any rising merchant, joined, drank, dined, and scratched, and the St. Andrew's Society scratched back. Early in the summer of 1773 he left his actors performing their benefits at the close of the summer season in New York to sail to Charleston, where he arrived in late July and initiated a subscription scheme to build a new theatre, as he had done in Annapolis.[10] The new subscription scheme took quickly, and within a matter of weeks he had his lease and contractors. When the St. Andrew's Society met on the 28th of August, Douglass was introduced to the club, according to the bylaws sponsored by two members of solid standing—perhaps even his new landlords, as he had secured his advances and that very day had signed a fifteen-year lease on a lot in Church Street, on very generous terms, with four other Scotsmen all of the same club. Securing the support of Charleston's Scottish "quality" was a strategic move for Douglass, who then returned to Charleston on November

25, 1773, in time for his initiation into the St. Andrew's Society on the 30th, when construction was finishing on his new theatre on Church Street.

The new playhouse would be, as its counterpart in Annapolis was, "handsomely supported." The clientele, by all accounts, represented the beau monde of Charleston (the first notice of the theatre's opening was an advertisement for a lost bracelet, "set with brilliants, Rubies and twelve strings of Oriental Pearls").[11] Alexander Hewatt (another Scot) wrote of those who gathered for Charleston's "assemblies, balls, concerts, and plays" as "companies almost equally brilliant as those of any town in Europe of the same size."[12] The new theatre proved the most elegant on the continent and the audiences so plentiful that Douglass did not need to advertise in the newspapers.

But such support came at a price. Douglass spent £7.7s for his membership dues at the club that night, another £5.12s for the dinner, and then his share of the punch grog on top. The out-of-pocket fees amounted to over £15 for one evening (when an actor's weekly wage was £4 or £5), but it appeared money well spent. In one sloshy night, Douglass became acquainted (and reacquainted) with South Carolina's exclusive economic and political elite, what Walter Edgar has called "a vast cousinage" of interrelated families, office-holders, and trading partners, and found his patronage for the winter season.[13]

Immigrant Scots had excelled at such social advancement since arriving in America. Robert Weir has exposed the fear of the monopolies of Scottish merchants and placemen; their dense domination of certain trades, tobacco in the Chesapeake, for example, and printing, coupled with the notoriety of Lord Bute's nepotism, made the Scottish immigrant an easy target of popular prejudice. Who joined the French, twice, to abolish the Protestant religion? asked "Virginianus" to the editor of the *Virginia Gazette*. Who framed the Stamp Act? Who corrupted Parliament? And who aimed at arbitrary power in every part of Great Britain? "The Scotch," triumphantly concluded the soliloquy.[14] Weir describes their clannishness as "a proverbial lament," and cites a petition in Mecklenburg, Virginia, of one Malachi Macalle "for expelling out of the country all Scotchmen, to which he had got 300 names."[15] In his play *The Fall of British Tyranny*, John Leacock described the fear of "Scotch politics, Scotch intrigues, Scotch influence, and Scotch impudence."[16] Pinkney's *Virginia Gazette* spoke for many when it described the Scotsman thus: "[W]hen he first is admitted into a house, is so humble that he will sit upon the lowest step of the staircase. By degrees he gets into the kitchen, and from thence, by the most submissive behaviour, is advanced to the parlour. If he gets into the diningroom, as ten to one but he will, the master of the house must take care of himself, for in all probability he will turn him out of doors, and by the assistance of his *countrymen*, keep possession forever."[17] Such a trajectory had been many a Scot's progress, including, some would say, the Earl of Bute, as it had been for Douglass, from "your humble servant" entering New York, soliciting permission to leave, defending his profession, building his networks through "the assistance of his countrymen," to finally dining and drinking among the highest tiers of colonial society. This insidious practice extended to the elite levels of government as well. One letter to the *Virginia Gazette* complained that the Scots had clogged up the king's ministry: "[I]t is rare now-a-days to see the good old English names of Cavendish, Manners, Sackville, Pelham, Howard . . . in any of the new appointments that take place. On the contrary, Stewart, Murray, Keith, McCoy, Campbell, Hay, Drummond . . . are the favorite names which now weekly adorn our Court Gazette."[18] A London account, reprinted in many American newspapers, reported a "patriotic commoner has in contemplation to bring a bill next session into parliament to disqualify Scotchmen from representing English counties or boroughs for the future."[19] And as the resentment rose, the tighter this knot of Scots became. During the early years of the Revolutionary War, when Robert Munford penned his play *The Patriots*, he presented a scene of three Scotsmen—McFlint, McSqueeze, and McGripe—all hauled into a people's court to account for their want of support for the patriot cause. When McFlint inquires of the committee, "What is our offense, pray?," the court is roundly informed, "The nature of their offense, gentlemen, is, that they are Scotchmen; every Scotchman being an enemy, and these men being Scotchmen." When McGripe pushes for proof of their loyalty, Brazen, the committeeman, retorts, "Proof, sir! We have proof enough. We suspect any Scotchman, suspicion is proof, sir!"[20] That the subnational Scotsmen remained a political clan who would all hang together in this new crisis of nation was an accusation a long time in the making. And here they all gathered in one tavern in 1773 Charleston, "scratching," on the eve of a great reckoning.

Two important men headed the membership list of Charleston's St. Andrew's Society that November: the governor of South Carolina, William Lyttelton (honorary), and the lieutenant governor, William Bull (present), on whom Douglass counted for the license to open business, as he had a decade earlier. A cordial nod assured each of their (well-regulated) winter's entertainment. The attorney general of the colony, Sir Egerton Leigh, also attended that night, a man whom Douglass already knew on good terms from his *Heart of Oak* crossing. Detractors of Leigh (like Henry Laurens) might sneer at him for reveling with actors, but as he was a major office-holder of the city and Grand Master of Charleston's Freemasons, Leigh proved a powerful supporter of the theatre.[21] In gratitude, Douglass would donate the proceeds of a night's performance as a charitable benefit for the Union Kilwinning Lodge of Masons. The (former) speaker of the house, Peter Manigault, was also a St. Andrew's man whose family had been supporting Douglass for the past decade, as were many of the principal men of the town who would be his patron base: John Rutledge, Douglas Campbell, Robert Rowand, John Deas, David Deas, Charles Cotesworth Pinckney (Provincial Congress 1775, later general of the American forces), James Michie, John Stuart (superintendent of Indian affairs), William Moultrie (Provincial Congress 1775, later General Moultrie, who was also admitted to the Society that same night), Rawlins Lowndes (current Speaker of the House, chief judge, Provincial Congress 1775), and the visitor Adam Lord Gordon. Some would remain loyalists, others American patriots. Their allegiances would cut across their Scottish heritage, even here where Scottish heritage seemed to have the greatest currency. It would take an event of enormous magnitude to disrupt the dense network of Scotsmen in America, and it had just landed in the chests of "Bohea" tea.

The St. Andrews club convened at Dillon's tavern, later Mrs. Swallow's tavern (same establishment, new owner), so Robert Dillon was also on the membership list, as was Robert Wells, the printer and journalist who had his hand in much of the doings of the town, including Douglass's. Wells printed the playbills and sold tickets for the theatre, in exchange for box seats. Wells served as the club's secretary, as well as the Freemasons', for many years. David Deas, with whom Douglass had also sailed, was the treasurer of St. Andrew's. John Deas, his brother, held the presidency of the St. Cecilia Society, that equally exclusive association which sponsored the Charleston concert series and to which Douglass contributed his best singers; and Robert Wells, again, served as that club's secretary. The organist for the St. Cecilia Society, Peter Valton, also a St. Andrew's man, traveled to Charleston with Henry Gunn on the *Heart of Oak*. Douglass would lend Valton four of his best singers for Valton's benefit concert at the St. Cecilia's and promote the publication of Valton's sonatas at Wells's print shop; and Valton would play for Douglass at the theatre.[22] The four St. Andrew's men from whom Douglass leased his theatre in Charleston would each receive a benefit night, donated by Douglass. Thick as Scots, they said.

One finds these kinds of social networks all across the colonial American landscape. The amiable history of these clubs illuminates both the building and the rupture of colonial society. The same quorum of names of the Charleston St. Andrew's Society shared much of the roster of the 120-member core of the St. Cecilia's Society, that city's Freemason lodge, and many of the same names are found on the officer list of the colony's militia.[23] The Charleston elite intersected along many lines, governmental, civil, mercantile, and social, and this held true for the other colonies as well; and where they made their reckoning, it rippled across the highest levels of society.

New York likewise boasted a chapter of the St. Andrew's Society, and Douglass participated when in residence there. Its membership lists included a similar sampling of the colony's ruling elite, of diverse political backgrounds: the former governor, James Glenn, Lord Dunmore (governor of New York and president of the club in 1770–1771), the long-standing lieutenant governor, Cadwallader Colden, and his son David Colden, his brother Alexander Colden, Dr. Peter Middleton—all active loyalists; Philip and William Livingston, Hon. Richard Morris, William Alexander (Lord Stirling)—all active patriots, along with an abundance of military officers, judges, reverends, doctors, and ship captains whose alliances we do not know.[24] William Livingston, who would command the militia of New Jersey; Philip Livingston, who would sign the Declaration of Independence; Lord Stirling, who would rise to the rank of major general in the Continental Army; and Andrew Elliott, a member of the governor's executive council of New York and superintendent of all imports and exports in British America, later lieutenant governor of the province of New York, who, after the surrender, would return to Scotland; and Hugh Gaine, the

Scotch-Irish printer who published the rules of the Society and who would waffle on his position before throwing in with the British in occupied New York, all sat together at the St. Andrew's Society. Presidents of the Society, William McAdam (1772–1773) and William Alexander (Lord Stirling, 1761–1764), both dedicated patriots, would share the club with Alexander Colden (1764–1766) and Peter Middleton (1767–1770), both ardent Tories. And so it was in Charleston. Men would throw in with one side or the other, would commit their lives and fortunes to the cause, and this commitment, this reckoning, what William Nelson has called "the crisis of allegiance," would happen with relative speed.[25]

We can check this with a small sampling from the evening preserved in the tab above. These are unusual cases, I grant, but three new members were initiated that evening—David Douglass, William Moultrie, and a Cherokee chief, Oucconnastotah—and the range of their commitments illustrates the reckonings that followed. William Moultrie (1730–1805), of an established Charleston family, had fought against the Cherokees in the Anglo-Cherokee war of 1761. He was one of the forty-five members of the General Committee, originally created to enforce the non-importation association. He was a colonel in the Charleston militia in 1774 and would in the brief time ahead deploy that militia in defense of the city against the British. His military service on behalf of the American cause attained for him the highest rank in the Continental Army, major general, and after the war he was elected governor of South Carolina.

Admitted the same night as Moultrie and Douglass was Oucconnastotah, "the great warrior chief of the Cherokee Nation."[26] During the French-Indian Wars, Oucconnastotah (ca. 1710–1783) was a captain in the French army and waged a fierce campaign against the British, including against Moultrie. He was responsible for the attack on Fort Louden—and the first Native American to capture a British fort. One celebrated peace treaty carried him as far north as upper New York to visit the Mohawks, and Oucconnastotah and his party were hosted in New York City—by David Douglass at the John Street Theatre, both on their journey north and again when the party returned. On one occasion in New York, after a night of watching plays, Douglass invited Oucconnastotah onto the stage to share a war dance and prepared the audience for the respect owed the Cherokee chiefs.

Oucconnastotah's separate peace treaties, however, lasted only as long as they served his people's trading interests. His alliances shifted easily, and under his leadership the Cherokees waged campaigns against both the French and British backcountry settlers, against the Choctaw armed by the French, against the British armed by the French, and on their own against the British and later against the Americans. In New York, at the John Street Theatre, he was accompanied by John Stuart, the superintendent of Indian affairs, and at the outbreak of the Revolutionary War, Stuart fought for the king and was suspected of using his position with the Cherokees to incite a guerilla campaign against the Americans. Stuart's property in Charleston would be confiscated by the Provincial Congress of South Carolina; the man who carried out the confiscation was William Moultrie. And they were drinking together that night.

And then there was Douglass himself, who cautiously declared no position but whose subsequent royal appointments in Jamaica (a loyalist colony) suggest a deep investment in British rule. Tories, Whigs, loyalists, radicals, opportunists, fence-sitters, and Scotsmen—all Scotsmen: all dining, toasting, and scratching, while the first winds of war brought the tea cargos into harbor. How loyalties would be sorted had a great deal to do with how these various St. Andrew's men conceived of their positions—to each other, to Great Britain—and much of this shaping would be displayed around them in unavoidable rituals and commodities, including those of the third initiate that evening, Douglass. On the last night of November, there were two new things in Charleston: tea and a theatre.

On November 30, with a small flotilla of ships carrying a cargo of East India tea making landfall in Charleston and in Boston, tea would have been a difficult subject to avoid, and perhaps even harder to talk about. In the weeks to come, tea would be a crucible of so many reckonings: where one stood, a deep and divisive question, was asked publicly and privately, over and over again, in so many forums.

And so it was, friendship and family, household by household, club by association: the vast network of patronage that built and sustained so many careers was ripped asunder. When the tea arrived in British America, the tensions with Great Britain escalated, and emergent notions of a stand against Whitehall's policies began to unknot the ties of this proverbial Scottish clannishness. The Scots, like the rest

Great Reckonings in Small Rooms

of colonial America, would not function as a subnational population, but rather Scotsman by Scotsman would draw his line of alliance at the expense of so many networks. As in Scotland in '45, it would soon be a time for declaring alliances. "Private friendships are broken off," James Allen of Philadelphia confided to his diary, and in that sentiment one can only lament how quickly the dense webs unraveled: St. Andrew, St. Cecilia's, the Annapolis Jockey Club, the Homony Club.[27]

How each arrived at his position is a private matter that few, even among the writers of the period, publicly discussed. Still, there were public moments when this reckoning was prompted, invited, tested. Toasting the king's health, for example, or taking tea after the boycott, or which lyrics one chose to chorus in a public voice: small, quietly coercive moments that demanded and declared a position.[28] There were public venues for working out that private position: in coffeehouses, for example, spirited debates caffeinated the nights; in clubs, toasts were raised, honored, refused, or reluctantly joined. But for a quieter, safer rehearsal, a testing of who stood where, there was the theatre. The new theatre on Church Street opened in the thick of the tea crisis, and it remained open until the blockade of Boston and the election of delegates to the first Congress. During this winter of reckonings, the new theatre would be instrumental in rehearsing positions, preparing the rupture to come, in unfashioning and refashioning the new identities.

"EXIT WITH TEA BOARD"

Several letters from London by the Packet say "the ship with the TEA, for your Port, will sail about the 12th or 15th of September" so that we may hourly expect her. Last Wednesday embarked on board the Sea Nymph, South Carolina, the American Company.
South Carolina Gazette, November 30, 1773

The Scotsmen with their various allegiances were barely sober from the annual dinner when, in the early morning hours of December 1, 1773, the ship *London* dropped anchor in Charleston harbor with its cargo of 257 chests of tea. Charlestonians knew this ship was daily expected and were preparing a response. Broadsides had already been in circulation for a week, deploring the act and warning stamp masters and commissioners against compliance. Fresh handbills were stuck up at the coffee houses in town on the 30th "menacing destruction to any person who should accept a commission for the sale of East India Company's tea, or be in any way accessary thereof."[29] The previous month, on November 28, "Junius Brutus" (Peter Timothy?) had written in a special edition of the *South Carolina Gazette* devoted to the tea debate, protesting the tea tax and a Parliament determined "to raise a revenue, out of your pockets, against your consent, and to render assemblies of your representatives totally useless."[30] The concerns of "Junius Brutus" would have been on the lips of many present at the dinner.

Once the tea ship arrived, more handbills circulated, calling for a general meeting at the Exchange the following day to determine a popular course of action, a gathering described by one historian as "one of the most significant events in the coming of the Revolution to South Carolina."[31] The meeting, at which Christopher Gadsden and Charles Pinckney were present, passed resolves to prevent the cargo from being unloaded. In response, "Gentlemen of Trade" (the city's most important merchants, including David Deas) also met at Mrs. Swallow's and organized the Charleston Chamber of Commerce to "coordinate opposition to the boycotts." Just below the Chamber's advertisement, the first theatre notice appeared: "The new Theatre in this town will be opened on Monday next, with *Word to the Wise* and *High Life below Stairs*."[32] Agitated mechanics and Liberty Boys threatened both ship and ship captain, until the *London* shifted its mooring to deeper waters. The captain, Alexander Curling, refused to sail without unloading his goods, Lieutenant Governor Bull was determined to collect the tax if the tea was sold, traders were determined to sell it, and the Liberty Boys threatened merchants who consigned tea. Then more ships arrived; on December 13 the *Magna Carta* (irony not lost) docked, carrying "Green and Bohea TEAS," tea kettles, and tea china.[33]

The whole affair stood at a hostile impasse when the news from Boston upgraded the contest to a state of urgency. On December 16, patriots in Boston had devised their own solution to the problem of tea by dumping it all in the harbor. Of this John Adams wrote proudly: "This is the most Magnificent Movement of all. There is a dignity, a Majesty, a Sublimity in this last effort of the Patriots that I greatly admire. The People should never rise without doing something to be remembered."[34] In Charleston, Gadsden and his radicals were embarrassed that they had not made more of the opportunity; the South Carolina city was, after all, the only port in America in which tea was actually landed.[35] Henry Laurens, by contrast, thought the Boston Mohawks "wily Cromwellians."[36] John Drayton recalled how several successive popular meetings were called throughout December "that the sense of the community might be better collected."[37]

Back and forth went the debates, some thinking as "friends of liberty" on one night, and considering the matter as private merchants on another. They were working out where they stood. "All this evinced a desire," wrote Drayton, "of not entering hastily into measures."[38] Committees, now well established in their protocols, met across the colonies. Men adopted resolves, such as Philadelphia's articulating the "duty of every American to oppose this attempt."[39] Such actions publicly alerted traders to the troubles to be encountered if they chose to traffic in the "baneful weed." Ship captains carrying cargos of tea to Philadelphia and New York returned to England without attempting to discharge their loads. Not so in Boston, obviously, but not so in Charleston, either, where Captain Curling with his 257 chests received a spirited letter that threatened to solve his dilemma by burning the ship. For his part, the captain had the names of Charleston merchants who ordered the tea, and the threat of making them public was as real a danger as firing the ship. It looked like the Stamp Act all over again, and people spoke of it as such.

Any ship entering the port had twenty days to clear its cargo, but none of the consignees were forthcoming, and when its legal period expired, the burden would fall to the collector to seize the cargo for nonpayment of duties. That day was the 21st of December. The immediate showdown was frustrated when Bull, under cover of night, moved the disputed cargo into the basement of the Exchange for nonpayment of customs, avoiding a "Charleston Tea party." Though there was, in America, not a single chest of the new East India tea to be taxed, there was plenty still in stock, and what to do with it was the subject of several meetings of the merchants and planters, and grand meetings of the inhabitants of Charleston, resolving that the tea in "Captain Curling's ship ought not to be landed," and reconfirming "[n]ot to receive or have anything to do with the said tea."[40] Peter Timothy reminded his Charleston readers that in Boston notices were posted threatening destruction to any person meddling with the sale of the cargo."[41] Lexington, Massachusetts, burned the tea in a common bonfire, and Charlestonians entertained that solution as well.[42] The very next night after Bull locked Curling's cargo in the Exchange, the theatre opened "to a polite and crowded" audience.

So what happened, in the midst of this contest over tea, when a popular London play called for tea service onstage before a very powerful, deeply divided audience? In the parlor settings of so many comedies of manners, tea was a routine piece of stage business, and such moments occurred rather frequently in the opening weeks of the winter season in Charleston. The humor of the opening night's afterpiece, *High Life below Stairs*, concerns the running abuse of an aristocratic household by its servants. Suspecting foul play in his pantry, the master stages his own absence and returns, disguised as a new servant, in time for a party thrown by the valet, Philip, who entertains his guests as lord of the manor:

> PHILIP: Well, ladies, what say you to a dance, and then to supper?
> Have you had your tea?
> ALL: A dance, a dance! No Tea, No Tea.[43]

The lines might have rung for a chuckle or two, but tea was the new dividing line between British and Americans, between Whigs and Tories in the audience. Who nodded, who frowned, who laughed, who worried, who watched the many tea scenes in these plays imported from London revealed private convictions by means of public displays. These were moments in which, through which, convictions could be consolidated. In late December 1773, "Have you had your tea?" was precisely the question that wedged and splintered the networks of all these convivial gatherings.

A small moment in the next performance, *Cross Purposes*, raised precisely the same question:

> CHAPEAU: William, bring chocolate. *[Enter Servant.]* Or would you rather have tea, Robin?
> ROBIN: No, thank you, Mr. Chapeau, chocolate if you please. I have left off tea for some time. (1.1.34–36)

Again, on December 30, Douglass and the American Company presented Garrick's *The Clandestine Marriage*, in which a protracted tea conversation is staged. Act 2 begins with a *valet de chambre* and a chambermaid mimicking the manners of their masters. Brush, the valet, makes chocolate in his room; the maid has had her tea already but enters carrying the tea board. The tea sits steeping, while the two sip chocolate and slander their betters, but the scene concludes abruptly with an invitation raised and flatly declined:

> BRUSH: Will you drink tea with me in the afternoon?
> CHAMBERMAID: Not for the world, Mr. Brush.—I'll be here to set all things to right—but I must not drink tea indeed—and so, your servant.—*[Exit with tea board.]* (2.1.63–64)

Innocent lines (and small moments, each of them), but suddenly even these small acts were dangerous.

In the months ahead there would be many public documents generated exactly to this point. Thomas Jefferson drafted one such: "It is further our opinion that as TEA, on its importation into America, is charged with a duty, imposed by parliament for the purpose of raising a revenue, without the consent of the people, it ought not to be used by any person who wishes well to the constitutional rights and liberty of British America."[44] Even the most pronounced patriots, like John Adams, nonetheless found it difficult to give up. Clear into June 1774 Adams inquired of his hostess, "[I]s it lawfull for a weary Traveller to refresh himself with a Dish of Tea, provided it has been honestly smuggled, or paid no Duties?" To which his landlady replied sharply: "No sir, we have renounced all Tea in this place." She poured him coffee instead: "And I have drank Coffee every Afternoon since, and have borne it very well. Tea must be universally renounced. I must be weaned, and the sooner, the better."[45] Exiting with tea boards may be a patriotic position, but it follows first the display of the tea. A boy stands in a small scene in *A Bold Stroke for a Wife* (performed twice that winter in Charleston), with coffee in one hand and asks: "Fresh coffee Gentlemen, fresh coffee?" And in the other: "Bohea-tea, Gentlemen?"[46] "Which will you drink?" asked the stage, in a tableau of the crisis to come. Who nodded, who hissed, who laughed, who jeered? Did these governors and royalists, patriots, militiamen, and traders, and fence-sitters look about at each other and take straw polls? Could they measure the temperature of the times by the response in the playhouse?

The tea issue simmered throughout the winter, in Charleston and elsewhere, and all through the winter season the question echoed on the stage. The loud cries for non-importation were met with a response from a merchant association to protect their trading interests: "We learn that the merchants of this town have formed themselves into a society by the name of the Charlestown chamber of commerce. . . . David Deas, Esq. Treasurer."[47] To counter the Chamber of Commerce, a popular (extralegal) committee was formed in mid-January 1774 to enforce the non-importation of tea. Its forty-five members (among them Gadsden, Moultrie, Lynch, and Rawlins) recalled its genealogy in the Wilkes clubs of 1769, and it would later be called the "Join-or-Be-Ruined Committee."[48] In Philadelphia a similar civic body had just formed with the threatening name "Committee of Tarring and Feathering," and had sent its first letters of introduction to the Delaware pilots regarding the landing of tea.[49] These "associations" would be a notorious force in the days ahead. Abroad, Parliament threatened individual colonies, punished others, closed the port of Boston, and passed the Coercive Acts; and tea seemed to be the fuse that smoldered and hissed as it crawled to a great powder keg. William Smith of New York mused, "I suppose we shall repeat all the confusions of 1765 and 1766."[50] For Abigail Adams in Boston it was quite clear that the tea crisis would precipitate a civil war. Writing to Mercy Otis Warren on December 5, 1773, she noted first: "The tea that baneful weed is arrived. . . . This weed of slavery." Then the dire visions of war follow, inspired by a piece of theatre: "Many, very many of our Heroes will spend their lives in the cause, with the speech of Cato in their mouths, 'What a pitty it is that we can dye but once to save our country.'"[51] To Mrs. Adams, the arrival of the tea was the arrival of the war, and that war would look like a play.

And in the theatre in Charleston those drawing-room comedies played on, with their servants and tea boards poised. Perhaps the most aggressive staging of the tea question is found in a perfectly coercive scene in Isaac Bickerstaff's *School for Fathers*, produced in Charleston on March 4, 1774, when young Diana is pouring, pursuing, and pushing tea on Mr. Harmon:

> DIANA: Well come, let us go into the drawing room and drink tea and afterwards we'll talk of matters.
> HARMON: I won't drink any tea.
> DIANA: Why so?

HARMON: Because I don't like it.
DIANA: Not like it! Ridiculous.
HARMON: I wish you would left me alone.
DIANA: Nay, p'rthee.
HARMON: I won't.
DIANA: Well will you if I consent to act as you please?
HARMON: I don't know whether I will or not.
DIANA: Ha ha ha, Poor Harmon. (2.5.390–400)

Given everything we know about the vocal nature of eighteenth-century audiences, what kind of response might these exchanges have invited? Did Douglass excise such lines from the text? I think not, because the plays that he altered he advertised as such, as with Foote's *Mayor of Garratt* (advertised "with alterations").[52] To play them without recognizing topical applications would be foolish, to acknowledge them dangerous. True enough, Charleston was not Boston, where they were circulating a new song celebrating the victory:

Rally Mohawks! Bring your axes,
And tell King George we'll pay no taxes
    On his foreign tea;
His threats are vain, and vain to think
to force our girls and wives to drink
    His vile Bohea![53]

But Charleston did have the very public forum of a crowded theatre in which actors displayed the most volatile issue of the day, on a tray, asking, "Will you drink it?" A curiosity should be noted: the tea is always declined—"I must not drink tea" they say repeatedly onstage. Or deferred (as in *The Suspicious Husband*: Ranger: "Your tea is a damned while a coming. You shall have no tea now, I assure you." [4.4]). The theatre, by its license, may have been commercially and constitutionally incapable of taking a position on the matter, but its position was determining positions. "I don't know whether I will or not" was the reply that might have been on many minds during the mid-winter months of reckoning season. That small, fraught, deeply thoughtful moment of the actor standing with the tea tray in one hand, coffee in the other: all the politics of identity and crisis of allegiance hung on the decision.

If drinking tea was a political reckoning onstage, how did theatregoers witness the toasting to the king? This too was part of stage traffic; throughout the season that very moment finds expression, as in the opening business of *The Recruiting Officer*. Douglass played Sergeant Kite, the recruiter, throughout his long career:

SERGEANT KITE: I hope gentlemen, you won't refuse the King's health?
ALL MOB: No, no, no!
SERGEANT KITE: Huzza, then! huzza for the King!

What did the house say to that, performed as it was for the Charleston militia, who would train as British and fight as Americans, who gathered in the theatre that night to celebrate the anniversary of the repeal of the Stamp Act? Consider the complexity of this one gesture. During the Stamp Act a man could be (and sometimes was) tarred and feathered for drinking the king's health.[54] But upon that act's repeal, the king's health was restored to the table and routinely toasted. By 1774, the gesture had again become dangerous. The play originally celebrated an early-century war with Spain, but was now somewhat dated, and likely was read with more topical applications. So what version of the king, exactly, was being toasted on that night? Did they toast the original toast of the play, to Queen Anne? Their own King George III, who repealed the Stamp Act? The king that was, the king as he should be? The once king, the past king? Was it an index of current allegiance? Or an allegiance to the idea of kingship, but not the current office-holder? In the imaginary, who is raising glasses, and who is sitting on his hands?

"A TEST OF PUBLIC FEELING"

Why, they deserve to be hanged. I was told they were in a private room, shut up. The person who told me, says he, peeped through the key hole, and saw them wink to each other, and then drink.
ROBERT MUNFORD, *The Patriots* (1776?)

The departing governor of Maryland, Sir Robert Eden, had been as easy and convivial a governor as any colony could hope for, host of many a guest at turf and table, sideboard and side boxes, and on his departure he presided over a dinner for the principal men of the city. His affability notwithstanding, he was still a Crown-appointed governor, and in the fall of 1774 when he departed, reckonings had already been made and great friendships were beginning to sever. A few Whigs accepted the invitation to his farewell, out of long friendship, but they recoiled at the first toast:

> When the cloth was removed, Eden rose, and as usual, gave the first toast: "His Majesty George III." It was customary to drink their toast *standing*. Now it was considered a test of public feeling. Though every man raised his glass, it was returned to the table in silence. When the company was about to retire in an unpleasant mood, [Thomas] Johnson invited the company to dine with him the next day, provided the Governor had no engagements, and would form one of the party. Eden tried to excuse himself, but Johnson would not listen. The next day, the same party met again at dinner. Johnson arose to propose the first toast. He said the King usually received the first honors on such occasions, but as it was more in accordance with his own feelings, and that of his guests, *except the Governor,* he would propose the *Independence of the Colonies.* Eden was startled. He turned pale, sat down his glass, and soon retired. That night a cargo of tea was burned in the harbour of Annapolis.[55]

That exact moment—that first public declaration of position—must have played out repeatedly between 1774 and 1775, when all across British America reckonings were made to unhyphenate those British-American identities. Earlier that fall (September 1774) the delegates could still toast the king at the outset of the Congress—reluctantly, perhaps, but no one went on record declining the courtesy.[56] That position soon shifted. The difficulty in tracking such a private and dangerous decision was that many, like some of the more radical members of Congress, went on toasting His Majesty's health long after their hearts were no longer in it. Up to 1774, everybody may still have been drinking loyalist toasts, but some were more loyal than others. None were more transparent in their duplicity than the Sons of Liberty.

When the Sons of Liberty met in New York to celebrate the repeal of the Stamp Act (March 1770), they concluded their evening with forty-five toasts, and later listed them for print. The first toast was, according to the published sheet, to the king. Though more revealing toasts followed (to Alexander McDougall, to John Wilkes, "to the memory of the Scotch Barons in the Reign of Robert the First"), they began where decent loyal subjects should, with the king.[57] But somebody who was present took exception with their published narrative of the night and disclosed to the editor an alternative account, particularly in regard to the business of the toasts, documented with a list drawn up, apparently, to prompt this soggy population through forty-five distinct bumpers. This list, quoth he, disclosed a different agenda entirely: "The first and second toasts which those *loyal* Sons of Liberty *actually* drank, as appears from a printed Copy of them for the Day, were, 1st May the American Colonies fully enjoy the British Constitution. 2nd the King, *as the Head and Preserver of the Constitution.*" In the public record, they were good loyal subjects toasting the health and long life of their sovereign, but clearly they were a very different body in their meetings, their clubs, their celebrations, and it was in the toasting that these two agendas parted ways.[58]

By the time the war started, toasting the king was grounds for arrest and incarceration. Robert Munford might sport at arresting a Scottish tinker for "drinking the King's health" but that is exactly how States Dyckman was arrested. After the fighting had broken out between America and England, Dyckman had been with a small party of loyalists drinking to "the damnation of the King's enemies" at Cartright's Inn, Albany, on the king's birthday when the party was overheard; the intention of this gathering was passed on, and soon a group of Sons of Liberty intruded and arrested the lot.[59]

So what happens in the playhouse when the king is toasted onstage? Consider the same moment in Dodley's *The King and the Miller of Mansfield* (staged twice in Charleston on January 8, 1774 and again on February 10, 1774.) Here is the Miller and the disguised king pledges his own toast:

> MILLER: Come, Sir, you must mend a bad Supper with a Glass of good Ale: here's King Harry's health.
> KING: With all my Heart. Come, Richard, here's King Harry's health; I hope you are Courtier enough to pledge me, are not you?

RICHARD: Yes, Yes sir, I'll drink the King's Health with all my
Heart. (1.7.1–9)

And so they drink. And so did many in clubs outside the theatre. And many others sat and waited, politely perhaps, or not, and others still who toasted with no heart for it, for form's sake, or fear's sake, or just simple incredulous indecision. But how do we read their intentions in an act so ordinary and so profound? How does one stage allegiance to Great Britain, or resistance to the king, in such times when intentional, or not, such moments as toasting] would be read with a political appetite that positioned the company and the audience in the crosshairs of nationalism? How does one raise a British flag onstage (as in *The Reprisal*), or toast a king, or declare as the newly enlisted ensign Charles Dudley does in Cumberland's *The West Indian*, "I prefer the service of my king to that of any other master," or stage a rebellion, as is at the heart of every history play that same season, or kill a king onstage and not, at some level, be read locally?

DRUMMING FOR SOLDIERS

Earlier that spring, a similar "test of public feelings" transpired in Charleston, toasts and all, with the lieutenant governor, William Bull, proposing the king's health to the principal men of the city, in this case the officers of the Charleston militia. It was a curious and to some degree duplicitous evening, a tad premature for many to declare positions publicly. Still, reckonings were in the air. Minds were being made up, and a few moments in this process are legible.

On March 18, 1774, the anniversary of the repeal of the Stamp Act, another social gathering graced the tables of Swallow's Tavern: the Charleston militia. After their drill and dress parade before the lieutenant governor, the citizen soldiers enjoyed a pastime with good company, with a dinner sponsored by Bull and the officers. They consumed volumes of madeira, port, and beer, and Bull, as was his place, proposed the toasts: the king's health, then the queen's, then the royal governor's. Peter Timothy, who reported on the evening, did not record who, if any, abstained, but rather related the willingness of all present to live "in loyal and harmonious joy" and did so with such an excess of zeal that one begins to suspect something entirely ironic is afoot. The protestations for peace seem just a little too vocal to be sincere.[60]

But there were, in fact, two dinners that evening. The first with the governor present, when the "many loyal and constitutional toasts were drunk." Then the party adjourned to the theatre to watch George Farquhar's *The Recruiting Officer*, after which "they returned to the Mrs. Swallows, to supper."[61] We have no records of this second meeting, and that is the inviting part. No list of the toasts on this occasion, who proposed, who stood, who declined, as if, one may be tempted to conclude, the first gathering was the public, official show for the lieutenant governor, and the second a more private affair. Between the two, the Charleston militia, who had polished their drills and paraded their readiness (against whom?), watched a play about the recruiting of soldiers occasioned by the anniversary of the first American victory over British policy.

The anniversary and its annual celebration was not entirely a present moment; it was itself a reenactment, an attempt to recapture the original euphoria of the repeal back in 1766. Each year since the spirit of that victory had been stoked with celebrations that marked the elation of that glorious spring when Parliament "caved to colonial demands."[62] It was the first American populist victory, mythologized annually with toasts, dinners, celebrations, and fireworks, much of which, like the "Hearts of Oak" they sang, had lost something of the original efficacy and a great deal of loyalty eight years and several miscarried acts later.

Originally, the citizens of New York had voted to erect a statue of King George III for repealing the Stamp Act. That same population was now less than two years away from pulling it down and melting it for cannonballs. This erosion of loyalty would have percolated through much of the evening, finding its moments to leach out as high irony. Indeed, celebrating the proto-victory in the thick of the tea crisis may already have been a coded performance whose texts ostensibly declared loyalty (the toasts proposed by the lieutenant governor), but whose gathering was attended with a substratum of dissent. Certainly there were officers present who were drinking the king's health with one hand and preventing the distribution of the king's tea with the other.[63] Certainly there were officers present who would use their military commission in the service of American liberty. Certainly there were officers and militia present who had very different ambitions for the mustering of munitions. Indeed, even the raising of recruits and the training of a new militia may themselves have been riddled with the same irony.

This day Colonel Charles Cotesworth Pinckney mustered men and toasted the king and governor, but once the war officially commenced, Pinckney would volunteer for the Continental Army and fight valiantly to defend Charleston. Where was he in his own reckoning on this evening? Were traces of that conversion from loyalist to patriot present that evening of the anniversary of the repeal? Macartan Campbell, the St. Andrew's officer who commanded the Light Horse that day, was another Scotsman, but a Charleston patriot of the revolution. He would break with most of his Scottish community and would be unequivocally American once the war commenced. Members of the assembly, who also joined the dinner, including Pinckney and William Moultrie, had forced the lieutenant governor's hand when they insisted that the £1,500 of the public treasury that had been promised to the radical John Wilkes should be paid, against the governor's objection, and that mini-triumph may also have been part of the celebration that evening. Pinckney was among the council members who had voted for the original Wilkes fund in 1769, the last installment of which Bull still denied as late as a week before the militia dinner. Bull had written harshly of the matter but a week earlier, and one cannot imagine that the wounds had healed much.

Many of those same officers and men of that militia praised for their "armed maneuvers" would use their training for military action against Great Britain, and the rupture would happen very quickly. But this was not Boston; these were not British troops quartered in their houses, camped on their Common, locking up their harbors, firing on their citizens. These were Charleston militiamen, ostensibly organized to prevent slave uprisings, Indian attacks (though William Bull had just written to the Earl of Dartmouth on March 10, 1774, that "I have not received any accounts of mischief being done by the Indians since the 23rd of January"), and some vague threat of "the Spanish," drilling and mustering on the threshold of a monumental decision that had, for some, already begun.[64] They were training with arms, and nobody was openly speaking about why the need for a standing militia at

182]   CHAPTER TWELVE

this time, only to be ready, as was their charge—that and news of the British fleet en route to seal off Boston harbor.

What we do hear is a kind of "speaking through." The drilling of the Boston militia spoke through the fear of another war with France. In October 1774, when the Continental Congress was in its inaugural session, South Carolina imported large quantities of gunpowder and munitions, and Timothy assured his readers the weapons were needed because of "the extraordinary warlike preparations of the Spanish."[65] Peter Timothy spoke through the Spanish threat. Pamphlets routinely spoke through classical references—Cato, Junius Brutus, Caesar, Sejanus, Catiline—in their quest to speak of London, King George, and tyranny. Plays routinely spoke through their subjects. *The Tars of Old England* speaks through the threat of the French; *The Recruiting Officer* speaks through the threat of the Spanish, recycling the now-resolved conflicts of the Seven Years' War and the War of the Spanish Succession. Nobody overtly alerted the readers or auditors that Caesar equaled King George, that the French threat had become the British threat, that the warlike Spanish all wear British redcoats; they were simply understood to be analogous, to be, in Georg Lukacs's phrase, "the pre-history of the present."

The theatre was one of the more potent forums for speaking unspeakable things. Caesar and Cato, recruitment and rebellion, tea and toasting, the strained models of the subject-monarch relationship, all find their most concentrated circulation on the stage, nodding and winking through a network of analogies that all seem to find their essential narrative framework in a playhouse that presents and makes present the critical thresholds of identity. This imagining constituted a rehearsal of the revolution, making the unthinkable a little more thinkable. This is what John Adams had in mind when he wrote of the revolution occurring first "in the minds of the people": a gradual imagining of enormous changes.

All this season of plays and convivial gatherings could be read as just so many innocent diversions—just the Masons watching *Cato*— were it not that occasionally somebody went public and gave up the code that everybody already knew. Once transparent, the code forever abdicates its innocence. William Bull wrote to the Earl of Dartmouth in England in August of 1774 that his assembly, radicalized by the Boston Port Bill, was now requesting guns "for the frontier," they claimed, with a very clear understanding they could be used elsewhere:

> They had prepared a message to me, which the prorogation prevented, to desire I would purchase a number of small arms to be given to many poor Irish and others in our western frontiers, with ammunition upon the apprehensions of an Indian war. Whenever that appears to me unavoidable, I shall take every step in my power to enable them to defend themselves. It is not improbable but many of the poor Irish may have been White boys, Hearts of Oak or hearts of Steel, who have been accustomed to oppose law and authority in Ireland, may not change their disposition with their climate, and may think of other objects than Indians. In the warmth of argument, which is an artful method of extracting secrets, words are sometimes incautiously dropped which convey ideas of extremities in case of their failing in the expectations of redress.[66]

So while the colony's militia desired to hone its skills on new arms and ammunition provided by Great Britain, the Heart of Oak boys—themselves transported rebels from Ireland—were hinting at extremities, and the assembly requested arms with other enemies than Indians in mind, the lieutenant governor watched cautiously and proposed loyalist toasts that were honored (in word at least) by many who were also members of the Wilkes Club, or candidates of the Mechanics Association (Pinckney), the General Committee (Moultrie), or Christopher Gadsden's corps (the artillery company). All pledged their loyalty and training in arms, and who was winking at whom? Great preparations, great reckonings are made in such little rooms.

Farquhar's *Recruiting Officer*, a well-known comedy about the chicanery deployed in drumming up soldiers for the king's wars, certainly celebrated soldiering, but it also staged the very coerciveness of the long day's activity. The officers had underwritten the dinner at Mrs. Swallow's, the officers proposed all of the loyalists' toasts, and the officers sponsored the night at the theatre as well, including the selection of the play. The coercion reenacts that of the play itself, positioning the sponsors as so many recruiting officers, cajoling, coercing, entrapping, and signing the rank-and-file militiamen, over a great quantity of drink, and sealing the deal with a toast to the king. Philip Fithian, the New Jersey tutor, recorded the worries of many of his neighbors that same spring: "The lower class of people here are in tumult on account of reports from Boston, many of them expect to be press'd and compelled to go and fight the Britains!"[67] In the play, Sergeant Kite (played by Douglass) does exactly this, plying his prospects with drink; they toasting the king and queen, declare their loyalty louder with each successive pint, and sign on until sobriety reveals the chicanery and nullifies the contract. The irony—exposed only later—is that of course one can celebrate soldiering on both sides of the war. And lest we render it solely a loyalist play, we should recall that *The Recruiting Officer* was one of two plays staged by Washington's officers at Valley Forge, while British soldiers enjoying their ease in Philadelphia that winter staged the very same play.

These fantasies of polite assemblies in taverns and playhouses in the winter of the tea crisis, toasting the king and governor, quickly gave way to a more radical agenda that surprised even William Bull, and the rapidity of the sea change should alert us that the change had already been under way for some time before surfacing. A scant three months after the dress parade, "the greatest concourse of Charlestonians ever assembled" gathered to vote on members to send to the first Continental Congress. The king's birthday (June 4) came and went in Charleston with an enforced show of official support—cannons fired, Bull hosting another dinner—but utterly without popular support. Wrote Bull, "[N]ot a single house was illuminated."[68] The small moments in the theatre had documented this unmaking of British identity, this shedding of old affiliations and expectations, and the fashioning of something new: Americans.

The drumming for soldiers that played that late March night in the theatre had undergone the same transatlantic sea change. What had once served in Queen Anne's time to satirize the enlisting of soldiers for foreign wars had been refashioned into something cautiously duplicitous. Recruitment had commenced all right, but not for the queen's army. The play had now become a portmanteau, a trunk that packs and unpacks from both ends. The duplicity of such texts that season allowed the radical realignment to cohabit with and within the traditional sphere of discourse for so long, to pack in and pack out in the same small rooms.

THE HOUSE OF TWO DOORS

Let me italicize the duplicity within the Church Street theatre building itself. The theatre did not sell tickets directly; they were available at the printer's shop of Robert Wells, or the box-keeper's house, John Calvert. These two names were published in all three of the city's newspapers on January 28, 1774, April 25, 1774, and May 10, 1774, and advertised on the playbill for the May 11, 1774, Masonic benefit of *Cato*. By design or by coincidence, Wells was known to be ultra-royalist, and Calvert ultra-radical.

The latter was one of Christopher Gadsden's Sons of Liberty men. A small merchant, brewer, and bookkeeper, Calvert kept the books for the theatre and seating lists for the boxes and sold tickets, primarily to box-holders, which meant that his house was the point of entry for the elite. He was remembered as one of "the original 26 Liberty Tree Boys, to pledge resistance to Great Britain," back in 1765. His radicalism was not mollified by the general prosperity of the early 1770s, and when the Revolutionary War broke out he served on the Council of Safety; later, he was appointed the first secretary of the South Carolina navy, wounded at the battle of Beauford in 1779, and expelled from Charleston during the British occupation for refusing to take the oath of allegiance to the Crown.[69] He was, in short, a deeply committed patriot.

If theatre-goers objected to Calvert's politics, they could purchase tickets from a hardened loyalist, Robert Wells. When Calvert was assembling with the Sons of Liberty in 1765, Wells had declared publicly, "I wish to be under the direction of the British Parliament and not our little Provincial Senate aping the grandest Assembly in the world without Knowledge, skill, power or any other requisite almost."[70] Wells would lose his business at the outbreak of hostilities and retreat to England, where his family would claim compensation from the Crown as displaced loyalists.

Perhaps the politics of the ticket-seller didn't matter to the purchaser. But I find it curious that two ordinary Charlestonians whose politics were farther apart could not be found: both sold the tickets, both doors led to the same theatre, yet that theatre played the same play to two very different audiences. How one watched that play may have had a great deal to do with what door one entered.

Consider one very public play, the benefit night for the Masonic lodge—the most advertised evening of the season. For that occasion, the play was Addison's *Cato*, a play, as it happens, the American Company had not performed for many years (retired in March 1768) and the only play in a fifty-eight-play repertory not chosen by the manager—a play that appealed greatly to more than one audience and was known by every literate person on the continent. That Douglass did not choose the piece and that it had been dropped from the repertory may tell us something about how audiences read and heard this play. The *Cato* purchased from Robert Wells would not be same play as the *Cato* purchased from John Calvert. To the radicals, *Cato* would function as Abigail Adams read it, to inspire martyrs to the love of liberty and die, like Nathan Hale, with a line of *Cato* on their lips. Indeed, the muscular, charismatic speech of Sempronius would work remarkably well to inspire fervent patriotism, and we find it quoted as such, by patriots up and down the colonies:

> When liberty is gone,
> Life grows insipid, and has lost its relish.
> Oh, could my dying hand but lodge a sword
> In Caesar's bosom, and revenge my country,
> By heav'ns I could enjoy the pangs of death,
> And smile in agony. (2.3.13–18)

"Huzza!" said the Whigs, while the loyalists rolled their eyes. Surely they knew these words were spoken by the most disreputable character in the play, the dissembler who betrays Cato to traitors and then betrays the traitors? Sempronius, like Iago, is a highly unstable and untrustworthy site from which to declare a position. Cato, after all, had failed; his rebellion and his little senate collapsed and he committed suicide. So was this a loyalist tale of the dangers of dissent? Or was Abigail Adams right to find in it inspiration for martyrdom in the pursuit of liberty?

Cato was followed by an after piece, *The Reprisal, or Tars of Old England*, originally written during the Seven Years' War to vilify the French. It was a jingoistic celebration of the might of the British navy, but featured a disaffected Scotsman (played by Douglass), a refugee from the '45, now a loyalist abetting in the rescue of an English family from French privateers. The piece was studded with maritime anthems, such as "Hearts of Oak," except, as we have seen, the song now hosted dual sets of lyrics that so thoroughly cohabited in the same melody that they too, like the playhouse and the plays within it, would serve both audiences. And so when Stephen Woolls, the finest tenor of the company, sang "Hearts of Oak," one can only wonder which version of the song the actor sang, the traditional lyrics celebrating the might of Great Britain, or Dickinson's lyrics inspiring commercial resistance? Or a parody of Dickinson's parody, or a parody of that parody? Did they declare a position, or diminish by parody all positions? And who was listening to who was singing which lyrics? And was the chorusing a reckoning of sorts? Which version would Sir Egerton sing, that master Mason whom no one loved? And to oppose him, which version would the other Masons sing? What was the militia singing? Because which version they chose to sing, voice by voice, choice by choice, had everything to do with the final installment of the American transformation.

Whatever was going on in this house of two doors, it was very popular. The Church Street Theatre was crowded, night after night, right down to the last performance (May 19, 1774), when Douglass was still complaining of gentlemen sitting on the stage: "[I]t is almost impossible that the Performers can do their Characters that justice their Duty to the Publick requires, when the stage is crowded, as it has been for several nights past."[71]

I ask of their reception, not because so much ink has been spilled in the quoting of *Cato* in the Revolution, but because *Cato* was only one of a season of plays that openly played with rebellion. Consider its company for that last season: *Henry IV, Part 1, King John, Douglas, Tamberlane, Julius Caesar, King Lear, Richard III, The Earl of Essex, Macbeth,* even *Romeo and Juliet* might embody the civil broils topically. It remains a curious feature of the American Company's last season in America, but as the hostilities between the two cultures became increasingly pronounced, the theatre began to represent rebellion plays with a concentration unseen in the repertory before 1774. Six of their last ten plays took for their theme the subject/monarch relationship, and the violent rupturing of that contract. Douglass was playing with rebellion, and it wasn't pretty. What I have been suggesting is that these were not innocent nights in the playhouse, but rather part of the great reckonings of identity. I want to close with a final case study, the last professional play in British America.

MARKETING REBELLION

The complexity of the political situation meant that the season's appeal never lay in its unabashed commercialism, contrary to what David Mays has concluded ("in short, whatever paid, played").[72] Public businesses had their positions, and those positions were generally known. Newspapers, for example, jockeyed for business in a partisan town by proclaiming on their masthead, as Isaiah Thomas had, "Open to All Parties, Influenced by None," although every reader knew where the editor stood on the "American question."[73] Isaiah Thomas established the *Massachusetts Spy*, a newspaper expressly devoted to "the free use of the press . . . especially when its productions tend to defend the Glorious Cause of Liberty." The printer promised his readers "great regard will always be paid to such political pieces as tend to secure to us our invaluable rights and privileges."[74] By contrast, the *Pennsylvania Ledger*, a loyalist paper, prominently displayed the royal coat of arms in its banner. Members of the public often knew where public institutions as well as private merchants stood on important issues. Thus, where the theatre stood in its final season in colonial America is worth asking, so long as one asks it in a way that acknowledges the complexity of the problem. By its license, the theatre could not engage in overt positioning (Douglass's permission was dependent on Crown-appointed governors). But something deeply coded was afoot, and once asked, everything becomes a cipher for uncoding it. Douglass's choice of printers (Robert Wells) is fair inquiry, as are the associations he supported, such as St. Andrew's, and their affiliations; the politics of his landlords (Wells, Michie, Rowand, all loyalists); and even the location of the theatre itself: on the corner of Church and Tradd Streets, sharing a block with Robert Wells's bookstore and the residences of Robert Wells, Colonel John Stuart (lot 106 Tradd), George Rouppel (the postmaster and customs officer for the port), David Deas (lot 128 Tradd), and Robert Rowand, all loyalists, and, incidentally, the same block where Douglass and his wife also lodged, at Mrs. Dawson's.[75] George Saxby, the stamp distributor, whose house was the scene of a

Sons of Liberty riot during the Stamp Act, also lived on Tradd Street.[76] Indeed, during the Revolution this block of Tradd Street between Orange and Church Streets came to be known as "Tory Row."[77] This is not to imply that location itself was a marker of ideology; but in a time of great reckonings, such associations of politics, company, and neighborhood would have been read in this way, with a sophistication greater than our own, and so it behooves us to listen to the period's associations with the theatre.

The following two moments may reveal something of the theatre's own reckoning. Jacob Mordecai lived in Philadelphia between 1762 and 1784 and saw his first plays there in the spring of 1773. Some years later he wrote a brief impression of the Southwark Playhouse that included this telling observation: "British band formed the orchestra, 12 Regimental [illegible] centinels [sic] stood near the stage. Boxes one on each side."[78] Mordecai also names some actors and the plays—Hallam, Henry, Woolls, Morris—that clearly identify the performance he witnessed as the American Company's productions of *The Beaux' Stratagem* and *Catherine and Petruchio*, on March 17, 1773, a benefit for Mr. and Mrs. Morris. Mordecai notes a British band (from one who lived through the Revolution, this suggests a military band), and British sentinels "near" the stage. This was the spring Douglass staged *The Conquest of Canada*, with full military onstage. On several occasions in that spring of 1773, the British military were all over the theatre in Philadelphia, and again in New York in the summer of 1773, with the bands of the Twenty-Third Regiment or the Welsh Fusiliers providing the orchestra.[79] Does being chummy with the regiment make the theatre a royalist space? Of course not; but lining the stage with sentinels implicitly governs the codes of conduct within that space. Were they there to keep the peace, or to provoke? Was Mordecai watching the plays, or watching plays through the British military?

William Alexander Levingston, (a modest New York leather merchant) took a page from his account book ("60 hides I carried in the waggon £72.0.0") and recorded all the plays of the American Company in New York from April through July 1773. He noted the ones he attended (most of them), as well as the few he missed, and what songs were performed, what Masonic prologues and epilogues. Midway through the list he notes, "Theatre Royal in New York, these plays were performed in April, May, and June."[80] The fact that a leather merchant described the company as a "Theatre Royal" suggests that the notion of the playhouse as a Crown patent theatre was in circulation, or that its position in the division of British and America was unambiguous. A theatre under Crown protection would solve issues of legitimacy, but in 1773 royal protection (in New York) and a military presence (in Philadelphia) would also firmly position the theatre as an appendage to Crown interests.

The subsequent history of the American Company would seem to bear this out. Once the company left America, they would travel to Jamaica, a declared loyalist island. There they would pursue their last best market: the British military. At one later point in Jamaica the military even staged a benefit for the acting company. Douglass would eventually leave the stage and assume various positions with the British colonial administration of Jamaica, including that of His Majesty's printer. His subsequent position would be very clear—a royalist of the first order—but that was not a position he openly declared in the spring of 1774 in Charleston.

As the conflict heated up, though the theatre may not have openly declared an allegiance, the stories chosen all had one inevitable end: the plays themselves were already trapped by a genre that was itself circumscribed by royal authority. Tragedy, in particular, was already predisposed to royalism. *Cato, Julius Caesar, Henry IV, King John*, all played in Charleston in the spring of 1774, may contest the legitimacy of the current monarchy, but monarchy itself is the structured resolution of tragedy; without it lies only a landscape of civic and moral chaos. In tragedy, even historical tragedy, moral order is restored with kingship, a structural model of thinking that would be of little use to a generation conceiving of a nation without kingship.

As the American Company's last season closed with the electing of delegates to the First Continental Congress in May of 1774, the repertory increasingly reflected on the dangers of civil war: *Julius Caesar, Macbeth, Tamerlane, Cato, Douglas*, and *King John*. Shakespeare's *King John* (the King John of the Magna Carta contract) proved the last play professionally performed in America, on May 19, 1774. In a key scene, Philip Falconbridge, the illegitimate son of Richard Lionheart (called here "Bastard') attempts to suppress a rebellion against King John:

BASTARD (Lewis Hallam): Now hear our English King,
For thus his Royalty doth speak in me.
. . . .
. . . Know the gallant monarch is in arms,
And like an eagle o'er his eyrie towers,
To souse annoyance that comes near his nest.
And you degenerate, you ingrate revolts,
You bloody Neroes, ripping up the womb
Of your dear mother England, blush for shame. (5.2.128–153)[81]

Is this the last word of the theatre in America prior to the Revolution? The ingrate revolts of the play do not blush for shame (though one can imagine no little squirming in the boxes), but commence their unpromising contest of war—Alarum, drums, the drop scene of war, and enter Melun, the French count, wounded, soon to expire, whose dying breaths again upbraid the rebels:

MELUN (to the English rebels): Fly, noble English; you are bought
 and sold.
Unthread the rude eye of rebellion,
And welcome home again discarded faith;
Seek out King John and fall before his feet. (5.4.10–14)

And indeed, the ingrate rebels have a change of heart and return in humility to King John, unthread their rebellion, and are forgiven their trespass.

Perhaps with such fantasies in mind Douglass closed the season by sending Lewis Hallam off to London to recruit more actors and purchase new scenes, promising his American patrons a "theatrical force thitherto unknown."

[CHAPTER 13]

Christopher Gadsden's Wharf

Charleston, Summer 1774

• • •

THE FOUR-HORSE PHAETON

If one sought out the ten wealthiest people in colonial America in 1774, nine of them could be found within a carriage ride of Charleston. In spite of the vigorous join-or-die committees, boycotts, and nonimportation agreements elsewhere in the colonies, at the close of May 1774 business had never been better in Charleston. In spite of recent turmoil (the last two years had seen a plummet of tobacco prices as much as 50 percent, which led to tightened credit and foreclosures in many southern and middle colonies), Charleston was prospering. By population, it was the fourth largest city in America, but by far the wealthiest per capita.[1] Josiah Quincy, Jr., traveling down from Boston, described the city in the winter of 1773–1774 as "in grandeur, splendour of buildings, decorations, equipages, numbers, commerce, shipping, indeed in almost every thing, it far surpasses all I ever saw, or expected to see, in America," an observation echoed by many foreign visitors.[2] Three hundred fifty ships "lay off the town," noted Quincy, "and the new exchange which fronted the place of my landing made a most noble appearance."[3] Walter Edgar notes that in 1774 there were 148 carriage-makers in Charleston, a figure that astonishes when compared to the two or three able carriage-makers in the capital of Virginia, for example.[4] Diversified crops of rice and indigo shipped out at unprecedented volumes, prices held strong, and demand was high. The affluence of the town was seen in the goods that filled newspaper advertisements, wharfs, and the storefronts of Charleston.

At the close of May 1774, Thomas Jefferson penned his first serious political tract, *Resolutions against Trade with England*, in which he advocated for "a complete stop to all imports from Great Britain," excepting only necessaries like gunpowder and medicine. But the *South Carolina Gazette* at the same time advertised for nothing but a decadent array of British offerings: "superfine broadcloths," "superfine flour," fowling pieces (just imported), hosiery, fashionable silks, optical instruments, upholstered chairs, paints, oil, glass, madeira wine, all enticing the reader as "the latest from London." Everybody, it seemed, was a merchant, whose last ship from London was bringing the very latest genteel goods directly to Charleston residents. Anyone with a trade could get in on the import game, and most did.

The Charleston men with whom Douglass had sailed to London a decade earlier—David Deas and Dr. Carne—were traders, but now even the ship captain Henry Gunn offered imported wine for sale, dockside. There were goods everywhere, including a brisk business in slaves (five ads deep), a commerce underwrote the production of raw agricultural goods, such as rice and indigo, and afforded all these high-end items. Here in Charleston in May of 1774, amid talk of a total boycott of British goods, Bristol Beer, silk umbrellas, Gloucester cheese, newly fashioned ribbons, superfine millinery, luxury craftsmen, carriage-makers, and coach-painters were available. Here were huge fortunes built on transatlantic trade. And Thomas Jefferson, two colonies to the north, was advocating a general boycott of all British goods? The papers in Charleston where Douglass had just finished his most successful season suggested that nothing would stop the trading.[5]

Douglass too rode high on the wave of the latest goods. His season in Charleston had been an enormously lucrative one, financially, socially, and professionally. When Douglass had first entered New York back at the close of 1758, he had been little better than a stroller defending his gentility: "Mr. Douglass, the director of the company, is of a good family, and has a genteel and liberal education; and if we may judge from behavior, conduct, and conversation, has better pretensions to the name of a gentleman in every sense of the word, than he who so politely and generously lavishes the appellation of vagrant and stroller on him."[6]

Now, fifteen years later, he had arrived at a certain gentility. He was David Douglass, Esquire ("Yesterday arrived in town from Charleston, David Douglass, Esq: Manager of the American Company of Comedians").[7] He now owned seven theatres in five colonies outright; he enjoyed strong relationships with seven colonial governors and mixed with the best of colonial society from Charleston to New York. He drove a four-horse phaeton through a one-street town (Williamsburg), a half mile from playhouse to church pew. He had become carriage folk in a colony where, as Philip Fithian described, "almost every Gentleman of Condition keeps a chariot and Four."[8] When he left Williamsburg in 1772, he advertised the carriage for sale, with an emphasis on its genteel display: "A Genteel Pheton, not more than eighteen months old, in excellent order, very strong and newly lined and painted. There is a harness for four horses, made not above 9 months ago, genteelly ornamented with brass plates, etc."[9]

That was the beautiful thing about America: many immigrants learned they could refashion themselves. Wigs, carriages, manners, and titles could all be acquired and displayed by those who would seem to be what they had only just become. The speed of such a transformation, once generational, was accelerated in America, compressed, as we have seen, into a span of a dozen years. America had become a culture of reinvention. The road to Esquire was greased with money, character, and "scratching" networks of acquaintances. Douglass was not the only one who had done very well by it, and they were getting rich.

THE NEW WHARF

[M]any affecting circumstances in my little Family intervening those together with a large Wharf or rather, quay, the largest in America, which I undertook at first to relieve my Mind for the almost insupportable Loss of my eldest son, a very promising youth of about sixteen years old, has so taken up my attention that unless when the Assembly was sitting I very seldom appear'd in Publick.
CHRISTOPHER GADSDEN to Samuel Adams, May 23, 1774

On March 7, 1774, the *South Carolina Gazette* reported that the "stupendous work . . . was nearly completed." Peter Timothy was referring to the largest new building project in Charleston: Christopher Gadsden's new wharf. It was extraordinary, 840 feet long, truly, as Gadsden described to Adams, the longest wharf in America, long enough, he claimed, for no less than thirty ships to load or unload simultaneously, built from 3,500 pilings, beached with 14,000 bushels of oyster shells, with warehouses large enough to store 10,000 pounds of rice.[10] The *Gazette* called it "the most extensive of the kind ever undertaken by any one man in America." It was the culmination of an eight-year project and represented a substantial investment in sustained transatlantic trading from one of the most radical representatives of South Carolina. In the words of David Ramsay, the future son-in-law of Henry Laurens, the wharf in the summer of 1774 was "just beginning to yield an interest on the immense capital expended in building it. His [Gadsden's] whole prospect of reimbursement was founded on the continuance of trade."[11] If Christopher Gadsden, the most vocal supporter of non-importation in the colony, was still investing at this scale in transatlantic trade, the prospect seemed quite good for others.

Timothy used Gadsden's new wharf to summarize the prosperity of Charleston in the opening of 1774:

> Besides the stupendous work now nearly completed by Christopher Gadsden, Esq. at the north end of this Town which is reckoned to be the most extensive of the kind ever undertaken by any one man in America, it is amazing to observe the other improvements that have within a very few years past been made here and are daily carrying on. More than six new and commodious Wharves have been added to our water-front. In the same period a great Assembly Room has been built, and within six months past an elegant Theatre established by which a Company of Comedians are handsomely supported.
>
> White Point is almost covered with houses, many of them very elegant. Several excellent academies have been established for the education of the Youth of this Province; great attention is also paid to the Fine Arts, the St. Cecilia Society warmly patronized music, while many Gentlemen of Taste and Fortune are giving the utmost Encouragement to Architecture, Portraiting and the ingenuous [sic] performances of the first capital Landscape Painter that visited America, whose works will do him Honor. And shall it be said that such a People will suffer themselves to sink into Slavery?[12]

The prosperity and refinement of the town—its wharfs, its theatre, its music, its very gentility—would surely be enough to forestall the rebellion. So thought Peter Timothy, and so thought Douglass, who signed a fifteen-year lease on his new theatre, had just imported from London "a set of most superb habits" ("at immense expense," he was quick to add), and promised Charleston an even better season on his return.[13] When his company closed, a summary of the season was penned for the *South Carolina Gazette* (Timothy), but in his insistence on staying on the lips of colonists elsewhere, Douglass had the review of the Charleston season sent to Williamsburg, where it was reprinted in the *Virginia Gazette* of June 16, 1774:

> On Friday last [19 May] the Theatre, which opened here the 22d of December, was closed. Warmly countenanced and supported by the publick, the Manager and his Company were excited to the most strenuous efforts to render their entertainments worthy of so respectable a patronage. If it is considered how late it was in the season before the house could be opened, the variety of scenery and decorations necessary to a regular theatre, the number of plays represented (fifty-eight) and that almost every piece required particular preparations, it must be confessed that the exertions of the American Company have been uncommon, and justly entitle them to those marks of publick favour that have, for so many years, stamped a merit on their performances. The Choice of Plays hath been allowed to be very judicious, the Director having selected from the most approved English Poets such Pieces as possess in the highest Degree the *Utile Dulce,* and while they entertain, improve the Mind by conveying the most useful Lessons of Morality and Virtue. The Company have separated until the Winter, when the New York Theatre will be opened, Mr. Hallam being embarked for England to engage some recruits for that service. The year after they will perform at Philadelphia, and in the winter following we may expect them here with a theatrical force hitherto unknown in America. Scratch me, countryman! and I'll scratch thee.

What strikes the reader is not that the summary is so full of praise, that it is so full of production details and itineraries, that it appears to have been composed by Douglass to advance the currency of the company as a solid, longstanding, moral, and useful accessory to colonial life, but rather how forward-looking it is for colonies on the eve of chaos. Douglass was formulating a three-year business plan while at the same time the colonies were electing delegates to their first extralegal Congress and the British warships sent to seal off Boston Harbor were within sight of land.

Of course, none of the plans came to pass, but one very astute and very well-connected man of business in a town of traders had a hard look at the situation, the new wharfs and crowded theatres, and concluded in May of 1774 business in America would be just fine.

Then, on the first day of June, the port of Boston was closed, and following the lead of Samuel Adams, radicals across the colonies began to propose a total cessation of trade with Great Britain. But the first gesture of solidarity took on a more solemn and determined aspect. In Virginia, on June 1, the House of Burgesses declared and observed a day of "Fasting, Humiliation, and Prayer," an expression honored in many other cities as well. Philadelphia also closed its shops, muffled its bells, and lowered its colors to half-staff in solidarity with Boston.[14] The grammar of the gesture—fasting and prayer—was Jefferson's brainchild, borrowed directly from the days of the English civil war, and it meant, in spirit at least, that with a single unifying gesture the vibrant trading business of Charleston, Philadelphia, the tidewater towns of Virginia, tied themselves to the embargo of Boston Harbor. Just a few weeks into that summer, all across the colonies, general assemblies were convened to elect delegates to attend a general congress in Philadelphia, to determine what action should collectively be taken in response to the closing of the port of Boston.

News of the threat of a general boycott spread across the colonies. When Virginia broker James Robinson learned that the townspeople of Boston had determined "to stop all importation from and exportation to Great Britain and every part of the West Indies," he wrote, "In answer to this proposition the committee of Philadelphia required time to collect the sentiments of the inhabitants of not only the city but colony on a measure of so great importance. The inhabitants of Annapolis entered warmly into the proposal and have made some violent resolves, besides putting a stop to all exports and imports."[15]

And so it went, colony by colony, with "violent resolves," as the new lyrics to "Hearts of Oak" boasted:

> Our purses are ready
> > Steady, friends, steady,
> > Not as slaves, but as freemen our money we'll give.

But to the rank-and-file merchants and large traders, this talk of a general cessation of trade was hot-headed and spelled the downfall of both parties. Even among the five delegates South Carolina had elected, only Christopher Gadsden was uncompromising about a total boycott. The business was watched anxiously by many a merchant, including Robinson, who wrote apprehensively to his trading partner on June 1, 1774:

> Letters are to be written to the representative of each county to take the opinion of the people on this important affair. What determination they may then come to is uncertain. It is said that a non-importation agreement will be entered into, as well as resolutions to suspend at some future day exporting any commodities to Great Britain. As the consideration of this affair is thus delayed some are of the opinion that something decisive may be done at Boston before then. Meanwhile our violent patriots, of which there are a number, will cool and they will consult reason and their own interests in the measures then embraced.[16]

Gadsden lobbied hard to ensure support for the plight of Boston, but the moderates in-house quashed a complete boycott of British goods. This vote was echoed when the proposal arose in Philadelphia as well, with Gadsden initially alone of the five South Carolina delegates in his support for the boycott. By the close of the first Congress in 1774, however, the delegates had agreed to a complete boycott of British goods, and Gadsden, writing to Samuel Adams in Boston, swore off his new wharf. "I would sooner see every inch of my Quay (my whole fortune) totally destroyed."[17] Ships like the *Heart of Oak* would not be bringing in their neat Windsor chairs and superfine silk, their British porter and latest plays. South Carolina would be vigilant in its non-importation at a cost to the economy so devastating it is nearly incomprehensible. In the year that followed, import revenues plummeted catastrophically, from £378,116 in 1774 to just £6,245 in 1775, a staggering 98 percent reduction of trading income in one year.[18] Trade effectively stopped.

To the surprise of many, merchants like Gadsden and Laurens were, in the end, more patriot than mercantile.

"SUCH SUDDEN AND GREAT CHANGES"

After the professional theatre season closed, students in Charleston, to do their part to generate fervor, undertook several amateur productions of—what else?—*Cato*. On June 29, 1774, pupils of James Thomson, formerly of New Jersey College (now Princeton University), performed *Cato* "in the presence of several hundreds," while six weeks later students of Oliver Dale presented, once again, *Cato*, in the rented Church Street Theatre.[19] Not without irony, this brace of *Cato*s would be the last full productions of a play in America before the outbreak of the war.

And all across the colonies something extraordinary was happening. "The People are at last roused," wrote Edward Rutledge.[20] Reckonings great and small had made patriots of merchants, Bostonians of Virginians, and Americans of them all. A great storm of organized protest was refashioning the social landscape of British America. Many of those involved in its administration were the most baffled by the intensity of this sudden change. In July of 1774, William Bull wrote to the Earl of Dartmouth of the emergent resolve that would define this new American:

> I beg your lordship's permission to observe, and I do with great concern, that this spirit of opposition to taxation and its consequences is so violent and so universal throughout America that I am apprehensive it will not be soon or easily appeased. The general voice speaks discontent, and sometimes in a tone of despair, as determined to stop all exports to and imports from Great Britain, and even to silence the courts of law, foreseeing but regardless of the ruin that must attend themselves in that case, content to change a comfortable for a parsimonious life, to be satisfied with the few wants of nature if by their sufferings they can bring Great Britain to feel. . . . Such sudden and great changes in the manners of an extended thriving people, among whom the Gazettes are filled with such variety of articles for luxury, is scarce credible.[21]

And so the articles of luxury sat idle, in huge new warehouses, on huge new wharfs. Even Charlestonians were learning parsimony.

Still, it wasn't likely to happen, something violent. Even the delegates, hot as some of the patriots were, were nonetheless circumscribed by a popular mandate. Instructions had been issued that the delegates were to seek the restoration of their natural rights as Englishmen. Spitfire candidates like Gadsden were moderated by sensible voices like Mr. Rutledge. This fit would pass. As Douglass sailed out to New York to prepare his next theatre for the next season, past Christopher Gadsden's new wharf, two ships deep, it didn't seem likely that all this trade would really stop over a dispute in Boston. But then, the port of Charleston wasn't blockaded.

The acting company dispersed for the summer. Lewis Hallam sailed back to England to recruit more actors; Douglass and his wife sailed to New York to prepare the John Street Theatre; the last of the company sailed to Philadelphia, on Captain Blewer's *Sea Nymph*—with them, two of the delegates to the great congress, Gadsden and Lynch.[22] The morning that the *Sea Nymph* sailed from Charleston, like everything to come, was both hopeful and deadly. The departure of Gadsden and Lynch (and their humble actor companions) that Sunday morning was met with a vigorous sermon at St. Michael's delivered by Reverend John Bullman, who denounced the pair from the pulpit as traitors to Great Britain. The denunciation was received by an indignant congregation, who called for Bullman's immediate resignation. When the *Sea Nymph* hoisted anchor, it was sent off with a discharge of seventeen cannons. As they cleared the new wharf, actors and delegates watched the salvos from the fort. One of the salutes exploded prematurely, burning three men; one died of his wounds.

[CHAPTER 14]

The Second America
New York, Winter 1774

• • •

Many people of Property dread the Violence of the lower sort.
William Smith, 1774

This is not only reducing everybody to a level, but it is entirely reversing the matter, and making the mob their masters.
"Extract of a Genuine Letter to a Gentleman from His Friend at New York," December 1774[1]

By the end of the summer of 1774, British America was in a state of revolt, and none of its administrators seemed to know how to ratchet down the conflict. Overlapping tiers of authority (traditional and self-anointed) troubled the notion of authority itself. The Crown governors of Massachusetts and New York had left their provinces in the hands of local lieutenants and General Gage had taken up his position in Boston, while the elections of delegates, the new Congress, their resolves, and the committees they created to enforce their resolves offered new stratigraphies of power. The British troops found a counterpart in colonial militias, drilling, training, recruiting, and clearly repurposed. The governors all knew that the election of delegates to an anonymous American Congress was illegal, but they also knew they could do nothing to prevent it without exacerbating the conflict. The more thoughtful assumed it was best to let the delegates meet—that the result would be a petition of grievances; Parliament would propose a compromise, perhaps a repeal; and these new, local, extra-legal "congressmen" would step down and the familiar order would be restored. But the civic investment prior to the Congress proved tumultuous and frightening to many. Towns convened ad hoc committees of representatives to resolve on issues to deliver to other representatives. The organizational apparatus of the Stamp Act protests appeared inadequate now, and citizens cobbled together new, often improvised structures. In New York, the Committee of Fifty-One commandeered and replaced the Committee of Five, and by the fall of 1774 it had expanded to the Committee of Sixty. Alexander McDougall, on the authority of none of the newly minted committees, convened the town of New York for an emergency meeting in the Fields (now City Hall Park) "where every friend to the true interest of the distressed country is earnestly requested to attend when matters of the utmost importance to their Reputation and Security as Freemen will be communicated."[2] McDougall presided, young Alexander Hamilton is rumored to have spoken, and the recently elected Committee of Fifty-One might well have thought, "What on earth is he doing and by whose authority is he making resolutions?" It was that kind of chaos. The newly extra-legal and self-empowered Committee objected to this even newer extra-legal self-empowered Assembly, and then called their own meeting to re-collect McDougall's new base. The Merchant Association responded with a further meeting, producing their own resolves, and so it went, layers upon layers of new men, new committees, self-declared, self-fashioned, and clearly potent. This succession of competing bodies occupied most of July 1774—and would be the reason, wrote William Smith, impatiently, that New York "lagged behind all the rest" in arriving at some consensus on how to act in concert with the other colonies.[3] One satirist captured the frenzy with a broadsheet of resolutions:

> Meeting of the Sons of Liberty, New York, 27 July 1774:
> 1) Resolved, that in this general time of resolving we have as good a right to resolve as the most resolute. . . .
> 15) Resolved: Lastly, that every Man, Woman, or child who doth not agree with our sentiments whether he or she or they understand them or not, is an Enemy to his Country, wheresoever he was born and a Jacobite in Principle whatever he may think of it and that he ought to be tarred and feathered if not hung, drawn, and quartered all statutes, laws, and ordinances whatsoever to the contrary notwithstanding.[4]

What was one humble theatrical manager to make of that, stepping into New York, as Douglass had, in the first week of July? A man or woman could not walk into a coffeehouse without finding it clogged with committeemen drafting resolves and threatening those who violated them; urgent notices and damning broadsides, thicker than playbills, choked the town; and the tavern greatrooms, like Hull's, that once hosted concerts, Freemasons, and St. Andrew's nights now stood as the makeshift curia, forums, and floors of citizen-senates. Robert Honyman arrived in New York a few months later, and his summation was brief: "Politics, Politics, Politics! There are numbers of hand bills, advertisements, extracts of letters on both sides daily and hourly printed, published, pasted up and handed about. Men, women, children, all ranks and professions mad with Politics."[5] It was a vital time for insurgent democracy, but they were not forming an insurgent democracy. They were participating in the formation of something new, violent, perhaps marvelous, but at that moment utterly anarchic, certainly extra-legal, and by most definitions treasonous.

In the midst of this affray, David Douglass quietly unlocked the John Street Theatre, moved in the scenery, gathered his actors, and waited for a sensible outcome from this Congress, that they all might get back to work. Philip Livingston had proposed one such sensible solution. His pamphlet, *The Other Side of the Question*, appeared in New York bookstalls and coffeehouses in 1774. Livingston asked that once petitions and remonstrations to the Crown had failed, as they likely would, "the question is reduced to this short alternative: which is most advantageous, commerce or freedom? One or the other we must forego."[6] Not driven solely by commercial interests, Livingston believed, like many others, in the "ridiculous" nature of an independent America. It would, he thought, fall into civil war in a month, and by the look of the streets of New York, a month would be a generous allotment for failure. Giving up the embargo meant at least a return to commerce, a return to some prosperity, and avoiding bloodshed and the lasting damage of a civil war on two fronts (one against Great Britain, then against each other). The Livingston plan seemed to many merchants a sensible solution. But merchants were not in control. John Adams, who met Livingston in New York en route to the Philadelphia Congress, dismissed both his ideas and their author, as a "great rough rappid [rabid] mortal. . . . Seems to dread N. England—the levelling spirit &c. Hints were thrown out of Goths and Vandals."[7]

There were other sensible notions afloat, notions that many considered workable, nonviolent solutions to the American problem. Some governors were talking favorably of Joseph Galloway's proposal for a Union, like that of Scotland, with its own parliament ("Grand Council"), its own "president-general" (to be appointed by the king), and its own representation and local administration, but answerable to the king and Parliament. Cadwallader Colden wrote favorably of the plan, as did William Franklin of New Jersey; more importantly, so did the Earl of Dartmouth. A few members of the Congress supported it, but alas, sighed Colden, "A fatal pride and obstinacy seems to have governed them. The delegates from Virginia were most violent of any. . . . These southern gentlemen exceeded even the New England delegates."[8] Galloway's proposal was not only quashed but expunged from the Congressional record, and Galloway resigned from Congress "despised and condemned by all."[9] The fearful, agitated march to violent independency seemed to be inevitable.

The first Congress issued a series of resolves that affected trade across the colonies, including the eighth resolution, which targeted gaming, horse-racing, and (Douglass's trade) theatre. If Congress was to be honored as the authority in America, theatre would be over until the dispute had been settled. But as the summer became fall, and fall nudged into winter, that dispute grew more and more violent.

Into this agitation stepped the last thing an unemployed manager needed: actors just off the boat, recruited from London, including a cousin of the Hallam family, Thomas Wignell. What promises they had received to lure them across the ocean at such an unsettled juncture one can only guess, but here they were, the "theatrical force hitherto unknown," an ironic counterpoint to the build-up of British troops. Indeed, the new actors had traveled on the *Lady Gage*, a ship named for the general's wife and owned by Sir William Howe, who would command the British military against the rebellion in America. William Dunlap, chronicler of the early stage, recounts that Thomas Wignell received the news sitting in the barber's chair, cleaning up after the transatlantic voyage, only to discover that there would be no brilliant and prosperous season after all, that all the theatres in America were closed and likely to remain so.[10]

Such was the vigilance in the streets and barber stools that even Wignell and other (unnamed) new actors were noticed. The *New York Journal* of December 15, 1774, suggested, in its politely dangerous way, that if their manager were ever to count on support in this city again, he would do well to honor the congressional resolution: "As a number of players have arrived in the Lady Gage, from London, and it is reported that they are to act among us this winter, I beg leave through the channel of your paper, to invite the attention of the public to the eighth article of the association, agreed upon by the Continental Congress." The author, "Pro Patria," went on to accord Mr. Douglass the following respect, but also served him notice: "From my knowledge of Mr. Douglass's urbanity, I am persuaded he would not wish to give any offence to the good people of this city, whose favour he has formerly experienced, and who may hereafter render him more essential service, and I doubt not such an application, as I have mentioned above, will have a proper effect." And if that courtesy were not enough, the paper concluded with as clear a threat as it could print: if Douglass did not heed this advice, it would have "consequences—which, if we may judge from what happened in 1765—may be very disagreeable." No one needed to be reminded that "what happened in 1765" was the complete destruction of Douglass's Chapel Street Theatre at the hands of the Sons of Liberty. Lest all that courtesy go unnoticed, the *Journal* reminded its readership (particularly Mr. Douglass) that the Committee had recently shut down two puppet shows, and were on their way to closing an auction of books. "Pro Patria" also raised the issue that had been unspoken for years when he characterized the new actors as goods that fell under the prohibition of the 10th congressional resolution. All goods (already en route) were to be sent back, stored, or sold by the General Committee. The wording was polite, the concept somewhat ambiguous (actors as goods?), but the threat was very real and equally transparent:

> The present importation of players, is doubtless in consequence of orders sent in proper season, though they have arrived after the first of December; but as they are neither "goods nor merchandize" I imagine they do not come within the tenth article of the association; however, as it is the proper business of the committee, and one principal end of their appointment, "attentively to observe the conduct of all persons touching this association," I think they ought to interest themselves in this matter; and by a decent remonstrance to the manager endeavour to prevent the breach of the association said to be intended, and its consequences—which, if we may judge from what happened in 1765 [*recte* 1766] may be very disagreeable."[11]

Perhaps the men of the "Association," these vigilantes patrolling the conduct of the populace, could not pen a proper letter, but dangling clause after clause made their point with great clarity. These committeemen scarcely knew what to make of actors but damned them nonetheless. They labeled them as marked goods, condemned in the popular imagination as imported luxuries in a time of boycott, despite any letters of authority Douglass might secure.

Since the departure of William Tryon the previous spring (1774), the nominal authority of the city resided with the enduring Cadwallader Colden, now in his eighties, but clearly the real dominion lay elsewhere. The optimism of playing through the times may seem ludicrous now—when militiamen from New England to Virginia were seizing gunpowder and carrying off cannons from forts—but the optimism of a winter season of plays—and all it represented—appeared far less ludicrous than a war with Great Britain.[12]

THE SECOND AMERICA

Of this new population of unmannered Americans, these Goths and Vandals, Dr. Myles Cooper, the Anglican priest and president of King's College, New York, would write at great length. They were a class he never knew, a second America, quite unlike the rising and respectful students he taught, these other Americans, like McDougall and these Sons of Liberty boys, those whose fortunes and families were not up to the admission standards of the college, indeed, were so below the expectation of education that their presence in his institution, in any capacity but service, was itself unthinkable. And for Cooper, rightly so. There was, for him, a natural order to society, those who governed and those who were governed. Education, refinement, income, and leisure—the hallmarks of gentlemen—qualified the former, the America he knew, while labor and ignorance were those of the other America, a second America. Mark Longaker has documented the values expressed in the curriculum Cooper initiated, with less emphasis on theology and more on refinement.[13] Class was, for Cooper, a fixed rule of society. The dismantling of class distinction in the years preceding the Revolution deeply offended this Oxford-educated man. Upon his arrival in America, early in the 1760s, he noted that "the insolence, and brutal abuse of Rank, Titles, and Power" felt both shocking and lamentably all too familiar to him. "No man of common observation who has crossed the Atlantic," he wrote, glossing a poem of his own composition, "can have failed to remark, the great Difference between the Manners of the lower and middling sort of people in England, and of People of the same classes here."[14] Cooper would lay into this "Second America," this population of overreaching, undereducated "men undefin'd by any rules," with a scathing portrait of a rebellion by an underclass "born to be lodg'd, and cloth'd and fed / by other toils than toil of the head." After that same population of unlettered Vandals had threatened to slit his nose and cut off his ears, Cooper would conclude that this rebellion was unframed anarchy, composed entirely of men dislodged from their proper spheres and stations, controlled by the puppet-masters at home (New York) and in Philadelphia, this raw thing, this American mob, made of men

> Deprav'd, who quit their sphere
> Without Remorse, or Shame, or Fear,
> And boldly rush—they know not where.[15]

That same mob now drove Cooper from his college, threatened his life and livelihood; the president of King's College and Anglican priest was obliged to retreat to a British ship for his own safety.[16] The man in whose care Washington had placed his stepson, young Jacky Custis, now found his life threatened for speaking his opinions to those who were, in his estimation, unqualified to enter his college.

David Douglass may or may not have agreed with Cooper's politics (the two men were well acquainted), but both knew firsthand the same crowd of "gaping mobs," if only from the same theatre. Cooper attended plays at the John Street Theatre, wrote at least one prologue for Douglass, and participated in the benefit Douglass hosted for the hospital under construction next to the college, to which Douglass (and the actors) had donated funds. In the microcosm of the playhouse, Douglass found himself troubled by the same rude class of "gallery gods," to the extent that he initially placed constables in the gallery before he closed it entirely. Shutting up the gallery meant a truncation of another sort, sealing off the theatre from the lower (dis)orders.

> The repeated Insults which some mischievous Persons in the Gallery have given, not only to the Stage and Orchestra, but to the other Parts of the Audience, call loudly for Reprehension, and since they have been more than once ineffectually admon-

ished of the Impropriety of such a Conduct in a public Assembly, they are now (for the last Time) inform'd that unless the more regular and better disposed People, who frequent that Part of the Theatre will interfere either by turning out the Offenders, or pointing them out to the Constables, who attend there on purpose, that they may be brought to Justice, the Gallery for the future must be shut up.[17]

Cooper and Douglass were not the only ones who saw the metaphor of the playhouse: a world ruined by an unmannered underclass who broke out of their proper sphere, and once untethered, rankly abused the public. These disorders marked an utter evacuation of respect for place, rank, title, and the courtesies owed to the public. These gallery gods represented the antithesis of everything the theatre taught. William Smith exclaimed over "what a pass the Populace are arrived. Instead of that Respect they formerly had for the King, you now hear the very lowest Orders call him a Knave or a Fool."[18] They threw eggs from the gallery of the John Street Theatre at actors and audience members alike. In the Southwark Theatre in Philadelphia, in a gesture of the leveling spirit, the gallery gods tore up the spikes that divided the boxes from the gallery.

Apprehension about this second America grew widespread, and not just among loyalists, though their contacts with this new force were often the most violent. Josiah Martin, the last colonial governor of North Carolina, wrote to the Earl of Dartmouth from New York in November of 1774: "The people of consideration feel too late their ill policy in having made it [the mob] so consequential and omnipotent in the time of the disturbances occasioned by the Stamp Act and fear now to attempt, as much as they wish, to resume the power with which they then conspired to arm the multitude, that they now see a monster of their own creation become formidable to themselves, usurping dominion."[19] The colonial governors reporting to the Earl of Dartmouth throughout the fall of 1774 routinely reached the same unsettling conclusion: this monster mob was the creation of the gentry, and it had now outgrown them. "They [the gentry]," wrote Gouverneur Morris to John Penn, "stimulated some daring coxcombs to rouse the mob into an attack upon the bounds of order and decency. These fellows became the Jack Cades of the day."[20] They told each other this tale, told Whitehall and the administrators of America and the colonial governors. This story resurfaced with some regularity: once the "principal men" during the Stamp Act had rehearsed the "lower orders" to cease the honoring of place and privilege (their proper spheres) and take up the concerns of government, there was no returning to their docility after the repeal. Though they, the gentry, recognized there was little that qualified this new breed of the street to take up government, the latter would, nonetheless, be ministers, and in this, the farce turned tragic.

"Poor reptiles!" wrote Gouverneur Morris to John Penn. "It is with them a vernal morning, they are struggling to cast off their winter slough, they bask in the sunshine, and ere noon they will bite, depend upon it. The gentry began to fear this. . . . Farewell Aristocracy. I see, and I see it with fear and trembling, that if the dispute with Britain continue, we shall be under the worst of all possible dominions. We shall be under the dominion of a riotous mob."[21] So too feared William Smith, and so too Philip Livingston, who articulated his dread of the "Levelling spirit" in *The Other Side of the Question*.[22] Henry Hulton could only sigh over America lost: "[T]hey have become depraved before they have been refined."[23] A force had been unloosed, and it could not be contained by order of British law. The codes of authority had all been quite unhinged, and old laws were now unbinding.

This new second America may have been inspired by the populism of the Stamp Act, but its power and violence had grown and its civility had diminished. The straw effigies of Stamp Act protests gave way to flesh-and-blood targets. Alexander McDougall emerged as a force in the militant New York that largely replaced the old oligarchies of assembly- and councilmen like the Livingstons and Delanceys. For all his uncouth behavior, McDougall, son of a dairyman, merchant and privateer, rose quickly in the committees of this new order that set little stock by manners. Yet he could shock even his own committee with the violence of his ideas. As a committeeman, McDougall convened a large population in the Fields for an ad hoc meeting to propose a series of resolutions that even his committee rejected, for example, supporting the destruction of James Rivington's loyalist print shop. These were the same Sons of Liberty who drank toasts to the "Liberty of the Press" back in 1770, when a free press meant expressing views in concert with their own.[24] Within his own coffeehouse cabal he suggested, "What if we prevent the landing [of tea] and kill the Governor and all the Council?" MacDougall's apparently earnest proposal for a mass murder to protest a three-penny tax on tea no one was compelled to drink demonstrates the utter erosion of order by 1774.[25]

At the close of 1774, New York, and indeed all the colonies, were a powder keg, and the maniacs all had matches. "Every man who will not drink 'destruction to his King,'" wrote one at the close of the year, "is a Tory and liable to tar and feathers. In the east and southern provinces they are in actual rebellion, raising troops, and seizing ammunition in the most daring manner; the common people are mad. . . . [A]s the fever is quite high, a little bleeding is absolutely necessary."[26]

Of course there would be no more theatre. While that may seem a frivolous concern, the loss of everything the theatre had stood for was not. The great social networks that stretched across the British Atlantic and bound this society would all be severed. The codes of class and conduct, station, and rank that held it all together would shatter asunder; the very fabric of a common English culture would be shredded in the leveling of the new America. The models of etiquette, manners, and civility that marked station and shaped polite society would also become unnecessary, and in one violent spasm be rendered obsolete. It would indeed become, as Marc Egnal and Joseph Ernst put it, "a revolution of the lower class against a plutocracy."[27]

It would be, as Peter Oliver feared, "a world turned upside down." Theatre, rather than a finishing school for polishing manners and class aspirations, would be stigmatized as "British" and an aristocratic indulgence in ways the Virginia, Maryland, and South Carolina gentry had never conceived. But there was nothing inherently disruptive about theatricals, even in times of war, given the seasonal nature of warfare at the time. Soldier companies and professionals alike had played, for example, right through the French-Indian War. The British would enjoy their theatricals every winter of the Revolutionary War, occupying Douglass's theatres in New York and Philadelphia, and making their own in Boston. Middlekauff has argued that such prohibitions as the eighth resolution were Boston clauses, through which New England values had been promoted into becoming American values.[28] But this was not so much New England morality as a leveler's distaste for distinction.

Maybe because Douglass knew them as a polite and genteel society, he was less prepared for the loud words and rash gestures they were now making in Philadelphia and on the streets of New York. This was no longer a trade dispute over taxes, goods, and duties; these men had set up an extra-legal American authority in opposition to the British government. Take tea or leave it; stamps, boycotts, and mobs aside, this talk was now treasonous. Men would hang for this. The sober voices of moderation, like that of John Dickinson, or Galloway, or Cooper, had given way to open talk of armed resistance. His (former?) patrons in Philadelphia were forcing issues of allegiance, and that was a dangerous game to enter upon hastily. Even General Gage, a rather sensible man with an American wife, was shocked by the violence of it all. He wrote to Lord Dartmouth from Boston on November 15, 1774, "The proceedings of the Continental Congress astonish and terrify all considerate men."[29]

A dozen years earlier, when Douglass had changed the name of his company of actors from "The London Company" to "The American Company," the distinction at the time was geographic, not political. He was claiming an acting circuit—the colonies—and protecting his monopoly against rival companies. What was happening in Philadelphia was a radical redefinition of America: "American" had suddenly ceased to describe exclusively a place and had now come to signify an identity, a position, a position increasingly in direct and quite likely now armed opposition to Great Britain.

Douglass was a lowland Scot, who, as a young man, had seen the '45 and its aftermath. He had been a printer's apprentice in Edinburgh when printers were jailed for being pro-Scot. He had already assimilated once. He had since made a career out of selling the latest London culture, that is, British culture, in speech, poise, carriage, and ideology. Like many disaffected Scots of his generation, he had learned to make a living out of becoming British. He had made a business out of making British-Americans British and making Americans Londoners abroad. Were they all expected now to declare yet another new nationality? To give over their refinement to become the American rabble? Was he somehow now expected to refashion himself again, and then—God help him—to refashion this rabble-audience into cultured Americans? With what, if not British culture? There were few acceptable American plays and no currency for them. Thomas Godfrey's *The Prince of Parthia*, one of the few dramas penned by an American for performance, had played exactly once in Philadelphia and was politely retired.[30] Douglass sold British theatre, British culture, and now he found himself on the wrong side of the nation who needed none of it. When the Reverend Jonathan Boucher addressed the radicals of Virginia, he pleaded that they were all still a "British community." But he and others overestimated the ties that bound them, and Boucher found himself without a pulpit, Cooper without a college, Douglass without a theatre, and thousands without direction or order.

It all seemed incomprehensible: the associations, the boycotts, the complete embargo on imported goods that was so contrary to the commercial desires that had created the British-American economy. American merchants had spent the last three decades developing the markets for fine London goods, and now a Congress of lawyers was interdicting all that? Fleets of ships out of Newport, Charleston, and New York sailed each week packed with raw goods and brought back fine goods, superfine goods, and everybody was getting rich at it. And then it all quite suddenly ceased, because of a three-penny-a-pound tax on tea?

Henry Pelham wrote from Boston to his half-brother, the painter John Singleton Copley, then living in London: "It is inconceivable the distress and ruin this unnatural dispute has caused to this town and its inhabitants. Almost every shop and store is shut. No business of any kind is going on. . . . The clothes upon my back and a few dollars in my pocket are now the only property which I have."[31] William Mylne in Maryland concurred: "Trade is in a manner stopped."[32] It went from Gadsden's wharf to this, in six months? The unthinkable had come to pass; "the merchants," as David Ramsay wrote with some befuddlement, "put far behind them the gains of trade, and cheerfully submitted to a total stoppage of business in obedience to the recommendations of men, invested with no legislative powers. . . . They counted everything cheap in comparison with liberty and readily gave up whatever tended to endanger it. . . . The animation of the times raised the actors in these scenes above themselves."[33]

The very ship that carried over the new actors, the *Lady Gage*, carried a cargo that—after December 1—had been declared unmerchantable, and was to be auctioned rather than unloaded. The actors too had become unmerchantable. If that were not disappointing enough for the importers, discovered among the cargo were crates of firearms and gunpowder. When the weapons were discovered—Scottish customs inspector Andrew Elliot (a St. Andrew's man) opened the first case—a mob confiscated them. He in turn alerted the merchant to whom the munitions were addressed, who gathered loyalists and recovered them.[34] Such was New York at the close of 1774. One month later, armed patrol boats cruised the harbor, guaranteeing that British goods were not unloaded.

Just when Douglass, through his character, his connections, and his perseverance, had succeeded in building up a sustainable theatrical marketplace; just when he had overcome the moral opposition to his business, cultivated a reputable company and a well-to-do audience, and enjoyed operating in America without a rival company; just when he had every expectation of enduring success—theatre and apparently everything it stood for was officially banned. This was not a case of courting the governor or the mayor to weigh in against the Quakers; this act applied to the entire continent, and was beyond appeal until the very conflict itself was resolved. Nothing remained for him to do but gather his company, secure his letters, and wait it out in some polite and loyalist elsewhere until the storm passed.

When Douglass had first arrived in North America, he had been praised for ushering in the arts, a civilizing force, to the wilds of America:

> See! Genius wakes, dispels the former Gloom,
> And shed Light's Blaze, deriv'd from Greece and Rome!
> With polish'd Arts wild Passions to control;
> To warm the Breast, and humanize the Soul![35]

Whatever virtues art may have accomplished, at the close of 1774 it looked like the last stand of civility had fallen.[36]

As the new year dawned, the American Company had only one place left to go: back to the islands, to Jamaica, from whence they had come sixteen years earlier. At least one knew where Jamaica stood. At a town meeting on December 6, 1774, the freeholders and inhabitants of Kingston had resolved that they were "heartily attached to the royal house of Hanover, as the guardians of the civil and religious liberties, of the whole British empire; and that we esteem it our duty, to render true and faithful allegiance to George the Third, King of Great Britain, as our only rightful Sovereign."[37] Boatloads of loyalist refugees from the colonies were retreating to Jamaica, and the actors would be among them.[38]

The first notice of the company's departure was posted in Rivington's *Gazette* in early January: "The Company of Comedians, with Mr. Douglass, the manager, are preparing to embark for the island of Jamaica, and they will not return to the continent until its tranquility is restored." Complications beset them, and the item was retracted the following week.[39] Douglass was waiting on a last character letter that he did not secure until the end of January. Sir Basil Keith, governor of Jamaica, later replied to Cadwallader Colden: "Sir, a few days ago I received your favour of the 28th of January. I am at present at a considerable distance from the Towns; but on my return which will be in five or six weeks hence; I will with pleasure give all my countenence and protection to Mr. Douglass and his Company."[40] That letter effectively transferred what patronage Douglass had left from one uncertain governor to another. Without it, there would be no business at all. Colden had described the events of New York at the close of the year to Lord Dartmouth as "a dreadful situation." "It is in the power of a few People at any Time to raise a Mob. . . . If we are not rescued from it by the Wisdom and Firmness of Parliament, the Colonies must soon fall into Distraction and every Calamity annex'd to a total annihilation of Government."[41]

It was time to leave. The gallery gods had broken from their proper spheres and no constabulary on earth could contain them again.

[EPILOGUE]
Final Reckonings
New York, January 1775

• • •

To the public. Whereas my wife, American Liberty, hath lately behaved in a very licentious manner, and run me considerably in debt, this is to forewarn all persons from trusting her, as I will pay no debts of her contracting from the date hereof. . . .
To the public. Whereas my husband Loyalty hath, in a late advertisement, forewarned all persons from trusting me on his account, this is to inform the public that he derived all his fortune from me, and that by our marriage articles he has no right to proscribe me from the use of it. My reason for leaving him was because he behaved in an arbitrary and cruel manner and suffered his domestic servants, grooms, foxhunters, &c to direct and insult me.
"American Liberty," *Virginia Gazette*, January 20, 1774

Not many at the time thought the marriage between Britain and America would really come to such a nasty divorce, but having come to it, fewer understood how deep or costly the separation would truly be. James Robinson, the hopeful tobacco-broker, wrote in that spring of 1775: "[I]n what manner this unnatural and alarming contest betwixt Britain and the colonies may be settled I know not. However I think it must be settled some way or other in 12 months."[1] Mercy Otis Warren gave it a few months; Henry Laurens, writing in January of 1775, thought the whole thing would be over "before the fashions change."[2] But Benjamin Franklin proved the more prescient; he thought the dispute would take a full decade to settle, and he was precise to a year.

The war that became a revolution put an end to so much work of so many lifetimes. What had been generations in the building came down in the spasm of a season. Businesses, and those lovely social networks that facilitated them as a cultured society of potential mobility, vanished. "Private friendships are broken off," James Allen confided to his diary. The famous Jockey Club, the Homony Club, St. Andrew's—all set aside for a decade or more and the old alliances utterly broken.[3]

Thousands lost the very roofs over their heads; once-prosperous merchants found themselves reduced to the shirts on their backs;

citizens became refugees seeking shelter where they could find it. Of Christopher Gadsden, the Charleston merchant who had invested so much capital toward his future business, no man was more active in adopting the resolutions of Congress; as David Ramsay wrote, "[F]ew men lost more by them [i.e., the resolves] than he did."[4] Merchant James Beckman wrote to his London purveyors that he could make no spring order until "proper redress of American Grievances is obtained."[5]

William Mylne, a builder, had traveled to New York looking for work. He arrived about the time Douglass and the actors were leaving. He too would depart empty-handed. As he wrote on March 1, 1775: "I have been here a fortnight in this place, as far as I can judge I have not any prospect of being employed as an architect, these troublesome times have put a stop to building."[6] Actor Thomas Wignell would not see a payday for six months. An equally poignant portrait is painted in the diary of John Harrower, who had come to Virginia earlier on a four-year indenture. His contract was purchased by a Fredericksburg planter, and Harrower was set up as a schoolteacher. By perseverance, thrift, and diligence, he saved enough money to bring his wife and their children to Virginia from their native Shetland Islands. Poor man, just as his term expired and he planned on acquiring land of his own, the war broke out. The seas grew unfriendly to travelers, and the prospects of Harrower, like those of many young men in America, were dashed on the rocks of revolution.

While the war brought ruin to many, it made the careers of others. A Boston bookseller, Henry Knox, was radicalized by the British troops' occupation of Boston. He closed his shop and enlisted in Washington's Continental Army. It was Knox's outlandish idea to surprise the thinly manned Fort Ticonderoga, not so much for its strategic position but for its massive cannons, left over from the French-Indian War a dozen years earlier. He and a small force of volunteers successfully captured the fort and dragged the forty-eight pieces of heavy artillery back to Boston on sleds. He rose quickly in the army under Washington, attaining the rank of brigadier general.

Above all, the opening months of 1775 were the last call and final reckoning for choosing sides. Many colonists, immigrants and Americans, Scottish and British expatriates, farm boys and fishermen, merchants and lawyers, made personal decisions to take up "the Glorious

Cause." Douglass did not. There is no indication what his feelings were on the matter. Other artists sided with the revolutionaries: John Trumbull and Charles Willson Peale both enlisted for the Americans; Captain Peale served with the Philadelphia militia, joined Washington at Valley Forge, and painted a few miniatures between skirmishes.[7] The Reverend John Rogers preached a rousing sermon for independence in New York where not a third of the population shared his politics.[8] Thomas Paine donated the proceeds of his enormously popular pamphlet *Common Sense* to buy mittens for the troops at Quebec.

The young Alexander Hamilton left King's College to join the artillery unit at Fort George; he was nineteen. Three faculty members from William and Mary College in Virginia joined the Continental Army when the war began.[9] Two others of the same institution both returned to England. Reverend Naphtali Daggett, an old professor of divinity at Yale, got off a few shots at the British before he was clubbed.[10]

Volunteers from all over the colonies committed themselves, some at great personal expense. Thomas Byrd, son of William Byrd III of Westover, resigned from the British navy in 1775, even though his father disinherited him for it, and joined the Continental Army. He served as aide-de-camp to General Charles Lee and through this choice lost his share of one of Virginia's most sizeable fortunes.[11] Christopher Marshall, of Philadelphia, was excommunicated from his pacifist Quaker community when the congregation "denied the lawfulness of defensive warfare."[12] Marshall joined the Committee for Safety and hosted many of the Congress in Philadelphia.

These private reckonings made for uneasy divisions. Many families and business partnerships split. One of Douglass's Scottish patrons, Dr. Alexander Garden in Charleston, remained a deeply committed loyalist, while his son and namesake became a patriot and served as a major in the provincial army of South Carolina. The same proved true for the loyalist printer, Robert Wells, and his patriot son. Lieutenant Governor William Bull, who remained in South Carolina, had two patriot nephews who opposed him and joined with Charles Cotesworth Pinckney in securing the colony's arsenal.[13] Peyton Randolph became the first president of Congress, but his brother John remained a loyalist, served as the king's attorney for Virginia, and departed the colony with the governor. If the painter Peale was radicalized, William Williams, who had painted scenes for Douglass in Philadelphia, was "loyalized." He left New York for London in disgust in 1775 when his two sons joined the American army. And so the country went, household by household.

Others had positions declared for them. Many office-holders, for example, were bound by their oaths of allegiance to support the Crown, in spite of their inclinations to the contrary. This population included civil servants, like William Eddis, surveyor and governor's secretary, and rectors like Jonathan Boucher, both of whom served by royal appointment.[14] In many cases citizen committees declared positions for their constituents. Rebel representatives in Annapolis resolved that "every person who should refuse to contribute to the purchase of arms and ammunition for the use of the country before the 1st of this month [February 1775] shall be deemed an Enemy to America and his name published in the *Maryland Gazette*."[15]

Nor was neutrality an option. Jonathan Boucher adopted this position initially, but his congregation consisted almost entirely of Whigs, and when his dissent was not as vocal as his congregation's, he became, in his words, "a marked man." When he was approached to give a sermon "to recommend the suffering people of Boston to the charity of my parish" and refused, he was arrested and presented before the Committee for Public Safety, known as Tory headhunters. It was only by the grace of his eloquence that Boucher was acquitted.[16] Cadwallader Colden II, son of the former lieutenant governor of New York, also determined on a course of impartiality, nonetheless winding up in Kingston jail as a loyalist (condemned as much by his name as any actions); but he remained steadfastly neutral. From jail he wrote to John Jay of his "Determined Resolution to keep a Clear Conscience by Takeing [sic] no active Part on Either Side of the Controversy, yet it Seems I have a full Share of Punishments."[17]

Douglass's agent in New York, Hugh Gaine, printer of the *New York Mercury*, was deeply divided. Like many, he tried to join the strongest party and at one point belonged to both. Once the war broke out, Gaine established a second newspaper in Newark, New Jersey, by the same name but with a decidedly Whiggish slant. The Newark edition ran for only a few months, September to November 1776. His rival, James Rivington, suffered the most for his split loyalties. Identified as a Tory in the spring of 1776, his print shop was vandalized and his types smashed. He did not have business again until General Howe captured New York and he reopened as a loyalist paper. But his Tory slant, in the end, proved just a front, as he was later discovered to have been an American spy, smuggling strategic news to General Washington wrapped in his newspapers.

Douglass's Charleston landlord, the printer Robert Wells, was a devoted loyalist. When the war came, he swore he would never leave his house, "while two stones were standing." But the local Sons of Liberty left no stone unturned, and Wells escaped to England. His daughter sold off the rubble, put the money into five casks of indigo, and tried to follow. Her ship was captured by the British as an American privateer and towed back to New York. His son, John Wells, Jr., took over the newspaper as an American sympathizer, until the British occupied Charleston, and then he did an about-face and changed the name of the paper to the *Royal Gazette*.[18]

But in this final hour of reckoning, neither Douglass nor any of the actors in his company—as many as twenty of them—endorsed the cause on one side or the other. Some of the actors, certainly Lewis Hallam and John Henry (whom John Bernard recalled as having the posture of a "former British soldier"), were able-bodied men in their thirties at the time; they would play both sides of the contest, claiming loss of property as loyalists to the British, and some years later, when they returned to New York, declaring loyalty to the American cause. The only actor who remained in America was Thomas Wall, whose story remains particularly elusive. He left the American Company not to take up arms but to continue acting, with a solo series of lectures. As a camp follower of the military, he remained, like Brecht's Mother Courage, commercially attached to the war. At some point by late 1777, Wall was captured, but neither side claimed him, and he ended up in Charlottesville with the British military prisoners. Here he joined or formed an amateur theatrical group, and many "tiresome hours this man help'd us to pass over in the wilds of Virginia, by acting on a little theatre the officers erected at the Barracks," wrote one British prisoner to Governor Thomas Jefferson.[19] On one occasion, the company invited the governor and his wife to the performances. The prisoners were later moved to Frederick, Maryland, where Wall received some unfriendly official attention for claiming rations for himself and his family. The official report concluded of Wall that "the British say he doth not belong to them; but he is their Country man."[20]

Most of Douglass's actors remained performers tied to a company and to the lifestyle they had established under Douglass's management. They may have imagined that the conflict would eventually resolve in a compromise. Or perhaps Douglass knew enough about tragedy to know how rebellions generally ended. Having played *Cato* for fifteen years, he knew that the fifth act always ended in suicide. And he had seen this offstage as well: a lifetime of self-appointed over-reachers and quashed rebellions. The Jacobites under Bonnie Prince Charlie, the great gathering of the clans, the doomed Highland Scots, the Irish, the Caribs, Indian uprisings, slave rebellions, servant rebellions, all rose up and all subsided in the end. Why should the American scenario play out any differently? Did Douglass in 1775, like thousands of other Scotsmen in America, look on "General" Washington as anything but another hopeful, heroic, but ultimately doomed Highlander?

By early 1775 the company had been out of work for eight months and could wait no longer; on February 2, 1775, they boarded the sloop *Sally* and embarked for Jamaica "until the unhappy differences that subsist between the mother country and her colonies in America subside" (a phrase cribbed from the proceedings of Congress, published on January 30, 1775). American patrol boats skimmed the harbor of New York. It was the first day after the ports were "officially" closed to all British goods. Captain William Watson's ship *James* had arrived the day before and was prohibited from unloading its cargo. After several clandestine attempts, he left New York for Jamaica.[21]

As the company sailed out of sight of the troubled land, one by one, all Douglass's theatres were pulled down or repurposed. Up the Chesapeake in Annapolis, his lovely theatre was already being converted for the use of St. Anne's parish church, while the town militia was using his old theatre. William Mylne heard the militiamen drilling with drum and fife late into the night: "They muster everywhere, I could get no sleep for some time at Annapolis for the noise of their drums and fifes exercising in an old Playhouse close by where I lodged."[22] Douglass would not reopen his beautiful theatres there or in Philadelphia, New York, Charleston, or Williamsburg. The latter would be dismantled for its bricks. And the Charleston house would supply "Five loads Benches from Play house to State house, ord[ere]d by Calvert." This was John Calvert, who had kept the books and sold the tickets for the theatre in Charleston last summer, now parting out the new Church Street Theatre, bench by bench.[23] One by one the theatres of Douglass's circuit, his monopoly, were being dismantled to help fund the rebellion. Would this be the end of it all? The bricks and iron spikes that separated the classes pilfered for redoubts, the lead gutters melted for bullets? Would the civilizing force of American theatre transform into bullets and billets?

"The first act of violence on the part of the Administration in America, or the attempt to reinforce General Gage this winter or next year, will put the whole Continent in arms, from Nova Scotia to Georgia," thought John Dickinson; and so it did.[24] British troops marched on the ammunition stores in Lexington and Concord, and the continent did indeed appeal to arms. "To Arms! To Arms! is the Language here!" wrote Philip Fithian, as he traveled through Pennsylvania just three weeks after the Revolutionary War began at Lexington and Concord. Taxes were being imposed on all estates to raise money for arms and ammunition.[25] The debates were over; blood had been shed. The days of associations and pamphlets were past; resolutions and declarations were passing. The contest of the emerging American nation would now be settled by force of arms.

Theatre as a civilizing force in British America was over, as was the notion of a British America. The British would now be an occupying force in a great contest of nation, and the theatre—there would still be plenty of theatre—would become a tool of that warfare: the theatre of war, the theatre in war, and that theatre would shape the war. But that is the subject of another story.

[NOTES]

PREFACE

1. The dimensions of this painting in its original frame are 56 in. × 46 in. Its provenance is traced at the Dewitt-Wallace Decorative Arts Museum, Colonial Williamsburg, acq. no. 1956-296A&B.

2. We have an account book for the British military who occupied the John Street Theatre for winter seasons during the war and, being the military, kept meticulous records of every salary, property, and fashionable piece of costuming, but nothing of that sort has survived for the career of Douglass or any actor prior to the Revolution. Thomas Wall, during and after the Revolution, would jot a few financial notes on the back of the playbills in the Maryland Historical Society Collection; nothing comparable exists for Douglass and the American Company.

3. His appointments include Master of the Revels (1777), Printer to the Assembly (1779), Master in Ordinary (1784), and Justice of the Quorum for St. Catherine's Parish (1785).

4. A full inventory of the effects of David Douglass is registered in Inventories, liber 76, folio 81R, Jamaica National Library, Spanish Town, Jamaica; and his will in Wills, liber 61, folio 5R.

5. David Ross to William Hamilton, RH15/44/136, National Archives of Scotland, Edinburgh. (A 26-in. board would make a single 8-ft × 5-ft 5-in. flat.)

6. Hodge 175.

7. Kolve 108.

PROLOGUE

1. The letter has not survived, but a record of the receipt of it has. After the Revolution, William Dunlap, one of America's first playwrights, recorded it this way: "The Resolution of Congress was conveyed to Douglass in a letter from the President, Peyton Randolph, and the Committee of New York gave him likewise notice of the same" (Dunlap 64).

2. Ford et al., *Journals of the Continental Congress*, Resolution viii, 23 October 1774.

3. The Annapolis Bill of Association was dated 23 May 1769, and the Virginia Non-importation Agreements 22 June 1770; both are discussed below.

4. When Gordon Wood notes that American revolutionary leaders do not fit the reckless, bloodthirsty mold of other radicals (Lenin, Robespierre, Mao Zedong), he refers to their gentility ("they made speeches, not bombs; they

wrote learned pamphlets, not manifestos" (*Radicalism* 3). Wood is recognizing a refinement, even in revolution.

5. "Many people go from Boston to Newport to see the plays," Nathaniel Ames notes in his diary for 14 September 1761; and in his memoranda for the month: "Boston People flock up to Newport to see the Plays by the English Actors" (1:69, 63). Dr. Robert Honyman's journal for 1775 records the distance as forty-five miles, and his coach ride, albeit in the snow, took thirteen hours (Honyman 39).

6. Washington's association with the theatre was the subject of an early study, Paul Leicester Ford's *Washington and the Theatre*. For Jefferson's theatre-going, see my "Thomas Jefferson and the Colonial Theatre."

7. Abigail Adams to John Adams, 19 August 1774 (Butterfield 1:143); John Adams, 20 June 1774 (*Diary* 96).

8. For example, Mercy Otis Warren, *The Adulateur* (1772); John Andre, *The Blockade of Boston* (performed January 1776); Hugh Henry Brackenridge, *Battle of Bunker Hill* (1776).

9. Eddis, 8 November 1774 (letter xviii). The force and ubiquity of this *theatrum mundi* trope is, in part, the subject of Jeffrey H. Richards's *Theatre Enough*.

10. "Washington understood this art very well, and we may say of him, if he was not the greatest President, he was the best actor of presidency we have ever had. His address to the states when he left the army, his solemn leave taken of Congress when he resigned his Commission, his Farewell Address to the people when he resigned his presidency: these were all in a strain of Shakespearean and Garrickal excellence in dramatic exhibitions." JA to Benjamin Rush, 21 June 1811 (Schutz and Adair 180–181).

11. Abigail Adams to Mercy Otis Warren, 5 December 1773 (Butterfield 1:88–89).

CHAPTER 1

1. Hickey 134–135. The club is briefly summarized in Lord 17–18.
2. John Adams counted fifty-six members of the first Congress, twenty-two of whom were lawyers. *Diary*, 29 August 1774.
3. Eddis 136.
4. Cresswell 44–45.
5. Adams, *Diary* 106.
6. Copley 98.
7. Davies 8:207 (5 October 1774).
8. Cresswell 42, 44.
9. Hoffman 2:737.
10. Devine 142.

11. The titles are but a sampling. A more fulsome collection can be found in Bailyn, *Pamphlets of the American Revolution*.

12. Adams later wrote of the argument: "The people of America had been educated in an habitual affection for England, as their mother country; and while they thought her a kind and tender parent, (erroneously enough, however, for she never was such a mother,) no affection could be more sincere. But when they found her a cruel beldam, willing like Lady Macbeth, to 'dash their brains out,' it is no wonder if their filial affections ceased, and were changed into indignation and horror." John Adams to H. Niles, 13 February 1818 (Adams, *Works* 282).

13. John Adams to Abigail Adams, Philadelphia, 20 September 1774 (Butterfield 1:161).

14. *South Carolina Gazette*, 27 December 1773.

15. From Samuel Foote, *The Mayor of Garratt*, played last in Charleston, 30 December 1773 and 21 February 1774.

16. Jay 3.

17. Lieutenant Governor William Bull to Earl of Dartmouth, 20 January 1775 (Davies 9:30); Devine 141.

18. The Committee responded on 18 November 1774. "Address to the Committee of Mechanics, New York," Jay 31–32.

19. Cadwallader Colden to Earl of Dartmouth, 5 October 1774 (Davies 8:207).

20. James Robinson to William Cuninghame, 20 August 1774, GD 247/58, Scottish Record Office, Edinburgh.

21. James Murray to Charles Steuart and James Parker to Charles Steuart, 28 December 1774, MS 5029, Letters of Charles Steuart, National Library of Scotland, Edinburgh.

22. The earlier Committee of Correspondence was succeeded in November 1774 by the Committee of Sixty, or Committee of Inspection. "Rules, &c. of the St. Andrew's Society, at New York, in the Province of New York . . . for the Year 1770," 13. See Morrison 258 for the year 1761.

23. Colden 55:281–282.

24. The accounts of the destruction of the Chapel Street Theatre are chronicled in Johnson and Burling 248–250. "Pro Patria's" letter was published in the *New York Journal*, 15 December 1774.

25. JA to AA, 28 August 1774 (Butterfield 1:144–145).

CHAPTER 2

1 *New York Mercury*, 16 October 1758.

2. For the early performance records, see Johnson and Burling. Relating to

the Anglophone islands, see Richardson Wright 33–47; to the Leeward Islands, see Johnson, "The Leeward Islands Company."

3. *New York Gazette*, 16 October 1758.

4. William Smith 1:226.

5. William Livingston et al. 257, 405.

6. Of these, John Adams would write: "The two great families upon whose motions all their politics turn were the Delanceys and the Livingstons" (Adams, *Diary* 103). For a canvassing of the social dynamics of the ruling families, see Kierner, *Traders and Gentlefolk*; the Cruger family and the new theatre are treated in Nathans 31–32.

7. *New York Gazette*, 22 December 1758; *New York Gazette*, 23 February 1761; Sedgwick 119.

8. *New York Mercury*, 6 November 1758.

9. From Pierce Egan's *Life of an Actor* comes the following note: "This theatre [Richmond] was probably the same that stood on the declivity of the Hill, and was opened in the year 1756 by Theophilus Cibber, who to avoid the penalties of the Act of Parliament against unlicensed comedians, advertised it as *A Cephalic Snuff Warehouse!—The General Advertiser*, July 8, 1756, thus announces it:—Cibber and Co.; Snuff merchants, sell at their warehouse, at Richmond Hill, most excellent cephalic snuff, which taken in moderate quantities (in the evening particularly) will not fail to raise the spirits, clear the brain, throw off ill humours, dissipate the spleen, enliven the imagination, exhilarate the mind, give joy to the heart, and greatly invigorate and improve the understanding! Mr. Cibber has also opened at the aforesaid warehouse (late called the theatre) on the Hill, an *histrionic academy* for the instruction of young persons of genius in the art of Acting; and purposes, for the better improvement of such pupils, and frequently with his assistance, to give public rehearsals—without hire, gain, or reward!" (220n1).

10. *New York Mercury*, 11 December 1758.

11. Odell 76.

12. *New York Mercury*, 1 January, 8 January 1759.

13. Odell 105–106.

14. *New York Mercury*, 8 January 1759. But see Ireland 1:80, who claims Mr. Singleton to be the author.

CHAPTER 3

1 Hickey 197–198.

2. For Washington on Barbados, see the "Barbados Journal" (Washington, *Daily Journal*). For Hamilton's introduction, see Chernow 43. A less generous introduction can be seen in Governor William Tryon's letter to Samuel Ward, governor of Rhode Island, on behalf of a manager of a strolling company of

actors: "Sir—Mr. Mills, who is the manager of a company of comedians, intends to solicit your permission to act in some parts of your Government. He has therefore entreated me to mention their behaviour during their stay here of six months, which, as far as I have understood, has been decent, orderly, and proper. I am, sir, your most obedient servant, Wm. Tryon." Saunders 8:786–787.

3. Paine xix.

4. Anne Arundel County Records, EB-2, 95–127, Maryland State Archives, Annapolis.

5. For more detailed data on the Scottish immigrant communities in America and the Caribbean in the eighteenth century, see Karras.

6. The company was likely playing in New Jersey in the early months of 1759. Both John Bernard (141) and William Dunlap—the latter, born in Perth Amboy, recalled those who knew the players there—record it as such. John Durang claims the company traveled to Providence, Rhode Island, sometime in 1759. For a full discussion of this claim, see Johnson and Burling 189. For Colden's support, see the *Connecticut Gazette*, 22 August 1761: "New York: Last week his honour the Lieutenant Governor was pleased to give Mr. Douglass permission to build a theatre, to perform in this city the ensuing winter."

7. Quoted in Scott 87.

8. The best summary of his brief tenure remains Nicholas B. Wainwright's "Governor William Denny of Pennsylvania." Wainwright's assessment of Denny's career is succinctly summarized in his concluding line: "He [Denny] was in all respects a wretched governor" (198). For Denny's career among the Dilettanti, see Kelly's *The Society of Dilettanti*.

9. William Denny to Mrs. Abigail Edwin, 27 January 1757 (Denny 104).

10. Bridenbaugh 58, 60.

11. Ibid. 144–145.

12. Manuscript from the Gratz Collection, Historical Society of Pennsylvania, Philadelphia.

13. "Petition Respecting the Theatre," 1759, in Hazard 659–660. For a biography of Williams, this interesting and traveled figure, see Dickason.

14. Hornblow 24.

15. Pennsylvania's first prohibitions against the theatre had been ratified in the colony in 1682, repealed in England in 1692, reratified in 1699 and 1700, repealed again in England in 1705, reratified in Pennsylvania in 1706, repealed in 1709, prohibited again in 1711, and repealed again in 1713. See Pollock 4–6.

16. Klepp and Smith 70.

17. Wroth 80–81.

18. The history of Sterling's colonial career is best told in Lemay 257–312.

19. Ibid., 260–261, 306–308.

20. Such were the reflections of John Bernard, *Retrospections on America*, 78.

21. *Memoir of the Life of Josiah Quincy* 479 (11 May 1773).

22. Burnaby 37.

23. Tinling 697–698.

24. Thomas Jefferson to Louis M. Girardin, 15 January 1815 (Jefferson, *Papers of Thomas Jefferson, Retirement Series* 8:1, 200).

25. The earlier minutes are missing; one sheet remains from the winter of 1762. Douglass's induction into the Masonic order is covered in Johnson, *Absence and Memory in Colonial American Theatre* 99–108.

26. Paul Leicester Ford 19.

27. "Journal of a French Traveler" 742.

28. Governor Francis Fauquier to the Lords of Trade, 3 November 1765, Colonial Office Series 5, 1331:139, PRO, London.

29. Robinson wrote of his agents "doing a great deal of business at our General Courts." Devine 11–13.

30. This advance subscription seems to have been one of Douglass's more useful marketing tools, though not his brainchild. A subscription-based advance was first initiated by the Murray-Keen Company, who introduced the idea to Williamsburg in 1751 (*Virginia Gazette*, 29 August 1751). Lewis Hallam, Jr., would use the same scheme in Jamaica in 1779.

CHAPTER 4

1 One recalls Alexander Pope's portrait of rural life: "old fashioned halls, dull aunts, and croaking rooks"; quoted in Porter 55–56.

2. Peter Manigault to Ann Ashby Manigault, 1 November 1750 (Webber 181–182).

3. A small cottage industry has grown up around this phrase, most accessibly T. H. Breen's *The Marketplace of Revolution* and "'Baubles of Britain.'"

4. Bushman 410. Despite the enormous scope of Bushman's work, he curiously overlooks the theatre entirely.

5. Flavell 117.

6. Adams, *Diary* 109.

7. Quoted in Phillips 359.

8. Flavell 130.

9. Gordon Wood discusses this "truncated society" at great length in *The Radicalism of the American Revolution*.

10. *South Carolina Gazette*, 1 March 1773.

11. For a larger discussion on the desire for theatre in the provinces, see Johnson, *Absence and Memory in Colonial American Theatre*.

12. Luffman 119. See also the note on the introduction of theatre in Provi-

dence, Bahamas—to which "they owe their deliverance from Gothic rudeness" in Johnson and Burling 128.

13. Signed, "A Free Thinker," *Pennsylvania Chronicle*, 16 February 1767.

14. A fine example comes from the *Virginia Gazette* (Purdie-Dixon) of 2 April 1772: "Mr. Kelly's new comedy, 'A Word to the Wise' was performed at our Theatre Last Thursday, to a very crowded and splendid Audience. It was received both Nights with the warmest marks of Approbation; the Sentiments with which this excellent Piece is replete were greatly, and deservedly, applauded; and the Audience, while they did Justice to the Merit of the Author, did no less Honour to their own refined tastes. If the comick writers would pursue Mr. Kelly's Plan, and present us only with moral Plays, the Stage would become (what it ought to be) a school of Politeness and Virtue."

15. *New York Journal*, 7 January 1768.

16. For larger conversations on the material culture and the refinement of colonial America, see Bushman.

17. "The Life and Character of General Arnold," extracted in *Continental Journal*, 18 October 1781.

18. This process is noted in Gustafson 216, and more thoroughly charted in Longmore 7, 8.

19. Little documentation exists for the Caribbean circuit in the early 1750s, but see Hill 21–27; Richardson Wright 26–30.

20. It is also quite likely that the young Washington had indulged in that Virginian tradition of amateur theatricals, reading plays in social gatherings. See Paul Leicester Ford 18.

21. Royal Theatre account books, New-York Historical Society, New York.

22. Washington, *Daily Journal* 52.

23. Wood, *Radicalism* 198.

24. Eric Richards 112.

25. Russell 24; see also Mackay 30.

26. She delivered the epilogue for the Freemasons in New York on their annual night of John the Evangelist, 28 December 1753. *Pennsylvania Gazette*, 15 January 1754.

27. See Goring 91–113.

28. Sheridan 4.

29. Ibid. 13.

30. Pottle 28, 65.

31. Ibid. 47.

32. For Sheridan's *Lectures* ordered for the new college in Providence (later Brown University): "list of books for the College Library," MS A9410, James Manning Papers, John Hay Library, Providence, RI. For a sampling of bookstore

advertisements: *Pennsylvania Chronicle*, 6 August 1770; *Boston Chronicle*, 25 April 1768; *Virginia Gazette*, 25 February 1768, *Georgia Gazette*, 26 September 1765; *New York Mercury*, 22 April 1765. For those who couldn't purchase, the *Lectures* were available in the Philadelphia Library Company, *Pennsylvania Chronicle*, 25 December 1769.

33. *New York Gazette*, 1 February 1768.

34. "Examination of Benjamin Franklin in the House of Commons, 13 February 1765" (Greene 73).

35. Quoted in Kammen 270.

36. Bernard 45–46.

37. "[The West Indian] tis [sic] really a prety [sic] performance and afforded me an hours [sic] or two of very agreeable entertainment." AA to Isaac Smith, Jr., 20 April 1771 (Butterfield 1:76–77).

38. Graydon 71–72.

39. Ibid. 88.

40. Boucher, *Reminiscences* 80.

41. Ibid. 66.

42. "London. Mr. Garrick, we are told, will appear in the character of Lear next week, a part which, it was feared he had relinquished, as he has not played in since his return from Italy." *Virginia Gazette*, 4 February 1768. Or, "Mr. Foote (for the first time since his late misfortune) appeared on Tuesday night in men's cloaths, but was obliged to support himself on a couple of sticks. His leg is cut off considerably below the knee." *South Carolina and American General Gazette*, 29 August 1766.

43. Papenfuse 670.

44. Iredell 1:35; see also 1:42.

45. John MacPherson to William Patterson, 30 September 1771, "Extracts of the Letters of John MacPherson," *Pennsylvania Magazine of History and Biography* 23, no. 1 (1899): 51–59.

46. See, for example, his reviews in the *Boston Gazette*, 25 August 1765.

47. *Pennsylvania Gazette*, 22 January 1767.

48. Ibid.

49. *Maryland Gazette*, 6 September 1770. See also Rivington's *Royal Gazette*, 8 December 1779.

50. One finds this expression frequently in the provinces of England as well. Joseph Greene, a pastor in Stratford-upon-Avon, penned several prologues for visiting strolling companies in the late 1740s, lamenting in his playful way the theatre the provinces did not enjoy, as well as the occasion for showboating one's London urbanity:

> You who the sweets of city life have known
> How far beyond the pleasures of this town!

Who in a coach to London-plays have roll'd
Or with your Ladies o'er a side box loll'd;
With such grimace, methinks I hear you say,
"How these d—mned strollers murder a good play?
Where's Wilke's gaity, or Oldfields grace,
Or comick Cibber's foppish meagre face?
I wonder what the plague these bunglars mean!
They've no trap doors, nor scarcely shift a scene."

Fox 29; see also 33–34.

51. Iredell 1:128.
52. Bernard 149.

CHAPTER 5

1 The *Newport Mercury* advertised unclaimed letters (6 October 1766).
2. Ketchum 10.
3. Her death, in Jamaica in April of 1777, had been frequently misprinted as occurring in Philadelphia in 1773. The historiographical issue is rehearsed in my *Absence and Memory in Colonial American Theatre* 204–210.
4. Gifford's provincial career is chronicled in Johnson and Burling 312–317.
5. *Virginia Gazette*, 4 February 1768.
6. Bernard 182.
7. Our best source on income for the provincial theatre in America comes from a collection of playbills of Thomas Wall in the Maryland Historical Society, over the print of which Wall has written the proceeds of the evening and charges (expenses of the house).
8. William Wignell, memorandum book, Historical Society of Pennsylvania, Philadelphia.
9. Bridenbaugh 3.
10. George Owen Willard 6.
11. The *Boston Gazette* prints a long letter dated Newport 18 September 1761 that opines on Douglass's strategies to secure permission to play.
12. George Owen Willard 7.
13. Ibid. 6.
14. *Connecticut Gazette*, 22 August 1761.
15. *Boston Gazette*, 21 September 1761.
16. George Owen Willard 6.
17. News from Philadelphia, reprinted in the *New York Gazette*, 4 August 1766.
18. Quoted in Lemay 308–309.
19. Rankin 72.
20. *Star and Public Advertiser*, 7 September 1763; Curtis 61.
21. Hospital, *South Carolina Gazette*, 21 May 1763; inoculation, *South Carolina*

Gazette, 25 June 1763, 23 July 1763; quarantines, *South Carolina Gazette*, 23 July 1763; landlords and lodging, *South Carolina Gazette*, 28 July 1763.

22. *South Carolina Gazette*, 5 November 1763.

23. "Dr. Watts' Remarks on Playhouses and Midnight Assemblies," *South Carolina Gazette*, 19 November 1763.

24. *South Carolina Gazette*, 10–17 December 1763.

25. "Extracts from the Journal of Mrs. Ann Manigault," *South Carolina Historical and Genealogical Magazine* 20, no. 3 (1919): 205.

26. Colden 55:281–282.

27. The botany connection was encouraged by the ascension of George III in 1760, whose minister, Lord Bute, was an enthusiastic botanist, and whose residence at Kew would become the royal gardens. See Robert Olwell, "Seeds of Empire," in Mancke and Shammas 263–283.

28. Edgar 174.

29. Huguenot Society of South Carolina 60.

30. *Lloyd's List*, 2962, Friday, 1 June 1764.

31. Tobias 67.

CHAPTER 6

1 For example: Douglass signed his name "Esq." in the Galt-Pasteur Apothecary Shop Account Book on 23 December 1770 (Rockefeller Library, Williamsburg, VA, p. 13), as well as the account book of William Bradford, Philadelphia printer, on 22 April 1771 (William Bradford account book, Historical Society of Pennsylvania, Philadelphia); *Massachusetts Spy*, 15 July 1774: "New York, last Wednesday afternoon Capt. Ogilvie arrived here in a schooner . . . in whom came David Douglass, Esq., Manager of the American Company"; see also *New York Gazette*, 15 June 1778. Other actors included William O'Brien, who married above his class and "ruined" his aristocratic wife, reported 27 May 1773, in Rivington's *Gazette*: "The New Farce of Cross Purposes to be performed tomorrow was written by William O'Brien, Esquire, formerly of Drury Lane theatre; a gentleman who, with his amiable consort, Lady Susan, Daughter of the Right Honorable the Earl of Ilchester, resided several years in this city."

2. Quoted in Marble 4–5. Daniel Defoe has left a similar caricature of a newly minted Lord: "I am William Lord Craven, my father was Lord Mayor of London, and my grandfather was the Lord knows who"; quoted in Flavell 196.

3. Eddis 66; Boucher, *A View* 183–184.

4. Quoted in Weir, *Colonial South Carolina* 286–287.

5. Philip Wright xii, xiii.

6. This process of self-invention (more properly, "self-describing") in early America is the subject of a series of case studies gathered up in Hoffman, Sobel, and Teute.

7. "The ship *Heart of Oak*, Henry Gunn, master . . . for Passage, having extraordinary accommodation." *South Carolina Gazette*, 12 November 1772.

8. Technically, Laurens was a major partner in the venture, but the ship was built in South Carolina and Laurens oversaw its construction and launch. It was registered in London, 11 November 1763, with the owners listed: Henry Laurens, James Laurens, John Edwards, John Savage, and John Rose; Laurens had the major share. "Naval Office Shipping Lists," 1764–1767, 70.

9. Olsberg 232.

10. Hugh Thomas 10; Rawley 413.

11. For Laurens's career in the slave trade, see Hugh Thomas 265, 268–270; for his disengagement, see McDonough 22–24, 94–95.

12. Advertisement in the *South Carolina Gazette*, 5 November 1764.

13. Williams 212. For Valton's career in Charleston, see Butler. Laurens was an officer in St. Cecilia's.

14. Even Henry Laurens's domestic slave Scipio changed his name on his shipboard crossing to London accompanying the young John Laurens. When he disembarked, Scipio was now Robert Laurens. The story of the passage is told in Flavell 13.

15. Laurens to Isaac King, 3 April 1764, 7 May 1764 (Laurens 4:268–270).

16. For a brief account of the life of Egerton Leigh, see Calhoon 193–219.

17. Leigh's own words on the matter: "I am a downright Placeman" (Leigh 2).

18. Calhoon 210.

19. See Calhoon and Weir.

20. *The Man Unmasked* and "Satire in the Dramatic Mode," advertised for publication in the *Gazette* of 25 May 1769.

21. Laurens 9:332.

22. Deas and his brother also just purchased land, two thousand acres, on the Altamaha River, bordering on two sides land owned by Henry Laurens and purchased from him, and jointly owned another tract with Laurens. A third Deas, Robert, architect and builder, was the carpenter building Henry Laurens's new house at Ansonberg.

23. Laurens 4:225.

24. Ibid. 4:115n5.

25. London news reprinted in *New York Post-Boy*, 5 July 1764.

26. *Virginia Gazette* (Purdie-Dixon), 30 April 1772. Of the status of wigs, see John Adams's comment on William Livingston: "A plain man . . . wears his hair, nothing elegant or genteel about him." *Diary*, September 1, 1774.

27. Records of the Charleston St. Andrew's Society, Special Collections, College of Charleston, Charleston, SC.

28. Joseph Johnson 234.

29. The Sons of Liberty in Boston, gathered to celebrate the anniversary

of the opposition to the Stamp Act, sang the tune after fourteen toasts. "News from Boston," *Connecticut Journal*, 14–21 August 1770. For a summary of the fulsome life of the song, including its Tory parodies and the second-generation Whig parodies, see John Dickinson 424–432.

30. For more on the song's circulation and many revisions, see Davidson 189–193.

31. Mackraby 493.

32. Edmund Burke, Speaker to the House of Commons, 22 March 1775 ("Speech on Moving Resolutions for Conciliation with America"), in Burke 464–471.

CHAPTER 7

1 The *Heart of Oak* was sighted off Gravesend on 30 May 1764 (*Lloyd's Evening Post*, 1 June 1764), but did not touch land again until 14 June 1764 (*Public Advertiser*, 19 June 1764).

2. Robert Weir's survey of colonial American newspapers concludes that the average delay in reportage from London was nearly eighty days. Weir, *Last of American Freemen* 189, table i.

3. "Hallam's scheme, at the time, was thought to be perfectly Utopian, and was the subject of green-room jest and *jeu d'espirit* while he was organizing the details in London." Charles Durang, "The Philadelphia Stage from 1749 to 1821," serialized in the *Philadelphia Sunday Dispatch*, 1854.

4. The best brief genealogy on the extended Hallam clan is still Highfill 2 (chart).

5. The account of the death and trial is derived from Appleton 30–33.

6. Haslewood 1:142–143.

7. The summer work had not always been strong. Tate Wilkinson lamented that "the little motley troop from London" (to which he belonged) "certainly deserved more attention and encouragement than was bestowed." He, of course, was writing of his own experience, and "not even my Orestes, nor Mrs. Barrington's Andromache, could attract a sufficient audience." They were, however, at the high end of the benefit season, owing to their popularity. Tate Wilkinson: "Wignell, because he was a good stroller, punctually paying his bills and understanding the art of application and solicitation, was, however, certain of a good benefit. So too were the Barringtons, who were able to make a big show, amazing 'the eyes and ears of the little streets with a very handsome one horse chair' in which every noon they 'took a genteel airing.'" (quoted in Rosenfeld 255).

8. *The Thespian Dictionary* (168) would claim that the first Hallam tour netted £10,000 and that her father owned a string of theatres, but this was clearly an exaggeration.

9. Published in the *New York Gazette and Weekly Post-Boy* as London news of the previous year, 6 May 1765.

10. *The Secret History of the Green Room* has little kind to say of their marriage, mentioning only the affairs of both parties that strained relations (Haslewood 1:142–143). Miss Hallam entered the 1764–1765 season at Covent Garden still single; by her benefit (24 April 1765) she had declared her marriage. The quote is from Garrick's adaptation of *The Country Wife* (4.3).

11. See the *North Briton*, #46, 12 November 1763. For a study of Wilkes and his political activism, see Peter D. G. Thomas.

12. Bailyn, *Pamphlets of the American Revolution* 70–73. For a further discussion of the Wilkes riots, see Stevenson 81–94.

13. Bradford 177.

14. "This day is publish'd and sold by Hugh Gaine, on Rotten Row; an Authentic Account of the Proceedings against John Wilkes, Esq; . . . Also the North Briton, No. 45. Being the Paper for which Mr. Wilkes was sent to the Tower. Addressed to all lovers of Liberty." *New York Mercury*, 8 August 1763.

15. Wheeler 37–38.

16. *Public Advertiser* (London), 10 August 1775.

17. Harrington 341.

18. *South Carolina Gazette*, 3 October 1768.

19. Henry Laurens to Thomas Franklin, 26 December 1771 (Laurens 7:21).

20. *Connecticut Gazette–New London*, 25 August 1769 (reprinted from the *Chronicles of Liberty* [London]).

21. *London Evening Post*, 10 May 1764.

22. *St. James Chronicle*, 12 May 1764.

23. The events of the early summer are summarized from *The Annual Register, or a View of the History, Politics, and Literature for the Year 1764*. Their first airing would of course be in the many daily and weekly newspapers. See Rudé.

24. Epitaph reprinted in Stone and Kahrl 648.

25. Hickey 44.

26. The actor's addresses are advertised for Miss Hallam's benefit, 25 April 1764.

27. Highfill 1:130–131; Winston 66.

28. William Douglass, "Notes to the Theatric Tourist," Theatre Museum Library, 1:37, 57; Hare 59.

29. The wartime career of Wall is discussed below.

30. Wilkinson 2:96–97.

31. *The Musical Companion*; *The Warblers Delight*.

CHAPTER 8

1 Literature on the Stamp Act is extensive; I am relying primarily on Morgan and Morgan, Peter D. G. Thomas, and Maier.

2. Silverman 92. I am relying on newspaper reports for the ships' arrivals. No passenger lists survive for either ship, but see note 6 below.

3. George Saxby was a Charleston merchant who had served the colony with a series of appointments over the last decade including councilman, assemblyman, and receiver general. He had received this latest appointment while in London. George Grenville foolishly thought American agents would go down better with their countrymen. Watson 25–26.

4. *South Carolina Gazette*, 31 October 1765. Timothy's *Gazette* has been variously described as "the leading organ of the South Carolina protest movement" (McDonough 53) and "the conduit pipe" of radical ideas (William Bull's report to the Board of Trade, 3 November 1765), while Henry Laurens termed his involvement in the mob action as the "prompter of the play" (Laurens to James Grant, 1 November 1765 [Laurens 5:36]). Timothy's own claim as the conduit of radicalism is best articulated in his own letters; Timothy 17–18.

5. For the full account, see Laurens 5:29–32.

6. Robert Wells published the announcement in the last edition of the *South Carolina Gazette* before the act was to become effective. "On Friday [25 October] last Mr. Douglass, director of the Theatre in this town, arriv'd from London with a reinforcement of his company." There is little documentation on Captain Robson and the *Carolina Packet*—no record in the Registry of Ships, nor in the South Carolina Shipping and Maritime Database (1765, p. 180) for either ship or captain, nor in the maritime reports carried in the *South Carolina Gazette*. Beyond his own claim, it is not clear which ship Douglass and company sailed on. The announcement of his arrival with Captain Robson may simply have been to distance himself from Saxby.

7. The most thorough newspaper account is printed in the *Pennsylvania Gazette* of 2 January 1766 ("News from South Carolina").

8. *South Carolina Gazette*, 31 October 1765.

9. Laurens 5:40; Edgars 209. The ubiquity of the resistance can be better seen in the more provincial ports. See the *Pennsylvania Journal*, 28 November 1765, for an example from St. Kitts, where the stamps were later burned (*London Daily Advertiser*, 12 February 1766).

10. *South Carolina and American General Gazette*, 23–31 October 1765.

11. James Poyas, account and letterbook (1764–1766), MS 34/325, South Carolina Historical Society, Charleston.

12. Peter Thomas 141.

13. Morgan and Morgan 187.

14. William Bull to the Lords of Trade, 3 November 1765, Manuscripts of the House of Lords, 14 February 1766, quoted in Morgan and Morgan 188.

15. "Lieu. Governor Colden's life daily threatened by the Sons of Liberty," observed Captain Montresor; quoted in Ketchum 165.

16. Montresor 362 (4 April 1766).

17. "News for New York," *Pennsylvania Gazette*, 10 April 1766.

18. *Maryland Gazette*, 22 May 1766; see also *New York Post-Boy*, 8 May 1766, and *New York Gazette*, 12 May 1766.

19. Adams, *Diary*, quoted in Ketchum 157.

20. *Pennsylvania Gazette*, 27 March 1766.

21. Benjamin Franklin and David Hall, account books, 1:25, 26 (12 April 1754–27 May 1754), Historical Society of Pennsylvania, Philadelphia. As the Philadelphia editorialists wrote, "their playbills are everywhere"; Jackson 199.

22. Morgan and Morgan 195.

23. Morgan and Morgan 196; Marble 27.

24. *South Carolina Gazette and Country Journal*, 17 December 1765.

25. "To the Public," South Carolina Historical Society, Charleston.

26. *South Carolina Gazette*, 28 March 1769, quoted in Godbold and Woody 66–67.

27. Mrs. Ann Manigault, MS 12/99/3, 18 (19 December 1765), South Carolina Historical Society, Charleston.

28. Royall Tyler, the "first" American playwright (*The Contrast*), wrote in his autobiography of *Cato*'s attraction even in Boston: "Among this general abhorrence of dramatic writing there was one play suffered to be read, and those austere men who would rather have had a pack of cards in their house than a volume of Shakespeare still suffered their children to read Addison's Cato." "The Bay Boy," in Peladeau 143.

29. Garden 208.

30. Sellers 189.

31. Weir, *Colonial South Carolina* 296.

32. Mrs. Ann Manigault, MS 12/99/3, 18–20, 209, South Carolina Historical Society, Charleston.

33. For example, Morgan and Morgan: "[I]t was only the coolness of the officers within [Fort George, New York] that prevented the American Revolution from beginning on November 1, 1765, with an attack on it" (206).

34. Garden 208.

35. *South Carolina Gazette*, 15 April 1766.

36. "Extracts of a Letter Received from Barbados," *Gentleman's Magazine* (London) 36 (1766): 425.

37. Alleyne 63–64.

38. Thomas Usherwood to the Earl of Denbigh, Letterbooks of the 6th Earl of Denbigh, CCR 2017/C243, pp. 30–31, Warwickshire County Record Office, Warwick, England.

39. Cresswell 38.

40. Alleyne 64.

CHAPTER 9

1 Middlekauff 156; Bailyn, *Ideological Origins* 117. The notion of crests and troughs in the struggle is best captured by William Smith, Jr., the historian of New York. Writing of Alexander McDougall's arrest, Smith allowed that "before this alarm our zeal for liberty began to languish. . . . [W]e were all composing ourselves for a nap of security—there was a necessity for fresh oil to quicken that expiring lamp" (75–76). Silverman refers to these as "quiet" and "loud" times (162).

2. Wood, *Radicalism* 169.

3. Iredell 1:420–421.

4. Graydon 132.

5. Tatum 278.

6. Bailyn called this work "the most influential pamphlet published in America before 1776" (*Ideological Origins* 100–101).

7. John Dickinson 34, 130.

8. William Franklin to Benjamin Franklin, 10 May 1768, quoted in Lucas 72.

9. Quoted in H. T. Dickinson 67.

10. *Boston Evening Post*, 9 November 1767, quoted in Breen, *American Insurgents, American Patriots* 208, who develops this anti-consumption campaign around the character of the "virtuous consumer" at some length.

11. The tedious legislative journey is traced in Johnson and Burling 94–98.

12. *Pennsylvania Gazette*, 31 July 1766.

13. *Pennsylvania Gazette*, 5 March, 12 March 1767; *Pennsylvania Chronicle*, 9 March, 30 March 1767.

14. *Pennsylvania Gazette*, 5 March 1767.

15. And indeed, the old fight would continue in America, under the same terms in the same city by the same Synod. Nearly thirty years later, Henry Wansey would observe of the new Chestnut Street Theatre, Philadelphia, that the Synod of Quakers petitioned to have it prohibited, unsuccessfully. Wansey 127.

16. *Gentleman's Magazine*, May 1764.

17. Mackraby 494 (20 June 1770).

18. Thomas Wharton to B. Franklin, 7 February 1767 (Franklin 14:29–30). See also Hutson 81–82.

19. *Pennsylvania Chronicle*, 30 March 1767.

20. *Pennsylvania Chronicle*, 11–18 May 1767.

21. Walker 410.

22. *New York Gazette, or The Weekly Post-Boy*, 3 December 1767.

23. "To the Printer," reprinted from *Providence Gazette* (New York), 9 January 1768.

24. *New York Journal*, 10 December 1767; see also *New York Journal*, 17, 24, 31 December 1767.

25. *New York Journal*, 17 December 1767.

26. *New York Gazette*, 1 February 1768.

27. *New York Journal*, 7 January, 1768. This perception of extravagance is also discussed in Nathans 33–34.

28. Withington 27–28.

29. Washington, *Diaries* (ed. Fitzpatrick) 2:272.

30. *New York Gazette, or Weekly Post-Boy*, 17 December 1767.

31. *New York Gazette, or Weekly Post-Boy*, 24 December 1767.

32. Quoted in Bailyn, *Ideological Origins* 103.

33. "Philander," *New York Journal*, 28 January 1768.

34. *New York Journal*, 25 January 1768.

35. *New York Gazette and Weekly Post-Boy*, 20 August 1767.

36. *New York Mercury*, 10 April 1769.

37. Ibid.

38. Ireland 1:54–55.

39. Garden 267–268.

40. David G. Martin 71.

41. *Boston Evening Post*, 9 March 1767.

42. *Boston Gazette*, 30 March, 6 April 1767.

43. Bradford 116. Andrew Eliot had something to do with this bill. He wrote to Thomas Hollis boasting of his energies exerted to prevent the theatre; "Letters from Eliot to Hollis," in Massachusetts Historical Society 403–404. Hancock would continue to resist the introduction of theatre through the early 1790s. Two letters by John Quincy Adams to his father document his fierce opposition. JQA to JA, 8 December, 16 December (Butterfield 1:340–341, 348–350).

44. Quoted in Wood, *Radicalism* 88.

45. Francis Bernard to Lord Hillsborough, 2 October 1768, quoted in Unger 126.

46. *Boston Evening Post*, 13 March 1769.

47. Ramsay 1:68–69.

48. Rowe 189 (24 June 1769). For the St. John's Night gathering, see the *Boston Post-Boy*, 19 June 1769.

49. For the various social capacities of Colonel Ingersoll's Bunch of Grapes Tavern, see Rowe 118, 153 (merchants); 119, 258–259 (Freemasons); 146, 153, 214 (Charitable Society).

50. Ibid. 190–191.

51. Oliver 63.

52. Original letter in Harvard Theatre Collection, reprinted in Odell 152.

53. David Douglass to William Bradford, 2 June 1770, Bradford correspondence (1770), Historical Society of Pennsylvania, Philadelphia.

54. Henry Drinker to James Abel, 26 May 1770 ("Effects of the Nonimportation Agreement in Philadelphia" 45).

CHAPTER 10

1 The activities of William Verling and the New American Company are discussed in Rankin 140–152 and chronicled in Johnson and Burling 286–289.

2. James Robinson to David Walker, Falmouth, 11 July 1770 (Devine 31–32, 78–80).

3. *Virginia Gazette* (Purdie-Dixon), 21 June 1770.

4. David Walker, 17 April 1770; James Robinson to William Henderson, April 1770 (Devine 28).

5. *Virginia Gazette* (Purdie-Dixon), 21 June 1770.

6. As was Fauquier merchant Bennet Price's concentrated experience, of June 1769 (Devine 7).

7. William Byrd, "Progress to the Mines," 22 September 1732 (Byrd 341–342).

8. Washington, *Diaries* (ed. Fitzpatrick) 2:384.

9. The escalation of hostility is summarized in Middlekauff 202–205; the episode of the "liberty pole" is treated in ibid. 192–193.

10. The time line for most colonies is ably rehearsed in ibid. 182–183.

11. The phrase is from Washington's handwriting added to the document on the sheets he circulated through Fairfax County; Fitzpatrick 16.

12. Henry Drinker to Abel James, 9 December 1769 ("Effects of the NonImportation Agreement in Philadelphia" 41).

13. Though concentrating on wartime experiences across the lines, some of these notions of the influence of civility are expanded in Van Buskirk. I am borrowing the notion of "technologies of empire" from Ryan.

14. Bernard 87–92.

15. Jefferson, *Papers* 1:7.

16. Bear and Stanton 1:205.

17. Ibid. 1:210–211.

18. Malone 56.

19. Washington, *Diaries* (ed. Jackson and Twohig) 2:245–246.

20. Ibid. 2:248.

21. Washington, *Diaries* (ed. Fitzpatrick) 2:125.

22. *Virginia Gazette* (Purdie-Dixon), 5 April 1770.

23. Middlekauff 182.

24. *Virginia Gazette* (Purdie-Dixon), 7 June 1770, reprinted as "News from New York" (10 May 1770).

25. See Butterfield 1:73n2 for a long inventory of the effect of non-importation on English manufacturing.

26. Bonomi 276.

27. "Effects of the Non-importation Agreement in Philadelphia" 41.

28. "The large orders, which are sent here [London] for tea perplex the mind of every friend to our interest or reputation," wrote Isaac Smith to John Adams; Butterfield 1:70 (21 February 1771).

29. Hiltzheimer 22.

30. Association of Virginia Burgesses, 22 June 1770, Manuscript Division, Library of Congress, Washington, DC.

31. Oliver 61.

32. "To the Ladies" (1769), in Moore, *Songs and Ballads* 49.

33. Isaac 193.

34. Tyler, "Hudson Muse to T. Muse" 241. Colonel Henry Basset and Andrew Skinner Ennalls, the men referred to, were both friends of Washington; the later would petition Washington two decades later for a post as treasurer with the newly established US Mint (Ennalls to GW, 18 February 1791 [Washington, *Papers* (Presidential Series) 382–383]). The brilliance of Virginia assemblies was also noted by Jonathan Boucher.

35. *Pennsylvania Chronicle*, 24–31 October 1772.

36. Rowland 1:143.

37. *Maryland Gazette*, 6 September 1770.

38. Association paper of 22 June 1769, Broadside 35, Maryland Historical Society, Annapolis.

39. A review of the company for this 1770 season is preserved in the *Maryland Gazette* of 6 September 1770.

40. Wood, *Radicalism* 35.

41. Haulman 145.

42. "General Accounts of Receipts and Disbursements for the Two Last Seasons" (1782), broadside, New-York Historical Society, New York. The silk for Mrs. Williams and other essentials are found in the Theatre Royal account books for the year 1778, in which, again, nearly £3,800 in ticket sales was taken in and a mere £140 dispersed in charity; Jared Brown 93n36.

43. James Robinson to David Walker, Falmouth, 11 July 1770 (Devine 31–32).

44. Henry Drinker to James Able, 29 April 1770 ("Effects of the Non-importation Agreement in Philadelphia, 1769–1770" 42).

45. Roger Atkinson to John Ponsonby, 19 November 1769, Atkinson letter-book, Rockefeller Library, Williamsburg, VA.

46. Weir, *Colonial South Carolina* 303.

47. The Methodist preacher Joseph Pilmore found preaching in the theatre too hot and moved the benches outside; Pilmore 151.

48. Cadwallader Colden to the Earl of Dartmouth, 7 December 1774, writing of the Continental Congress (Davies 7:217).

49. GW to George Mason, 5 April 1769 (Washington, *Papers* [Colonial Series] 177–181).

50. Ibid.

51. Withington 22.

52. For Basset, see Kneebone 383–384. He rode with Washington on the Braddock campaign and accompanied Washington to the theatre, several occasions of which Washington recorded. For Jefferson, see Bear and Stanton 1:254, 262–263; for Washington, see *Diaries* (Jackson and Twohig) 3:24–26; "Letter from Hudson Muse, of Virginia, to His Brother, Thomas Muse, of Dorchester Co., Maryland."

53. Sir William Nelson did not sign it, but allowed he was an "associate in principle." Van Horne 34. For the full text of the Virginia Association for Nonimportation, see *Journals of the House of Burgesses* xl–xliii.

54. For the shareholders of the earlier theatre, see Tyler, "The First Play-House in Williamsburg" 29–30.

55. *New York Gazette*, 1 February 1768.

56. The Lee house, formally known as the Ludwell-Paradise House, block 18, lot 7, Duke of Gloucester Street, was next to the capital. "Notes from the Meeting of the President and Masters of the College, 11 April 1771."

CHAPTER 11

1 Association paper of 22 June 1769, broadside 35, Maryland Historical Society, Annapolis: "We the subscribers, his Majesty's loyal and dutiful Subjects, the Merchants traders, freeholders, Mechanics and other Inhabitants of the Province of Maryland, seriously considering the present State and Conditions of the Province, and being sensible, that there is a Necessity to agree upon measures as may tend to discourage, and as much as may be, prevent the Use of foreign Luxuries and Superfluities, in the Consumption of which, we have hitherto too much indulged ourselves, to the great Detriment of our Private Fortunes, and in some instances to the ruin of families, and to this end to practice ourselves and as much as possible to promote, countenance and encourage in others, a Habit of Temperance, Frugality, Oeconomy, and Industry."

2. Douglass's description of the theatre was published in the *Maryland Gazette*, 13 June 1771.

3. *Maryland Gazette*, 4 October 1770.

4. *Maryland Gazette*, 12 September 1771.

5. *Maryland Gazette*, 6 September 1770.

6. *New York Journal*, 28 January 1768.

7. Boucher to Washington, 18 December 1770 (Washington, *Papers* [Colonial Series] 413–417. For Jacky Custis's pocket expenditures, see Washington, *Diaries* (ed. Jackson and Twohig) 2:271 (September 18).

8. Washington's cashbook for the week records the damage: "By sundry tickets to the plays, [£]1"; followed by additional notes of expenditures: "Oct 5: By Douglass's Compy £1. 19. 0"; Paul Leicester Ford 23.

9. Boucher, *Reminiscences* 65.

10. Ibid. 71.

11. Ibid. 66.

12. *Maryland Gazette*, 6 September 1770.

13. *Maryland Gazette*, 4 October 1770.

14. For Nancy Hallam's performance, see "YZ," *Maryland Gazette*, 6 September 1770; Eddis 202–215 (letter xx).

15. For a brief history of this social club, see Shields 198–208.

16. Records of the Homony Club of Annapolis, folio 68, Historical Society of Pennsylvania, Philadelphia, reprinted in the *American Historical Record* 1:295–303, 301–302 (July 1872). See also Silverman 240.

17. "XY," *Maryland Gazette*, 6 September 1770.

18. *Maryland Gazette*, 7 November 1771.

19. The "self-taught" epithet may be a bit of a misnomer, as Annapolis merchants, recognizing his great talent, had funded Peale a trip to London in 1767 to study with Benjamin West. This application for a club portrait is related in the memoirs of the Homony Club, *American Historical Record* 1:302.

20. Charles Carroll to Charles Carroll, Jr., 7 May 1771 (Hoffman 2:569).

21. *Maryland Gazette*, 20 August 1772.

22. Earl of Hillsborough to Deputy Governor Robert Eden, 3 October 1770 (Davies 2:198).

23. For a summary of the breakdown of non-importation in Maryland, see Scharf 118–119. For Drinker's comments, see Henry Drinker to James Abel, 26 May 1770 ("Effects of the Non-importation Agreement in Philadelphia, 1769–1770" 44).

24. Annapolis, 11 October 1770, reprinted in the *Virginia Gazette* (P&D), 25 October 1770.

25. Charles Carroll, Jr., to Charles Carroll, Sr., 9 August 1771 (Hoffman 2:579).

26. Eddis 106–110 (2 November 1771).

27. Washington, *Diaries* (ed. Jackson and Twohig) 3:178–182.

CHAPTER 12

1 Receipt of tavern bill, St. Andrew's Society, 30 November 1773, "Notes of the Charleston St. Andrew's Society," Special Collections, College of Charleston, Charleston, SC.

2. The Society met on 28 February, 31 May, 31 August, and 30 November each year.

3. Boucher, *Reminiscences* 137; Boucher to Washington, 6 August 1775 (Washington, *Papers* [Revolutionary War Series] 252–255). Van Buskirk offers similar accounts in New York.

4. Crèvecoeur 342–343.

5. The records are housed in Special Collections, College of Charleston, Charleston, SC.

6. "An Address Delivered in the First Presbyterian Church before the St. Andrew's Society of the City of Charleston on Their Centennial Anniversary" (Easterby 74).

7. Curiously, this tag line is usually omitted in the many source books (including my own) that reproduce the public letter Douglass published in the *South Carolina Gazette* of 30 May 1774, reprinted in the *Virginia Gazette*, 16 June 1774.

8. *Public Advertiser*, 2 November 1773.

9. Extract of a letter, reprinted in the *South Carolina Gazette and Country Journal*, 5 January 1773. "Scratch for Scratch is a game well understood by all Political Adepts," wrote the *St. James Chronicle*, 9 March 1773. This definition is not found in Dr. Johnson's dictionary, as it is usually conceived to be a Scottish variant.

10. *South Carolina Gazette*, 26 July 1773: "On Friday last arrived the Brig Betsey, Captain Schermerhorn, from New York, in whom came . . . Mr. Douglass, Manager of the American Company of Comedians who, we hear, proposes to erect a theatre here."

11. *South Carolina Gazette*, 27 December 1773.

12. Hewatt 2:296–297. The construction of the new theatre on Church Street coincided with the arrival of a visiting Baptist preacher, Mr. Piercy. He undertook a series of "evening lectures" against the pleasures of the playhouse now rising just a few lots away from the Charleston Baptist church. Recycling old arguments, moral and economic, he laid the blame at the feet of the lieutenant governor and the council for not disallowing the project. Several of his parishioners penned letters in objection to the new playhouse, and once it opened initiated a bill in council to have it suppressed. The bill was quashed.

13. Edgar 123.

14. "Virginianus," *Virginia Gazette*, 21 July 1774.

15. Weir, *Colonial South Carolina* 123. See, for example, the soliloquies of "Vir-

ginianus," *Virginia Gazette* (Rind), 21 July 1774. "James Gilcrest to Capt. James Parker, Halifax, Dec 22 1774," *William and Mary Quarterly*, 1st ser., 13 (1905): 69.

16. Leacock 1.2.
17. *Virginia Gazette*, 20 October 1774.
18. *Virginia Gazette*, 20 May 1773.
19. *New York Journal*, 5 November 1767.
20. Canby 461.
21. "His [Leigh's] spirits have been lately supported by a company of Players who have been fleecing this town since November last, who when they do not entertain him at the theatre (where, by the by, he has met with much disrespect), get drunk with him at his own house"; James Laurens to Henry Laurens, 3 March 1774 (Laurens 332).
22. Valton arrived in Charleston on the return leg of the *Heart of Oak* passage that Douglass had sailed on in 1764; benefit concerts: November 13, 1765, again in February 1774; the sonatas (original compositions of Valton's) were advertised in the *South Carolina Gazette* of 10 October 1768 and the *New York Mercury* of 10 January 1769. "Those intending to encourage this work to send their names to the author, to Mr. Gaines, or to Mr. David Douglass as soon as possible." Mr. Gaines is Hugh Gaines, New York printer; Douglass was in Philadelphia at the time.
23. John Moultrie, for example, a Scottish physician, was the first president of both the St. Cecilia's Society and the St. Andrew's Society; Robert Wells was secretary for both the Masonic Lodge—which was itself named after its Scottish charter, Union Kilwinning—and the St. Andrew's. The member lists between St. Andrew's, the Masons, and St. Cecilia's were extensively shared; a few names recognizable from this narrative include: David and John Deas, Alexander Garden, Rawlins Lowndes, Charles Cotesworth Pinckney, and Alexander Fraser. From Butler, appendix iv.
24. "Rules, &c. of the St. Andrew's Society, at New York, in the Province of New York: Adopted November 30th, 1764; With List of Members, Resident and Honorary, for the Year 1770," New-York Historical Society, New York.
25. Nelson 64.
26. The notes of the St. Andrew's Society of Charleston are recently donated and as yet uncatalogued; Misc. file, member lists, 1773. A transcription of the cumulative membership is also available. It is unclear when Douglass's association with the club began. The bylaws state (II: iii), "[N]o person shall be balloted for at the same meeting on which his application was presented (except on St. Andrews Day)," which would be less helpful in a close community in which Douglass was no stranger to most Scotsmen. That he leased land from four of the members on the day of the last quarterly meeting (28 August) might suggest that he was formally introduced in August and balloted in November. The full

deed (indenturement) of Douglass, Robert Wells, Robert Rowand, John Deas, and Alexander Michie is found in the Mesne Conveyance Office register, misc. 1779–1781, 46–50, Charleston County, Charleston, SC.

27. Brobeck 432.

28. For a fine period description of the protocols and expectations of toasting, see Chastellux 1:110.

29. *South Carolina Gazette and Country Journal*, 30 November 1773. Anti-tea broadsides had circulated as early as 23 November 1773, reprinted from Philadelphia and New York. *South Carolina Gazette and Country Journal*, 23 November 1773, concluding: "Freemen, American Freemen, can never approve it."

30. *South Carolina Gazette*, 29 November 1773.

31. See Godbold and Woody 110, to whom this discussion is indebted.

32. Fraser 136; *South Carolina Gazette*, 13 December 1773. For a summary of that winter's conflict between patriotism and mercantilism, see Lambert 15–17.

33. *South Carolina Gazette*, 13 December 1773.

34. Butterfield 2:85–86.

35. William Eddis, in Annapolis, for example, expected Charleston to treat the tea exactly as Boston had; Eddis 156–157 (letter xvi).

36. HL to JL, 18 January 1775 (Laurens 10:29).

37. Drayton 1:97–98.

38. Ibid. 1:98. Drayton traces the many meetings, resolutions, and debates over the landing of the tea that occupied the winter (97–100).

39. The Pennsylvania resolves are printed in Ramsay 1:91–92.

40. *South Carolina Gazette*, 20 December 1773; for a summary of the events, see Sellers 222–225.

41. *South Carolina Gazette*, 30 November 1773.

42. *Pennsylvania Gazette*, 24 December 1773.

43. *High Life below Stairs*, act 2. The lines were pointed enough to be excised in editions published after 1775. The 1780 London edition, for example, derived from the manager's book at Drury Lane, had excised the lines. Douglass would have acquired the 1770 published edition.

44. 27 May 1774 (Jefferson, *Papers* 1:108).

45. John Adams to Abigail Adams, July 6, 1774 (Butterfield 1:129–130).

46. Susanne Centlivre, *A Bold Stroke for a Wife*, 4.1; performed 21 February and 2 May 1774.

47. *South Carolina Gazette and Country Journal*, 28 December 1773.

48. The "Sign or Die" campaign is best summarized in Walsh 45–50.

49. Davies 7:28, v.

50. William Smith 1:158.

51. Abigail Adams to Mercy Warren, 5 December 1773 (Butterfield 1:88).

52. See, for example, *Rivington's Gazette*, 6 May 1773.

53. "Song from the Boston Tea Party," in Goss 123–124.

54. "At Trenton in West Jersey they tar'd and feather'd a man just for Drinking the King's health." Ambrose Barcroft, writing to his cousin, quoted in Hibbert 9.

55. "Reminiscences of Thomas Johnson," *Potters American Monthly* 1 (1872): 101.

56. Jones 1:476.

57. *New York Gazette*, 26 March 1770.

58. This is a three-edition squabble, beginning in the *New York Gazette*, 26 March 1770; rebutted in the *New York Journal*, 29 March 1770; and defended in the *New York Journal*, 12 April 1770.

59. Flexner 9.

60. *South Carolina Gazette*, 21 March 1774.

61. The day was described with some detail by Peter Timothy, *South Carolina Gazette*, 21 March 1774.

62. Ketchum 173.

63. William Moultrie and Charles Cotesworth Pinckney, who commanded the Charleston militia, had both urged the resolution that prevented the tea from being unloaded.

64. Bull to Dartmouth, 10 March 1774 (Davies 8:64).

65. *South Carolina Gazette*, 17 October 1774.

66. Bull to Dartmouth, 3 August 1774 (Davies 8:158).

67. Fithian 148.

68. Bull 200.

69. "The Calvert Family of South Carolina," genealogic and biographic report prepared by Robert Paslay, Jr., MS 30-04, South Carolina Historical Society, Charleston.

70. Weir, *Last of American Freemen* 287.

71. *South Carolina Gazette and Country Journal*, 6–13 May 1774.

72. Mays 148.

73. See, for example, Rind's *Virginia Gazette*.

74. Quoted in Martin 80–81. For Thomas's position, see Isaiah Thomas 164–165.

75. Douglass advertised his lodging in the *South Carolina Gazette*, 9 August 1773.

76. *Pennsylvania Gazette*, 2 January, 1766 (reprinted news from South Carolina).

77. Easterby 46. Robert Wells operated his bookstore out of 71 Tradd Street, and lived next door. Alexander Michie, Robert Rowand, and David Deas also lived on Tradd Street (Gould 27). When Wells attacked John Wilkes, he became, in his own words, "extremely offensive to the people of Carolina" (Wells ix).

His coverage of the Boston Massacre must have left his paper in many a patriot fireplace. Despite the stream of loyalism that poured out of the Wells press, his last two years in America (1774–1775) were his most profitable (Gould 29); he is loaning large sums of money and investing in long-term leases, including the theatre. For Robert Rowand's loyalism, see Laurens 11:213 (January 1776–November 1777). For the plat map, see Smith and Smith 235–256. For "Tory Row," see Harriot 172.

78. Bell 157–158. Mordecai later moved to Richmond after the Revolution and returned to Philadelphia for a visit quite late in life. During this latter visit, while reminiscing about the "old days," he was introduced to John Watson's *Annals of Philadelphia*. Mordecai read the work and commenced his own recollections, to be added as interleaves in the next edition of Watson's work. The plan never came to pass and Mordecai's notes went unpublished until 1971.

79. *New York Gazette*, 21 June, 5 July 1773.

80. "Theatre Royal in New York, these plays were performed in April, May, and June," MS, acc. 6 July 1946, New-York Historical Society, New York.

81. From Shakespeare, *The Complete Works* (Baltimore: Penguin, 1969).

CHAPTER 13

1 Edgar 161.

2. Quincy 72–73. Crèvecoeur, a decade later, is equally astonished by the sumptuous lifestyle (Crèvecoeur 158–159).

3. Quincy 195.

4. Edgar 164.

5. T. H. Breen quotes a "foreign visitor" (Jacob Duché) in 1774 who registered equal astonishment at the loaded wharfs in Philadelphia: "[E]very wharf within my view is surrounded with groves of masts and heaped with commodities of every kind from almost every quarter of the globe" (*The Marketplace of Revolution* 111).

6. *New York Mercury*, 28 December 1761.

7. *Virginia Gazette*, 21 July 1774.

8. Fithian 29.

9. *Virginia Gazette* (Purdie-Dixon), 30 April 1772.

10. Ibid. 95.

11. McDonough 137.

12. *South Carolina Gazette*, 9 January 1774.

13. "News from Charleston," *Virginia Gazette*, 10 March 1774.

14. "This being the day when the cruel act for blocking up the harbour of Boston took effect, many of the inhabitants of this city, to express their sympathy and show their concern for their suffering brethren in the common cause of liberty, had their shops shut up, their houses kept close from hurry and busi-

ness; also the bells at Christ Church were muffled, and rung a solemn peel at intervals from morning to night; the colours of the vessels in the harbour were hoisted half-mast high. . . . Sorrow mixed with indignation seemed to be in the countenances of the inhabitants, and indeed, the whole city wore an aspect of deep distress, being a melancholy occasion." Marshall 6 (1 June 1774).

15. James Robinson to Messrs W. Cuninghame & Co., 7 June 1774 (Devine 141–142).
16. Ibid.
17. Christopher Gadsden to Samuel Adams, 5 June 1774 (Gadsden 96).
18. Figures are from Sellers 229.
19. *South Carolina Gazette*, 4 July 1774; 19 September 1774.
20. Edward Rutledge to Mr. Izard, 21 July 1774 (Izard 2–3).
21. William Bull to Earl of Dartmouth, 31 July 1774 (Davies 8:153–154).
22. Crain 437; *South Carolina Gazette*, 19 September 1774.

CHAPTER 14

1 Printed in the *Morning Chronicle and Daily Advertiser*, 25 February 1775.
2. Jones 1:451–452.
3. William Smith 1:157–158.
4. Jones 1:465–466.
5. Honyman 31.
6. Philip Livingston 28.
7. Adams, *Diary* 107.
8. Colden 10:374.
9. Davies 8:238; Cadwallader Colden to Earl of Dartmouth, 7 December 1774; Earl of Dartmouth to Colden; quoted in Nelson 65, Nelson 69.
10. "He was sitting under his hairdresser's hands, when it was made known that all the theatres on the continent were virtually closed by this recommendation" (Dunlap 64–65).
11. *New York Journal*, 15 December 1774.
12. Governor John Wentworth of New Hampshire wrote a very detailed account to the Earl of Dartmouth narrating how his colony's militia carried off the province's supply of gunpowder and cannon, and attempted to dismantle the fort itself; Davies 8:248–251.
13. Longaker 149–150.
14. Cooper 37. Cooper's reflections on the "patriots" obliged him to retreat to a British ship, where "he thought fit to shelter himself from the resentment of a people who consider him the writer of several pieces highly injurious to the liberties of America"; *New England Chronicle*, 1 June 1775.
15. Cooper 4.
16. Ibid. 3.

17. *New York Gazette*, 3 May 1773. For similar disturbances in Philadelphia the previous year, see the *Pennsylvania Chronicle*, 31 October 1772.

18. William Smith 1:192.

19. Josiah Martin to Earl of Dartmouth, 4 November 1774 (Davies 8:226).

20. Jones 1:444.

21. Ibid. 1:445–446.

22. William Smith 1:188–192; Philip Livingston 25–29.

23. York, *Henry Hulton* 353.

24. The New York Sons of Liberty gathered on Monday, 19 March 1770, to celebrate the anniversary of the repeal of the Stamp Act (the 18th being the Sabbath). Early in their evening of forty-five toasts, between the "glorious revolution" and John Wilkes and Alexander McDougall, was their toast to the liberty of the press. *New York Gazette*, 26 March 1770.

25. William Smith 1:157–158. As the writer insisted in the *New York Journal* (8 December 1774), this "contest is not for what these traitors to their country would fain have it believe to be, but for our very lives, religion, and estates."

26. Extract of "A genuine letter to a gentleman from his friend at New York," 28 December 1774, in the *Morning Chronicle and Daily Advertiser*, 2 February 1775.

27. Egnal and Ernst 6.

28. Middlekauff 249.

29. Davies 8:232.

30. Thomas Godfrey's *Prince of Parthia*, performed at the Southwark Theatre, Philadelphia, 24 April 1767. Two weeks earlier, another American original, Thomas Forrest's *The Disappointment*, was scheduled for production at the same theatre but then withdrawn. Johnson and Burling 271.

31. Quoted in McCullough 8–9.

32. That was, of course, Boston, with a closed port; Ruddock 75.

33. Ramsay 1:135.

34. Ketchum 303.

35. *Maryland Gazette*, 6 March 1760.

36. In *Civil Tongues and Polite Letters*, chap. 9, "Toward the Polite Republic," David Shields traces the arduous rebuilding of polite culture, clubs, and societies after the war, but that would be the 1790s.

37. The full set of resolutions was published in the *New York Journal*, 15 December 1774. The British subjects of Jamaica, though expressing their sympathy for the disturbances in America, remained vigorously loyalist.

38. Lambert 269.

39. The departure notice was reproduced in the *Virginia Gazette* of 28 January 1775. Rivington's original has not survived. The retraction was published in the *New York Mercury* of 2 January 1775.

40. Colden 9:236–237.

41. Cadwallader Colden to the Earl of Dartmouth, 7 December 1774 (Colden 10:373–374).

EPILOGUE

1 James Robinson to W. Cuninghame and Co. (Devine 179).

2. "Yet I cannot but hope a few months may again restore us to such a peaceful state, that we shall no longer hear the din of arms"; Mercy Otis Warren to Harriot Temple, 2 June 2 1775 (Richards and Harris 50). Laurens 10:22.

3. Brobeck 432.

4. Quoted in McDonough 137.

5. Quoted in Ketchum 300–301.

6. Ruddock 76.

7. Miller 1:250–269.

8. McCullough 119.

9. Wallace Brown 189.

10. Daggett's story is told in Allen 303.

11. Tinling 2:803n1.

12. Marshall iii.

13. The nephews were Stephen Bull and William Henry Drayton; Zahniser 36.

14. Wallace Brown 173.

15. Quoted in Moore, *Diary* 4.

16. Boucher, *Reminiscences* 105–108. Boucher technically lived in Virginia, hence he characterized himself as a "Virginian" in his pamphlet *A Letter from a Virginian to Members of Congress*.

17. Cadwallader Colden, *Journal*, quoted in Crary 228–229.

18. Lambert 190–191.

19. —— to Thomas Jefferson, 27 February 1781 (Pleasants 91).

20. Major Phillips to Governor Thomas Jefferson, 12 August 1779; Fielder Gannt, Frederick, to Governor Lee, 1 February 1781 (Pleasants 46).

21. For more on the repercussions of Captain Watson's ship, see Rivington's *Gazette*, 16 February 1775, 2 March 1775.

22. Ruddock 75.

23. "Papers of the Second Council of Safety of the Revolutionary Party in South Carolina" 16.

24. John Dickinson to Arthur Lee, 27 October 1774 (Burnett 83).

25. Fithian 3.

[WORKS CITED]

ARCHIVAL SOURCES

Anne Arundel County Records. Maryland State Archives, Annapolis.

Association of Virginia Burgesses, June 22, 1770. Manuscript Division, Library of Congress, Washington, DC.

Association paper of June 22, 1769. Broadside 35. Maryland Historical Society, Annapolis.

Atkinson letterbook. Rockefeller Library, Williamsburg, VA.

Bradford, William, account book. Historical Society of Pennsylvania, Philadelphia.

Bradford correspondence. Historical Society of Pennsylvania, Philadelphia.

Charleston St. Andrew's Society, records. Special Collections, College of Charleston, Charleston, SC.

Franklin, Benjamin, and David Hall, account books. Historical Society of Pennsylvania, Philadelphia.

Galt-Pasteur Apothecary Shop account book. Rockefeller Library, Williamsburg, VA.

"General Accounts of Receipts and Disbursements for the Two Last Seasons" (1782). Broadside. New-York Historical Society, New York.

Gratz Collection. Historical Society of Pennsylvania, Philadelphia.

Homony Club of Annapolis, records. Historical Society of Pennsylvania, Philadelphia.

Manigault, Mrs. Ann, diary abstracts. South Carolina Historical Society, Charleston.

Manning, James, papers. John Hay Library, Providence, RI.

Mesne Conveyance Office, register. Charleston County, Charleston, SC.

"Naval Office Shipping Lists for the West Indies (Excluding Jamaica) 1678–1825: In the Public Record Office, London." East Ardsley, Yorkshire, England: Micro Methods, 1980.

Poyas, James, account and letterbook (1764–1766). South Carolina Historical Society, Charleston.

Robinson, James, letters. Scottish Record Office (now renamed National Records of Scotland), Edinburgh.

"Rules, &c. of the St. Andrew's Society, at New York, in the Province of New York: Adopted November 30th, 1764; With List of Members, Resident and Honorary, for the Year 1770." New-York Historical Society, New York.

Sixth Earl of Denbigh, letterbooks. Warwickshire County Record Office, Warwick, England.

Steuart, Charles, letters. National Library of Scotland, Edinburgh.

"Theatre Royal in New York, these plays were performed in April, May, and June." MS. New-York Historical Society, New York.

Wignell, William, memorandum book. Historical Society of Pennsylvania, Philadelphia.

PUBLISHED SOURCES

Adams, John. *Diary and Autobiography of John Adams*, vol. 2: *1771–1781*. Edited by L. H. Butterfield. Cambridge, MA: Belknap Press of Harvard University Press, 1961.

———. *The Works of John Adams, Second President of the United States, with a Life of the Author*. Edited by Charles Francis Adams. Vol. 10. Boston: Little, Brown, 1856.

Albanese, Catherine L. *Sons of the Fathers: The Civil Religion of the American Revolution*. Philadelphia: Temple University Press, 1976.

Allen, Thomas B. *Tories: Fighting for the King in America's First Civil War*. New York: HarperCollins, 2010.

Alleyne, Warren. *Historic Bridgetown*. Bridgetown: Barbados National Trust, 1978.

American Historical Record, and Repertory of Notes and Queries. 3 vols. Philadelphia: Chase and Town, 1872–1874.

Ames, Nathaniel. *The Diary of Nathaniel Ames of Dedham, Massachusetts, 1758–1822*. Edited by Robert Brand Hanson. 2 vols. Camden, ME: Picton Press, 1998.

The Annual Register, or a View of the History, Politics, and Literature for the Year 1764. London: J. Dodsley, 1765.

Appleton, William W. *Charles Macklin: An Actor's Life*. Cambridge, MA: Harvard University Press, 1960.

Bailyn, Bernard. *The Ideological Origins of the American Revolution*. Enlarged edition. Cambridge, MA: Belknap Press of Harvard University Press, 1992.

———, ed. *Pamphlets of the American Revolution: 1750–1776*. Vol. 1. Cambridge, MA: Belknap Press of Harvard University Press, 1965.

Bailyn, Bernard, and Morgan, Philip D., eds. *Strangers within the Realm: Cultural Margins of the First British Empire*. Chapel Hill: University of North Carolina Press, 1991.

Barker, Kathleen. *The Theatre Royal Bristol, 1766–1966: Two Centuries of Stage History*. London: Society for Theatre Research, 1974.

Barnes, James J., and Patience P. Barnes, eds. *The American Revolution through

British Eyes: A Documentary Collection. Kent, OH: Kent State University Press, 2013.

Bear, James A., Jr., and Lucia C. Stanton, eds. *Jefferson's Memorandum Books: Accounts, with Legal Records and Miscellany, 1767–1826*. 2 vols. Princeton, NJ: Princeton University Press, 1997.

Bell, Whitfield J. "Addenda to Watson's Annals of Philadelphia: Notes by Jacob Mordecai, 1836." *Pennsylvania Magazine of History and Biography* 98, no. 2 (April 1974): 131–163.

Berkeley, Edmund, and Dorothy Smith Berkeley. *Dr. Alexander Garden of Charles Town*. Chapel Hill: University of North Carolina Press, 1969.

Bernard, John. *Retrospections of America, 1797–1811*. New York: Harper and Brothers, 1887.

Bonomi, Patricia U. *A Factious People: Politics and Society in Colonial New York*. New York: Columbia University Press, 1971.

Boswell, James. *Boswell's London Journal, 1762–1763*. Edited by Frederick A. Pottle. New York: McGraw-Hill, 1950.

Boucher, Jonathan. *Reminiscences of an American Loyalist, 1738–1789*. Edited by Jonathan Bouchier. Boston: Houghton Mifflin, 1925.

———. *A View of the Causes and Consequences of the American Revolution*. London, 1797.

Bourdieu, Pierre. "Systems of Education and Systems of Thought." In *Knowledge and Control: New Directions for the Sociology of Education*, edited by Michael F. D. Young, 189–207. London: Collier Macmillan, 1971.

Bradford, Alden. *History of Massachusetts*. Vol. 1. Boston: Richardson and Lord, 1822.

Breen, T. H. *American Insurgents, American Patriots: The Revolution of the People*. New York: Hill and Wang, 2010.

———. "'Baubles of Britain': The American and Consumer Revolutions of the Eighteenth Century." In Carson, Hoffman, and Albert, *Of Consuming Interests*, 444–482.

———. *The Marketplace of Revolution: How Consumer Politics Shaped American Independence*. New York: Oxford University Press, 2004.

Bridenbaugh, Carl. "Colonial Newport as a Summer Resort." *Rhode Island Historical Society Collections* 26 (1933): 1–23.

Bridenbaugh, Carl, and Jessica Bridenbaugh. *Rebels and Gentlemen: Philadelphia in the Age of Franklin*. New York: Oxford University Press, 1965.

Brobeck, Stephen. "Revolutionary Change in Colonial Philadelphia: The Brief Life of the Proprietary Gentry." *William and Mary Quarterly*, 3rd ser., 33, no. 3 (1976): 410–434.

Brown, Jared. *The Theatre in America during the Revolution*. Cambridge: Cambridge University Press, 1995.

Brown, Wallace. *The King's Friends: The Composition and Motives of the American Loyalist Claimants.* Providence, RI: Brown University Press, 1965.

Bull, Kinloch, Jr. *The Oligarchs in Colonial and Revolutionary Charleston: Lieutenant Governor William Bull II and His Family.* Columbia: University of South Carolina Press, 1991.

Burke, Edmund. *The Works of the Right Honorable Edmund Burke.* Vol. 1. London: Henry G. Bohn, 1854.

Burnaby, Andrew. *Travels through the Middle Settlements of North-America, in the Years 1759 and 1760.* London, 1775.

Burnett, Edmund, ed. *Letters of Members of the Continental Congress.* Vol. 1. Washington, DC: Carnegie Institution, 1921.

Bushman, Richard L. *The Refinement of America: Persons, Houses, Cities.* New York: Alfred A. Knopf, 1992.

Butler, Nicholas Michael. *Votaries of Apollo: The St. Cecilia Society and the Patronage of Concert Music in Charleston, South Carolina, 1766–1820.* Columbia: University of South Carolina Press, 2007.

Butterfield, L. H., ed. *Adams Family Correspondence.* Vols. 1 and 2. Cambridge, MA: Harvard University Press, 1963.

Byrd, William. *The Writings of "Colonel William Byrd of Westover in Virginia, Esquire."* Edited by John Spencer Bassett. New York: Doubleday and Page, 1901.

Calhoon, Robert McCluer. "Critics of Colonial Resistance in the Prerevolutionary Debate, 1763–1776." PhD diss., Case Western Reserve University, 1964.

Calhoon, Robert M., and Robert M. Weir. "The Scandalous History of Sir Egerton Leigh." *William and Mary Quarterly*, 3rd ser., 26, no. 1 (1969): 47–74.

Campbell, Donald. *Playing for Scotland: A History of the Scottish Stage, 1715–1965.* Edinburgh: Mercat Press, 1996.

Canby, Courtlandt, ed. "Robert Munford's *The Patriots* (1776?)." *William and Mary Quarterly*, 3rd ser., 6 (1949): 437–503.

Carson, Cary, Ron Hoffman, and Peter J. Albert, eds. *Of Consuming Interests: The Style of Life in the Eighteenth Century.* Charlottesville: University Press of Virginia, 1994.

Carson, James Taylor. *Making an Atlantic World: Circles, Paths, and Stories from the Colonial South.* Knoxville: University of Tennessee Press, 2007.

Chastellux, Marquis de. *Travels in North America in the Years 1780, 1781, and 1782.* Edited and translated by Howard C. Rice, Jr. 2 vols. Chapel Hill: University of North Carolina Press, 1963.

Chernow, Ron. *Alexander Hamilton.* New York: Penguin, 2005.

———. *Washington: A Life.* New York: Penguin, 2010.

Colden, Cadwallader. *The Colden Letter Books, Part 1, 1760–1765*. Vol. 9 of the *Collections of the New-York Historical Society*. New York: New-York Historical Society, 1937.

———. *The Colden Letter Books, Part 2, 1765–1775*. Vol. 10 of the *Collections of the New-York Historical Society*. New York: New-York Historical Society, 1878.

———. *The Letters and Papers of Cadwallader Colden*. Vols. 50–56. New York: New-York Historical Society, 1917–1923.

Cooper, Myles. *The Patriots of North America: A Sketch*. New York, 1775.

Copley, John Singleton. *Letters and Papers of John Singleton Copley and Henry Pelham, 1739–1776*. Boston: Massachusetts Historical Society, 1914.

Crackel, Theodore J., et al. *The Papers of George Washington Digital Edition*. Charlottesville: University of Virginia Press, Rotunda, 2007–.

Crain, Timothy Mark. "Music in the Colonial Charleston, South Carolina Theatre, 1732–1781." PhD diss., Florida State University, 2002.

Crary, Catherine S. *The Price of Loyalty: Tory Writings from the Revolutionary Era*. New York: McGraw-Hill, 1973.

Cresswell, Nicholas. *The Journal of Nicholas Cresswell, 1774–1777*. Port Washington, NY: Kennikat Press, 1968.

Crèvecoeur, J. Hector St. John de. *Letters from an American Farmer and Sketches of Eighteenth Century America*. Edited by Albert Stone. New York: Penguin, 1981.

Crowley, John E. *The Privileges of Independence: Neomercantilism and the American Revolution*. Baltimore: Johns Hopkins University Press, 1993.

Cunningham, Noble E., Jr. *In Pursuit of Reason: The Life of Thomas Jefferson*. Baton Rouge: Louisiana State University Press, 1987.

Curtis, Julia. "The Early Charleston Stage, 1703–1798." PhD diss., Indiana University, 1968.

Davidson, Philip. *Propaganda and the American Revolution, 1763–1783*. Chapel Hill: University of North Carolina Press, 1941.

Davies, K. G., ed. *Documents of the American Revolution, 1770–1783*. 21 vols. Shannon: Irish University Press, 1972–1981.

Davis, David Brion, and Steven Mintz, eds. *The Boisterous Sea of Liberty: A Documentary History of America from Discovery through the Civil War*. New York: Oxford University Press, 1998.

Denny, H. L. L. "Memoir of His Excellency Colonel William Denny." *Pennsylvania Magazine of History and Biography* 44, no. 2 (1920): 97–121.

Devine, T. M., ed. *A Scottish Firm in Virginia, 1767–1777: The Correspondence of William Cuninghame and Co*. Edinburgh: Scottish History Society, 1984.

Dickason, David Howard. *William Williams: Novelist and Painter of Colonial America*. Bloomington: Indiana University Press, 1970.

Dickinson, H. T., ed. "Britain's Imperial Sovereignty: The Ideological Case against the American Colonies." In Dickinson, *Britain and the American Revolution*, 64–96. London: Longman, 1998.

Dickinson, John. *The Political Writings of John Dickinson, 1764–1774*. Edited by Paul Leicester Ford. New York: Da Capo Press, 1970.

Dillon, Elizabeth M. *New World Drama: The Performative Commons in the Atlantic World, 1649–1849*. Durham, NC: Duke University Press, 2014.

Donohue, Joseph W., Jr. *The Theatrical Manager in England and America: Player of a Perilous Game*. Princeton, NJ: Princeton University Press, 1971.

Drayton, John. *Memoirs of the American Revolution*. Charleston, SC: A. E. Miller, 1821.

Dunlap, William. *A History of the American Theatre*. New York: J. J. Harper, 1832.

Easterby, J. H. *St. Andrew's Society of the City of Charleston*. Charleston, SC: Walker, Evans, and Cogswell, 1929.

Eddis, William. *Letters From America, Historical and Descriptive: Comprising Occurrences from 1769, to 1777, Inclusive*. London, 1792.

Edgar, Walter. *South Carolina: A History*. Columbia: University of South Carolina Press, 1998.

"Effects of the Non-importation Agreement in Philadelphia, 1769–1770." *Pennsylvania Magazine of History and Biography* 14, no. 1 (1890): 41–45.

Egnal, Marc. *A Mighty Empire: The Origins of the American Revolution*. Ithaca, NY: Cornell University Press, 1988.

Egnal, Marc, and Joseph A. Ernst. "An Economic Interpretation of the American Revolution." *William and Mary Quarterly*, 3rd ser., 29, no. 1 (1972): 3–32.

Farish, Hunter Dickinson, ed. *Journal and Letters of Philip Vickers Fithian, 1773–1774: A Plantation Tutor of the Old Dominion*. Williamsburg, VA: Colonial Williamsburg, 1957.

Ferling, John. *A Leap in the Dark: The Struggle to Create the American Republic*. Oxford: Oxford University Press, 2003.

Fithian, Philip Vickers. *Journal of Philip Vickers Fithian*. Edited by Robert Greenlaugh Albion and Leonidas Dodson. Princeton, NJ: Princeton University Press, 1934.

Fitzpatrick, John C., ed. *The Writings of Washington from the Original Manuscript Sources, 1745–1799*. Vol. 3. Washington, DC: Government Printing Office, 1935.

Flavell, Julie. *When London Was Capital of America*. New Haven, CT: Yale University Press, 2010.

Flexner, James Thomas. *States Dyckman, American Loyalist*. Boston: Little, Brown, 1980.

Ford, Paul Leicester. *Washington and the Theatre*. New York: Dunlap Society, 1899.

Ford, W. C., et al., eds. *Journals of the Continental Congress, 1774–1789*. 34 vols. Washington, DC: Government Printing Office, 1904–1937.
Fox, Levy, ed. *Correspondence of the Reverend Joseph Greene*. London: Historical Manuscript Commission, 1965.
Franklin, Benjamin. *Papers of Benjamin Franklin*. Vol. 14. Edited by Leonard Labaree. New Haven, CT: Yale University Press, 1970.
Fraser, Walter J. *Charleston! Charleston! The History of a Southern City*. Charleston: University of South Carolina Press, 1990.
Freeman, Lisa. "The Social Life of Eighteenth-Century Comedy." In *The Cambridge Companion to British Theatre, 1730–1830*, edited by Jane Moody and Daniel O'Quinn, 73–86. Cambridge: Cambridge University Press, 2007.
Fulton, Richard M. *The Revolution That Wasn't: A Contemporary Assessment of 1776*. Port Washington, NY: Kennikat Press, 1981.
Gadsden, Christopher. *The Writings of Christopher Gadsden, 1746–1805*. Edited by Richard Walsh. Columbia: University of South Carolina Press, 1966.
Garden, Alexander. *Anecdotes of the Revolutionary War in America*. Charleston, SC: A. E. Miller, 1822.
Gibbs, Jenna M. *Performing the Temple of Liberty: Slavery, Theatre, and Popular Culture in London and Philadelphia, 1760–1850*. Baltimore: Johns Hopkins University Press, 2014.
Godbold, E. Stanley, Jr., and Robert H. Woody. *Christopher Gadsden and the American Revolution*. Knoxville: University of Tennessee Press, 1982.
Goring, Paul. *The Rhetoric of Sensibility in Eighteenth-Century Culture*. Cambridge: Cambridge University Press, 2005.
Goss, Eldridge Henry. *The Life of Colonel Paul Revere*. Boston: Joseph George Cupples, 1891. Facsimile edition, Boston: G. K. Hall / Gregg Press, 1972.
Gould, Christopher. "Robert Wells, Colonial Charleston Printer." *South Carolina Historical Magazine* 79, no. 1 (1978): 23–49.
Granger, Bruce Ingham. *Political Satire in the American Revolution, 1763–1783*. Ithaca, NY: Cornell University Press, 1960.
Graydon, Alexander. *Memoirs of a Life, Chiefly Passed in Pennsylvania, within the Last Sixty Years*. Edinburgh, 1822.
Greene, Jack P., ed. *Colonies to Nation, 1763–1789*. New York: McGraw-Hill, 1967.
Gustafson, Sandra M. *Eloquence Is Power: Oratory and Performance in Early America*. Chapel Hill: University of North Carolina Press, 2000.
Hare, Arnold. *The Georgian Theatre in Wessex*. London: Phoenix House, 1958.
Harrington, Virginia D. *The New York Merchant on the Eve of the Revolution*. Gloucester, MA: Peter Smith, 1964.
Haslewood, Joseph. *Secret History of the Green-Room*. 2 vols. London: J. Owen, 1795.

Haulman, Kate. *The Politics of Fashion in Eighteenth-Century America.* Chapel Hill: University of North Carolina Press, 2011.

Hazard, Samuel, ed. *Pennsylvania Archives.* 1st ser., vol. 3. Philadelphia: Joseph Severn, 1853.

Hewatt, Alexander. *An Historical Account of the Rise and Progress of the Colonies of South Carolina and Georgia.* 2 vols. London: Alexander Donaldson, 1779.

Hibbert, Christopher. *Redcoats and Rebels: The American Revolution through British Eyes.* New York: W. W. Norton, 1990.

Hickey, William. *Memoirs of a Georgian Rake.* Edited by Roger Hudson. London: Folio Society, 1995.

Highfill, Philip, Jr. "The British Background of the American Hallams." *Theatre Survey* 11 (1970): 1–30.

Highfill, Philip, Jr., et al. *A Biographical Dictionary of Actors, Actresses, Musicians, Dancers, Managers and Other Personnel in London, 1660–1800.* Vol. 1. Carbondale: Southern Illinois University Press, 1978.

Hill, Errol. *The Jamaican Stage, 1655–1900: Profile of a Colonial Theatre.* Amherst: University of Massachusetts Press, 1992.

Hiltzheimer, Jacob. *Extracts from the Diary of Jacob Hiltzheimer.* Edited by Jacob Cox Parson. Philadelphia: William F. Fell, 1893.

Hodge, Christina J. *Consumerism and the Emergence of the Middle Class in Colonial America.* Cambridge: Cambridge University Press, 2014.

Hoffman, Ronald, ed. *Dear Papa, Dear Charley: The Peregrinations of a Revolutionary Aristocrat.* 4 vols. Chapel Hill: University of North Carolina Press, 2001.

Hoffman, Ronald, Mechal Sobel, and Fredrika Teute, eds. *Through a Glass Darkly: Reflections on Personal Identity in Early America.* Chapel Hill: University of North Carolina Press, 1997.

Honyman, Robert. *Colonial Panorama, 1775: Dr. Robert Honyman's Journal for March and April.* Edited by Philip Padelford. San Marino, CA: Huntington Library, 1939.

Hornblow, Arthur. *History of the Theatre in America: From Its Beginnings to the Present Time.* Vol. 1. Philadelphia: J. B. Lippincott, 1919.

Huguenot Society of South Carolina. *Transactions of the Huguenot Society of South Carolina.* Vol. 4. Charleston, SC: Walker, Evans, and Cogswell, 1897.

Hutson, James H. *Pennsylvania Politics 1746–1770: The Movement for Royal Government and Its Consequences.* Princeton, NJ: Princeton University Press, 1972.

Iredell, James. *The Papers of James Iredell.* 3 vols. Edited by Don Higginbotham. Raleigh: North Carolina Division of Archives and History, Department of Cultural Resources, 1976–2003.

Ireland, Joseph. *Records of the New York Stage from 1750 to 1860*. 2 vols. 1866–1867. Reprint, New York: Burt Franklin, 1968.

Isaac, Rhys. "Dramatizing the Ideology of Revolution." In *The Revolution That Wasn't: A Contemporary Assessment of 1776*, edited by Richard M. Fulton, 186–202. Port Washington, NY: Kennikat Press, 1981.

Izard, Ralph. *Correspondence of Mr. Ralph Izard of South Carolina: From the Year 1774 to 1804*. Edited by Anne Izard Deas. New York: C. S. Francis, 1844.

Jackson, John W. *With the British Army in Philadelphia, 1777–1778*. San Rafael, CA: Presidio Press, 1979.

Jay, John. *The Correspondence and Public Papers of John Jay*. Edited by Henry Johnston. Vol. 1. New York: G. P. Putnam's Sons, 1890.

Jefferson, Thomas. *The Papers of Thomas Jefferson*. Vol. 1. Edited by Julian P. Boyd et al. Princeton, NJ: Princeton University Press, 1950.

———. *The Papers of Thomas Jefferson, Retirement Series*, vol. 8: *1 October 1814 to 31 August 1815*. Edited by J. Jefferson Looney. Princeton, NJ: Princeton University Press, 2012.

Johnson, Joseph. *Traditions and Reminiscences, Chiefly of the American Revolution in the South*. Charleston, SC: Walker and James, 1851.

Johnson, Odai. *Absence and Memory in Colonial American Theatre*. New York: Palgrave Macmillan, 2006.

———. "The Leeward Islands Company." *Theatre Survey* 44, no. 1 (2003): 29–42.

———. "Thomas Jefferson and the Colonial Theatre." *Virginia Magazine of History and Biography* 108 (2000): 139–154.

Johnson, Odai, and Bill Burling. *The Colonial American Stage, 1665–1774: A Documentary Calendar*. Cranbury, NJ: Associated University Presses, 2001.

Jones, Thomas. *History of New York during the Revolutionary War*. Edited by Edward Floyd De Lancey. 2 vols. New York: New-York Historical Society, 1879.

"Journal of a French Traveler in the Colonies, 1765." *American Historical Review* 26, no. 4, and 27, no. 1 (1921).

Journals of the House of Burgesses, vol. 11: *1766–1769*. Richmond: Virginia State Library, 1906.

Kammen, Michael. *Colonial New York: A History*. New York: Charles Scribner's Sons, 1975.

Karras, Alan L. *Sojourners in the Sun: Scottish Migrants in Jamaica and the Chesapeake, 1740–1800*. Ithaca, NY: Cornell University Press, 1992.

Kelly, Jason M. *The Society of Dilettanti: Archaeology and Identity in the British Enlightenment*. New Haven, CT: Yale University Press, 2009.

Ketchum, Richard. *Divided Loyalties: How the American Revolution Came to New York*. New York: Henry Holt, 2002.

Kierner, Cynthia A. *Traders and Gentlefolk, the Livingstons of New York: 1675–1790*. Ithaca, NY: Cornell University Press, 1992.

Klein, Milton M. *The American Whig: William Livingston of New York*. Rev. ed. New York: Garland, 1993.

Klepp, Susan E., and Billy G. Smith, eds. *The Infortunate: The Voyage and Adventures of William Moraley, an Indentured Servant*. University Park: Penn State University Press, 1992.

Kneebone, John T., ed. *Dictionary of Virginia Biography*. Vol. 1. Richmond: Library of Virginia, 1998.

Kolve, V. A. *The Play Called Corpus Christi*. Stanford, CA: Stanford University Press, 1966.

Konkle, Burton Alva. *Benjamin Chew, 1722–1810*. Philadelphia: University of Pennsylvania Press, 1932.

Lambert, Robert Stansbury. *South Carolina Loyalists in the American Revolution*. Columbia: University of South Carolina Press, 1987.

Laurens, Henry. *The Papers of Henry Laurens*. Edited by David R. Chesnutt. 16 vols. Columbia: University of South Carolina Press, 1968–2002.

Leacock, John. *The Fall of British Tyranny: or, American Liberty Triumphant. The First Campaign: A Tragi-Comedy of Five Acts*. Philadelphia, 1776.

Leigh, Egerton. *Considerations on Certain Political Transactions of the Province of South Carolina*. London, 1774.

Lemay, J. A. Leo. *Men of Letters in Colonial Maryland*. Knoxville: University of Tennessee Press, 1972.

"Letter from Hudson Muse, of Virginia, to His Brother, Thomas Muse, of Dorchester Co., Maryland." *William and Mary Quarterly* 2, no. 4 (April 1894): 237–241.

Livingston, Philip. *The Other Side of the Question; or, A Defence of the Liberties of North America*. New York, 1774.

Livingston, William, et al. *The Independent Reflector; or, Weekly Essays on Sundry Important Subjects, more particularly adapted to the Province of New-York*. Edited by Milton M. Klein. Cambridge, MA: Belknap Press of Harvard University Press, 1963.

Longmore, Paul K. *The Invention of George Washington*. Berkeley: University of California Press, 1988.

Lord, Evelyn. *The Hell-Fire Clubs: Sex, Satanism and Secret Societies*. New Haven, CT: Yale University Press, 2008.

Lucas, Stephen. *Portents of Rebellion: Rhetoric and Revolution in Philadelphia, 1765–1776*. Philadelphia: Temple University Press, 1976.

Luffman, John. *A brief account of the island of Antigua together with the customs and manners of its inhabitants . . . .* In *Letters to a Friend: Written in the years 1786, 1787, 1788*. London, 1789.

Mackay, James. *I Have Not Yet Begun to Fight: A Life of John Paul Jones*. Edinburgh: Mainstream Publishing, 1998.

Mackraby, Alexander. "Extracts from the Letters of Alexander Mackraby to Sir Philip Francis." *Pennsylvania Magazine of History and Biography* 11, no. 2 (1887): 276–287, 491–495.

Maier, Pauline. *From Resistance to Revolution: Colonial Radicals and the Development of American Opposition to Britain, 1765–1776*. New York: W. W. Norton, 1991.

Malone, Dumas. *Jefferson the Virginian*. Vol. 1. Boston: Little, Brown, 1948.

Mancke, Elizabeth, and Carole Shammas, eds. *The Creation of the British Atlantic World*. Baltimore: Johns Hopkins University Press, 2005.

Marble, Annie Russell. *From 'Prentice to Patron: The Life Story of Isaiah Thomas*. New York: D. Appleton-Century, 1935.

Marshall, Christopher. *Passages from the Remembrancer of Christopher Marshall*. Edited by William Duane, Jr. Philadelphia: James Crissy, 1839.

Martin, David G. *The Philadelphia Campaign, June 1777–July 1778*. Cambridge, MA: Da Capo Press, 2003.

Martin, Robert W. T. *The Free and Open Press: The Founding of American Democratic Press Liberty, 1640–1800*. New York: New York University Press, 2001.

Massachusetts Historical Society. *Collections of the Massachusetts Historical Society*. 4th ser., vol. 4. Boston: Little, Brown, 1858.

Mays, David. "The Achievements of the Douglass Company in North America, 1758–1774." *Theatre Survey* 23, no. 2 (1982): 141–149.

McCullough, David. *1776*. New York: Simon and Schuster, 2005.

McDonough, Daniel. *Christopher Gadsden and Henry Laurens: The Parallel Lives of Two American Patriots*. Selinsgrove, PA: Susquehanna University Press, 2000.

McInnis, Maurie D., and Angela D. Mack, eds. *In Pursuit of Refinement: Charlestonians Abroad 1740–1860*. Charleston: University of South Carolina Press, 1999.

Middlekauff, Robert. *The Glorious Cause: The American Revolution, 1763–1789*. New York: Oxford University Press, 1982.

Miller, Lillian B., ed. *The Selected Papers of Charles Willson Peale and His Family*. Vol. 1. New Haven, CT: Yale University Press, 1983.

Montresor, John. "The Journals of Capt. Montresor." Edited by G. D. Scull. In *Collections of the New-York Historical Society for 1881*. New York: New-York Historical Society, 1882.

Moody, Jane. "Dictating to the Empire: Performance and Theatrical Geography in Eighteenth-Century Britain." In *The Cambridge Companion to British Theatre, 1730–1830*, edited by Jane Moody and Daniel O'Quinn, 21–41. Cambridge: Cambridge University Press, 2007.

Moore, Frank. *Diary of the American Revolution, 1775–1781*. 1876. Edited by John Anthony Scott. New York: Washington Square Press, 1967.

———, ed. *Songs and Ballads of the American Revolution.* New York: Appleton, 1856.

Morgan, Edmund S., and Helen M. Morgan. *The Stamp Act Crisis: Prologue to Revolution.* Chapel Hill: University of North Carolina Press, 1995.

Morrison, George Austin, Jr. *History of Saint Andrew's Society of the State of New York.* New York, 1906.

Murdoch, David H. *Rebellion in America: A Contemporary British Viewpoint, 1765–1783.* Santa Barbara, CA: Clio Books, 1979.

The Musical Companion: Being a Collection of All the New Songs Sung at the Play Houses. London, 1765.

Nathans, Heather. *Early American Theatre from the Revolution to Thomas Jefferson: Into the Hands of the People.* Cambridge: Cambridge University Press, 2003.

Nelson, William H. *The American Tory.* Oxford: Clarendon Press, 1961.

Nivelon, François. *The Rudiments of Genteel Behavior.* 1737.

"Notes from the Meeting of the President and Masters of the College, 11 April 1771." *William and Mary Quarterly*, 1st ser., 5 (1897): 168–170.

O'Connor, John E. *William Paterson, Lawyer and Statesman, 1745–1806.* New Brunswick, NJ: Rutgers University Press, 1979.

Odell, George C. D. *Annals of the New York Stage.* Vol. 1. New York: Columbia University Press, 1927.

Oliver, Peter. *Peter Oliver's Origin and Progress of the American Revolution: A Tory View.* Edited by Douglass Adair and John A. Schutz. San Marino, CA: Huntington Library, 1961.

Olsberg, R. Nicholas. "Ship Registers in the South Carolina Archives, 1734–1780." *South Carolina Historical Magazine* 74, no. 4 (October 1973): 189–299.

Olwell, Robert. "Seeds of Empire." In *The Creation of the British Atlantic World*, edited by Elizabeth Mancke and Carole Shammas, 263–283. Baltimore: Johns Hopkins University Press, 2005.

Onuf, Peter S., ed. *Maryland and the Empire, 1773: The Antilon–First Citizen Letters.* Baltimore: Johns Hopkins University Press, 1974.

O'Quinn, Daniel. *Entertaining Crisis in the Atlantic Imperium, 1770–1790.* Baltimore: Johns Hopkins University Press, 2011.

———. "Theatre and Empire." In *The Cambridge Companion to British Theatre, 1730–1830*, edited by Jane Moody and Daniel O'Quinn, 219–232. Cambridge: Cambridge University Press, 2007.

O'Shaughnessy, Andrew Jackson. *The Men Who Lost America: British Leadership, the American Revolution, and the Fate of the Empire.* New Haven, CT: Yale University Press, 2013.

Ousterhout, Anne M. *The Most Learned Woman in America: A Life of Elizabeth Graeme Fergusson.* University Park: Penn State University Press, 2004.

Paine, Thomas. *Common Sense and Other Writings*. Edited by Gordon S. Wood. New York: Modern Library, 2003.

Papenfuse, Edward C., et al. *A Biographical Dictionary of the Maryland Legislature, 1635–1789*. Vol. 426. Baltimore: Johns Hopkins University Press, 1985.

"Papers of the Second Council of Safety of the Revolutionary Party in South Carolina, November 1775–March 1776." *South Carolina Historical and Genealogic Magazine* 4, no. 1 (1903): 3–25.

Peladeau, Marius B., ed. *The Prose of Royall Tyler*. Montpelier: Vermont Historical Society, 1972.

Phillips, Ulrich Bonnell. *Life and Labor in the Old South*. Boston: Little, Brown, 1935.

Pilmore, Joseph. *The Journal of Joseph Pilmore, Methodist Itinerant: For the Years August 1, 1769, to January 2, 1774*. Edited by Frederick E. Maser and Howard T. Maag. Philadelphia, 1969.

Pleasants, J. Hall, ed. *Journal and Correspondence of the State Council of Maryland, 1781*. Vol. 47 of *Archives of Maryland*. Annapolis: Maryland Historical Society, 1930.

Pollock, Thomas Clark. *The Philadelphia Theatre in the Eighteenth Century: Together with the Day Book of the Same Period*. New York: Greenwood Press, 1968.

Porter, Roy. *English Society in the Eighteenth Century*. London: Allen Lane / Pelican, 1982.

Pottle, Frederick A., ed. *James Boswell: The Earlier Years, 1740–1769*. New York: McGraw-Hill, 1985.

Quincy, Josiah. *Memoir of the Life of Josiah Quincy, Junior of Massachusetts, 1744–1775: By His Son*. 2nd ed. Edited by Eliza Susan Quincy. Boston: J. Wilson and Son, 1874.

Ramsay, David. *The History of the American Revolution*. Ed. Lester Cohen. 2 vols. Indianapolis: Liberty Fund, 1990.

Rankin, Hugh F. *The Theater in Colonial America*. Chapel Hill: University of North Carolina Press, 1965.

Ravenel, Harriott Horry. *Charleston: The Place and the People*. New York: Macmillan, 1906.

Rawley, James A. *The Transatlantic Slave Trade: A History*. New York: W. W. Norton, 1981.

"Reminiscences of Thomas Johnson." *Potters American Monthly* 1 (1872): 100–102.

Richards, Eric. "Scotland and the Atlantic Empire." In *Strangers within the Realm: Cultural Margins of the First British Empire*, edited by Bernard Bailyn and Philip Morgan, 67–114. Chapel Hill: University of North Carolina Press, 1991.

Richards, Jeffrey H. *Theatre Enough: American Culture and the Metaphor of the World Stage, 1607–1789*. Durham, NC: Duke University Press, 1991.

Richards, Jeffrey H., and Sharon M. Harris, eds. *Mercy Otis Warren: Selected Letters*. Athens: University of Georgia Press, 2009.

Ritchey, David, ed. *A Guide to the Baltimore Stage in the Eighteenth Century: A History and Day Book Calendar*. Westport, CT: Greenwood Press, 1982.

Rosenfeld, Sybil Marion. *Strolling Players and Drama in the Provinces, 1660–1795*. Cambridge: Cambridge University Press, 1939. Reprint, New York: Octagon Books, 1970.

Rowe, John. *Letters and Diary of John Rowe, Boston Merchant: 1759–1762, 1764–1779*. Edited by Anne Rowe Cunningham. Boston: W. B. Clarke, 1903.

Rowland, Kate Mason. *The Life of George Mason, 1725–1792*. 2 vols. New York: G. P. Putnam's Sons, 1892.

Rozbicki, Michal Jan. *Culture and Liberty in the Age of the American Revolution*. Charlottesville: University of Virginia Press, 2011.

Ruddock, Ted, ed. *Travels in the Colonies in 1773–1775, Described in the Letters of William Mylne*. Athens: University of Georgia Press, 1993.

Rudé, George. *Wilkes and Liberty: A Social Study of 1763 to 1774*. Oxford: Clarendon Press, 1962.

Russell, Phillips. *John Paul Jones: Man of Action*. New York: Brentano's, 1927.

Ryan, Dermot. *Technologies of Empire: Writing, Imagination, and the Making of Imperial Networks, 1750–1820*. Newark: University of Delaware Press, 2013.

Saunders, William L., ed. *The Colonial Records of North Carolina*. 10 vols. Raleigh, NC: P. M. Hale, State Printer, 1886–1890.

Scharf, John Thomas. *History of Maryland from the Earliest Period to the Present Day, 1765–1812*. Hatboro, PA: Tradition Press, 1879.

Schutz, John A., and Douglass Adair, eds. *The Spur of Fame: Dialogues of John Adams and Benjamin Rush, 1805–1813*. San Marino, CA: Huntington Library, 1966.

Scott, Jonathan. *The Pleasures of Antiquity: British Collectors of Greece and Rome*. New Haven, CT: Yale University Press, 2003.

Sedgwick, Theodore. *A Memoir of the Life of William Livingston*. New York: J. J. Harper, 1833.

Sellers, Leila. *Charleston Business on the Eve of the American Revolution*. Chapel Hill: University of North Carolina Press, 1934.

Shaffer, Jason. *Performing Patriotism: National Identity in the Colonial and Revolutionary American Theatre*. Philadelphia: University of Pennsylvania Press, 2007.

Sheridan, Thomas. *A Course of Lectures on Elocution*. London, 1762.

Sherman, Susanne K. *Comedies Useful: Southern Theatre History, 1775–1812*. Williamsburg, VA: Celest Press, 1998.

Shields, David S. *Civil Tongues and Polite Letters in British America*. Chapel Hill: University of North Carolina Press, 1997.

Silverman, Kenneth. *A Cultural History of the American Revolution*. New York: Thomas Y. Crowell, 1976.

Smith, Alice R. Huger, and D. E. Huger Smith. *The Dwelling Houses of Charleston, South Carolina*. Philadelphia: J. B. Lippincott, 1917.

Smith, William. *Historical Memoirs of William Smith*. Edited by William Henry Waldo Sabine. 2 vols. New York: Colburn and Tegg, 1956–1958.

Stevenson, John. *Popular Disturbances in England, 1700–1832*. 2nd ed. London: Longman, 1992.

Stone, George Winchester, Jr., and George M. Kahrl. *David Garrick: A Critical Biography*. Carbondale: Southern Illinois University Press, 1979.

Tatum, Edward H., ed. *The American Journal of Ambrose Serle, Secretary to Lord Howe, 1776–1778*. San Marino, CA: Huntington Library, 1940.

The Thespian Dictionary, or Dramatic Biography of the 18th Century. London: T. Hurst, 1802.

Thomas, Hugh. *The Slave Trade: The Story of the Atlantic Slave Trade, 1440–1870*. New York: Simon and Schuster, 1997.

Thomas, Isaiah. *The History of Printing in America: With a Biography of Printers, and an Account of Newspapers*. New York: Weathervane Books, 1970.

Thomas, Peter D. G. *British Politics and the Stamp Act Crisis: The First Phase of the American Revolution, 1763–1767*. Oxford: Clarendon Press, 1975.

———. *John Wilkes: A Friend to Liberty*. Oxford: Clarendon Press, 1996.

Timothy, Peter. *Letters of Peter Timothy, Printer of Charleston, South Carolina, to Benjamin Franklin*. Edited by Douglas C. McMurtrie. Chicago: Black Cat Press, 1935.

Tinling, Marion, ed. *The Correspondence of the Three William Byrds of Westover, Virginia: 1684–1776*. 2 vols. Charlottesville: University Press of Virginia, 1977.

Tobias, Thomas J., ed. "Charles Town in 1764: The Letters of Moses Lopez." *South Carolina Historical Magazine* 67, no. 2 (April 1966): 63–74.

Tyler, Lyon G., ed. "The First Play-House in Williamsburg." *William and Mary Quarterly*, 1st ser., 24, no. 1 (July 1915): 29–31.

———, ed. "Hudson Muse to T. Muse, April 19, 1771." *William and Mary Quarterly*, 1st ser., 2, no. 1 (July 1893).

Unger, Harlow Giles. *John Hancock: Merchant King and American Patriot*. New York: John Wiley and Sons, 2000.

Van Buskirk, Judith L. *Generous Enemies: Patriots and Loyalists in Revolutionary New York*. Philadelphia: University of Pennsylvania Press, 2002.

Van Horne, John C., ed. *The Correspondence of William Nelson, as Acting Governor of Virginia, 1770–1771*. Charlottesville: University Press of Virginia, 1975.

Wainwright, Nicholas B. "Governor William Denny in Pennsylvania." *Philadelphia Magazine of History and Biography* 81, no. 2 (1957): 170–198.

Walker, Lewis Burd. "Life of Margaret Shippen, Wife of Benedict Arnold." *Pennsylvania Magazine of History and Biography* 24, no. 4 (1900): 401–429.

Walsh, Richard. *Charleston's Sons of Liberty: A Study of the Artisans, 1763–1789.* Columbia: University of South Carolina Press, 1959.

Wansey, Henry. *The Journal of an Excursion to the United States of North America, in the Summer of 1794.* Salisbury, England, 1796.

The Warblers Delight: Being a Select Collection of the Most Favourite Songs, Duets, Catches, Airs, and Cantatas, That Have Been Sung . . . at the Theatres, Ranelagh, Vauxhall. London, 1765.

Warren, Mercy Otis. *The Plays and Poems of Mercy Otis Warren.* Edited by Benjamin Franklin V. Delmar, NY: Scholars' Facsimiles and Reprints, 1980.

Washington, George. *The Daily Journal of Major George Washington, in 1751–2.* Albany, NY: Joel Munsell's Sons, 1892.

———. *The Diaries of George Washington.* Edited by John C. Fitzpatrick. 4 vols. New York: Kraus Reprint, 1971.

———. *The Diaries of George Washington.* 6 vols. Edited by Donald Jackson and Dorothy Twohig. Charlottesville: University Press of Virginia, 1976–1979.

———. *The Papers of George Washington*, Colonial Series, vol. 8: *24 June 1767–25 December 1771.* Edited by W. W. Abbot and Dorothy Twohig. Charlottesville: University Press of Virginia, 1993.

———. *The Papers of George Washington*, Presidential Series, vol. 7: *1 December 1790–21 March 1791.* Edited by Jack D. Warren, Jr. Charlottesville: University Press of Virginia, 1998.

———. *The Papers of George Washington*, Revolutionary War Series, vol. 1: *16 June 1775–15 September 1775.* Edited by Philander D. Chase. Charlottesville: University Press of Virginia, 1985.

Watson, Alan D. "Placemen in South Carolina: The Receiver Generals of the Quitrents." *South Carolina Historical Magazine* 74, no. 1 (January 1973): 18–30.

Watson, John Fanning. *Annals of Philadelphia and Pennsylvania, in the Olden Time.* 2 vols. Philadelphia: Whiting and Thomas, 1856.

Webber, Mabel, ed. "Peter Manigault's Letters." *South Carolina Historical Magazine* 31, no. 3 (July 1930): 171–183.

Weir, Robert M. *Colonial South Carolina: A History.* Millwood, NY: KTO Press, 1983.

———. *The Last of American Freemen: Studies in the Political Culture of the Colonial and Revolutionary South.* Macon, GA: Mercer University Press, 1986.

Wells, William Charles. *Two Essays . . . with a Memoir of His Life.* London: Archibald Constable and Co., 1818.

Wheeler, Joseph Towne. "Reading Interests of Maryland Planters and Merchants, 1700–1776." *Maryland Historical Magazine* 37, no. 1 (March 1942): 26–41.

Wilkinson, Tate. *The Wandering Patentee*. Facsimile of the 1795 London edition. 2 vols. London: Scolar Press, 1973.

Willard, George Owen. *History of the Providence Stage, 1762–1891*. Providence: Rhode Island News Co., 1891.

Willard, Margaret Wheeler, ed. *Letters on the American Revolution, 1774–1776*. Boston: Houghton Mifflin, 1925.

Williams, George W. "Eighteenth-Century Organists of St. Michael's, Charleston." *South Carolina Historical Magazine* 53, no. 4 (October 1952): 212–222.

Willis, Eola. *The Charleston Stage in the XVIII century, with Social Settings of the Time*. Columbia, SC: The State Company, 1924.

Wilson, Kathleen. *The Sense of the People: Politics, Culture and Imperialism in England, 1715–1785*. Cambridge: Cambridge University Press, 1995.

Winston, James. *The Theatric Tourist*. Facsimile of the first and only edition of 1805. Edited by Iain Mackintosh. London: Society for Theatre Research, 2008.

Withington, Ann Fairfax. *Toward a More Perfect Union: Virtue and the Formation of American Republics*. Oxford: Oxford University Press, 1991.

Wood, Gordon S. *The Idea of America: Reflections on the Birth of the United States*. New York: Penguin, 2011.

———. *The Radicalism of the American Revolution*. New York: Vintage Books, 1993.

Wright, Louis B. *The Cultural Life of the American Colonies, 1607–1763*. New York: Harper and Row, 1957.

Wright, Philip, ed. *Lady Nugent's Journal of Her Residence in Jamaica from 1801 to 1805*. Kingston: University of the West Indies Press, 2002.

Wright, Richardson. *Revels in Jamaica, 1682–1838*. New York: Dodd, Mead, 1937.

Wroth, Lawrence C. *A History of Printing in Colonial Maryland, 1686–1776*. Baltimore: Norman T. A. Munder, 1924.

York, Neil Longley. *Henry Hulton and the American Revolution: An Outsider's Inside View*. Boston: Colonial Society of Massachusetts, 2010.

———. *Turning the World Upside Down: The War of American Independence and the Problem of Empire*. Westport, CT: Praeger, 2003.

Zahniser, Marvin R. *Charles Cotesworth Pinckney: Founding Father*. Chapel Hill: University of North Carolina Press, 1967.

Zall, Paul M., ed. *Comical Spirit of Seventy Six: The Humor of Francis Hopkinson*. San Marino, CA: Huntington Library, 1976.

[INDEX]

Note: Page numbers in *italics* refer to illustrations.

Adams, Abigail, 7, 9–10, *175*, 187
Adams, John, 8, 12, 14, 15, 17, 43, 103, 128, 134, 171, 174, 204
Addison, Joseph, *Cato*, 8–9, 15, 90, 109, 111, 186, 187, 200
Alexander, William (Lord Sterling), 167, 168
Amherst, Jeffrey, 18

Barbados, 7, 46–47, 94, 106, 109, 112, 138
Barrington, Ann, 84–85
Bernard, Francis, 128–29
Bernard, John, 50, 55–56, 136
Boston, Massachusetts, 11, 114, 128–31, 134, 198–99
Boston Massacre, 134, 140
Boucher, Jonathan, 53–54, 71, 152–58, 161, 213, 219
Bradford, William, 54, 105, 131
Bull, William, 66, 76, 98, 102, 166, 171, 180, 182, 183–84, 185, 200, 218
Bunch of Grapes Tavern, 129–30
Bute, Earl of. *See* Stuart, John (Earl of Bute)

Calvert, John, 186, 221–22
Carne, Samuel, 76, 78, 194
Carroll, Charles Jr., 13, 155, 157, 159
Charleston, South Carolina, 4–5, 15, 63–68, 104–11, 160–67, 193–94, 195–97
Chase, Samuel, 6, 151

Church Street Theatre, 170, 186, 188
Colden, Cadwallader, 16, 17, 26, 65, 71, 102, 104, 148, 167, 205, 207, 215
Continental Congress, 1, 4, 12, 13, 90, 212
Cooper, Myles, 14, 159, 207–9
Cruger, John, 20
Cunninghame, William, 16
Custis, Jacky, 152–53, 158–59

Dartmouth, Earl of, 13
Deas, David, 75–77, 166, 171, 175, 189, 194
Deas, John, 77, 163, 166–67
Delancey, James, 20
Denny, William, 26–30
Dickinson, John, 4, 14, 78–79, 113, 114, 116–17, 122, 125, 222
Dillon's Tavern (Robert Dillon), 90, 110, 163, 166
Douglass, Sarah (formerly Sarah Hallam), 18, 20, 57–58, 72, 81, 84
Drinker, James, 140
Dunmore, Lord. *See* Glen, James (Lord Dunmore)

Eddis, William, 7, 12, 32, 55, 155, 219
Eden, Robert, 45, 139, 159, 177–78
Elliot, Andrew, 167, 204

Fauquier, Francis, 36, 38
Freemasons, 6, 31, 37, 130, 166

[271]

Gadsden, Christopher, 15, 108, 171–72, 195–200, 217
Gage, General, 2, 14, 102, 129, 202, 222
Gaine, Hugh, 89, 167–68, 219
Galloway, Samuel, 152–53
Garden, Alexander, 65–67, 109, 127, 218
Garrick, David, 21, 48, 55, 72, 91–92
Gifford, Henry, 58
Glen, James (Lord Dunmore), 167
Goddard, William, 105, 121
Godwin, James, 53
Green, Jonas, 32
Grenville, George, 95–96
Gunn, Henry, 72, 77, 98, 194

Hallam, Adam, 92
Hallam, Isabella (Mrs. Mattocks), 84–86, 94
Hallam, Lewis Jr., 19, 20, 55, 64, 84, 94, 112, 220
Hallam, Lewis Sr., 57, 64, 82, 84
Hallam, Nancy, 108, 142–44, *144*, 154–57
Hallam, Sarah Smyth. *See* Douglass, Sarah
Hallam, Thomas (actor), 82–83
Hallam, Thomas (Lieutenant), 103–4
Hallam, William, 21, 84
Hamilton, Alexander, 25, 203, 218
Hancock, John, 8, 114, 128, 130
Henry, John, 131, 220
Henry, Patrick, 8, 9, 133
Hickey, William, 11, 25, 92
Homony Club, 34, 54, 155–57
Howe, William, 130, 205

Jamaica, 214–15, 221
Jay, John, 15, 16

Jefferson, Thomas, 4, 7, 37, 133, 136–38, 174, 193
Jockey Club, 77, 157–58

Knox, Henry, 217

Laurens, Henry, 15, 34, 72–76, 78, 90, 97–98, 101–2
Leigh, Egerton, 74–75, 77, 166
Livingston, Philip, 6, 16, 20, 167, 204
Livingston, William, 6, 20, 167
Lynch, Thomas Jr., 42, 76
Lyttelton, William Henry, 64, 166

Macklin, Charles, 82–83
Manigault, Anne, 65, 67, 108, 110
Manigault, Peter, 42, 166
Mason, George, 132, 143, 148–49
Mattocks, George, 85–86
Mattocks, Isabella. *See* Hallam, Isabella (Mrs. Mattocks)
McDougal, Alexander, 12, 90, 203, 210–11
Moncrief, Major James, 127
Montresor, Captain, 102
Moody, John, 93
Morris, Gouverneur, 209–10
Moultrie, William, 166, 168, 169, 175, 182, 184
Munford, Robert, 133, 145, 165, 179
Muse, Hudson, 142, 145
Mylne, William, 217, 221

Nelson, William, 149
New York: Chapel Street Theatre, 100–103, 113, 206; Cruger's Wharf Theatre, 20–24; John Street Theatre, 2–3, 12, 122–27, 168–69, 204
Newport, Rhode Island, 6, 59–61

Oliver, Peter, 130, 211
Osbourn, Henrietta, 58, 93–94, 109
Ouccannastotah, Cherokee Chief, 168–69

Paca, William, 6, 151
Peale, Charles Willson, 51, 143–44, 152, 156–57, 218
Penn, John, 118, 120, 131
Philadelphia: Society Hill Theatre, 27; Southwark Theatre, 44, 115, 118–19
Pinckney, Charles Cotesworth, 42, 166, 182, 184, 218

Quincey, Josiah Jr., 34, 134, 193

Randolph, Peyton, 2, 6, 7, 16, 37, 139, 218
Rivington, James, 210, 219–20
Robinson, James, 13, 133, 146–47, 198–99, 216
Ross, David, 119
Rutledge, Edward, 43

Saxby, George, 78, 96, 189–90
Sharpe, Horatio, 31–32, 36
Sheridan, Thomas, 48–49, 93
Smith, William (historian), 19
Smith, William (provost), 28, 31
Sons of Liberty: Boston, 11; Charleston, 4, 101–2, 108–9; New York, 17, 100–104, 113, 134, 178–79, 203
St. Andrew's Society, 6, 16, 77, 160–68
St. Cecilia's Society, 52, 66, 73, 77, 108, 167

Stamp Act, 4, 15, 19, 50, 71, 95–111
Sterling, James, 32–35
Stevens, George Alexander, 122, 130
Stuart, John (Earl of Bute), 87, 97, 164–65
Swallow's Tavern (formerly Dillon's), 162–63, 166, 180–81, 184

Thomas, Isaiah, 189
Timothy, Peter, 97, 172–73, 180, 195
Tomlinson, Ann, 102
Tomlinson, John, 102–3
Townshend Acts, 114, 126, 134, 139
Tuesday Club, 32, 34

Upton, Robert, 83, 93

Valton, Peter, 73, 108, 167
Verling, William, 26, 109

Wainwright, Sarah, 86–87, 108
Wall, Thomas, 57, 59, 93, 220
Warren, Mercy Otis, 175
Washington, George, 2, 4, 6–8, 36–38, 45–48, 63, 132–33, 136, 138–39, 148–49, 153, 161
Wells, Robert, 99, 104, 163–64, 166–67, 186, 189, 218, 220
Whitefield, George, 28, 48, 119
Wilkes, John, 87–91, 163
Williams, William, 218–19
Williamsburg, Virginia, 36–38, 63, 132, 141–42, 146–50
Woodmason, Charles, 70, 108, 114
Woolls, Stephen, 58–59, 87, 188

Index [273

STUDIES IN THEATRE HISTORY AND CULTURE

Actors and American Culture,
  1880–1920
  By Benjamin McArthur
The Age and Stage of George L. Fox,
  1825–1877: An Expanded Edition
  By Laurence Senelick
American Theater in the Culture of the
  Cold War: Producing and Contesting
  Containment
  By Bruce McConachie
Athenian Tragedy in Performance:
  A Guide to Contemporary Studies
  and Historical Debates
  By Melinda Powers
Classical Greek Theatre: New Views
  of an Old Subject
  By Clifford Ashby
Czech Theatre Design in the Twentieth
  Century: Metaphor and Irony
  Revisited
  Edited by Joseph Brandesky
Embodied Memory: The Theatre of
  George Tabori
  By Anat Feinberg
Fangs of Malice: Hypocrisy, Sincerity,
  and Acting
  By Matthew H. Wikander
Fantasies of Empire: The Empire Theatre
  of Varieties and the Licensing
  Controversy of 1894
  By Joseph Donohue
French Theatre Today: The View from
  New York, Paris, and Avignon
  By Edward Baron Turk
From Androboros to the First Amendment:
  A History of America's First Play
  By Peter A. Davis

The Jewish Kulturbund Theatre
  Company in Nazi Berlin
  By Rebecca Rovit
Jews and the Making of Modern
  German Theatre
  Edited by Jeanette R. Malkin
  and Freddie Rokem
Kitchen Sink Realisms: Domestic Labor,
  Dining, and Drama in American
  Theatre
  By Dorothy Chansky
London in a Box: Englishness and
  Theatre in Revolutionary America
  By Odai Johnson
London's West End Actresses and
  the Origins of Celebrity Charity,
  1880–1920
  By Catherine Hindson
The Making of Theatrical Reputations:
  Studies from the Modern London
  Theatre
  By Yael Zarhy-Levo
Marginal Sights: Staging the
  Chinese in America
  By James S. Moy
Melodramatic Formations: American
  Theatre and Society, 1820–1870
  By Bruce A. McConachie
Meyerhold: A Revolution in Theatre
  By Edward Braun
Modern Czech Theatre: Reflector
  and Conscience of a Nation
  By Jarka M. Burian
Modern Hamlets and Their Soliloquies:
  An Expanded Edition
  By Mary Z. Maher

*Molière, the French Revolution, and
the Theatrical Afterlife*
By Mechele Leon

*The Most American Thing in America:
Circuit Chautauqua as Performance*
By Charlotte M. Canning

*Music for the Melodramatic Theatre
in Nineteenth-Century London
and New York*
By Michael V. Pisani

"Othello" and Interpretive Traditions
By Edward Pechter

*Our Moonlight Revels: "A Midsummer
Night's Dream" in the Theatre*
By Gary Jay Williams

*The Performance of Power: Theatrical
Discourse and Politics*
Edited by Sue-Ellen Case
and Janelle Reinelt

*Performing History: Theatrical
Representations of the Past in
Contemporary Theatre*
By Freddie Rokem

*Performing Whitely in the Postcolony:
Afrikaners in South African
Theatrical and Public Life*
By Megan Lewis

*Poverty and Charity in Early Modern
Theatre and Performance*
By Robert Henke

*The Recurrence of Fate: Theatre and
Memory in Twentieth-Century Russia*
By Spencer Golub

*Reflecting the Audience: London
Theatregoing, 1840–1880*
By Jim Davis and
Victor Emeljanow

*Representing the Past: Essays in
Performance Historiography*
Edited by Charlotte M. Canning
and Thomas Postlewait

*The Roots of Theatre: Rethinking Ritual
and Other Theories of Origin*
By Eli Rozik

*Sex for Sale: Six Progressive-Era
Brothel Dramas*
By Katie N. Johnson

*Shakespeare and Chekhov in Production:
Theatrical Events and Their Audiences*
By John Tulloch

Shakespeare on the American Yiddish Stage
By Joel Berkowitz

*The Show and the Gaze of Theatre:
A European Perspective*
By Erika Fischer-Lichte

*Stagestruck Filmmaker: D. W. Griffith
and the American Theatre*
By David Mayer

*Strange Duets: Impresarios and Actresses
in the American Theatre, 1865–1914*
By Kim Marra

*Susan Glaspell's Poetics and Politics of
Rebellion*
By Emeline Jouve

*Textual and Theatrical Shakespeare:
Questions of Evidence*
Edited by Edward Pechter

Theatre and Identity in Imperial Russia
By Catherine A. Schuler

*Theatre, Community, and Civic
Engagement in Jacobean London*
By Mark Bayer

*Theatre Is More Beautiful Than War:
German Stage Directing in the
Late Twentieth Century*
By Marvin Carlson

*Theatres of Independence: Drama,
Theory, and Urban Performance
in India since 1947*
By Aparna Bhargava
Dharwadker

*The Theatrical Event: Dynamics of
Performance and Perception*
By Willmar Sauter
*Traveler, There Is No Road: Theatre, the
Spanish Civil War, and the Decolonial
Imagination in the Americas*
By Lisa Jackson-Schebetta
*The Trick of Singularity: "Twelfth Night"
and the Performance Editions*
By Laurie E. Osborne

The Victorian Marionette Theatre
By John McCormick
*Wandering Stars: Russian Emigré
Theatre, 1905–1940*
Edited by Laurence Senelick
*Writing and Rewriting National
Theatre Histories*
Edited by S. E. Wilmer